11/16

It Is Well

OTHER TITLES BY JAMES D. SHIPMAN

Constantinopolis
Going Home

It Is Well

JAMES D. SHIPMAN

LAKE UNION
PUBLISHING

Published by Lake Union Publishing, Seattle

www.apub.com

Amazon, the Amazon logo, and Lake Union Publishing are trademarks of Amazon.com, Inc., or its affiliates.

ISBN-13: 9781503939479
ISBN-10: 1503939472

Cover design by Shasti O'Leary Soudant

Printed in the United States of America

I dedicate It Is Well to a variety of people. I want to thank my amazing editor, Danielle Marshall, and Lake Union Publishing for all of their support. I want to thank my family for putting up with my quirky writing schedule and my quirkiness in general. I want to thank my readers for their support. Lastly, I dedicate this book to all the people who lived through World War II, surviving perhaps the greatest storm in human history. As they leave the stage in ever-increasing numbers, the generations that follow look to them in awe and appreciation.

PROLOGUE

Grand Army of the Republic Cemetery
Snohomish, Washington
Saturday, September 23, 1939

She was finally dead. Jonathan stared at the casket. He knew his wife's body was inside, but Helen was gone. As Pastor Miles delivered the eulogy, Jonathan stood in stunned silence, unable to hear the words.

For two years cancer had consumed her, until she withered into the emaciated creature that rested so close to him now. He felt surprise at the depth of his grief. How could the pain sting so sharply when there had been so much time to prepare? There was guilt, too, standing in the shadow of relief. There would be no more agony, no more screaming in the night when torment rocked her. Even as she begged for the end, her body had betrayed her and clung with viselike claws to life.

Jonathan shook his head, trying to drive the blackness from his mind. Family huddled protectively around him. He stared beyond them and down the grassy hill, thinking of all the people buried here: generation after generation of families who'd grown up and died in this quiet corner of America. Farther down, the Snohomish River crawled by with ashen waters mirroring the overcast sky. He tried to focus on something, anything.

Pastor Miles continued to speak, talking about the Beecher family, about church, about Jonathan's store. Their eyes met, and Jonathan saw the compassion in his friend's glance. As the service concluded, Jonathan bent his head in prayer, asking God to protect his family, to give him strength in the months and years to come, and even in the midst of his grief, to protect his country as war clouds gathered over Europe.

The funeral directors from Bauer's came forward. They removed the centerpiece from the casket and then, with a cranking mechanism, jerkily lowered the coffin into the grave below. Jonathan felt a gentle hand grasping at his. It was his daughter, Mary, tears cascading hotly down the slope of her cheeks. He recognized in her face the same shock and disbelief he felt. Behind her were her two older brothers, Matthew and Luke, themselves young men. They stood together in silence, saying a final good-bye to Helen Beecher, wife and mother, dead at thirty-eight years old.

The Beechers remained after everyone had left, nodding an occasional good-bye until they had the cemetery to themselves except for the groundskeepers. The rain drizzled on, the irritating sprinkle so familiar in rainy western Washington. Finally, after what seemed hours, the grave was filled in. Jonathan trod forward with measured steps and firmly shook the hands of the workers, then led his family to his truck. They drove the mile into town in silence, turning left on Avenue B and up a slight incline to their home—a modest Victorian built in the late nineteenth century.

Soon they were inside, still not speaking to one another. Jonathan moved into the kitchen in silence and washed the dishes, a chore he had shared with Helen hundreds of times. He felt weak. The hot water scalded his hands. He clasped them together as the fiery liquid burned him, enduring the searing cleanse.

"Pa?" The voice startled him. Only one person called him that: Matthew. Jonathan wanted to be alone with his grief, but he knew he had business with the boy. He shut off the water and faced his oldest son. Matthew stood in the kitchen doorway, his arms pressed gingerly against the jamb, watching Jonathan for a few moments. The boy worked his pocked jaw back and forth unconsciously, his frame a narrow stick beneath a burning match of hair.

"I'm sorry, Pa." His voice swallowed air and spurted out syllables in hesitant echoes.

"I'm sorry, too, Son. But don't feel bad for me—be sorry for your mother. She was taken from us far too soon."

"I thought about your question, about coming home. I've kicked it around. I can talk now if—"

Jonathan launched in, not waiting for his son to finish. "I never understood why you left right out of school. Why Boise? Why construction?"

"Pa, I'm not going back to talk about all that again."

Jonathan took a step forward, his hands fencing Matthew in. "We don't have to visit the past. What's important is you're here now. You've come back to us. I didn't know if you'd make the funeral."

"Of course I did. I'd have come earlier, but . . ." He stopped midsentence. Matthew's jaw jerked, sending a roll under the skin of his cheek. He looked away.

Jonathan forged on. "I could use you here, Matthew. The past couple years have been very tough on all of us, particularly on your sister—she's so young."

"She's fifteen."

"She's younger to me. Anyway, she's not you, Matthew—you're a hard worker. You always have been. I need help. I can't afford to pay for outside help at the store. What do you say about sticking around?" Jonathan waited, hoping. He needed his son now more than ever.

Matthew glanced around. "The house still looks the same."

"I've never understood why you left."

"I needed . . . I needed to get away. I'm different from you. I didn't want to be born, live, and die without traveling more than ten miles from my house."

"I've traveled more than that . . ."

"More than what?" asked Matthew, laughing. "More than ten miles? Yes, Pa, you've traveled to Seattle a few times, maybe even Tacoma? What's that, sixty?"

"I never saw a point. Home is home. What's out there for me?"

"A whole world to see. So far I've only worked in a few states. That may change soon."

"What do you mean?" Jonathan asked sharply. *I'm losing him.* He knew it in his heart, but he hoped he was wrong, that Matthew might reconsider at the last moment. He took another step forward, trying desperately to gather the harvest of his son.

"Our company picked up some overseas contracts out in the Pacific. With the war starting in Europe, I think people are getting a little jumpy. The military is a bunch of eager beavers building out there—airfields mostly. Company asked me to help out."

"That's an even better reason to come home now. A war is no place to be. I joined up last time around and was darn lucky we never got overseas. Some folks didn't come back."

"I'm not going to be anywhere near the war, Pa," said Matthew, pacing like a furious tin soldier wound too many times. "The Pacific is as far away from the fighting as I could possibly be. How would it be better if I was at home, waiting to be drafted? If I was working for you and the war did start, they would snatch me and Luke right up. I'm in a necessary job now, a civilian job. Not that I would shirk fighting, if it came to that."

Jonathan reached toward him, his hands spread in a wide arch to calm the storm. "Matthew, please. I need you here. We need you at the store. Times are tough and getting tougher. Without your mom . . ."

"What about Luke?"

"You know Luke. I love that boy, but he's worth a quarter day's work at best, if I can keep him focused. Half the time he doesn't show up. Last week I caught him at the store passed out under a blanket with the Baxter girl. Both of them naked as the day the Lord made them."

Matthew laughed. "Well, at least some things never change."

"Can't you think it over just a bit more?"

"I can't, Pa. I just can't. I love you, but this isn't my home anymore. In some ways . . ."

"In some ways what?"

Matthew looked at his dad for a moment and then came forward, extending a timid hand, his eyes scanning the ceiling. He whispered plaintively, "Please let's not talk about it anymore. Give me your blessing."

Jonathan weighed the request in his mind. Matthew didn't want to leave without his father's permission. If he could just keep Matthew home for a month or two, he might never depart again. *Can I deceive my boy to protect him?* If he pushed, Matthew might obey him. He always had. Jonathan remembered his frail son growing up, never a leader but always loyal, hardworking, kind. Matthew deferred to his father in all things, and Helen would quickly correct him if he didn't. Jonathan might wish for a bit more fire in the boy, but it simply wasn't there. No, he wouldn't force him. He couldn't live with himself if he overpowered his son's will for selfish reasons. *God's will be done.*

Jonathan took Matthew's hand, looking in his eyes for a moment. There were words he yearned to say, but he held them back. He roughly embraced him, not wanting to let go.

"You've got my blessing, boy. But always remember you have a home here. It's getting dangerous out there, more than you realize. If you get a sniff of war coming, promise me you'll catch a ship home straightaway."

Matthew laughed in short, nervous spurts as he turned away. "I know it is, Pa, but I'll be in paradise—the Pacific. Europe is half a world away."

Jonathan didn't answer.

"Fine, if it makes you feel better, I promise. If things get hot, I'll get out of there and get my tail home."

They talked for a few more minutes about inconsequential things. His stay had been too short. He wanted Matthew home for another month—if he couldn't have him permanently. That wasn't going to happen. Jonathan watched his son leave. He would stay another day or two, but the moment had passed. They would not talk about this again.

Jonathan lurched to the sink and fumbled for the faucet to drown out his tears. He couldn't shield Matthew any longer. A storm was coming.

CHAPTER ONE

Snohomish Free Methodist Church
Snohomish, Washington
Sunday, December 7, 1941

Jonathan stood wedged between his children in the back pew of the Snohomish Free Methodist Church. The Beechers' place of worship rested on Mill Avenue near the Pilchuck River. It was a simple structure, long of tooth, with faded walls drawn warily up to a pine pulpit. Light fanned through stained glass, haloing the disciples in various scenes from the gospel. A hundred people huddled inside, murmuring a hymn. As melancholy music drifted around him, Jonathan thought of the past two years of his life.

He had survived. The first crushing months had gradually led to a dull ache as he grew used to his life alone. The pain stabbed at him sharply each holiday and flared up with random memories: a place, a song, anything that reminded him of his life with Helen. He continued his work each day at the hardware store, using the comforting monotony of his daily duties to blanket his grief.

As time passed, friends and family moved on. He wasn't asked about Helen anymore. Some even suggested he find a new wife. He was still young after all, barely forty-five. But he couldn't remarry. He would be a widower for life. He still felt the anguish of her long illness again as he thought of the day she passed. Now he toiled sunrise to sunset, hemmed in by the towering walls of routine.

The children grieved in their own ways. Mary took it harder than Luke. She was seventeen now and a senior in high school. She had taken over many of her mother's duties, doing most of the cooking and cleaning. She smothered her grief with flurries of work and storms of frenzied social activity. *Too many boys in her head,* thought Jonathan. His daughter longed for a prince and a family. He kept her emotions from carrying her away with the firm foot of his will. Plenty of time for that nonsense after school and college. He'd planned the education for Matthew, but no matter. She was smart. She'd be the first in the family.

Luke handled his mother's death much more easily, or so it seemed to Jonathan. He let life roll off of him. He was the kind of young man who never worked too hard and was always up to no good. A year out of high school, Luke had neither the inclination nor the aptitude for work. He wanted to play. In his latest antics, he and some friends had broken into the local auction house and led a cow across the street to the high school, releasing it to wander the halls overnight. Somehow Luke seemed to endear himself to others, rather than anger them. He had a bounty of friends and was popular with the girls. Jonathan dragged him out of bed to work each morning at the store and babysat him throughout the day.

Then there was Matthew. Jonathan hadn't seen his oldest son in two years, not since the funeral. Matthew had worked in the Philippines constructing and maintaining airfields, then moved on to Wake Island in the middle of the Pacific. They were supposed to finish their work no later than the spring of '42, and then Matthew intended to head home for a few months. Jonathan hoped his son would come home to

8

stay—maybe get a job that would keep him out of the war that raged in Europe and that everyone feared was coming to America.

Jonathan wondered how much longer the United States could stay out of the mess. They heard more and more about Japan—a place most people in Snohomish would be hard pressed to find on a map. War news blackened the papers. If the conflict came, he had to get Matthew home.

Jonathan shook his head. What was he doing? He never let his mind wander during the sermon. He chastised himself and looked up, concentrating on the words that today focused on the prodigal son. Jonathan smiled to himself, thinking of Matthew again. Pastor Miles worked himself up toward his conclusion. He was a fiery mountain looming over the congregation, his voice ripping linen.

The sermon concluded, and the basket was passed around. Jonathan pulled a dollar from his wallet and dropped it in. He gave all he could. They were not a wealthy family. He worked hard to make ends meet with the store, but there were plenty of bills chasing him. Mary watched him put the money in and reached up, squeezing his arm, smiling at the sacrifice.

With the service complete near noon Jonathan filed out, his kids lingering to visit with some of their friends. There was a small area past the sanctuary where coffee was served and the crowd would visit for a spell before returning home for the day. Jonathan poured himself a cup and chatted with a neighbor, his mind still a little distracted. Soon he saw Pastor Miles coming out, his face gliding above the heads around him.

"Ah, Jonathan, how are you today?" he asked in his booming, jovial voice.

"I'm fine, Pastor. How are you?"

"Well enough, my friend. Well enough. We have a new employee you may see around here now and again. Ah! Here she comes. Jonathan

Beecher, let me introduce you to Sarah Gilbertson and her daughter, Margaret."

Standing like a wilted blossom in the shadow of the pastor was a woman in her thirties. She clung to a girl as frail as she was. Jonathan stepped forward politely and extended a hand to greet her. She offered her left hand, which he took, glancing down for a moment at her right. He noticed it was covered in a glove. He tore his eyes away, but she had caught him looking. Her pale cheeks reddened.

"It's very nice to meet you, Mrs. Gilbertson," he mumbled, not knowing what else to say.

"It's nice to meet you, too, Mr. Beecher."

"Sarah is going to be cleaning our church every week and also doing some sorting out of our archives from the basement. Jonathan here takes care of the church grounds for us, something he's kind enough to do for free," explained Pastor Miles.

Sarah's daughter looked up shyly at Jonathan, and he winked at her. She jolted in surprise, then moved closer to her mother. Jonathan chuckled and turned to Sarah. "I probably won't see you around too much. I usually try to cut the lawn early on Saturday morning. Of course, the grass doesn't need any mowing at this time of year. I don't think I've seen you before. Where are you from?"

"I'm from Everett, but I've—"

Jonathan's attention was suddenly pulled away as he heard a commotion on the other side of the room. People were gathering around and shouting.

"Excuse me. I'm sorry, but . . ." He took a step back.

Sarah started to say something but seemed to change her mind. "It's okay. I'll talk to you some other time."

He nodded distractedly and turned away, drawn swiftly to the murmuring crowd.

"What's going on?" he asked.

"We've been bombed," said Pete Brandvold, one of Jonathan's friends, his face a bleached canvas. "The Japanese bombed us in Hawaii!"

Jonathan felt his heart sink. "What are you talking about? Are you sure?"

"It's all over the radio. They attacked Pearl Harbor this morning."

Jonathan stood in shock, not knowing what to do. The storm was coming to all of them, and there was nothing he could do to stop it.

Before long the humming grew as everyone seemed to talk at once. Mary and Luke ran up together, wondering what was happening. Jonathan explained.

"This is the worst possible news!" said Mary. "Why would the Japanese attack us?"

"They're all joined up with the Nazis," said Luke. "The Germans probably talked them into it."

Someone turned on the church's radio, and soon quiet fell over the congregation again. They all stood together as one body, listening to the stories coming over the airwaves. The general situation seemed confused, but it was clear that the Japanese had indeed attacked the American fleet at Pearl Harbor. Potentially thousands were dead, and the Japanese had sunk a number of ships. There was no word of any other attacks so far, and the broadcaster was not certain whether any Japanese soldiers had landed in Hawaii.

"How far is Wake Island from Hawaii?" asked Mary. "Is Matthew okay?"

"Don't worry, dear," said Jonathan. "Wake is thousands of miles from Hawaii. I'm sure he's fine." He didn't tell Mary that Wake Island was actually *closer* to Japan. Ever since the moment he heard about the attack, he had thought of Matthew. The United States and Japan were now at war. Matthew worked on a military airfield in the thick of the war zone. He wondered if there was any way to get a hold of his son, to make sure he was okay. They had only communicated by mail. Was there a telegram service on Wake? A telephone? Would he be able to even send a telegram or call in such an emergency?

"What's wrong, Father?" asked Mary.

Jonathan realized he needed to focus on things closer to home. He placed a hand on Mary's shoulder. "Nothing, dear. I was just thinking about a few things. Don't worry about this. The president will know what to do. We are far away from Japan. They could never reach here." He wondered if that were true.

Luke paced back and forth, his face red, his fists clenched. "We're going to get them! We're going to teach those damned Japs a lesson!" A few voices echoed in agreement.

Pastor Miles moved to the front of the room and raised his hands.

"I've been your pastor for twenty years now, since just a little after the last war. We've been through a lot together, all of us. Some good times, mostly hard ones. Through it all, we've kept our faith, we've kept this church going and this town alive." He looked out over the crowd, keeping his voice composed and measured. There was pain in his eyes as he spoke.

"I don't know what's in front of us now. But we have to stay calm. We need to pray and put all of this in the Lord's hands. Then we will have to do our part. Hard times are coming again. If things come along like I guess they will, we will be saying good-bye to our young men for a long time to come. Some may never come back. We may be in for even worse."

A moan rose from the crowd as he said these words. Jonathan grimaced. *Please, Lord, not one of my boys.*

"There's been plenty of bombing in Europe, plenty of civilian folks getting killed as well. We need to be ready for all of this. Ready as a church family. Ready as a community. Now I want you all to go home and be with your children, with your mothers and fathers. Make this a day of family and a day of prayer. We will have a special service tomorrow night at seven." He finished with a prayer, and soon the congregation was filing out of the church and heading home, although some people continued to cluster outside to discuss the news.

Jonathan talked for a while with Pete. Pete had sons in their twenties as well, and both men knew what the war would mean for them.

"Whole thing's a mess," said Pete.

Jonathan nodded. "Has to be faced."

Pete swung a soft blow at his friend's arm. "Least we're too old for this one. I don't suppose we'd do any good tromping around a battlefield complaining about our sore backs and tired bladders."

Jonathan chuckled. He thought back to his army days. How different he would look now in the same uniform.

Pete's forehead creased in a severe fold. "Course there's the boys to think of. I guess they'll all be hot to join. No way to stop them, is there? Wouldn't be patriotic."

As if fulfilling that prophecy, Jonathan noticed Luke nearby in a pack of young men. He paced about with a nervous energy, his hands clutching a phantom rifle, and, as Jonathan watched, took aim at some invisible enemy. *It's already starting.* Jonathan collected him swiftly and drove the family home.

All afternoon they stuck close by the radio, listening to the reports as more details were learned about the attack. So far it did not appear there was a land invasion in Hawaii or anywhere else, but the airplane attack on Pearl Harbor was massive, and the damage to the fleet was almost incomprehensible. They sat in stunned silence, Mary clinging to her father. Luke paced back and forth, eyes darting, teeth clenched.

Mary eventually tired of listening and climbed the stairs to take a nap. Jonathan knew it was time to talk to Luke. He walked over and shut off the radio, then turned and sat down on the sofa, facing his second son.

"I saw you talking to some of the other boys. What's the mood?"

Luke kept up his furious pace. "We're all as angry as we could be. Those Japs are crazy, attacking us. We all can't wait to join up and give them a licking."

"And you?" Jonathan asked, his voice a measured tick of the pendulum.

Luke's feet stilled, though his hands snapped open and shut like steel cages. "I have to join. You know I'd never walk away from a fight. They attacked us. They killed Americans for no reason. We have to show them what happens when you pick a fight with us."

Jonathan looked at his son for a moment, then leaned forward and slowed the beat of his voice. "I know how mad you are and how upset all the boys are, but I want you to wait."

Luke's eyes bulged. "What are you talking about? I'm joining now. We all are. As soon as we find out where and when, we're going over together." He wagged an accusing finger. "Do you want them to think I'm a coward?"

"You're not a coward, Luke. Everyone knows that. But I want you to wait a few months. Matthew's already in harm's way. I need you here at the store. Mary, too. I want you to wait until we know more about what all this is going to be about. Trust me, I was like you, too. I rushed out and joined the army during the last war. Then it turned out there were too many of us, and I ended up guarding tents in Alabama for a year with the snakes and the heat. There's going to be too many boys joining up this time as well. Better to wait and sign up when you're needed. Stick it out here for now. Put in some full, hard days at the store. Work up to it."

"Dad, I have to go. All my friends will be going. I'd be the laughingstock of Snohomish."

"You're not going to go!" said Jonathan, raising his voice. He took a deep breath to calm himself. "You're going to listen to me *for once*, and you're going to wait. Do you understand me?"

Luke looked at his father for a few moments and then lowered his head. "Yes, sir," he muttered, then stormed out of the room.

Jonathan felt terrible. Did he really have the right to tell his son he couldn't go to war? He wanted to protect Luke, but he also wanted to keep his son safely at home for his own reasons. He was torn with guilt. He fell to his knees and prayed for guidance, asking God to lead him to the right decision and also to protect all the people going to war and the families of all the dead and wounded in Hawaii.

"Are you okay, Father?" It was Mary. He looked up and wiped away the tears that had fallen silently. She drew closer and embraced him. Jonathan buried his face in her arms and held her tightly for a few moments.

"All the boys will be leaving," she said.

He looked up. "What do you mean?"

"I graduate in six months. Every boy is going to leave this town at just the wrong time."

"You should be worried about Luke."

She laughed. "Does he want to join? He won't last a day."

"All boys want to play war."

"You don't want him to?"

"I want him to be protected. I want our family safe."

"Maybe other dads will feel the same. Maybe there'll be a few left behind."

"What are you talking about?" he asked.

She sighed. "It doesn't matter." She squeezed his hand. "I don't think you're right, Father. He'll have to go. Maybe not now, but sometime. They all will."

Jonathan knew she was right; he would have to let Luke go. Still, he could wait awhile. "I didn't say no. I told him to wait. We should see what happens next. We'll know more in the next few days. It won't hurt him to sit back for a week or two, or even a few months. In the meantime, we can all work as hard as we can at the store. If he does leave, I won't have any help at all there."

"You'll have me, Father. I can help some on the weekends even this year, and I'm free once summer comes. We will make it through one way or another. I'll always be here for you. There won't be anything else for me to do anyway."

He held Mary closer. He loved her strength and her joy. He held on to her as he was trying to hold on to Luke. He had them for a little while. But he knew everything was about to change forever.

～

Jonathan brought his family back to church the next evening for a special service. They arrived a half hour early, and he was surprised to see the building already full beyond capacity. He had never seen so many people here at one time, even on Easter. The din of conversation clanged throughout the sanctuary. He heard snippets of talk about President Roosevelt's speech and the declaration of war on Japan.

He felt a tap on his shoulder and turned around to find the woman Pastor Miles had introduced him to yesterday. He struggled to recall her name.

"Hello," he finally uttered, feeling vaguely uncomfortable with this stranger encroaching at such a troubling time.

"Hello. The pastor asked if I could find you and see if you could bring up the big coffeepot and some extra trays."

He watched her, a little surprised. She'd been here only a day or two and was already telling him what to do? He grunted. "I know where they are."

"Thank you. Could you get those right away?"

Get those right away. Who was this stranger? "I'm sorry, I don't remember your name . . ."

She looked up at him and smiled. "It's okay. It's Sarah. And you're Jonathan, correct?"

"Yes." The smile disarmed him a bit. She wasn't trying to be rude or bossy. He chastised himself. *Keep your pride under control. She's just trying to help out. You don't own the church—even the pastor can't make that claim.*

She turned and led him through the crowd, then down the steps into the basement. He watched her as she walked in front of him. She wore a white blouse traced with flowers and a tan skirt that danced around her ankles. Her clothing overwhelmed her slight frame. He noticed her right hand was concealed again, this time in a white cloth.

They reached the storage area where the dishes and coffee were kept. Sarah reached up and pulled down two protruding trays. Using her left hand to grasp their edges and balancing the load with her right, she teetered and nearly fell. Jonathan took a step forward.

"Can I help you with those . . . your hand."

"My hand is *just* fine," she said with ice in her voice. "As you can see, I manage."

"What happened to it?" he asked. *Where had that come from?* "Never mind, it's rude of me to ask."

"No, it's quite all right. I caught it in the wringer of my washing machine," she explained woodenly. "It happened years ago. I keep it wrapped because it's not very pleasant for people to see, but I learned long ago how to get by with it. If only people wouldn't stare."

He'd stared. "Does it bother you still?"

"A little in damp weather, which is most of the time around here." She laughed a little.

"I've been hurt plenty of times at the hardware store," Jonathan said. "There's always something heavy landing on me. I broke my arm one time when a stack of cedar tumbled down on me, but I've been lucky, nothing permanent."

She watched him for a second, then set her dishes down, giggling a little. "Look at us talking about our trivial woes when the world is falling apart."

"You're right. We've not much right to complain."

"Are you worried about the attack? About the war?" she asked.

"A little," he said. "I have a son out in the Pacific, working on an island called Wake. I don't know how to contact him except by letter. I tried calling his company today in Boise, but nobody answered."

She looked in his eyes for a moment. "I hope he will be safe. What about your other boy? What's his name? Luke? He must be in his twenties."

"He is—just twenty."

"Is he going to join up? That's all I've heard about in the past day."

"He wants to. I've asked him to wait a bit, and he agreed. I want him to do his duty, but I don't think he has to rush into things. There will be more than enough young men trying to join for months to come."

"How awful to have two sons that might end up in the war. You must be terrified."

"I wish none of this was happening. But I don't know what I can do about it. You're the lucky one—with only a young daughter to worry about."

"Yes . . . the lucky one." She turned then and picked back up the trays, moving swiftly past him and out of the storage room. He wondered if he had offended her in some way. He reached up to the top shelf and pulled down the big coffeepot. He nearly fell over, adjusting to its weight. Why did they store this monster up so high?

Back upstairs, he checked his watch—it was almost seven. He filled the pot with water and plugged it in to begin the brewing. Then he milled back through the crowd, looking for his family. The congregation shuffled into the sanctuary, making his progress more difficult. He found Mary, and they sat down in a pew, leaving a space for Luke.

After the crowd settled down, Pastor Miles led the congregation in prayer.

"I come to you today with resolve and anger in my heart. We are facing a war against an evil people who attacked us without provocation. For two years we've watched Hitler plow over Europe, killing millions of innocent, peace-loving people. Something has to be done about it. Our president spoke to us today. He needs us. We will be called on to rise up and fight these Japanese. We will have to send our sons out to war. We might even face them right here on our shores. Make no mistake, folks—this is no distant threat. We in Snohomish must be prepared for invasion.

"Earlier today I met with other church leaders and with our city government and police. They want volunteers to form a local patrol. We need to be ready in case the Japs attack us here. I have a sign-up sheet prepared for volunteers. If you have a good hunting rifle or at least a pistol, more the better, but we can use any man willing to help. Once we have all the names we will set up a system of regular patrols.

"Another thing we talked about at the meeting today—we need people to cover up their windows at night, starting immediately. We can't let lights show the enemy where our cities are from the air. So please go home tonight and cover all your windows with blankets or paper or anything you have. Our patrols will be watching for light at night, and we will let you know if there is a problem." The pastor looked out at the congregation. Tears framed his face.

"I don't know how long this will last. We have to be prepared for anything. We will certainly suffer grave loss, including some of our boys. But we have God on our side. Our nation was built on a foundation of faith and freedom. We may suffer defeats, but we will never lose this war."

A great cheer came up from the crowd. Jonathan felt an outpouring of love. He was deeply affected to see Pastor Miles so emotional. The pastor had been their leader for so long, and he was strong for them, but he had never cried in front of them, as far as Jonathan knew. Mary leaned against her father, tears falling from her face as well. He held her closely as the pastor turned to some passages from the Bible, then led the congregation in a hymn.

When the service was over, the crowd filed out again. Jonathan checked the coffeepot to ensure everything had functioned correctly, then spoke with a few neighbors. The people lingered for more than an hour. Afterward Jonathan remained behind to help clean up. As he put away chairs and stacked the cups, he saw Pastor Miles coming out of his small office. They shook hands warmly.

"Very nice message tonight."

"Thank you, Jonathan. How are you holding up?"

"I'm doing okay. I'm worried about Matthew."

"Have you had any word from him?"

"Not yet."

"I'm sure he will be fine. I will include him in my prayers tonight."

"Thank you. What was the mood at the town meeting you went to?"

"Folks are having a rough time of it. Nobody is quite sure what to do or what might be coming our way. I didn't say much tonight, but the mayor's pretty worried about a possible invasion. They are digging entrenchments at the waterfront in Everett, and the navy's patrolling the strait."

"Do they really think it might be that serious?"

"Nobody knows. I take it the military didn't expect them to be able to get to Hawaii. If they can get that far undetected with a bunch of ships, what would stop them from landing along the West Coast?"

Jonathan hadn't realized the possible threat of invasion was so real. "Well, I signed up to help out. Lots of people did."

"I had no doubt they would. Everyone's ready to fight. These Japs may find they bit off more than they can chew. If they land here, they are going to run into thousands of citizens with rifles and plenty of ammo. This would be no easy place to take and harder to keep."

"I hope you're right."

"Thanks again for helping out with the coffee."

"You're welcome. Sarah would've had trouble with that coffeepot—that thing weighs more than my truck. She seems like a nice enough lady. I met her daughter, too, but not her husband."

"She's just like you, Jonathan. She lost her husband, just as you lost your wife. Her man was killed on the green chain a few years ago at Weyerhaeuser. She had a house in Everett, but she sold it and moved here. She does some seamstress work out of a little rental. Frankly, I don't know how she is making ends meet. She has that little girl, too. I couldn't say no to her doing a little work for us after she told me her whole story."

Jonathan nodded. *That's why you're my pastor.* He was the best kind of man. "You're right as always. Charity must come first." Jonathan looked at his watch. "Well, I suppose I'd best get home. I had a delivery late today, and I'll be in early, putting everything away."

Jonathan shook hands again and left. Mary and Luke must have hitched a ride with friends. He climbed into his 1936 Ford pickup and drove the few minutes back to the house. When he walked through the front door, he found Mary in the kitchen, warming up some pie for a bedtime snack.

"Hello, Father. Wasn't that a wonderful sermon tonight? Can you believe how everyone is coming together?"

"It was amazing to see. So many people there, too. Where's Luke?"

She frowned. "I thought he was with you?"

"No. I didn't see him after the service."

"I didn't, either."

Jonathan felt a prick of fear. Where was he? It was too early to panic. Luke could be anywhere. He was always out with friends. "I better go out looking for him. Don't wait up—you've got school tomorrow."

Jonathan returned to his truck and started it up. Soon he was driving around town, looking for Luke. He asked a few of Luke's friends, but nobody had seen him. For the next several hours Jonathan drove, stopping by houses and his son's favorite places around Snohomish. Still no luck. There was a chance he might be out cavorting as he so often was, but Jonathan was sure this time that wasn't true. Luke was gone. He had left for war.

CHAPTER TWO

The blaring of bugles jolted them. Matthew Beecher was in the breakfast line with hundreds of others, civilian and military, when they heard the alarm. Everyone froze for a moment; then chaos erupted. Matthew dropped his tray, the food tumbling to the floor. He turned and ran toward the exit, jamming with dozens of others all trying to stream out of the narrow doorway at the same time. He made it outside and discovered dark, ominous clouds rolling overhead.

Matthew was a civilian worker with the Boise firm Morrison Knudsen, but like many others, he had volunteered to help the military defend the island. For months he had trained with marines on one of the .30-caliber machine gun positions. Wake had received a contingent of 450 US Marines in August 1941. Since that time, under the strict hand of their commander, Major Devereux, they had worked ten to twelve hours a day, seven days a week, preparing the defenses of the island. The major wasn't popular with the men, who felt he pushed them too hard. However, he had done much to build a defensive perimeter. Just how much was about to be seen.

Matthew ran a mile to his post, a circular pit surrounded by sandbags with a .30-caliber machine gun poised in the middle. His position lay on the north end of the airfield. Corporal Jensen and Private First Class Schmidt were already there, preparing their weapon for an attack. Matthew wondered if this was just another drill, one of dozens they had endured recently. Jensen blinked rapidly through his dense spectacles as he hopped over the sandbags and fumbled for an ammunition belt. They fed one end of the ribbon into the left side of the Browning M1919; then Jensen cocked the bolt with a sharp metallic clang.

"What the hell is going on?" asked Matthew.

"Not sure," said Jensen. "Could be another drill, but I heard someone say that the Japs hit Hawaii."

Matthew felt electric needles of anxiety stab his neck. Months of fear unleashed now in a single moment. If that was true, then they were at war and the Japanese might be coming here next. Surely they wouldn't attack this sandbar in the middle of nowhere? He hadn't signed up for this. He just wanted his civilian hazard pay and to get the hell out of here.

They sat in restless silence for hours as the morning advanced. Matthew strained his eyes upward, but the clouds blanketed the sky, almost touching them. They heard the sound of aircraft approaching. Jensen fixed the machine gun toward the noise, but it was just the four F4F-3 Wildcats coming in to land and refuel. Soon another four fighters took off, leaving eight on the airfield, spread about 150 yards apart.

Right before noon Matthew heard engines again, and he craned his neck to spot the Wildcats above. A blinding flash over the airfield drew his attention, followed a moment later by a tearing explosion. Staccato detonations pounded the airstrip. Crushing shock waves struck him in rapid succession. Jensen shouted and squinted through his Coke-bottle glasses as he unleashed fiery tracers into the sky. Matthew followed the arcing light, but if the marine was aiming at something, he couldn't tell. Rifle and machine gun fire rattled as batteries around the island erupted to life.

After what seemed like a lifetime, the flashes sputtered and ceased. The small-arms fire continued in ragged bursts until this, too, gradually faded. Matthew looked out at the airfield. The grounded Wildcats were burning. He saw figures in twisted heaps on the field, bodies on fire. He choked, and hot vomit erupted down his shirt. Jensen lay crumpled against the sandbags, his head buried in his knees. Black smoke billowed from the Pan Am facilities and the hospital. He glanced at his watch. The attack had lasted twelve minutes. Matthew put a dazed hand into his pocket and removed a cloth, rubbing absently at his shirt as he struggled to take in the carnage.

"I think we better see what we can do to help," said Jensen, having recovered from the initial shock. "Matthew?"

He couldn't reply. His jaw, ever twitching, was frozen solid. His teeth were clamped, welded together. He shivered.

"Matthew," Jensen repeated.

He felt a bony hand clasping his shoulder. The marine corporal hovered over him, his distant pupils staring down sand-smeared lenses. He shook his head, trying to drive the fog from his brain. His friend was right; they had to do something for the others. He willed himself to his feet and followed Jensen toward the fire and smoke.

For the rest of the day Matthew worked as fast and as hard as possible. Burned bodies writhed, with screams of agony echoing from the chasms of open mouths. A marine was lying against the wall of the Pan Am terminal, trying to hold in his stomach, his eyes full moons awash in shock.

Night hid the horrors, but not the shrieks of misery. Matthew labored endlessly, assisting with the wounded and bringing water and food to the men. Then he returned to assist the marines on the machine gun when the attacks resumed. All the firing seemed futile, although the marine aviators claimed to have shot down two Japanese planes, exacting a little revenge. Matthew was proud of their pilots, who seemed superhuman. They kept going up again and again, getting little sleep. The ground crews struggled to keep the planes operational sortie after sortie.

Because of the attacks and the damage to their housing, everyone had taken to sleeping at their posts or in the brush. They ate cold food for the most part, which was brought out by civilian contractors volunteering to assist with logistics. Two days passed.

Late on December 10 Matthew saw Major Devereux along with Navy Commander Cunningham, who had just taken over command of the island's defenses in late November. The commanders were touring the defenses near the airfield, surrounded by a squad of marines. Matthew joined the others in a ragged cheer. He wanted to rush up to salute them, but he was exhausted.

On December 11 ships appeared to the south of the island. Matthew and his gun crew laboriously lugged their machine gun and ammunition past the airfield and into the brush near the southern beach. Matthew hoped that the ships were American, but feared the worst. Soon it was clear that the ships, which numbered about fifteen, were Japanese. This fleet could mean only one thing: the enemy was here to invade the island.

Orders passed from group to group to hold fire. Not that the machine gun could have done anything to a ship, but Matthew knew Wake had a number of five-inch coastal guns. They waited. His heartbeat coursed through his veins, throbbing in his ankles and wrists. His exhaustion fell away, and he looked out with crystal focus. They were coming—not vague dots of silver in the air, but landing ships filling the horizon.

The vessels crept closer and closer. When would the order come to attack? The fire from those ships would be murder at this range.

A marine artillery piece roared, then another and another. Plumes of water erupted near the enemy ships. One of the bigger transports exploded and disintegrated. Matthew watched in disbelief as the craft belched flame and flipped angrily over before sinking into the blood-churned waters of the Pacific. The Japanese vessels returned fire, and shells erupted on the beach—sand, fire, and limbs jumbling into the air around him.

Jensen cocked the .30 caliber and fired short bursts of tracers, arcing the machine gun high so that the shells rained down on the looming ships' decks. Another ship exploded, smoke bellowing out of a gashing hole in the hull.

Then a miracle happened: Matthew thought his eyes deceived him, but before long it was clear the Japanese ships were slinking away. The marines kept up a fierce fire, but the enemy guns slackened as the vessels shrunk to dots on the horizon.

A loud cheer erupted as the guns fell silent. Matthew's own cry rattled dryly in his throat. They'd done it. He didn't know how. He flung himself down on the sand, his eyes shut. He dug his fingers into the wet, grainy beach. Waves licked his feet. He breathed the acrid air. He felt a thud as Jensen landed hard next to him. The corporal's wheezy laugh was interspersed with coughing, and they held hands tightly, clinging to each other—to life.

They were elated. They had beaten back the Japanese. They had taken hell from the enemy, and they had suffered casualties, but they still held the island. They were veterans now. They had some grit. They'd laughed and bled and died together among the bombs and the bullets.

On the night of December 13 Matthew and his gun crew carried their weapon back to their original position. They set the gun back up and then lay against the sandbags, enjoying their first hot food in a week.

Matthew was exhausted. He had never been more scared in his entire life. At the same time, he felt exhilaration. Thank God that Jensen and Schmidt were here. He couldn't have handled all of this without them. He wondered about his family back home. His pa must be worried sick. He remembered the conversation he had with his dad the night of his mother's burial. He smiled at the irony—what a great decision to travel out to the "peaceful" Pacific.

Schmidt had left to check in and returned as darkness was falling. "You won't believe it," he said.

"What?" asked Jensen.

"Sounds like we're heroes. A message came in to Cunningham. The military is real proud of us. We're about the only ones out here that have been able to stop the Japs so far."

"For now," said Jensen. "We got real lucky this last time around. I doubt that will happen again."

"We won't have to worry about it—I have other news," said Schmidt. "A fleet is coming to relieve us." He looked up at Matthew. "They're gonna take all the civilians off, too. Looks like a few more days of this bombing malarkey, and you'll be home free."

Matthew felt relief for the first time since the morning of December 7. They were going to be rescued. Soon he would be home in Snohomish a hero. He promised he'd never leave again.

∿

As the December days passed, the initial elation faded away. The Japanese kept up a daily bombing of the island, gradually reducing the buildings to rubble. The remaining fighters were shot up or suffered from mechanical failures until none were flyable.

Private Schmidt was killed in one of the raids, and his duties were taken over by a middle-aged civilian contractor named Julius "Babe" Hoffmeister. Babe was stocky, short, and shorter tempered. He was balding, and his face was ruddy from the sun and also, according to his own words, from a lifetime of "the bottle." Babe had come out to Wake to earn some extra money and also to get away from the temptation of alcohol, as the island was supposed to be dry. However, after the first attack, he had gathered all the alcohol he could find and hidden it around the island. He would occasionally disappear from their post and come back in a decidedly happier mood. Jensen couldn't stand Babe, and the two were constantly squabbling. Matthew felt differently.

"Pass me some crackers, kid," said Babe as the three men crouched against their sandbags in the late evening.

Matthew reached into the ration bag they had received for the day and pulled out a smaller brown bag, then handed some stale crackers over to Babe.

"Only a few days now until Christmas," said Matthew. "Where is our relief fleet?"

"They're coming," said Jensen. "They're supposed to be here any day."

"Bah! That's what the heads have been saying for two weeks now. There ain't no fleet coming. That's the truth." Babe turned his head to Matthew. "Don't let this boy fill your brain with garbage. He doesn't know a damn thing."

"Better his head with garbage than yours with hooch," retorted Jensen. "You've been at it again today. Gone for hours and then back with your brains in the fog. What if the Japs had come while you were out nursing a bottle? I need you here, and I need you sober."

"What difference does it make, *Goggles?* We're almost out of ammo, anyway. Almost out of food. Japs will be here in no time, and to hell with your phantom fleet."

Jensen started to rise, and Matthew thought the two men might come to blows. He quickly moved between them. "Come on now, fellas. Babe don't mean anything. We've all been through plenty this month. More than we signed up for; well, at least more than Babe and I did. Jensen's right—the fleet left Hawaii weeks ago. It'll probably be here tomorrow. They're bringing guns and supplies and a batch of more marines."

"And if they do by some miracle arrive, they'll be taking us off this whore of an island," said Babe. "When I get back to the States, I'll move to Nebraska. I don't want to see an ocean again so long as I live."

"To the relief fleet," said Jensen, raising his canteen of water.

"To the fleet," answered Babe, and the two men clanged their tins together.

Matthew sat back, relieved. He'd had to step in a few times now to stop these two from fighting. He liked both of them, although for very different reasons. Jensen was a professional, a true marine who had joined up long before there was any threat of war. He was in his late twenties, and he embodied everything Matthew would love to be: confident, strong, self-assured.

Babe was grumpy and funny, sarcastic and lazy. Matthew appreciated him because despite all of this, he had a good heart. He enjoyed watching Babe complain away the days, shirking his work and looking for any excuse to dodge out for a few hours of "recreation."

Babe was so different from Matthew's father. Jonathan was more like Jensen: faithful, simple. Pa believed in himself and in God and didn't worry about too much outside of that. Matthew had watched his pa put up with a lot in life, more than Matthew felt he could handle himself. Perhaps that was why he liked Babe. Babe was weak, but he kept on fighting in his own way, resisting even in his terror and weakness. Matthew understood those feelings all too well.

They talked away the hours into darkness, relieved there wouldn't be another attack that day. Soon they were lying back against the sandbags, under a few wool blankets and a crude canvas cover. Matthew slept between Babe and Jensen as if to keep them from killing each other in the night.

Rough hands shook him awake. He bolted up abruptly and blinked his eyes. It was still pitch black.

"Wake up!" The voice was Jensen's. "Wake up! The Japs are here again! There's a fleet off the south coast!"

"How do we know they ain't ours?" asked Babe, his voice a groggy growl.

"No way they come in this close without radioing in to the commander. It's a Jap fleet. Get up! We've got to get this gun over to the beach right now."

Matthew pulled himself up and pushed the blankets away. He fumbled in the darkness for his boots and slipped them on, tying them as well as he could. As he stood up, he saw the bobbing of flashlights in the distance as men ran south toward the airfield and the beaches beyond. Babe was still fumbling around. Matthew helped him collect his shoes.

Soon his small group had gathered the .30 caliber, along with its stand and the ammunition, and were moving through the dimly lit darkness toward the beach. Matthew felt the fear coursing through him, and he fought hard to drive it away. He had grown accustomed to the air raids, but this was something different. Japs were coming to the beach. Wake would be invaded and possibly overrun. He had heard a rumor: the Japanese never took prisoners. Today could be his last day alive.

They reached the brush above the southern beach a few minutes later. All around them marines were digging into position with rifles, just at the edge of the sand. There were no lights on here, and they worked as quickly as possible in the blackness. Matthew glanced out. He could see the lights of dozens of ships—a huge fleet was out there. The fear welled up fiercely. He looked to the east, trying to gauge the time. It must still be several hours before dawn. His group kept up their frantic labor and finally had the machine gun assembled and loaded with an ammunition belt. Now they waited.

The minutes tortured Matthew. He didn't know how long they sat there, but he thought it must have been hours. However, when he looked again to the east, the sky was still shrouded in darkness.

Night turned to day. In a moment the brightest light illuminated the ocean. Matthew blinked from the sudden change and realized that the marines had flipped on the searchlights they had pre-positioned on the beach. When he adjusted to the light, he stared in shock and terror—the ocean was full of small craft storming toward the shore, each one full of enemy soldiers.

The beach exploded with the sound of gunfire and artillery as the marines poured fire into the landing boats. A craft exploded a few hundred yards in front of Matthew, and bodies flew in every direction. He could see other men in the boats taking fire, and the screams echoed above the clamor of the guns. He wanted to turn away, wanted to run, but Jensen needed him, Babe needed him. He was surprised to see the middle-aged contractor cool under fire, feeding the belt to Jensen while the marine swung the machine gun rapidly in a wide arc, seeking targets.

Matthew felt nothing could survive such a fury of gunfire, but the boats kept creeping closer. Another open craft exploded from an artillery shell, but then the first vessel hit the beach and belched out a squad of Japanese soldiers advancing roughly on the dry sand, raking the defenders with fire.

Now Matthew could hear the sound of bullets and the screams of the wounded in the bushes. Airplanes roared above, and then the rapid detonations of bombs laced the beach. He felt a euphoric sense of calm course through him. Sound faded. Colors and shapes swam into sharp focus. He smelled the salt air mixed with acrid smoke and the sharp, metallic whiff of blood.

The Japs were advancing off the beach. Jensen kept up his fire, mowing down the enemy. An ammo belt finished, and he turned to Babe to ask for another. As Jensen did, his body flew backward as if he'd been struck an invisible blow. Matthew rushed over to the marine and saw, with shock, a gaping hole in his chest. Blood pumped out of the wound in pulsating fountains and washed out of his mouth. One of his lenses was cracked, and through the other an eye strained white and bulging in agony. Matthew knelt down to take his friend's hand. Jensen's fingers clutched his desperately.

"Jensen, can you hear me?" Matthew screamed. "Jensen!" He clawed at the marine's shirt, tearing the cloth, his hands awash with hot scarlet liquid.

The marine's chest heaved, and he coughed and gurgled. With a wild thrash his body jerked, then was still.

"Let's get the hell out of here." He heard Babe's voice behind him.

"What do you mean? Leave him?" Matthew demanded. His mind reeled. The thudding beat of his heart washed over him in crushing waves. He breathed in the explosions. He couldn't move.

"We have to go now!"

Babe placed a hand on his shoulder, but Matthew jerked it away. "I'm not leaving him!" Sand kicked up in front of him as bullets hissed by.

Babe lunged, his meaty fingers ripping at Matthew's hair. He jerked Matthew's head toward Jensen. "Look at him, kid. He's gone! There's not a damned thing you can do for him. Now you look at me, and you listen good." He gestured at the machine gun. "I don't know how to run that damn thing, and neither do you. We're no good here, and we're no good dead! Let's get the hell out of here!"

Babe tossed Matthew harshly back down and scrambled into the brush. Matthew lay stunned across Jensen's chest. He felt a sticky, tepid wetness soak his hair. He retched violently into the mud. His heart crushed against his ribs. Searching for breath, he launched himself into the undergrowth.

Matthew soon caught up with Babe. They broke out of the brush and scrambled onto the edge of the airfield. Men ran in every direction. The landing strip smoldered, concrete jutting in jagged angles from gaping craters. A fighter swooped down on them, bullets exploding in rapid trails. Matthew flung Babe to the ground as the shells raced by. A car on the edge of the field was hit and erupted in flame.

They fled and made their way to a depot, locating a small cart they loaded up with food and ammunition, pausing to recover themselves and wolf down some rations.

"I can't go back out there," said Matthew. His shaking had increased, and he flinched with each explosion. Babe wrapped an arm around him, a chuckle escaping his lips.

"I don't have you figured, kid. First you won't leave Jensen in the middle of hell out there, and now you don't want to go back?" He turned Matthew toward him. "We can't fight them with guns. We don't know how. But we can help out in our own way. We can do this. Just stick close to me." He pulled Matthew to his feet, and they piled the last of the supplies onto the cart.

The cart was heavy, so it took them quite a bit of time to move past the airfield and back to the brush beyond. The situation had changed dramatically since they left. They had expected that the Japanese might have overrun the positions, possibly that they could have even taken the island, but it appeared everywhere that miraculously, the marines were winning the fight.

As the fighting tapered off, men milled around in the aftermath, trading gossip. They learned that tiny Wilkes Island, divided from Wake by a narrow channel, had also been invaded but was now entirely in the hands of the marines again. Somehow they'd done it. They had driven off the first wave, just as they had defeated the first invasion fleet back on December 11.

The men helped themselves to the food, water, and supplies. Spirits were high as they shouted and slapped each other on the back. They moved about, wildly intoxicated by the victory. As Matthew and Babe chatted with them, the firing seemed to fade entirely away.

"Well, it looks like we've beaten them off again," said Babe. "Maybe our own damned fleet will show up now, and we can still get off this sand spit."

Matthew clamped his friend on the shoulder. He felt his arms ripple and shiver. He opened his eyes in wonder. The sky, an azure canopy, lay close above. A light breeze kissed them. The sun's heat licked at his neck and head. He breathed in deeply the briny heavens. *I'm alive.*

They sat down with a couple of the marines, sharing out a little food and washing it down with brackish water. They saw in the distance Major Devereux advancing with an escort of soldiers. Matthew was surprised to see a white flag. The major approached Matthew and the other men.

"What's going on, sir?" asked one of the marines.

"It's over. We surrendered," answered Devereux. His face was pale. Matthew realized that the men around their commander were Japanese. The soldiers looked like gargoyles, glaring in hatred at the Americans. They fanned out quickly, surrounding them in a forest of steel bayonets. They barked, growling in anger, lunging in sharp jabs.

Babe turned to the commander. "What the hell are you talking about, sir? We licked 'em."

"No, we didn't," responded the major, his voice gruff and measured like footsteps crackling over broken glass. "You've fought hard, but we can't stop them. I had word from Hawaii. The relief fleet turned back.

If we kept fighting, they would have killed every last one of us. I had no choice but to call it quits. I did this for us all."

"We should have fought on, sir," answered the marine, spitting into the sand. The major didn't answer but instead turned and moved along. Now Matthew could see other groups of Japanese soldiers quickly spreading out among the stunned marines. He couldn't believe it. They had won the battle, but somehow it hadn't made any difference. The Japanese were here, and Wake was lost. Matthew thought of all the rumors he had heard. Stories of Japanese cruelty and execution. *My God, what will happen to me now?*

～

Matthew and Babe, along with the others, were quickly corralled by Japanese soldiers wielding bayonets. The enemy screamed at them and motioned with their hands over their heads. Matthew lifted up his hands and marched with a group of twenty or so Americans toward the airfield. They were guarded by two Japanese soldiers who kept shrieking at them and striking stragglers with the butts of their rifles. A marine fell. The guard was like a hawk swooping down on his prey. He lashed out with his bayonet, pinning the marine's hand to the ground. The marine moaned in agony. The others could only watch in horror as blood spread in greedy rivulets from the wound. The guard kicked the marine in the stomach, then ripped the bayonet out of his hand and fired into his chest. A crimson volcano erupted from the marine's torso as his back arched and his boots thrashed against the sand. Then he was still.

The prisoners gaped, and a collective groan escaped them. The guards whipped around and screamed, herding them away from the grisly scene. Matthew was terrified, his mind reeling. He had just witnessed a senseless murder. *They will kill me for a trifle—for nothing at all.*

Soon they arrived in the middle of the airfield where an ever-growing crowd of prisoners had gathered. The Japanese motioned them, civilian and military, to remove their clothes and place them in a pile. Soon they all stood naked in a mass as more and more American prisoners arrived.

"The bastards are going to kill us," said Babe, whispering into Matthew's ears. "No reason to strip us otherwise."

Matthew wondered if his friend was correct. Why would they take all their clothes away? He felt wretched and trembled with fear. Now that the battle was over, he no longer felt that unexpected calm. He was afraid. He didn't want to die. He was so young. He had so much he wanted to do in life. Why hadn't he listened to his father and stayed at home? Now he was going to die out here, and his family would never know what had happened to him.

The day grew warmer as the sun climbed in the sky. The Japanese started pulling men away from the crowd. The guards were furious spiders, weaving rope up and down the lines until the men were lashed together. Once the prisoners were bound, the Japanese led the small groups away to sit down in clusters around the airfield. Eventually they reached Matthew, and he was pulled together with twenty others. They were led over to the pile of clothing.

Responding to the unintelligible shouted commands, the group grabbed what they could and quickly dressed. Matthew picked up a marine's shirt and some white civilian shorts. The shirt was huge on him, but the shorts fit. He wanted to find some shoes, too, but they were driven away too quickly.

A Japanese soldier came up to Matthew and turned him roughly around with his hands. Matthew felt a wire pulled tightly around his neck. The wire was jerked back until he choked and gagged. Matthew clutched at his neck, fighting to pry a finger in between his throat and the wire. When he finally managed to wedge in a pinkie, he pulled hard, opening a fraction of space. He could breathe again, although he remained closely trussed.

The guards barked sharp, singeing commands at them in their incomprehensible language and pushed them all toward an empty spot on the airfield. Once they reached the location, they were shoved to the ground.

Matthew glanced to his right. As luck would have it, Babe was next to him. "What's going to happen to us?" he asked.

"I don't know, kid. I don't know." Babe's face was pale white even in the sun, cheeks drained of the rosy blood vessels that usually patterned them.

A mass of Japanese appeared out of the brush. They were carrying machine guns, stands, and ammunition. They went to work and soon had set up six guns directly in front of the prisoners, each ten yards apart. The soldiers manned the guns, their fingers on the triggers. Matthew couldn't believe it. So they were going to die after all. He was afraid to die, fearing the pain and sorrowful that everything in his life was about to go away. He felt tears rolling down his face, and he heard himself sobbing. He tried to hold back the fear, but he couldn't.

"Hush now," whispered Babe. "No sense in giving these bastards the satisfaction. Everything's going to be okay, Matthew. We're going home."

He felt the furious piston of his jaw cracking reflexively. His gaze darted back and forth at the angry eyes of the gun barrels. He tried to pray, like he knew his father would, but the words just wouldn't come to him. He heard others around him doing the same. He wondered if he would feel anything or if the darkness would just wash over him. He waited and waited, but the bullets didn't come. The soldiers were still there, fingers on their triggers, but they had not fired. They were waiting for something, an order probably.

The sun labored heavily across the sky. The tension in the air would not release. Matthew almost wished they would just pull the triggers, to let this agony end.

A Japanese soldier walked through the line of guns and toward the prisoners, like a teacher in front of his many failed students. A sadistic smile pierced his mouth. He cleared his throat and spoke to them in a thick accent.

"American prisoner. You have shamed yourself by surrender. You deserve nothing but death. You are lucky. Our emperor has gracefully presented you with your life. You will be spared."

The soldier smiled again and moved his arm in a sweeping arc over them: a tyrant sparing the condemned. He laughed to himself and turned, walking casually away with a whistle on his lips. The other Japanese soldiers returned to the machine guns and began dismantling them, as the prisoners were to be held by regular guards holding rifles. A murmur of relief spread among the prisoners. Matthew felt happiness course through him. They were going to live! Whatever awaited them in captivity, they could survive. There was hope he would see his family again. That he would see home.

"I guess they aren't done with us yet, boy," whispered Babe. "You keep your chin up now."

Matthew turned and gave a little smile to Babe. He was so thankful his friend was here. *Dear God, I can't be alone.* He couldn't handle this without Babe. He felt shame in that. His pa didn't need anyone, not even their mother. It was their mother who always *needed*. Matthew did, too; he was not his father.

Hours passed. They baked in the terrible heat. There was no water and no food. Matthew's tongue dried up in his mouth, and he felt the scorching sun in his throat. He could hear coughing and the groans of the men, some of whom were wounded but not receiving medical care.

Day turned to night. The temperatures dropped, and soon they were cold. Clouds embraced them, and a tropical rain fell. At least there was a little water. They were able to turn their heads up a little and catch some drops on their tongues; never enough, but it helped take some of the agony away.

The night enveloped them. The moans increased. Finally, dawn came. Matthew hoped that with the new day something would happen, but the Japanese did nothing. The sun rose again, and soon they went from freezing to burning. Their skin was poached from the day before, and still there was nothing to slake their burning thirst. The Japanese brought out some gasoline drums filled with water. They marched up and down the line, giving each prisoner a small cup. The water was hot and tasted of oil, but it was the greatest thing Matthew had tasted in his whole life.

Day passed again into night. Matthew tried to whisper to Babe, but his throat was so parched that no sound would come. The middle-aged man seemed to be suffering even worse in the extreme temperatures. His head was drooping, and at one point he fell over, choking the man next to him. A Japanese guard came into their midst and struck Babe's back with the butt of his rifle, screaming at him. At last his friend pulled himself back up.

After another agonizing night the dawn came again. It was December 25. Christmas, Matthew realized. Memories welled up, images of home and presents and family. How different this year was. Was he going to die on Christmas? He didn't know how much longer they could survive out here.

About midday the Japanese came through again with water. This time Matthew was handed a little bread as well. He gulped the water greedily, then devoured the small crust of bread. More Japanese surrounded them and began shouting again, motioning for them to rise. The Americans stumbled slowly to their feet, a great moan rising from the crowd. They were herded away from the airfield and back toward the buildings near the north tip of Wake.

As they approached the buildings, the Japanese began sorting them into small groups and cutting their bonds. Once they were untied, the prisoners were pushed toward individual structures. Matthew stayed close to Babe, and they were herded into a small building that was previously used as a shop for the contractors. There were already prisoners inside, and everyone scrambled as best they could to find a spot to sit or lie down. There were no beds and no blankets, and the roof was partially caved in, but compared to the exposed airfield, this was paradise. Babe pulled Matthew over to a corner and then collapsed. Matthew sat next to him, resting his back comfortably against the wall. They were alive.

CHAPTER THREE

Beecher's Hardware Store
Snohomish, Washington
Saturday, April 18, 1942

Jonathan swept the sidewalk in front of Beecher's Hardware Store, one hand holding an envelope against the broom handle. He stood on the corner of First Street and Avenue C, right next to Bickford Motors, in the heart of downtown Snohomish. He was proud his store stood in the best part of town.

His eyes skimmed the glass and brownstone buildings that belonged to so many old families. He could see the Kit Kat Café, the New Brunswick Hotel, and the Cathcart Building. Farther down, across Avenue D, was the livery and the mammoth Snohomish Iron Works. His eyes lingered on the Snohomish Drug Company. The Gilbertsons owned it. Jonathan wondered whether Sarah Gilbertson was related to them. Maybe she was a second cousin or something? No, of course, Gilbertson was her married name, so she wouldn't be family after all.

Jonathan looked down again at the envelope he was holding. He placed his broom in one hand and pulled out the letter carefully as he returned to the interior of his store. It was from Luke. His younger son was in the middle of basic training at Fort Benning, Georgia. Jonathan remembered that long night back in December when he'd driven around the whole town looking for him. Luke had called the next day to tell him he was in Everett. He had tried to find an army recruitment office to join up, but they were all too full. Jonathan asked him to come home, but he refused. Only later in the week, after he had signed enlistment papers, did Luke finally return home. By that time, there was nothing Jonathan could do about it. His son was a young man, and whatever he thought about Luke's maturity, no matter what secret fears he kept, his son had made his own choice.

Luke hadn't left home right away. He stayed home through the early winter, waiting for his orders from the army. The decision to sign up seemed to have changed him, at least a little. He even put in an honest day's work at the store—well, at least half of one. In late March Luke finally shipped out, leaving Jonathan with nothing but worries about his two boys.

Matthew. Jonathan had heard nothing from his other son since the terrible news that Wake Island had surrendered. He had been so proud of Matthew when news reached the mainland of the heroic defense of Wake on December 11. Neighbors had stopped by to congratulate him. He had hoped to receive a letter from Matthew after this news, but he had not. Then came word of the surrender. Nobody seemed to know what had happened to the Americans on Wake Island since then. There were so many rumors about the Japanese. Stories of rape and murder. Of burying prisoners alive. Jonathan was sick with worry.

There was plenty of worry to go around. They were losing battle after battle to the Japanese. In Europe the Germans pushed farther into Russia, and in Africa they were poised to drive the British out of Egypt and capture the Suez Canal. The good guys were losing the war. In Snohomish the citizens prepared for an invasion that might come any day. Since Pearl Harbor they had learned just how unprepared

America was to defend itself. There were fears that if the Japs landed, the military believed it would not be able to stop them until the enemy reached Chicago.

Jonathan was doing his part. He had joined the night patrol and helped walk the streets, keeping an eye out for any suspicious activity and making sure that windows were properly blacked out. He was still helping at church as well, although he had less time to do so. Adding to his worries, the price of his hardware had risen substantially since the war started. Nails, tin, and iron were difficult or impossible to obtain. The store had never produced a bounty, but now Jonathan found it more difficult than ever to make ends meet.

He heard the jingle of the bell on the front door and turned to see who had come in. He smiled—it was Pastor Miles.

"Good afternoon to you, Pastor."

The pastor walked over and shook Jonathan's hand firmly. "Good afternoon, Jonathan. How are things?"

"As well as can be expected."

"Have you heard anything from Matthew?"

"Not a word." Jonathan's voice trembled as he answered. He struggled to keep his composure.

The pastor reached out a hand and squeezed Jonathan's shoulder. "You will, my friend. You will."

"What can I do for you today?" Jonathan felt better turning the conversation to the present. He didn't want to think about Matthew, what might be happening to his son.

"Well, I need some nails to repair a fence at home, and I also need a little favor."

Jonathan heard the front door open again. A police officer strolled in. Jonathan nodded. He knew the man a little: Robert something or other. He wasn't from Snohomish, but he'd been here for a few years now. Jonathan couldn't remember the man ever coming into his store before. "I'll have someone with you in just a moment." He turned. "Mary, can you come out and help?"

His daughter appeared out of the back office where she had been counting yesterday's receipts. Jonathan motioned her over to the customer, and then he turned back to the pastor, leading him to the nail bins.

"What size do you need?"

"About this size," said Pastor Miles, holding up a finger and his thumb.

Jonathan nodded. He dipped a small steel scoop into one of the bins and drew out some nails. He reached up with his other hand and pulled down a brown paper sack.

"Don't you want to know what the favor is?" asked Pastor Miles.

"I'm sure it's something important, or you wouldn't ask."

"Well, it is important, or at least it's something I can't do. I think you know we've been going through the church archives. I have boxes and boxes of the darned things in the basement. The thing is, my back isn't what it once was." He chuckled. "Then again, I wasn't ever much of a laborer. I need help pulling up all those boxes to my office, where they can be sorted. I was hoping you would be up for the job."

Jonathan looked at his friend skeptically. Pastor Miles was a hard worker, and the stories were that in his youth he was one of the strongest boys in town. Still, he was getting older. Jonathan realized if the pastor was having back trouble, it was probably a hard thing to admit. He placed a hand on the pastor's shoulder and gave him a brief squeeze, returning the reassurance the pastor had just given him about his son.

"Don't worry about it, my friend. I'll take care of it; although a strong guy like you, I doubt you need my help. When would you like me to come by?"

"Today or tomorrow would be great for the first set. I don't think it will take more than an hour here and there."

"I'll stay after church, then. I want to take a look at the lawn anyway. It's really starting to grow, and I want to cut it before the weather turns again." He thought of the grass and the spring rain. Wet Western Washington. If he waited even a few more days, the grass would grow unchecked, and when it was at last time to cut the lawn, the mower would slog through clumps of soggy grass.

Pastor Miles changed the subject to a couple of projects he needed to deal with at his house. Jonathan glanced over at Mary. She was chatting with the policeman. Something about the interaction bothered him. They were acting too familiar. The man arched his back and strutted back and forth like a rooster. Mary seemed entranced; she was laughing and cast her eyes away as he made some remark. Jonathan realized he hadn't been listening to the pastor. He nodded politely and made a couple of responses, but he couldn't focus. He kept his eye on the officer and his daughter. Finally, Mary moved to the counter and rang up the policeman's sale. He tipped his hat to her and left.

Jonathan finished his conversation with Pastor Miles and said his farewell. As soon as the pastor was gone, he walked back to the office where Mary had returned to work. He noticed immediately that her face was red from blushing. "What was that all about?" he inquired.

"Nothing," she said, but she kept her eyes down, her face a scarlet mask.

Jonathan's suspicions rose. "Do you know him?"

"No. Well, not really. I ran into him at a football game this fall. He used to date Katherine's older sister."

"What did he want today?"

She turned away. "Oh, look! I just found that shipment information you were looking for."

"Mary . . ."

She sighed. "He was picking up a hammer. It was nothing."

"Well, why did *nothing* take so long? You were helping him for ten minutes at least. For a hammer?"

"Are you keeping time on me now?"

Jonathan was surprised. Mary didn't talk back to him. She seemed to realize the same.

"I'm sorry, Father. He was . . . he was just asking how I was doing. He remembered me from the game. Now enough of these questions, Father. I have to finish this work."

Jonathan thought about saying more, but he let it go for now. He wondered what this *man* wanted with his daughter. He obviously enjoyed talking to her, and what was worse, she seemed as excited in return. She was too young, and this policeman was too old—nearing thirty.

Jonathan kept working for the rest of the afternoon. Mary remained busy in the office, and they didn't discuss the subject again. Near closing time a delivery arrived: white and yellow carnations in a basket for Mary. She danced down the aisles with them. There was no card, but Jonathan wasn't fooled—yet another thing to worry about. He would have to keep a very close eye on things from now on.

~~

Jonathan felt distracted the next morning at church. He had hoped he was making too much of Mary's excitement the day before, but when she had come down for breakfast that morning, she was a bright dawn shining through the house. She hardly spoke with him during their morning meal. She kept looking down at her plate with a glassy expression in her eyes, humming away.

Now, as they stood together in the sanctuary singing hymns, he saw the same smile out of the corner of his eye. His daughter was clearly smitten. She was far too young to be worrying about such things. She still had a few months left in her final year of high school. He knew it wasn't that unusual for someone to marry right after graduation, but he wanted more for Mary. She was so smart, excelling in every subject, particularly mathematics. He had hopes for her for college. She could become a teacher, maybe even a professor. Jonathan valued education. Neither of his boys was inclined toward college. Mary was his only hope.

He tried to concentrate on the service, but thoughts of Mary besieged him. All these dreams would be dashed if she married someone now. Her husband would expect her to stay home and tend to the house. He would probably want a family right away.

How should he handle things with Mary? He had thought his children would honor his wishes, but first Matthew, then Luke, had defied him. Now both boys were in harm's way, and Mary was in a different kind of danger.

The service was over before he knew it. He realized with guilt that he hadn't listened to the sermon at all. He chastised himself for his lack of focus. He didn't seem able to make any proper decisions lately. As they left the sanctuary, Mary sought out some of her friends, leaving Jonathan alone.

"Morning, Jonathan."

Jonathan looked up to see Pete. "Morning."

"I was watching you across the way during the service. You seem a little out of sorts today."

Pete always seemed to know when something was wrong. "As usual, you know me better than I seem to know myself."

"Is it the boys? What's wrong?"

"It's Mary."

"Mary? What could be wrong with her?"

Jonathan told Pete about the incident at the hardware store the day before.

Pete laughed and slapped Jonathan on the shoulder. "Is that all? You had me worried."

"I don't think it's a laughing matter."

"You haven't had a young daughter all grown up yet; that's all. You're feeling what every man has felt since God put us on this planet. She's your most precious possession, and she's caught the attention of another man. No father likes it when his daughter falls in love."

"It's hardly love," snapped Jonathan. "She just met him."

"Okay, okay." Pete put his hands in the air. "So it's not love. So it's meeting somebody for the first time. Who is he? You said he's a cop?"

"Yes. A Snohomish cop, but not a local kid. First name's Robert. Do you know him?"

"Yeah, I know him. Robert Miner. He's a kid from Shoreline, down south a bit by Seattle. Probably twenty-six or twenty-seven years old. He's been an officer for about four years." Pete's face darkened.

"What is it?"

His friend looked around, then leaned in and whispered, "It's probably nothing, but he don't have the best reputation. A bit of a ladies' man, they say. There's been rumors a time or two, also—rumors he's a little rougher than need be on the job."

That settled it for Jonathan. "I'm going to have to put an end to it, then. He's too old for her, and I don't want some man who doesn't have control of himself. Is he even a believer?"

"Don't know." Pete reached into his pocket and fumbled with a tobacco bag, drawing out a plug and shoving it into his cheek.

"Well, it doesn't matter. I'm going to have words with the boy."

Pete put a hand on Jonathan's shoulder. "Listen, my friend. You do what you think's best, but I figure you maybe want to think again about that idea.

"You really don't know how gals tick, do you? If you tell her she can't see this guy, you'll drive her right into his arms. She's just at that age where she wants to be free. You can't fix life up for her. She's got to earn her own bumps and bruises. If you try to stop her, then she'll just blame you, sure as can be."

Jonathan grunted. "Maybe he'll be gone to the army soon, and I won't have to worry about it."

"Doubt it. They're not going to take folks like police. Plenty of other people who aren't needed—they're gonna take them first. Best thing you can do is just stay out of it. Leave 'em be and hope the fire goes out on its own."

Jonathan thanked Pete. He didn't like what he had to say, but he was probably right. His friend had two married daughters, so he knew a thing or two about them. It seemed the tighter Jonathan tried to hold on, the more his children pulled away. Perhaps if he followed Pete's advice, the problem would sort itself out.

He heard a commotion and looked around, trying to understand what was going on as Mary ran up to him.

"Did you hear the news?" she asked.

"No, what happened?"

"It's all over the radio. We bombed Tokyo."

Jonathan felt elation. "Could it be true?"

"Why would they announce it if it wasn't? Such great things happening this week."

Finally, some good news, he thought. After more than four months of disasters, the loss of thousands of American lives and battle after battle to the Japanese, they finally had another victory. Carrier planes only had the range of a couple of hundred miles, so it was a wonder how the Americans had gotten close enough to stage an attack. The navy must have ventured in close to Japan. What a reckless and wonderful gesture. Jonathan soared with pride.

He looked at Mary, and she came forward to embrace him. They shared a moment of happiness, an easing of all the fears and disappointments of the winter. Jonathan thought of Matthew, hoping that this might be the turning point in the war that would bring his son back. He didn't know what he believed, but for now he would celebrate this first moment of happiness, the best news since the fall of Wake.

He let go of Mary. She smiled at him and ran off again with her friends. She was so young, so fragile and happy. He felt his concern rising again, but he knew Pete was right. He had already pushed too hard with his boys, and he had pushed them away. He couldn't do the same with his daughter. He must be patient. Much like the war, everything might look gloomy now, but time could change everything. He would watch and wait.

~~

Jonathan lingered on at church, visiting with a few of his friends. He asked Mary to hitch a ride home so he could remain behind and help Pastor Miles. The congregation talked excitedly about the Tokyo raid, but eventually the initial enthusiasm ebbed, and people drifted out of the church. Within a half hour he was alone with the pastor.

"This raid is a gift from God," Pastor Miles declared. "We needed something. I don't need to tell you how tense it has been here all winter—everything falling apart in the war and fear of invasion at every step. It's about time we scored a victory. Hopefully this will restore everyone's hope." Miles laughed, a mountain shaking. "I needed a little help myself. I figure the congregation would eventually want to replace me if I kept praying for victory with no results."

Jonathan joined in the relieved laughter. "Nobody blames you, Pastor. It's God's will. We will win this war when we are supposed to and not before."

"If we win it."

"Pastor . . ."

Pastor Miles held Jonathan's eyes for a moment. "History is full of decent people falling before barbarians. The Babylonian captivity, the fall of Rome, the fall of Constantinople, to name a few. We don't know what will happen, my friend." He sighed. "Still, there's hope. I was sure we would be invaded by now. There didn't seem like there was anything to stop them after Pearl Harbor. How many times did we drive out to the sound expecting to see Jap ships in the distance? Four months and, still, they haven't come. That gives me hope. This victory gives me still more."

Jonathan was surprised by what the pastor said. Sure, he had his own reservations, his own fears, but he kept those to himself. He didn't want to scare Mary, after all. He felt a little better knowing someone he trusted so much felt the same.

They continued chatting as they descended two flights of stairs to reach the cold dark of the church's lower basement. Ancient pulpits and pews stacked up against candelabras and communion casks. Piles of old books covered in cobwebs stood silent sentinels in the dark. The basement smelled of dust and decay. Pastor Miles shined a flashlight back and forth as he walked through the forest of rubbish. Jonathan followed him the length of the room until they came to the far wall. Rows of boxes held a noiseless vigil.

Jonathan whistled appreciatively. "That's quite a few. More than I thought."

Pastor Miles chuckled. "You don't have to move them all today. In fact, we can't deal with more than five or six a week. I'm just hoping each Sunday after church you could come down and carry up a few for me."

"Of course, Pastor. I'll get started right away." He paused a moment. "Before you go, did you hear about Mary?"

Pastor Miles grunted. "I did. Talking to that Robert boy? Do you want some advice?"

"Sure."

"Leave it alone. The more you poke a stick in there, the more she'll fight back."

Jonathan laughed.

"What's funny?"

"Pete said the same thing."

"Pete's a smart man. Now don't get me wrong, Jonathan. You're one of the best men I know. It's just . . ."

"I know what you're going to say."

"Good, then. I don't need to say it. Don't worry; these things take care of themselves over time." Pastor Miles shook Jonathan's hand firmly, then turned and lumbered through the rubbish and back up the stairs.

Jonathan took out his own flashlight and then walked up to the closest row. The containers were banker boxes. After putting down his flashlight, he wrapped his hands around one and lifted a little. It must have been jammed full of paper. The weight was significant. He picked up another and carried both at the same time, his right forearm holding up one side so he could still operate his flashlight with his right hand. He made his way through the maze in the basement and then walked back up the two flights of stairs to the main floor and to the pastor's office. The door was closed, and no one was nearby, so he pushed the boxes up against the wall to reach out with his left hand to turn the handle. The door slid open. He was surprised to see Sarah Gilbertson inside, sitting at the pastor's desk, a pile of documents under her arms.

"Oh, I'm sorry. I should have helped you," she said as she gently rose. Even the small office overpowered her, a solitary wildflower in a field of books and papers. "Here, let me clear off a place for you to put these down."

Jonathan nodded and moved into the study. He set the boxes against the edge of the desk and waited a few moments while Sarah cleaned up a spot for him.

"I here you go," she said.

"I didn't expect you."

She avoided his eyes. "Nor I, you. Pastor said he was going to carry all these up himself."

"He shouldn't."

"I know. He's not in any shape to. He tries to do most everything around here by himself. He pushes too hard."

Jonathan sat down in a chair across from the desk. He needed a moment to catch his breath. He smiled to himself. Pastor Miles wasn't the only one getting a little older. He would bring up one box at a time from now on.

The office was swelteringly hot—even in April. The air lay in heavy blankets over the room. A fan sputtered in the corner. Sarah sat back down and started her work again, her hand tapping out the letters of some document. Jonathan's eyes moved involuntarily down to her hand. The covered hand. Today she wore a white cotton mitten. He could make out the vague outline of her fingers beneath. His eyes moved up, and he saw with surprise she was staring at him, her eyes lancing through him. She caught herself and quickly glanced down. He coughed and sat a moment, unsure what to do. Finally, he rose from the chair.

"I'll be back with another box in a bit."

He left the office quickly and made his way back to the basement. He felt embarrassed. How rude to stare at her hand, to be caught staring a second time. What was wrong with him? He had most certainly made her uncomfortable. A poor woman who had done nothing to him. He chastised himself and uttered a quick prayer. *I will never look at that hand again,* he promised himself.

He grabbed another box and returned up the stairs toward the office. One box was much easier than two. He was certain she would be gone when he arrived. Or she would have angry words for him. She did not. She acted as if nothing was amiss, much to his relief. He set the box down and repeated the cycle again and again until all six boxes were in the office. She didn't look up or speak. He set the last box down and turned to go.

"Thank you."

He heard the voice again, delicate like a melody dancing lightly in his ear. He turned. She was looking up at him now, a shy smile on her face. He tried to read her expression. There was a certain hesitancy to her gaze, as if she wasn't sure she should be speaking to him. He wondered why. Or was it his imagination?

"What does the pastor have you doing?"

She looked down at her work, her left hand passing slowly over the papers. She had thin fingers, slight arms. She was frail. "I'm going through all these old boxes and sorting things out."

"What kind of things?"

"He wants to classify our documents more accurately. Pictures in one pile. Financial records in another. Letters, blueprints. Everything in a place."

"How long do you think it will take to get through it all?"

"I'm not sure. Months—maybe a year or more. I was surprised at how much they've collected here over all this time."

"We Methodists like to record things."

She laughed; her eyes mirrored moonlight on a midnight pond. Still, she did not look at him for very long, but instead glanced up for brief moments before looking down again.

"How are your boys?" she asked.

"Luke is fine, as far as I know. In the middle of boot camp in Georgia. I . . . I don't know about Matthew. I haven't heard anything from him since December."

Her face darkened. "I'm sorry. It was stupid of me to ask. Pastor Miles mentioned something about Matthew to me a while back. I had hoped you would've heard something by now."

"Not yet, but I hope to any day. He's a prisoner of the Japanese, I'm sure, but we've had no news. I keep sending letters to the war department and to Matthew's construction company, but so far nobody knows a thing."

"I'm sure it will turn out okay." She smiled warmly. He felt the heat of the office closing in on him.

"How do you deal with the temperature in here?"

"I haven't had to until now. It's so hot out today. I may have to move into the sanctuary this summer."

"And how is your daughter doing? What's her name again?"

"Margaret. That's kind of you to ask. She's doing well." Sarah leaned forward a little, her fingers still tracing little patterns on the paper beneath her.

"Are the kids treating her decent? It's not easy coming to a new town."

"She had a hard time at first, but she's made some wonderful new friends. It's easier for kids to meet new people."

"I'm glad. If she has any problems, please let me know. My youngest is in her last year in high school. We know quite a few of the parents and kids around."

"Thank you; that's very sweet of you."

Jonathan chuckled. "I don't think anyone has ever called me sweet."

"I don't believe that." She was leaning over even farther now, her entire attention on him.

He took a step back and cleared his throat. "Well, Mrs. Gilbertson. I know you have much to do, and so do I. Thank you for the nice talk, and I hope you have a good rest of the week." He nodded slightly to her and turned to leave.

"Thank you, Jonathan."

He nodded again without answering and left the room. He walked quickly down the hallway. He would normally have tracked down Pastor Miles and visited a bit more, but he felt anxious and overwhelmed. He walked out the door and into the unusually warm April afternoon.

∾

What had just happened? He was a widower of just a little over two years. In all that time he hadn't ever looked or felt anything about any woman other than the strictest friendship. He prided himself on his discipline and his honor. Now here he was, chatting away with this woman he didn't even know. He had looked at her arms, her shoulders, her hands. Worse, he had felt a warmth rise in him he'd never felt. *Don't think that.*

He felt guilt rising, hotter than the day. This woman was just another person. She didn't deserve to be gawked at and coveted. How could he expect his daughter to behave when he couldn't restrain himself? He would conduct himself like the perfect gentleman in the future. If not, then he would avoid contact with her. A simple change in his schedule and they need not run into each other at all.

After reassuring himself, he went on with his daily activities. Soon he was home with Mary, who was working on the laundry and preparing the evening meal. They went for a walk down past the Milwaukee train station and through downtown. They ran into Marshall Peterson and Mitch DePriest, two businessmen from nearby Marysville looking for directions to a Rotary function. During dinner Mary talked of school and friends and happenings around their small town. Jonathan smiled and listened, enjoying his daughter's company.

He climbed into his bed that night satisfied with another day. He said his prayers and closed his eyes, ready for sleep to overcome him. Despite his worries about Matthew, he smiled to himself as he fell into the darkness, watching delicate fingers dancing over a page.

CHAPTER FOUR

Fort Benning, Georgia
Thursday, May 7, 1942

Luke Beecher stood wrought iron straight in the back row of his platoon. He was terribly bored and sweltering in the humid heat. For weeks now, the men had marched and exercised while the noncommissioned officers screamed at them and cajoled them, informing them how stupid and weak they were and making certain comments about their mothers. This kind of talk had no impression on Luke. He knew he was special; he always had been. What most frustrated him was the constant attention. How could he get out of some of this training if they were watching him twenty-four hours a day? He had expected boot camp to be a lark. He had heard stories of how difficult the training was, but surely that wouldn't apply to him. He had always found his way out of the hardest work, usually by coddling up to the primary authority figure with compliments and using humor to win over his peers. The problem was, for the first time in his life, his charms seemed to be entirely lost on someone. That someone was Sergeant Dempsey.

Sergeant Dempsey was the platoon lead sergeant. A second lieutenant was technically in charge of the platoon, but he was rarely there, and nobody paid much attention to him. Dempsey was the person really in charge. He was regular army and had served in the military for more than a decade. He was everywhere, day and night. He moved rapidly on granite legs, with iron arms and a face carved of stone that never moved except to shout commands.

Luke had tried several times to joke with the sergeant and even to compliment him. Each time Dempsey had shouted Luke down, even sending the platoon on an extended run after Luke told the sergeant he admired his endurance. Not only was Luke making no ground with his platoon NCO, but the punishment run had angered a number of the men in his group.

Luke was totally unused to being disliked. He had strolled through life on his personality. Everything had gone his way. He had been his mother's favorite, adored by his little sister. The only other person who had seemed to see straight through his act was his father. Maybe that was what Sergeant Dempsey reminded Luke most of: his serious father who never believed his stories or excuses and never gave him a break like everyone else was wont to do.

Luke wasn't the only one unhappy with their sergeant. Whenever the platoon was alone, which was usually late at night after they were run ragged, they would fall exhausted into their bunks. After a few minutes the complaining would begin, always about the ceaseless exercise, the terrible food, and the tyrannical Sergeant Dempsey.

Now, as they stood at attention, Luke hatched the beginning of a plan. He didn't believe he would ever be able to bring the sergeant around to liking him. If he couldn't accomplish that, he needed to at least win over the men. How better to do this than to strike out against the object of everyone's loathing? He must figure out some way to pull a prank on Sergeant Dempsey. Something duly humiliating and so foolproof that it would never be traced back to him. Then after the men had all enjoyed the revenge, he could let slip a hint here and there, and soon everyone but the sergeant would know he was behind it. They might endure another punishment, but if the prank was good enough, nobody would care.

But what to do? He didn't have any close friends here yet to assist him. Worse, he had no access to anything besides what was in their gear. He also had no freedom. He couldn't simply sneak off to the store to pick up some items. He would have to make do with what was already in their possession, and he had to figure out a way to set up the practical joke without being detected.

They spent the rest of the day slogging through the mud and the fields. They finally arrived, exhausted, at a destination miles from camp, only to discover an obstacle course. Other NCOs blew whistles and screamed. The men were pushed with no break right onto the course, which required scrambling on all fours under barbed wire through more mud, swinging from ropes over yet more mud, climbing wooden walls, and high-stepping it through tires. Luke couldn't believe it. *What kind of a hell is this? I can't keep this up.* They could barely manage to work through the course, every man falling down at least once, all the while subjected to terrible profanity and ridicule by the sergeants. When they finally finished, the platoon was ordered to take a break.

Luke threw himself on the ground along with everyone else. The groaning was audible throughout the group. One person vomited. Others fell asleep. They stayed that way for what seemed only a moment before Dempsey was there, shouting for them all to get up. They were going to do the obstacles again! They were too tired, but they started to rise. Several men had to be woken up, and resisted.

Finally, they were all standing and ready to go through the course a second time. If the first trip through was agony, the second was hell on earth. Luke fell over again and again, unable to hold himself up or push himself forward in the mud. The screaming from the sergeants increased as the men tried to slog through the course, stopping occasionally to catch their breath, only to be shouted at to start all over again. By the time Luke finished, he couldn't even move. He slumped down in the mud at the end of the course, joined soon by others from his platoon. Nobody could shuffle out of the way.

No sooner had the last man finished than Sergeant Dempsey was there, screaming at them to rise and get back into file. The platoon collectively groaned. Two of the men couldn't get up. Sergeant Dempsey stood over them, shouting. He kicked one of the men in the stomach. Neither of them was able to stand. At last he simply ignored them, leaving them behind while he yelled at the rest of the platoon to march back to camp.

Luke stumbled along, trying to keep up. *I should never have signed up. Who does this bastard think he is? This isn't training. We're not going to fight a mound of mud.*

All along the way on the return trip, men fell out of line to throw up or collapse, simply too exhausted to continue. Each time, Dempsey halted the company, and they stood at attention until the soldier rejoined the ranks. The sun had set by the time they returned to their barracks. They were covered in reeking mud. Dempsey forced them to line up for roll call.

"You'll do without your dinner," ordered Dempsey. "You march together, fight together, die together, and eat together. If someone doesn't see fit to come back from training, then none of you need to eat."

"But they couldn't get up," complained one of the soldiers, a Private Erick Wenzel.

"Why didn't you help them up?" demanded Dempsey.

The men were silent, clearly confused.

"You're all part of the same team, the same platoon. If someone is down, you help them up. You take care of your fellow soldiers. Is that clear?" Dempsey raced up, his fierce stare a searchlight sweeping over them.

"Yes, Sergeant!" shouted the men in return.

"Next time you'll know what to do. But I'm going to let this lesson sink in real good. You can have a half-hour break. Then we will march back and pick up the rest of our platoon. When we get back, you can go to bed, *without* supper. By breakfast tomorrow you'll understand the point. Dismissed!"

The platoon uttered a collective groan and then stumbled together back into the barracks. The platoon housing was composed of a rectangular building with rows of cots lining the longer walls. A locked chest stood in front of each bed to stow each man's gear. At the end of the hall was a small enclosed room to the right that contained Sergeant Dempsey's office and quarters. To the left was another room containing the latrine.

Luke headed for the bathroom. Most of the men had simply fallen into their beds, not even bothering to remove their uniforms. Luke knew there would be hell to pay tomorrow if the blankets were soiled. He wanted to fall asleep, too, but he had to go to the bathroom badly, and he also wanted to take the time to remove his uniform to avoid further punishment. He shambled down the hallway with barely enough strength to keep going. He made his way into the latrine and stood over a toilet, leaning with one hand against the wall while he relieved himself. After he finished, he zipped up his trousers and gathered up the willpower to walk back to his cot.

He was just walking out of the latrine when he noticed that Sergeant Dempsey wasn't in his room. A sudden thought entered his mind. He looked around; nobody was nearby or seemed to be paying any attention to him. He stepped quickly into the sergeant's quarters. He had only a few moments and was taking a tremendous risk, but he didn't know when he would have another chance like this. Adrenaline coursed through his veins, and his heart thumped in his ears. He walked as quickly as his aching legs would carry him over to the sergeant's bunk. He looked around again and then pulled the blanket and the white sheet back. He crawled quickly into the bed and covered himself up: uniform, mud, and all. Once he was covered, he thrashed about, using his hands to pull the blanket and sheet up and down, removing as much of the wet, caked mud as his strength and time allowed. If he were caught now, he had no idea what might happen.

He counted to sixty and could risk no more. He pulled himself out of the bed, frantically straightened things as much as he could, and walked rapidly back to the door. Now for another dangerous moment. He peeked his head around the corner. Luck held again. Nobody appeared to be looking his way. He walked out of Dempsey's quarters and back down the corridor. Anyone observing him would simply believe he was coming back from the latrine.

Luke returned to his cot and removed his clothing down to his shorts and T-shirt. Private Wenzel was to his left, sitting on his bunk. Private Tony Bonelli on his right faced away, half asleep.

"Where'd you go, Beecher?" asked Wenzel, his piercing eyes watching him closely. Luke wasn't entirely comfortable with this recruit from Indianapolis, Indiana—he saw too much. Wenzel leaned across the space between their cots, pointing a wiry finger, his frame rocking back and forth rapidly like a jack-in-the-box. "Well?"

"I was using the latrine."

Wenzel stood and pointed a bony finger. "I was just in there; I didn't see you."

"You weren't looking with your eyes then. I was taking a crap."

Wenzel shrugged as if he were dismissing the matter. "Hell of a thing for the sergeant to cut off our dinner tonight. How are we supposed to run and do his damned calisthenics if we're too weak from hunger?"

"We'll be fine, you baby," said Bonelli, who lay back on his bunk with his eyes closed. "You'd think you never missed a meal before."

"Listen, fella," retorted Wenzel. "I've missed more than a few. But I don't whine every time something goes wrong like you New Yorkers."

"It's *Newark*, not New York."

"What's the difference?"

"If I wasn't too tired right now, I'd drag you outside and explain the difference."

"Dempsey's from New York," interjected Luke.

"*That's* the difference," said Bonelli. "If he was from Jersey, I'd have a talk with him and set things up real nice. We don't talk to the boys from over the river."

"All the good that would do," said Wenzel.

"We just need Sergeant Dempsey to have a little attitude adjustment," said Luke. "Maybe something will come along." He knew he was taking a risk saying that much, but he was very pleased with himself. Nobody had seen him, and he'd used the best possible resource available to prank the sergeant—the very stinking mud he had forced them to crawl in all afternoon. Now Luke simply could sit back and wait for the carnage. He readied himself for a very long evening. He was sure swift punishment was coming their way, but soon everyone would learn what had happened to the sergeant's bunk, and the men would be happy that one of their number had exacted a little revenge for everything they had suffered. Luke felt the same satisfaction all the way through the long march back to the obstacle course that evening. By the time they returned, it was near midnight and the men were exhausted and hungry. Luke collapsed on his cot and fell into an immediate sleep.

～

Luke sat bolt upright, assaulted by bright lights and screaming. His mind took a moment to process what he was hearing; then he realized with satisfaction what was going on. Sergeant Dempsey had found his little surprise.

"Get up! Get your asses out of those bunks this minute! I want everyone dressed and in line outside this barracks in sixty seconds! Move! Move! Move!"

The soldiers groaned but stood quickly, fumbling around with foggy heads for their gear. Luke hurried with the rest of them, but he felt no fear. He knew exactly what was wrong, and he was prepared for any punishment that might come their way. He felt content. He was sure everyone would appreciate the joke once the sting of this punishment was just a memory. He had played this game before with friends, with teachers, with parents. He knew what he was doing.

He slipped on his gear quickly and shuffled out the door into the darkness. A warm rain was falling hard, so hard that all the men were quickly drenched. They moved into position and then stood at attention. Sergeant Dempsey paced in front of them, looking at each recruit in the dim light, searching their faces. Luke was careful to keep his expression neutral. If the sergeant thought he was going to sniff him out with this game, he had another thing coming. Luke was an old pro.

Dempsey addressed them. "All right, scumbags. Someone here has a shitload of explaining to do. I went to my bed tonight, my sanctuary of rest. Only I didn't find my cot the way I left it, with pristine sheets. I found it full of mud. Now I wasn't born yesterday. One of you little bastards thinks he's mighty smart. I'm going to give you one minute to step forward and take your punishment like a man. I'm not promising any mercy. I *am* promising I won't take it out on everyone."

The sergeant looked at his watch and started the countdown. Luke could see the men out of his peripheral vision. The soldiers shifted uncomfortably. Everyone knew something terrible would be coming if someone didn't confess. The seconds ticked by. Nobody moved. The sergeant was back to searching their looks, clearly hoping to find a guilty party he could accuse. Luke felt nothing but exhilaration. Dempsey didn't know he had done it. What was more, surely someone would have ratted him out by now if they'd seen him leave the sergeant's room. He felt the thrill and the power course through him. He had truly gotten away with it.

The minute passed. The sergeant looked around for a few more seconds. "Okay, maggots! It looks like this platoon is full of cowards.

Nobody has the guts to admit what they did. Well, that's fine with me. I was looking forward to a little walk anyway. Go get your dummy packs. We're going for a twenty-mile march tonight. Tonight and every single night after, until the guilty party turns himself in. I don't mind waiting. I don't need any damned sleep anyhow. Now fall out on the double, and get those packs!"

Luke ran out with the rest of the men. They hurried into the barracks and retrieved their backpacks. They didn't have all of their combat gear yet, so the packs were stuffed with weights wrapped in towels to simulate an eighty-pound combat pack. Luke was feeling more nervous now. What did the sergeant mean about doing this every night? He hadn't expected that. He thought there would be one awful penalty and then that would be the end of it. This was different. If they did this every night, the men would never forgive him if they learned he was responsible. If someone had seen Luke but had kept his mouth shut so far, surely he wouldn't continue to do so with this threat.

The men loaded on their heavy packs, grimacing at the weight. Under the constant screams of Dempsey, they filed back out the door and into the rainy night. They assembled and began marching four astride, in total silence, out of camp and into the forest beyond. They were on a road, but it was so dark out they couldn't see well, and men continued to run into each other. Luke wasn't enjoying himself nearly as much. Every joint in his upper body ached from the unforgiving pack straps. Not only was he exhausted, but he also knew this wouldn't be the end of it. If Sergeant Dempsey carried out this threat, they might be marching night after night, perhaps all the way until training was over. They would never make it.

The sergeant led a punishing pace—faster than they had ever marched with their packs. Soon everyone was wheezing and coughing, sputtering with gasps of breath to keep up. The agony continued. When he didn't believe he could handle any more, Luke spotted the lights of camp in the distance just as dawn streaked the eastern sky. Thank God they were almost done! Ten minutes later they were back in camp and lined up again at attention.

"Are you prepared to come forward now and admit what you did? That was just one night. We will continue this over and over until someone tells the truth."

Another long silence ensued. Nobody stepped forward. Finally, Dempsey scowled and spat into the mud.

"That's just fine with me, maggots. You go get some rest. We'll take this back up tonight. Dismissed!"

The platoon stumbled back into the barracks, exhausted. They were far more tired than they had been after the obstacle course. Luke put his pack away quickly and fell into bed. Every inch of his body ached with fatigue. He didn't remember falling asleep.

In but a second the lights were back on. Dempsey was screaming at all of them to get up.

"It's morning, boys! Time to get up for your regular training. I suppose you thought you would get a little extra sleep after our march last night? You guessed wrong! Now listen here! There won't be one drop of extra sleep! You will do your regular training each day; *then* you will do our twenty-mile march in full packs every night! This will continue each and every night until the culprit admits what happened. Now get going, you little bastards!" Dempsey turned abruptly and left the room.

"When are you going to tell him?" Wenzel's voice lanced through Luke's heart. Somebody knew after all.

"What are you talking about?"

"I told you, I went to the latrine the same time you did. You weren't there."

"And I told *you*, I was there taking a crap. You must be blind as a bat."

"I'm not blind. I saw you weren't there, clear as day."

"No, you didn't."

"Did I forget to mention I also *saw* you come out of Sergeant Dempsey's room with a big smile on your face? That's probably an important detail I should've brought up before. So I'll ask again, when are you going to tell him?"

Luke was stunned. So he had been seen after all, and by Wenzel. He'd like to feel they were friends, but the truth was they weren't. The young man from Indianapolis kept to himself, taking what little time they had for breaks to read or write in a journal. Luke had made some attempts to get to know him better but always felt a wall between them. Now this man he didn't know held his life in his hands.

"I don't know what you think you saw, but it surely wasn't me." He looked at Wenzel threateningly. "You better not be mouthing off about this to anyone. You got it?"

"I won't say a word—not because you're threatening me. You're the one who'll have to live with this. I can't say I think much of you, though. A fella that can't take his medicine." Wenzel turned and walked rapidly away.

The men slogged through the next day, more exhausted than ever. At breaks, the grumbling increased. Men accused each other, vocalizing loudly what would happen when they found out who did all of this. Luke felt miserable and trapped. What was he supposed to do? He'd never had one of his plans fall apart like this. Dempsey was so different than anyone he had ever played with. He had strength and endurance that a teacher or parent simply didn't possess. And something else: he had power, total power. Luke felt a terrified panic rising in him. There didn't seem to be any way out. *And somebody knew.* He suffered through Wenzel's accusing stare every time they stopped for a break.

Luke survived the day somehow. He didn't know how he would be able to make the march again that night. He could barely keep his eyes open at dinner. His muscles were so sore he was hardly able to hold his silverware. They finished their meal and a short classroom lecture, then returned to their bunks. This was the part of the day when they were supposed to have a break, then lights-out. Instead Dempsey was already waiting for them when they arrived back.

"Well, ladies. I hope you had an enjoyable day. You could be resting right now, but some jackass coward has other plans for you. Enjoy a quick rest, then get your packs together. I've decided we will go twenty-one miles today. Tomorrow it will be twenty-two. You get the picture. Get your stuff together. We march in ten minutes!"

Luke gathered his gear. He heard the whisper behind him, the same as that morning.

"When are you going to tell him?"

Luke turned around. "I told you—I didn't do anything. Now shut your mouth!"

They lined up again in front of the barracks. The sergeant wasn't there yet. The grumbling increased, and so did the threats. Luke didn't know what to do. He'd never been in a situation like this. Should he turn himself in? What would happen to him? No, he couldn't do it. Dempsey was bluffing. He might march them another night or two, but finally he would stop. After a few weeks Luke might still be able to admit the trick. After a little time, surely the others would find it funny, would be glad they had all gotten away with it. At least he hoped so.

The sergeant appeared, and everyone came to attention.

"Well? How big of an asshole am I dealing with here? I can't imagine you would make your fellow soldiers march yet another night in heavy packs? What worm would make everyone lose another night's sleep? Go through another miserable day of training when you can barely move? Barely stand? Are you prepared to admit what you did? This is only going to get tougher on you."

Silence. Again nobody stepped forward.

"I guess that's it, then. We will be moving even faster tonight, so I hope you're ready."

"I did it. It was me."

Sergeant Dempsey turned around, triumph on his face. "Who said that? Who did it?"

Luke was shocked. He hadn't spoken the words. He looked to his right and saw a hand in the air. His heart sank. It was Private Bonelli. Probably the closest thing he had to a friend here. The tall Italian from Jersey hadn't had anything to do with this. He was taking the rap for everyone—for Luke.

Dempsey walked through the group and stood directly in front of Bonelli. "Finally admit it, do you? You scum-sucking piece of crap! You had the nerve to foul my bed! You're going to pay like nobody's business!" He barked at the rest of the platoon. "Get the hell back in your cots! Lights out now! Private Bonelli and I have business!"

Luke fell out with the rest of them, walking slowly back to the barracks. He felt shame as he'd never experienced before. He couldn't look at Private Wenzel or at anyone else. He lay in the darkness of his bed for hours, unable to sleep.

∿

Luke woke up the next morning feeling worse than ever. As the men dressed, he could hear a group planning how they would get back at Bonelli. His shame deepened. This was well out of hand. He couldn't admit what happened now. He wasn't even sure that Dempsey would believe him at this point. Maybe things would settle down, and Bonelli wouldn't be in too much trouble. Luke would never be able to confess what he did to the others. Nobody would be impressed now. If he kept his mouth shut, he could still hopefully avoid getting in trouble with all the guys. Could he live with himself?

They fell in for morning roll call. The sun was out and the sky blue. Soon Dempsey joined them, and that's when they saw Bonelli. He was covered from head to toe in mud. He was stumbling from exhaustion and had clearly been up all night. He had his full pack on and had been ordered to hold a rifle over his head. The sergeant ordered him to jog circles around the platoon during roll call.

"See how shitheads get treated?" Dempsey asked. "Private Bonelli thought he was clever. What's more, he was a coward. He let you all suffer for his bullshit prank. He's wiser now; I'll tell you that. He's spent all night figuring out what's what. After I'm done with him today, I'm sure you boys will have a few things to talk to him about."

That day Bonelli was always with the platoon, but in his full pack and with his rifle over his head. He fell often. Dempsey would scream at him until he finally rose back to his feet. At one point he passed out, and the sergeant had a soldier pour cold water on him until he came to. Then he started again, crawling at times, but he didn't quit.

Luke was in misery. He felt the hot guilt of Bonelli's suffering. He wasn't even able to enjoy the issuance of their guns that day. Each platoon member received a brand-new M1 Garand semiautomatic rifle. Dempsey instructed them on their new weapon, on the clip that would sound with a ping when the magazine was exhausted. The men spent the afternoon taking their rifles apart and cleaning them, over and over again. They were able to sit at tables and rest while they worked with interest on their new weapons. Bonelli had no break. He continued to march around them, hour after hour.

At each meal Bonelli tramped around the mess hall. He was not allowed in and got nothing to eat. He was only given enough water to keep him up. Luke couldn't stomach food that day, either—his tray lay untouched.

"When are you going to tell him?"

He heard the whisper again at dinnertime. He looked up. Private Wenzel was there, an inquisitor accusing.

"I told you—I didn't have anything to do with this." Luke couldn't say it with conviction. He realized he was in more trouble than he'd ever been in his entire life. He had no idea what to do about it. All he could think of was to keep his head down. He had to avoid this. If he admitted things now, he would be hated by everyone.

That night they returned to their barracks, except for Bonelli. The sergeant took him back outside for more punishment. Luke lay awake, filled with guilt and shame. Finally, in the early hours of the morning, Bonelli returned, exhausted, to his bunk. A few minutes later Luke heard rustling. He opened his eyes, and in the shadows he could see a group of recruits surrounding Bonelli's cot. The men grabbed Bonelli and lifted him up. Bonelli shouted out and tried to struggle, but he was exhausted, and there were too many. They were going to beat him, perhaps even kill him.

"Stop it! Leave him alone!" Luke barreled into them like an eagle scattering geese. Enough was enough. He couldn't take this anymore. Whatever the consequences, he couldn't let this man take any more of the punishment in his place.

"Stay out of this, Beecher!"

"I can't! He didn't do it! I did it!"

"What the hell are you talking about?" asked Mitch Congin, a huge, strapping man from a farm in Wayne, Nebraska.

"He took the rap for me. I wanted to come forward, but it was too late. It's not his fault. Ask Wenzel."

Congin turned to Wenzel, who was sitting up and watching. Wenzel nodded, a judge passing a sentence. "I saw it happen. I saw Beecher come out of the sergeant's room."

"Bonelli, is that true? Did you take the rap for Beecher?"

Bonelli hesitated, looking back and forth among the men. "I didn't know it was him. But I knew it was somebody. I just wanted it to end for all of us, and I figured if I took responsibility, Dempsey would finally stop."

Congin shook his head. "Well, I don't know if that's the dumbest thing I've ever heard, but it's one of the bravest. I owe you an apology." He extended his hand.

Bonelli took it, and the gang let him go. Congin turned to Luke. "Looks like we've got business with you instead."

Luke let it happen. He knew he deserved it, that there was nothing he could do to stop things. He was dragged into the latrine, where the men took turns beating him with their fists and then shoving his head in the toilet and holding him underwater until he nearly passed out. The pain was unbearable; the shame was worse. After what seemed an eternity he heard a shout.

"What the hell is going on in here?" The voice was Sergeant Dempsey's.

The men stood to attention. "Looks like we had the wrong man, Sergeant!" said Congin.

"What the Sam Hill are you talking about?"

"Beecher here admitted he did it, not Bonelli. Wenzel confirmed it."

Sergeant Dempsey focused on Luke, his eyes white-hot coals burning through him. "Why, you little shitbag. You let somebody else take the punishment for you. You let him run all night and all day while you sat back and stuffed your face with food and relaxed? What kind of cowardly nothing would do that to his fellow man? Finish up with him, boys. Then I'll take it from there."

The sergeant walked out, and the beatings resumed. Luke could taste his own blood. His left eye was swollen shut from the blows. A cut had opened up on his forehead where someone smashed his head against the lip of the toilet. He must have lost consciousness, because he woke up with Sergeant Dempsey looming over him alone in the latrine. He was ordered to put on his gear and his heavy pack and report immediately in front of the barracks.

All that night and the next day, Luke repeated Bonelli's agony. He went without food and was forced to constantly march around the platoon with his rifle high above his head. His arms were an unbearable fire of pain. His back and legs were gears mashed and grinding without end. Time lost all meaning. He marched on, enduring the screaming of the sergeant. Dempsey allowed the men to openly taunt him—to hit him and push him to the ground.

Darkness fell, but his torment did not end then. Dempsey sent another NCO out to march all night with Luke. He was still given no food, no water. His pack crushed him, his rifle a cross. He saw people he knew couldn't possibly be there: his father, his sister, his brother, Matthew, all watched him. He tried to reach them, tried to call out, but they were always just out of his grasp.

When he thought he could endure no more, he noticed an almost imperceptible lightening in the sky. Morning, finally. Luke was prodded back to the camp and ordered to change his clothes and report to Sergeant Dempsey again. He was barely able to move, but somehow he managed to change into a spare set of PT gear and dragged himself to the office, lurching to attention.

Dempsey ignored him for quite some time, and Luke was afraid he would fall over. He was so weak. His muscles trembled and jerked. Dempsey looked up.

"Well, what do you have to say for yourself, Private?"

"I don't know what to say. I thought I was being clever. I thought I would pull a trick and make the boys laugh. Things got carried away." Luke's eyes darted around, looking for a way out, for some angle he could pull. He was too exhausted.

"The trick was nothing. Do you think you're the first one to try to get back at me? I don't care about that crap. What I'm shocked by is that you didn't accept responsibility. I don't know what kind of man lets everyone else suffer just because they don't want to get caught. That would be bad enough, but it takes a special coward to let another man take responsibility in his place."

"I'm sorry, Sergeant. I feel terrible shame. I was so shocked when Bonelli came forward. Things moved quickly after that, and I didn't know what to do." Luke felt hot humiliation. He'd never been caught like this before.

"You make me sick, Beecher. You have no honor. I don't know if you will learn to have any or not. I thought about sending you home. A dishonorable discharge might be due in these circumstances—or a few months of hard labor. I thought about transferring you out of this unit as well. I've changed my mind. I want my eye on you. I want you to face these boys every day. You will live with any consequences they decide you deserve. You'll keep your mouth shut and walk the straight line. I'll teach you something about service and honor, if you are even capable of understanding what the hell I'm talking about. Let's see what happens to you. In the meantime, I'm assigning you to clean the latrines each and every day. You will have no weekend passes—ever. There will be no reprieve, no exceptions. When training is over, I'll see if you've learned a damn thing. Do you understand me?"

"Yes, Sergeant."

"Then get out of my sight! You can rest today. I want the latrines sparkling when we get back from training. You will have one meal only today. I'll have someone bring it to you in the barracks. I want you to think long and hard about everything I've said to you. I don't know if I've ever come across anyone like you. I don't like the smell. I'm giving you one more chance. One you don't deserve. You better take it. Do you understand me?"

"Yes, Sergeant."

"Get out of here, now, before I change my mind!"

Luke saluted and left the sergeant's office. He returned to the barracks, feeling more miserable than ever. He would have no passes for months. He would be stuck on this base and on latrine duty the entire time. He was hated by the sergeant and the men. How had things gone so wrong? He had always been beloved. He had gotten away with so many things through his good looks and charm. Now he knew what it was like to be rejected, to be loathed. He didn't know how he would survive this. He sat down on his cot, his head in his hands, and for the first time in years, he prayed.

CHAPTER FIVE

Bus Depot
Snohomish, Washington
Thursday, May 7, 1942

Jonathan sat at a table in the soda shop at the bus depot on Union
Avenue, on the river side of First Street. He drank coffee and pored over
his books. He had taken a break from his office and decided to walk
the few blocks to the soda shop so he could have some lunch and try
to sort through the ledger. His pencil moved up and down the register
in vertical strokes, too light to make a mark. He ran back through a
pile of bills, comparing the amounts to his figures. He was looking for
something. Any error. He was confused. There had to be a mistake in
here somewhere.

"Jonathan."

He looked up and saw Maxwell Weber, his landlord. Max was like
a Santa in a constricting brown suit, his face ruddy, with a bulbous
nose. He always wore fine clothing, wobbling up and down First Street
attending to his several properties. His face was perpetually red, and he
had a jolly, booming voice.

"Good morning, Max."

"Good morning." Max used to say *Guten Morgen* and lace his speech with other German words, but he had stopped abruptly when the war began. That was the extent of the change to his life as far as Jonathan could tell. He couldn't help but think of the Japanese family in Snohomish—the government had carted all of them off to resettlement camps in the first couple of months after Pearl Harbor. Max was a first-generation German with a lot of family still over in Europe. What was the difference? For whatever reason nobody seemed as interested in him or his family. Jonathan thought he knew why: Germans were still white.

"How are things at Beecher's Hardware?"

"Doing as well as can be expected."

Max gave him an understanding look. "I know, I know. Everything is harder to get, and nobody can buy what you do have. Am I right? It's the same all over, my friend."

"Times are tough for everyone right now."

"Listen, I don't want you to worry at all. If things get too bad, just come to Papa Weber. I won't let any of my businesses fail."

"Thank you. I'm sure I'll be okay, but I appreciate your concern."

"I mean it, Jonathan. America has treated me very well. I can afford to be generous. We can lower things and stretch them out. Please come talk to me if you need to." He took a step forward, placed his hands on the table, and leaned in, giving Jonathan a wink. "If you need help right now, just let me know."

"I appreciate it. I'm fine." Jonathan rose to shake Max's hand, then returned to his work. He searched for the register error for another couple of hours, then returned to his store. He couldn't find any mistakes. The numbers were correct. He sighed. No sense in worrying about things out of his control.

Late in the day a delivery arrived. Half the items he had ordered were unavailable. He reviewed the invoice. The shipment was dramatically higher in cost, some items by as much as 100 percent. How could he keep raising prices when people had less money? He signed for the items and then unloaded the materials.

In the late afternoon Jonathan decided to take a walk to clear his mind. He set the clock sign on the front door to an hour later, then locked up and stepped out onto First Street. He headed west, turning left at the iron works and crossing the Snohomish River Bridge. He walked along the road past the Darigold plant that processed much of the milk and other dairy products for local farmers, then down past the Seattle-Snohomish Mill and Nepa Construction. On his right the Harvey farm spread out before him. He felt better as he walked along, and he tried to push some of the dark thoughts out of his mind.

There was still no word from Matthew. He should have heard something by now. What if his son was dead? The thought raced through his mind as it had each day. No. Matthew was alive. He knew it. Matthew was a contractor, not a soldier. There was no reason he would have been involved in the fighting. The Japanese were not cooperating in providing prisoner information or allowing mail. Jonathan must be patient. At least Luke was still safe in training. The army wasn't engaged anywhere yet, and certainly the government would use the regular army and the National Guard units before throwing the new recruits into the fire.

Sarah. There was that name again, floating around in his head. Jonathan had avoided her since that last encounter in the pastor's study. Staying away was easy. All he had to do was take the boxes *before* the church service rather than afterward, and he didn't see her at all. She had attended church on Sunday. He had nodded to her from across the way but made no other attempt to engage her, and she had done the same. Hopefully she had sensed his distance, and some womanly instinct kept her at bay. Certainly Jonathan didn't feel he understood women very well. Even Helen had remained a mystery to him during their marriage, with her ups and downs, the storm clouds always on the horizon, waiting to strike with ferocity. He had endured her and loved her with his patience, his hard work, and his loyalty.

Endured her. What a terrible thought about the woman who had borne him three kids and suffered through two terrible years of cancer. She had taken care of the house and their family all those years. He must honor her memory. He chastised himself as he had so many times in the past. *She had every right to demand he stay loyal forever.*

Sarah. Avoiding her in his mind was far more difficult. Jonathan had prayed for God to take the thoughts away from him. Still, she returned again and again. He pushed her image away for the thousandth time. He was doing the right thing. If he was too weak to avoid her in his mind, then he would stay away from her in the flesh. In time the name and the face would fade. This must be a passing flaw. Jonathan had lived with such urges and thoughts all his life. He had never given in to any of them. He prided himself on his control. He had a promise to keep.

He felt better already as he reassured himself. His strength was all he knew, all he could depend on—that and his faith. The twin pillars of his life would see him through. He smiled to himself. He had weathered far worse during the Depression: the lack of work, the food shortages, the endless worry. He would survive this with his head down and by working hard.

Jonathan nodded to friends on the road as he returned to First Street. He was hungry. He headed for the Kit Kat Café.

As he was about to turn the corner into the restaurant, he froze. Inside sat Mary at a table. She was across from a man in a police officer's uniform—Robert Miner. They were sharing a slice of pie, their eyes focused on each other. Robert's hand slid across the table and brushed against hers; she moved away. His fingers were a tide advancing as they touched hers again. This time she didn't resist. His eyes lit with triumph, and a cat's smile spread across his face.

Jonathan turned and walked quickly away. They hadn't seen him. What was going on? She was eating lunch with this policeman, letting him touch her hand. Mary would never have allowed that at a first meeting. Jonathan realized she must have been seeing Robert for some time.

He felt anger rising. He started back toward the café but stopped himself. He didn't want to make things worse by confronting her in public. No, he would wait. Patience was a quality Jonathan had always possessed. Patience had saved him from making many mistakes. He would return to the store, and he would price the inventory tonight instead of tomorrow. He would think things over before he spoke to her. That way he wouldn't say or do something he might regret forever. First and foremost he feared he might drive Mary away—she was all he had left.

Jonathan spent the next couple of hours putting away the new stock, working well into the evening. He swept the floor and cleaned the bathroom. He exerted every measure of self-control and worked his hardest. Patience. Discipline. By the time he turned off the lights and locked the front door, he knew what he would say.

～

Mary was whistling away happily when Jonathan arrived home. The table was set. Warm and delightful smells emanated from the kitchen. He walked in to see what she had made. A roast steamed in a large pot, surrounded by potatoes and carrots in an ocean of gravy. Another pan contained a lightly browned loaf of freshly made bread, spilling over the edges, with butter drizzled along the top. He breathed in love and home. A fresh pie sat at an open window, the crust perfectly done. Apple pie. Helen's recipe. He had always loved Helen's pies.

Mary smiled at him. She glowed. He felt a twinge of pain. He didn't want to hurt her. He knew he was about to take away her happiness. He didn't want to, but he knew he had to stop this relationship before it went too far. Mary had a future. She didn't have to be just one more woman married and pregnant before nineteen.

They sat down to dinner. He felt like a coward. He didn't want to ruin this moment of happiness, even if it would only last a few more moments. He held her hands while he said the evening prayer, and then they started to eat. The roast was perfect, its rich aroma filling the room. He took a generous slice, along with the vegetables. He tore a chunk of the bread to sop up the gravy, nearly burning his fingers on the still-hot loaf. He was a monk nibbling piously at his food. Mary picked at hers. She had no appetite. The stony silence devoured them.

After they finished the meal, Mary cleared the plates. Jonathan kept his head down, avoiding her eyes. She returned a few minutes later with a slice of pie for each of them. Peach. He'd been wrong. He smiled. Peach was even better than apple. He placed his fork on the edge of the crust and pushed it down through the flaky crust. It slid through gently, and he lifted a bite to his mouth. The pie was still warm, the peaches ever so slightly crisp, the way he liked them. The crust was thick and soft, and crumbles of butter and cinnamon waltzed on his tongue. Helen's crust. She had taught all the children to cook, but most of all Mary. Jonathan closed his eyes and enjoyed the flavor, chewing slowly. He looked up at Mary. She sat across from him, smiling, enjoying his reaction to the pie.

He knew he couldn't wait any longer. He had to say something. He wasn't good at beating around the bush. He would just bring up the truth. "I saw you today. I saw you having lunch with Robert."

The color fled Mary's face, and her smile evaporated. "Let me explain."

"There's no explanation necessary, Mary. I saw his hand touch yours. You didn't pull away. Now, child, look me in the eyes and tell me the truth: You've seen him before this, haven't you?"

"This pie took so much time today."

"Mary. You've seen him many times."

She was quiet for a moment. "Yes."

"You did this behind my back."

Tears were streaming now down Mary's face. "Father, don't say that. Let me explain."

"There are no explanations you can make. I am not yelling at you. I want to face this head-on. You've made a mistake. We all make them. I'm disappointed in you, and you will need to be punished. But first you need to acknowledge that what you did was wrong, and you have to swear not to do it again before God. Promises *must* be kept."

"I've only seen him a couple times . . ."

"A couple times and he's touching your hand in public? I'm shocked, Mary. I might expect this kind of conduct from Luke but never from you."

"That's right," she said, her voice rising. "I'm always supposed to be the one who does everything right. I'm the one who stays at home, who takes care of you, who takes care of the house. Luke and Matthew can walk all over you, but I have to stay here and pick up the pieces!"

Jonathan felt his own anger rising, and he fought to control it. "You aren't even eighteen. You will live in this house, and you will follow my rules! I raised you to be honest, to follow your faith. What would your mother say?"

"My mother! What did she ever say other than to blame me or blame you or blame everyone around her?"

"How dare you speak ill of your mother!"

Mary burst into sobs and turned away. She ran up the stairs and slammed her bedroom door. Jonathan started to follow her but then held back. Patience. He went into the kitchen and cut another piece of pie. Mary needed to calm down. He couldn't let her comments about Helen stand. *Honor your mother and your father.* Still, he needed to focus on the problem itself and not get distracted.

Jonathan started in on the second piece of pie. The crust was cool now and a little flakier. The flavor had changed slightly, and he enjoyed this additional slice as if it were an entirely different kind of dessert. He closed his eyes, trying to remain serene and concentrate on the taste. He felt slivers of tranquility prick his soul. Patience always paid.

"Father." He heard Mary's soft voice from the hallway.

He opened his eyes. "Come in."

Mary came around the corner. Her eyes were red, and tear streaks still smudged her cheeks. "Can I talk to you?"

"Yes, of course."

"I'm sorry."

"Sorry for?"

"I'm sorry I deceived you. I should have come and talked to you about this in the first place. If you would just listen about Robert, I know you would find out that—"

"You're too young to date a man in his late twenties, Mary. It doesn't matter how wonderful you find him. The fact that he has seen you behind my back makes it that much worse."

"He didn't know."

"What?"

"I . . . I told him you knew, that you were okay with us spending time together." She trembled, a branch in a windstorm.

Jonathan was stunned. What had become of Mary that she would stack lie after lie like so many logs? *Patience.*

"You need to understand, Mary. You are still very young. I know you feel you are old enough to make the right decisions, but you still have a long way to go. I want a future for you. I want you to go to college. I want you to find a man at the right time."

"I want those things, too, but this is my life. You have to trust me."

What should he do? He had pushed Luke, and Luke had defied him. He had tried to stop Matthew from leaving, and his son had lovingly, gently refused. He didn't want to force Mary into a corner. He decided to bend. "I will agree you can see him in public places only. *And as friends only.* At least for now."

Mary flew into his arms and clutched him fiercely. "Oh, Father, you are so kind and sweet to me! Wait until you meet him. You'll love him. He's so wonderful, so strong and smart. I know you two will get along well."

"Let's not get ahead of ourselves. I said you could see him as a friend, in public for now. There's time for him to visit in another role down the road."

Mary clung to him. He loved the feeling, harkening back to when she was a child. "Thank you! Thank you so much!" she gushed.

"There's still the matter of your mother for us to discuss."

"I'm . . . I'm sorry about that."

"Why would you say something like that about her?"

She looked at him, her eyes searching his face. "It doesn't matter. I . . . I was just upset about Robert." She came back into his arms again, hugging him, holding him tight.

Jonathan smiled to himself. He would let the comment about Helen pass. He had solved the problem of Robert and reached an agreement with Mary. He hadn't required her to simply do what he originally wanted—he had given ground. Surely that would make the difference? He could keep an eye on the relationship, encourage Mary to keep moving at a slow pace. Once she was in college next fall, she would forget Robert. There would be school. There would be young students more her age. Distance and time would solve this problem for him.

Mary squeezed him one last time, then went back upstairs, almost bouncing away.

Jonathan closed his eyes again and took another bite of the pie. He breathed deeply in and out. He tried to pray, asking God to grant him wisdom. But his troubles galloped through his mind, and he found no solace.

∽

On Saturday Jonathan drove down to Snohomish Free Methodist to mow the lawn. He felt at peace. He turned left on Second Street and was met by the glorious kiss of the sun pouring out over Mount Pilchuck and the Cascades. The sky was an ocean of blue with the wispy whitecap of the occasional cloud.

He drove a few blocks, squinting at the brightness, then turned left on Pine. He waved at some passing pedestrians and whistled to himself, enjoying the quiet of the early morning. Soon he pulled up to the church. The parking lot was empty. Pastor Miles must be taking the day off or getting a late start. Jonathan scanned the lawn. The grass had grown several inches in just a few days. The combination of the spring warmth and ever-present rain in Washington assured prodigious growth in April, May, and June each year, until the heat of summer.

Jonathan walked to the shed behind the church. This outbuilding was ten feet by twenty with a tapered gradual roof and no windows. Paint had chipped off to expose raw wood in many places. *Time to scrape and repaint it,* he thought. Another project he didn't have time for. He smiled to himself. The Lord didn't love the idle.

He fumbled through his pockets and retrieved a ring of keys. He flipped through them until he found the right one, a small silver key that fit a padlock securing the double doors with a rusted central hinge. He opened the shed and found the lawn cutter, not much more than a steel pole with a handle and a series of circular blades on one end. Jonathan would have loved to have one of the power mowers that were out now. He'd even sold a few by special order. But such contraptions were for the rich— not for their humble church.

He marched the mower over to the lawn and commenced pushing it through the grass, grunting a little at the force necessary to drive it. He always found the work more exhausting until he found his groove. Soon he was moving along quickly, and his mind was free to wander. He loved manual labor for the time and liberty it provided him to think.

Matthew. Another day without a letter. Patience. Jonathan knew he had to remain disciplined, remain faithful. He prayed over and over for the strength to endure without knowing. He prayed for Matthew's safety and for his return home. He hoped wherever Matthew was that he knew his father was thinking of him, asking hourly for his protection and deliverance.

Luke. He thanked God his youngest son was safe. He hoped Luke was growing up and taking his training seriously. Jonathan smiled to himself, remembering the constant effort it took to make Luke do anything productive in the store. He would set him up with a task and come back an hour later to find the work unfinished and Luke chatting away with some pretty customer. Jonathan had tried to be stern with him, but Luke had a way about him—some aura that enabled him to stay out of trouble.

Then there was Mary. She was growing up far too fast. He was pleased with his compromise as he thought it over again today. She was so happy, flitting around the house, always smiling and teasing him. She had gone out with Robert for a walk one evening but had returned in less than an hour. She was following her promises. Jonathan still wasn't sure he was making the right decision. He was worried about Mary's future, concerned she would give up everything too fast—almost on a whim. What else could he do?

"Hello, Jonathan."

Jolted out of his thoughts, he stopped the mower. He knew that voice. There was Sarah, standing no more than ten feet from him. She was dressed in a peach dress with little white flowers. Her hair spilled over her shoulders. She had changed the style, he noted. Her lower arms were exposed, except for her right hand, which was covered as always, this time with a white gingham glove. Her calves ran a milky curve from ankle to fabric.

"Hello." He felt a buzz through his body, and his heart sang in his chest. He had never felt this kind of raw emotion. He pushed the feelings down.

"I haven't seen you in so long," she said.

"I'm fine . . . thank you. Yes, it's been a while."

"The boxes magically arrive each Sunday morning. You must make a special trip to avoid the crowd."

"It's easier to get that work done on Saturday after I mow, or early on Sunday. I . . . have things to do after worship."

"If you come when I'm there, I could tell you which ones I need. You're bringing them out of order."

"I didn't realize they are marked."

"Sometimes we miss things. How are your boys?"

"Luke is fine. Still in training. I haven't heard anything yet about Matthew."

Her face darkened a little. "I'm sorry. That must be terrible. I don't know what that's like."

"You've had some hard things happen to you. Just like me."

"That's true. But not like Matthew. My husband was there one day and gone the next. I was numb at first and then came the pain. But I knew all along what was happening. The not knowing must be unbearable."

Jonathan felt so drawn to this woman. She understood pain, like the pain he'd suffered. When Helen died, everyone gave their condolences, but so few understood the pain that wouldn't go away. He caught himself, controlling his thoughts.

"What are you doing at the church today?" asked Jonathan.

"I thought I would take a few things home and work on them there." She took a step back toward the building, nodding her head and smiling a little as she floated away. He watched her. She was so petite, so fragile, but she walked with grace, the sun shining around her as if she were an angel.

"Sarah."

She turned. "Yes?"

"Would you be free for . . . ?"

"For what?" He could see her eyes brighten. She was smiling at him, and he felt the warmth and dizziness rising to his head.

"Free for lunch sometime. I'd like to hear more about your husband . . . about your life."

"I would love to. I could go next week."

"Monday?"

"Monday would be wonderful. Should we meet here?"

"Yes, that sounds fine. At noon."

She beamed. She was even more stunning when she smiled. "Noon, it is."

She turned again and walked away. He watched her. He felt a wave of guilt. What on earth had just possessed him to do that? He was a widower. He had made commitments. What was it about this woman that unbalanced him so? He had done the right thing avoiding her, but now it seemed he had wiped out the effort of all this time in a moment. *Free for lunch sometime?* There was nothing for it. When she came back out, he would apologize. She would assuredly be hurt, but that was the way of the world. He had experienced a moment of extreme weakness. He would remedy that mistake immediately.

As the minutes passed he felt himself wavering. Was that really necessary? He didn't want to hurt her. *You can bend.* The thought occurred to him all at once. He had bent a little with Mary, and everything seemed better. Why couldn't he be friends with Sarah? It could never be more, but if he explained things to her, and she agreed, he could be around her. She was so like him: another single parent who had experienced death and loneliness and was facing the world without any help. She seemed to understand him.

The more he thought about this, the better he felt. That was the solution. He would talk to her, and if she would agree to friendship only, he wouldn't have to avoid her any longer. He felt relief and happiness. The back door of the church slapped closed, and Sarah returned, carrying a stack of papers up to her chin. Jonathan dropped the mower handle and walked quickly over to her. "Let me help you with those."

"Thank you." She smiled at him again. He brushed her hands briefly as he took the pile of documents away. He tried to think of something else as he followed her to her car. A breeze carried her perfume. She smelled light and fresh like a summer meadow. She opened the back door, and he gently placed the papers on the seat. He stood up. She was near him, facing him with her eyes waiting.

"I'll see you on Monday," he said.

"Monday, it is."

He watched her drive away and returned to the mower. He felt the guilt again, but he swallowed it. He had a plan. He wasn't betraying anyone or anything. *He would just bend a little.* Soon he was mowing away, thoughts tumbling happily through his mind. He didn't realize he was practically running, with a great grin on his face.

CHAPTER SIX

Silver King Café
Snohomish, Washington
Monday, May 11, 1942

Jonathan sat across from Sarah at the table at the restaurant on First Street and Avenue B, overlooking the river. He fidgeted with the glass of water in his hand as his eyes darted around the room. Several people he knew had already greeted him with appraising glances, and he bore stares from all around the restaurant. He hadn't thought about other people talking. Then again, what did it matter? He wasn't doing anything wrong after all. *You haven't broken any promises.*

"Where did you grow up?" he asked.

"In Everett. My parents had a house on Hoyt Avenue. Hoyt and Ninth."

Jonathan knew the area, the north part of town. Hoyt was a middle-class crossroad between the wealthier homes on Rucker and Grand to the west and the increasingly modest neighborhoods approaching Highway 99 to the east.

"What did your father do?" he asked.

"He still works as a printer at the *Everett Herald.*"

"Really? How interesting." The *Everett Herald* was the regional daily newspaper in the county, with an eastern office in Snohomish on First Street toward Brown's Theater and city hall.

"Your mother?"

"She passed away. A few years ago."

"Mine, too. Both my parents." Another tie that bound them. It was as if God put this woman right here into his life. *This could be a test of my faith.* He didn't want to think about such things right now.

"When did you meet your husband? I'm sorry; I don't even know his name. Maybe you don't want to even talk about him."

"His name was Jacob. I met him in high school, and we married a few weeks after we graduated."

"You must have waited awhile before you had Margaret?" Jonathan saw her face darken, and he realized what he had said. "I'm sorry; I shouldn't have asked that."

"No, you're just fine. We lost a couple of little ones before they were born. There was a time when the doctors didn't think we could even have a child. Then I became pregnant with Margaret, and by some miracle everything changed. She was born, and she was perfect."

Jonathan decided not to ask why she didn't have any more children after that. He changed the subject. "If you don't mind, tell me about Jacob."

She shifted in her seat a bit self-consciously but answered him. "Jacob was a regular man. There was nothing special about him or about either of us, really. We married very young. Too young, perhaps. We had some hard years at first as we learned to get along, adjust to life together. After that, things became easier. He was a hard worker. He was kind. He came home every night, and we sat together and talked. Sometimes we listened to the radio. He was exhausted so many nights from logging, but still, he stayed up with me. I loved him very much."

"How did you find out about . . . ?"

A cloud crossed her eyes. He hoped he wasn't pushing too far. "I was at home cleaning the house. Margaret was at school. I was scrubbing the floor of our kitchen, and I remember I was mad because he'd made such a mess under the table that morning. He had been eating breakfast with Margaret on his lap, and they were playing some silly eating game and making a clutter. I was cleaning it up later, and I was so angry at him. There was a knock at the door, and when I opened it, my dad was there, along with my minister. They were both crying. I knew the second I saw them he was dead. I don't know how, but I did. Here they were at the door, and everything had changed. You know the funny thing? All I could think about was what I had just been doing. I had been sitting there frustrated about nothing, and he was already gone." Tears came down her cheeks. Jonathan pulled his handkerchief out of his pocket and handed it to her.

"I'm sorry, Sarah. He sounds like a wonderful man."

She laughed a little through her tears. "It's funny because he's starting to fade a little bit. You wouldn't think that could happen, but it has. I try to hold on to every memory of him, but it's been almost four years now. Everything is starting to blur."

"I understand that feeling. You try to hang on to each memory, but they start to slip away. I feel guilty that I'm losing any part of Helen."

She nodded with understanding and leaned forward. "Tell me about your life here."

"I was born in town, and I guess I'll probably die here. I grew up on a farm on Fobes Hill. Our property looked out over the valley toward Everett. I could see the houses and the buildings on the horizon, and the Olympic Mountains on a clear day."

"Maybe you could see my house all along?" she teased.

"Perhaps not quite that far. My dad worked the farm, and he did some logging. I met Helen in high school, and we also married very young. I went to work at a sawmill at first and then in a hardware store. When all the bad times hit in the thirties, the owner was losing the store. I had saved up a little money, and I bought it from him. I changed the name to *Beecher's*, and I've been running the store ever since."

Sarah leaned closer, placing her elbow on the table and her good hand under her chin. "What about Helen?"

He felt a strange twinge. He was uncomfortable talking to Sarah about his wife. But he couldn't refuse—he had just finished asking her about Jacob. "Helen was a strong woman. She worked hard at the house and hard to take care of the children."

"Was she a loving woman?"

"She did her best. She was different. I think she was raised another way." Jonathan felt uneasy, as he often did when this question was asked. "She did her best," he repeated.

Sarah looked like she was going to say something and then seemed to change her mind. "If it's okay, can you tell me about her sickness?"

This was easier ground in some ways. "She . . . she found a lump. We went to the doctor, and they ran tests. It was cancer. They did everything they could to treat it. She fought hard. There didn't ever seem to be much chance. She lasted a very long time. Two years. She was as brave as anyone could expect her to be."

"What about you, Jonathan? How did you do during that time?"

"That doesn't matter. Of course the times were tough, but she was my wife. I had friends who came and helped some with the kids, with the chores. We made do. How could I even think about myself when she was going through all that?"

Sarah leaned in even closer. "That's very courageous and loyal of you, Jonathan. But there is always a *you* in there, also. Always."

He didn't agree with her, but it didn't matter. This was the perfect time to change the subject and talk about the two of them.

"At the end she asked something of me. Something that involved the future. That involves you in a way."

Sarah cocked her head, a little confused. "What's that?"

"She asked me to remain loyal to her. She asked me to never remarry. I promised her I never would."

Sarah flinched slightly, and her eyes darted down. Jonathan had dreaded telling her this. Still, if there was any chance for him to spend time with her, it *must* be only as friends.

"Jonathan, I know it might not be my place to say this, but that's not fair of her. How could she bind you with a promise like that for the rest of your life?"

He felt a little anger rise in him. *Patience.* "She had the right to ask. We were married for life before God. I didn't have to say yes. But I did. She spent her life taking care of me and the kids. She left this life early. She asked something of me for all her sacrifice, and I gave it. That's where you are part of this, Sarah. I like you. I respect you. I've never met a woman like you . . . well, at least not since Helen." *I shouldn't have said that.* "But please understand if we are going to have time together, you must promise me that it will be as friends and nothing more."

Sarah pulled back and sat straight up. Jonathan could see the conflicting emotions streaming across her face. "It's not fair," she repeated finally.

"It is the reality of my situation. I made her a solemn promise before God. If you and I are going to spend time together, if we are going to be friends, you must agree to this."

Her face was ashen now. He wanted to reach out to her, tell her it would be okay. How could he? If she declined, he must keep his distance. Every part of him prayed she would agree. He didn't know if he had the strength to stay away from her any longer. He was surprised by the intensity of his feelings, and he grew afraid she might walk out. He found himself hedging. "You don't have to decide right away."

She shook her head a little as if clearing cobwebs from her mind. She looked up, her eyes probing his. "No, I don't need time. I won't lie to you, Jonathan. I am very sad to hear this, but I will agree. I feel close to you. I . . . I have since the moment we met. Maybe it's because we both lost our spouses. Maybe it's more than that. All I know is I want to get to know you. I want to spend time with you. If . . . if the only way I can do that is as friends, then I will have to live with that."

He smiled, feeling relief. "Friends it is, then." He held out his right hand. She offered her left in return—her good hand. He shook it lightly. Her skin was soft and warm. Emotions drowned him, and he couldn't speak. The waitress appeared and delivered their plates. Sarah kept her eyes down, staring at her food, her cheeks red. Jonathan lifted his glass of water in a toast: "To friendship."

She raised hers in return, but didn't meet his eyes: "To friends."

～～

Jonathan and Sarah ate their meal in silence. He watched her, but she only looked up occasionally. He was sure she wasn't pleased with what he had said. But she would grow accustomed to the idea in time. He busied his mind with the joy of the future. They would be able to spend time together. He could share his life, his hopes and dreams with her. He wanted to know about everything in her life, everything she had experienced.

After their meal they took a stroll along First Street. Jonathan pointed out all the stores and told her things about the families that owned them. They walked past the Alcazar Theater advertising a slate of live shows. They stopped in Whitfield's Confectionary, and Jonathan bought her a box of chocolate before they resumed their walk. The afternoon was warm and pleasant. A light breeze caressed them, seeming to draw them deeper into conversation. Jonathan told her all about Matthew: his childhood, his unexpected decision to leave home, his travels.

"You must be so proud of him."

"I am."

"Terribly worried, too."

"Even more so. Still, how can I complain? These are difficult times. A few people we know have already lost someone. More will surely come. I haven't lost Matthew. I know he will come home to me someday. I just have to be patient."

In the late afternoon he drove her back to the church parking lot. Pastor Miles's car was there. Jonathan felt a little surge of embarrassment. His giant friend was always teasing him and would assuredly have something to say about Sarah. Jonathan let himself out of his truck and came around to open the door for Sarah. He picked up the box of chocolate he had purchased her and carried it as they walked to her car.

"Thank you so much for the wonderful day, Jonathan. It's been so long since I had someone to talk to and share with."

"You're welcome." He handed her the package. His hands brushed hers again, and he felt the dizziness. How could something so small and simple as a moment's touch create such a reaction in him? *It doesn't matter.* He smiled and opened her door for her. She lingered a moment and stood on her tiptoes, pulling him into a brief embrace. He helped her down into her seat, closing the door. *Farewell.* He didn't move as her car slowly left the lot. He watched until she was out of sight.

"Well, Jonathan, you must have quite a story for me." He closed his eyes. He had hoped to escape without an inquiry. He resigned himself and turned to see Pastor Miles filling the open doorway to the church.

"Nothing much to tell, Pastor."

"Oh, come on now. Come inside and have a little coffee. I want to hear all about it."

Jonathan reluctantly followed his pastor. He didn't really want to talk about all of this. Still, so many people had seen him today. Snohomish was a very small town; it was probably best to address this with those closest to him head-on. He felt doubts rising again. *This feels wrong. I may be going too far.* Perhaps this was another good reason to talk to the pastor.

In the office Pastor Miles gestured for Jonathan to sit down. He then left for the kitchen. Jonathan looked around. The room was small, with a veneer-maple wood paneling. A single steel desk sat in the middle. Tall, open shelves full of books and stacks of papers lined the walls. A table rested beneath the only window. The table was lined with boxes and files: Sarah's work. He smiled, thinking of her again. A few minutes later the pastor returned. He handed Jonathan a cup of coffee and put down one for himself.

"So, my friend, tell me all about it."

"All about what?"

Pastor Miles chuckled. "*All about what?* I've known you my whole life, Jonathan Beecher. Nothing ever changes in your life. Nothing. Except, of course, those things beyond your control. Today I noticed Sarah's car in the parking lot but no Sarah. Imagine my surprise when hours later you pull up, and Sarah is in your truck. Now that is a story I want to hear."

Jonathan grunted. "There's not much to tell."

"Well, tell me a little then."

"Sarah and I went to lunch."

"Funny thing, and I'm not disagreeing, mind you, but lunch usually is in the middle of the day. It's near six."

"We talked a little bit after. We're both widowed, after all."

"I'm well aware that you are a widower and she's a widow," said Pastor Miles, his eyes twinkling. "I was hoping you might have taken her to lunch before this."

Jonathan looked up in surprise. "What?"

"Oh, don't give me that. It's been two years, Jonathan, going on three."

"We're just *friends.*"

"I'm sure you are."

Jonathan watched his friend's face. There was a ruddy smugness on it. Well, he couldn't do anything about that. The whole cursed town was probably smirking at him. Like they didn't have anything else to do. He decided to change the subject.

"Any war news?"

Pastor Miles looked like he was going to try to continue the interrogation, then hesitated and said, "Haven't you heard?"

"No, is it bad?"

"The boys at Corregidor surrendered."

"I hadn't heard that. How terrible. That's about our last outpost in the Pacific, isn't it?"

"Pretty much. The Japanese own the whole thing, nearly all the way to Hawaii."

"At least they haven't come here."

"Not yet, anyway. Although, it seems like if they were coming, they would have been here by now."

"I heard the Brits are getting the same or worse," said Jonathan.

Pastor Miles nodded. "The Russians are falling apart, too. I don't know if they will last the summer."

"It's a miracle they lasted through December. Paper said the Nazis would take Moscow for sure."

Jonathan fiddled with a few of the documents on the desk. "Pastor, you know it's not something I've ever wanted to think about. It's not something any of us have ever wanted to think about, but could we lose this war?"

Pastor Miles was silent for a few moments. "I don't know. I don't think so, but it's been mostly bad news since we got into this thing. Our leaders keep telling us we are on the attack, that we are going to whip the Japs. The *Herald* tells us the same thing each morning when we get the news. The stories don't add up with the map. They've driven us out of half the Pacific, and the Germans seem to be beating up everyone in their path. I suppose it's possible we could lose."

"Why would God allow such a thing?"

"I don't know, Jonathan. We can't pretend to understand God's plan or ways. Just remember that we can't possibly see everything or the reasons that events happen in our world. There's been plenty of suffering by God's people. I don't think that's our future now, but you never know."

"Well, I guess we just keep praying about it and hope for the best."

"That's what I'm doing. And I'm praying for all our boys from Snohomish out there. I want each and every one of them to come back, but I'm afraid that may be too much to ask."

Jonathan rose. "I need to get going. Mary will have dinner made and will be worried if I'm not home soon."

"Have a good night, Jonathan. I'll pray for you, too, and for Sarah, of course."

Jonathan stopped and turned around. "It's a friendship, Pastor. Nothing more."

Pastor Miles chuckled, his hands raising in surrender. "I know, I know. So you've already told me." He still had that mischievous grin on his face.

Jonathan shook his head and smiled back. He didn't need to explain everything. He nodded a good-bye and left the church.

He was surprised when he pulled up to his property. No light poked out from the edges of the blackout curtains. Nobody was home. Mary should be home making dinner. He felt the hair on the back of his neck rise. What if something had happened to her? Here he was gallivanting all over Snohomish while Mary might be in trouble. He jumped out of the truck and entered the house. "Mary!" he called. She didn't answer.

He turned on some lights and went into the kitchen. There was no dinner and no sign of Mary. He called her name again and then walked to the foot of the stairs. He could feel his heart pounding out of his chest. He raced up the stairs and checked her room. She wasn't there. The bathroom door was open, and nobody was in it. Something was wrong. Mary was always home for dinner. Almost always, he reminded himself. Just like Luke. He felt a prick of fear. No reason to panic now; there were many possible explanations. Perhaps she was over at a friend's house doing some homework. He would call around. He stepped into his room to change clothes and saw it on the bed. A note.

He picked up the letter and scanned the contents quickly, his fear trampled by hot rage. She had betrayed him. Mary had broken her promise. She'd thrown everything away. His daughter had left him, left school, left everything—to run away and marry a man she hardly knew.

Jonathan whipped around and picked up a framed picture of Mary and him. He started to fling it against the wall but stopped in midmotion. He closed his eyes and breathed, willing himself to drive the anger away. He succeeded and then fell to the ground, sitting with his back against his bed, his head in his hands, weeping. He had lost all of them, his entire family. No matter what he did, they left him, they defied him. *I brought this on myself. She's done no more than I have. I held on too tight to Matthew and Luke. I gave Mary more rope, and she still betrayed me. I'm a failure.*

He sat there as darkness fell, alone and unmoving. Dawn's light found him still there, still staring out. The tears had dried. He felt exhausted and numb. He pulled himself to his feet, forgetting to change his clothes. He would return to work. He would endure somehow. As always, he must continue on.

CHAPTER SEVEN

Wake Island
Japan-Occupied Territory
Wednesday, May 6, 1942
(Across the International Date Line)

Matthew rode the tractor with Babe as they ran over foliage that had grown near the edge of the airfield. They were under the constant guard of the Japanese. Matthew was a little amused by the precautions. Where were they going to run? Wake was tiny and completely controlled by the Japs. The nearest islands were almost a thousand miles away and occupied by the enemy as well. Hell, the whole world might be under the rule of the Japs and Germans by now. They had no news of the outside except what they tried to sneak or what their guards would tell them. Not that anyone could make out more than a few words of Japanese in the first place. From what little they had learned, it sounded like their enemy had crushed America at every turn, taking island after island and destroying the US Navy in the process. There were even rumors of an invasion of the American mainland. Matthew tried to picture Japanese troops marching down First Street in Snohomish. He prayed to God his family and friends would never have to endure that.

Their own Japs treated them terribly. The Americans were forced to work long hours each day, rebuilding the island facilities and maintaining the airport. The marines had been removed from the island, along with most of the contractors, but the Japanese had kept 350 of the workers from Morrison-Knudsen who knew how to operate the heavy equipment. All the prisoners had lost weight. Since the invasion, more than twenty of the contractors had died. Still, they counted themselves fortunate: at least they knew Wake and what was here. Better what you understood than the uncertainty of captivity in China or Japan. Matthew wondered about the fate of his fellow civilians and all the marines the Japs had shipped off the island.

Matthew and Babe were among the "lucky" workers kept behind. Matthew stuck closely to Babe. The two tried to find labor details where they could stay close together. They kept barracks together as well. Babe had become like an older brother to Matthew, and he didn't know how he could have survived this ordeal without Babe's constant gruff complaining and sarcasm. His grumbling was reduced when he was able to steal away to one of his hidden caches of alcohol and sneak a drink or two. Then he would come back whistling and work away happily for the rest of the day.

Today was no exception. Babe had snuck away at the end of the midday meal break. He was gone for about twenty minutes. When he returned, a guard screamed at him and knocked him to the ground with a backhand punch to his face. Babe didn't seem to mind too much. They had all grown used to the beatings. He had made his way back to their tractor, a thin smile on his lips. Matthew knew why he was happy.

Now, late in the day, the effects of the alcohol were fading. Babe was starting to nod off. Matthew took over the driving and had Babe walk along the tractor to keep himself awake. Falling asleep during designated work times would certainly bring a full beating, perhaps even worse. Eventually the sun set, and it was too dark to continue. The guards moved forward and yelled at them in Japanese, prodding them with the ends of rifles and pointing to the barracks.

With the workday finally concluded, Matthew and Babe drove the tractor off the airfield to a crude wooden shed where equipment was stored and then walked off with a larger group of prisoners back toward the barracks. They grabbed their dirty bowls and lined up to receive their evening meal, a half ladle of watery rice gruel. Matthew remembered the first time he had tried to eat it and nearly retched, but now he greedily drank the contents, then rubbed his fingers along the edge of the bowl, making sure he had consumed every part of it. There was never enough food. Matthew had lost so much weight. He felt more exhausted and weak with each passing day, and he didn't know how much longer he could go on. Babe struggled even more as a middle-aged man. They huddled in a small circle, searching their bowls, hoping there might be a little more food they had somehow missed. There never was.

"These bastards are going to kill us," said Babe. "I can't take much more of this. Twelve-hour days every day of the week and this garbage to eat. What can they expect of us?"

"I don't think they care," said Matthew. "I think they figure when we surrendered we were already dead men. They're just getting a little extra work out of us. It's the same as if they'd just shot us down on the first day."

"Don't be talking that way now," snapped Babe. "You keep your head down and your mind on the job of staying alive. The war may not be going the way they say it is. They're liars, every last one of the slant-eyed devils. Any day now, we'll look out there, and it'll be our fleet lighting up the horizon."

"They'll kill us the day that happens," said Matthew.

"Maybe so, but it's our only chance to get the hell out of here. I hope they do show up, and I hope we survive it. I'll kill every last one of them with my own hands."

"Keep it down," whispered Matthew. "You know some of them understand us."

A few in the circle grunted agreement. Babe talked too loudly. The guards disliked him and looked for any excuse to beat him. The Americans loved him for it, but they also wanted to protect him.

"All this talking builds up a thirst in a man," said Babe, starting to rise.

"Don't go out there tonight," warned Matthew. "You're going to get caught one of these days, and they'll kill you."

"The only thing that'll kill me is if I don't go out. Now you keep a sharp eye out for me. I'll be back in a jiffy."

There was nothing Matthew could do. He knew arguing with Babe was useless. His friend needed his drink and couldn't seem to survive without it. Matthew nodded to the others and then crawled over near the wall. He set his back against the wood in a certain spot and then slowly pulled a few of the boards out of place and moved them aside. Earlier on, Babe had loosened some of them, allowing himself to sneak out and find his caches of liquor. It was a miracle he had never been caught, but the man seemed to lead a charmed life. Matthew kept his eyes forward, watching closely to make sure none of the guards were watching. He then moved aside just enough for Babe to crawl past him and out into the night.

"I'll be back in a few, Matthew. Give 'em a kiss if they come looking for me."

"Take care of yourself, Babe," whispered Matthew. "You're too careless with this."

Babe looked at him a moment, then placed his hand on his shoulder. "It's my little way of rubbing their nose in it. If they can't catch a fat, old drunk walking around on this island, how can they win the war?"

Matthew reached up and held on to Babe's arm for a moment. He didn't want Babe to go. Babe chuckled and then slipped into the darkness. Matthew quickly replaced the boards and then leaned back against the wall, worried about his friend. What would he do if Babe was caught out there? He couldn't handle things here on his own. He didn't have anyone else to rely on here. Sure, he knew many of the other men, but nobody like Babe.

Matthew closed his eyes, trying to strain his ears above the din in the barracks, waiting to hear the shouts that the Japanese had discovered Babe. His jaw worked back and forth involuntarily until his face was sore. A half hour passed, then an hour. He started to worry even more. Babe had never been gone this long.

Finally, he heard a slight scratching at the wall. Relief poured over him. That was the signal. Matthew scooted forward a couple of feet so that Babe could push the boards out. He kept an eye out, as before, for the guards. He felt his friend crawl past him, and then he turned to put the boards back into place. Once he was done, he could finally relax—they had not been discovered.

Matthew looked up to congratulate his friend and was surprised to see what looked like anger and fear playing across Babe's face.

"What's wrong?" Matthew asked.

"It's gone. It's all gone." Babe spat on the floor.

"What do you mean?"

"The liquor is gone. All of it."

"Did they find it?"

"No, they didn't find it, you nitwit," retorted Babe, as angry as Matthew had ever seen him. "I must have drunk the last of it. Damn it, I thought there was more. I thought it would last me until the rescue fleet came—or at least until they killed me. Now what the hell am I going to do?"

"Can't you quit?"

"I tried that already. Why do you think I came to this damn place? I came here to dry up. And I was doing fine until the cursed Japs came. That's what broke me. I can't quit again. I just can't." Babe put his head in his arms, covering his face. Matthew put a hand on his shoulder, but Babe shrugged it off. "Leave me alone, damn it! You're always bothering me, you little leech! I've got my own problems, and I don't need to look after a little sliver like you!" He turned and flopped down on his blankets, turning away to face the wall.

Matthew felt the sting of the rebuke. Babe had pushed him away before. He would tell Matthew that he was stifling him, that he didn't need anyone around. But then he would always come back and apologize. Matthew moved away from Babe and lay down on his own blankets and mattress stuffed with leaves. He knew there was no point in trying to talk to him again tonight. He would leave him alone and hope he came around in the morning. He had no idea what to do when someone needed a drink and couldn't get one. He'd heard stories of people going off the bottle. How could Babe do this? How could he work full days in the hot sun with no food while his body screamed for booze? Matthew whispered a silent prayer for his friend. God would find an answer.

～

The next morning Babe could barely get up. He slogged through the morning mealtime, refusing to eat or to speak to anyone. Matthew noticed his hands were shaking badly. After breakfast they walked out silently together. Babe swayed back and forth as if barely able to put one foot in front of the other. They made it to the tractor somehow. Matthew climbed on and then pulled his friend up.

"Just stay up on this thing today. I'll do the driving, and I'll get off and on. If they see you, just take over the driving for a spell."

"Don't worry about me," said Babe through gritted teeth. "You worry about yourself. I've worked longer than you've been alive, boy. I can handle myself."

But even as Babe said that, he could barely sit still. Matthew reached a hand up and steadied his friend. Then he started the tractor and threw it into reverse, moving out of the shed as quickly as he could so that the guards wouldn't get too close of a look at Babe.

Fortunately, they had the same job today as yesterday, which was to continue flattening the vegetation that grew so quickly in the tropical sun around the airfield. The task wasn't labor intensive, and they were both able to ride the tractor most of the time.

The sun rose, and the wind picked up, another typical day on Wake. Matthew kept one eye on the job and one eye on Babe throughout the morning and early afternoon. The hours dragged by, and it seemed the day would last forever. Matthew was sure Babe would topple off the tractor or that a guard would challenge them, but miraculously nothing happened.

"I'm dying, boy. I'm not going to make it," whispered Babe. He had grown pale, and the shaking seemed to be getting worse. His forehead dripped with sweat.

"You've got to hang in there, Babe. The day's more than halfway done."

"I can't do this another minute. I need something to drink. I . . . I need to rest." Babe groaned and tried to slump over in his seat, but Matthew propped him up.

"We can't rest, and there's nothing I can do for you. You have to keep going. They'll shoot you. You know they will."

"What difference does it make? I'll die without something to wet my whistle."

Matthew stopped the tractor and looked into his friend's eyes, pleading with him. "Don't say that. We'll figure something out tonight. There has to be something we can do."

These words seemed to calm Babe down, and he lapsed into quiet again. A few more hours passed. Somehow Babe stayed on the tractor. Soon the sun set, and they were met with the barking commands to quit work. When Matthew parked their machine, he had to assist his friend in getting down. Babe's back was soaked through with sweat, and he could barely walk. Matthew led him away from the shed and slowly back toward the barracks. Another contractor saw the situation and came up on the other side, grabbing Babe's arm near his elbow, and together the three of them shuffled toward the barracks. Again by some miracle the Japanese seemed not to notice what was going on. Any showing of weakness would bring beatings or even death. They made it into their building and to Babe's corner. They quickly laid him down and covered him with a couple of blankets. He immediately passed out, although the shivering continued. Without a word men hastened over and sat down in front of Babe, battlements blocking the view.

"Does anyone have any liquor? Anything we could give him?" asked Matthew. There was no answer. Any small amount of booze that was hidden was worth more than gold. At last, someone spoke up.

"I've a little," said John Gregory. John was a friend of Matthew's from Spokane, Washington.

"Could you get it?"

"It's not much," he said reluctantly. "I was kind of saving it for a special occasion."

"He's going to die without it."

John nodded and rose. He returned a minute later, and after looking around he produced a brown bottle that was almost empty. There was no more than a swig or two at the bottom.

Matthew patted John's arm in thanks and turned to Babe. He pulled his friend's head up slightly and then unscrewed the bottle. He poured the liquor slowly into Babe's mouth. His friend coughed and sputtered. Then he grabbed the bottle, pulling it back hard and drinking all the remaining liquid in a gulp. He looked up gratefully at Matthew and seemed to relax. Then his head fell back, and he was instantly asleep.

"Well, that takes care of tonight, but what the hell do we do now?" asked Martin Kelly, a contractor originally from Roseburg, Oregon.

"I don't know what to do," said Matthew. "How long does it take to dry out from the drink?"

"Many days, I've heard," said John. "Maybe weeks."

"We don't have days. If we sent him to the infirmary, they would probably just kill him," said Matthew.

"I have a friend who works there," said Martin. "I could make sure they keep an eye on him until he's better."

"Your friend won't be there all the time. What if something happens when he's not on his shift?" asked Matthew.

"Do you have any other ideas? Babe won't be able to work with you another day, I'll bet. There's no way he'll be able to stay here, either. They'd catch him, and then we'd be lucky if they didn't kill him right then and there."

Matthew thought about it. Martin was right. They had no choice. "Let's take him tonight then."

Martin and John helped Matthew bring Babe to his feet. His friend was unconscious, so they had difficulty moving him. They half dragged and half carried him to the barracks entrance, where they explained with hand gestures to the guard that their friend needed to go to the hospital. The Japanese soldier watched them warily for a few moments, then called another two guards over. They consulted in their barking, sharp language and then opened the door and motioned for them to leave.

The men carried Babe out of the barracks and over to the infirmary. The hospital consisted of a rectangular room with two rows of a dozen cots, each row pushed up against the longer walls. Dim lighting shone on a couple of civilian contractors, now serving as attendants, moving back and forth among the sick. Matthew gagged from the overpowering stench that hung ripe in the humid air. They carried Babe in and brought him to the nearest open cot, gently placing him on the bed. As they laid him down, he opened an eye.

"What's going on?" he asked, his eyes darting around.

"We've taken you to the hospital, Babe," explained Matthew.

He tried to rise, but Matthew held him down. "No, no, I'm fine. I don't want to be here. I'll die here."

"Don't worry," whispered Matthew. "Martin has a friend who will keep an eye on you. You need to rest and recover from that stuff. He'll take care of you until you're better."

Matthew could see the fear in Babe's eyes. "Please don't leave me. I know I'll die here. Can't you just find me some more hooch? Where did you find the stuff tonight?"

"I don't know of any more drink anywhere, Babe. Even if I could find a little, there'd be no more than another sip or two. You've got to get over the stuff. You can't do that in the barracks, and you're going to be too weak to work."

Babe tried to rise again and pushed Matthew's arms away. "You're trying to kill me, you bastard!" He cursed under his breath. He struggled, but Matthew pressed down with all his strength. John and Martin rushed to his side.

They heard the sharp clap of Japanese voices, and they froze. Matthew turned. One of the guards had seen the scuffling and come over to investigate. He shouted and motioned for them to move aside, his rifle pointed at them. Matthew whispered a warning to Babe. Then he slowly moved his hands up over his head, climbed off the cot, and stepped away. The soldier rushed forward, still shouting. He stuck the barrel of his gun in Babe's chest and prodded him, turning his head and shouting. An American orderly scrambled over and tried to get between the soldier and Babe. He had his hands up also and was speaking calmly, mixing in a Japanese word here and there.

"That's my friend," whispered Martin. "Let's step away slowly."

They all retreated a few steps, trying to move cautiously so they didn't increase the tension. The soldier kept shouting, *"Teishi!"* and motioning to Babe and then to the other contractors. Martin's friend kept his hands up, speaking slowly and gesturing away from the building. Eventually the soldier calmed down. He lowered his rifle and turned to stare at Martin and the others. He glared at them for a moment and took a step in their direction. Then he turned and strutted arrogantly out of the building.

They moved quickly to Babe again. This time Matthew's friend was calm, perhaps realizing the danger he was in.

"We're trying to help you," said Matthew.

"I know. I know that, and I'm sorry I snapped at you." Babe grabbed a fistful of Matthew's shirt and pulled him in. A furnace of fetid breath blew over Matthew. "You've been a good friend to me. You've been a son to me. I know you're trying to help me now. Although I think you've signed my death warrant."

"I don't know what else I can do. You can't work, and you can't stay. This is the only place where there's any hope. Please, Babe, just stay here and get better."

He looked up at Matthew, his eyes searching. "You're right, boy. Now get the hell out of here, and get back to work. Let Babe get some rest. I'll be back to work in a few days, stronger than ever. These zip-eyed little worms aren't going to stop me." He lay back, and his whole body collapsed into the cot. The fight seeped out of him.

Matthew grasped Babe's hand and held it tightly for a moment. "You take care of yourself tomorrow. I'll be back here at night. Try to keep yourself under control, and keep your big mouth shut."

Babe nodded a little by way of understanding, but he didn't speak again. Matthew squeezed his arm and then walked out of the hospital and into the night, tears falling unseen in the darkness.

∿

Matthew awoke early the next morning, hoping to visit Babe and make sure he was all right. However, the guard at the door of the barracks would not let him pass, and he couldn't make himself understood. He finally gave up with the call to the morning meal, and, after collecting a bowl of the same watery gruel, he sat down with Martin and John in the corner, where they wouldn't be overheard.

"I tried to get out of here early, but the damn guard wouldn't let me go," said Matthew.

"I'm not surprised," said John. "They're touchy as hell about anything unusual. Don't worry, though. After our breakfast I'll stop by the infirmary before I head out to work and check on him. I'll be coming out toward the airfield in the early afternoon, and I can tell you then how he's doing."

"I'd appreciate it. Still, I should try to make it over there before I head out to work."

"Are you kidding? You have no reason to be in the infirmary," said Martin. "If you're not careful, it'll be your head on the block. Don't worry about it. My orderly friend is a swell guy. He'll take care of things. You leave it to me, and I'll come see you after I check in on Babe."

Matthew didn't like it, but he didn't have a choice. It was not that he didn't trust John. He did, but he was terribly worried about his friend. He would have to wait. Maybe he could obtain permission to visit him this evening after dinner. He would try to find one of the guards who spoke a little English.

They finished their meager breakfast and then set off to work. Matthew didn't have a replacement for Babe, so he spent the day doing both jobs, which required much starting and stopping of the tractor as he jumped off to clear the stubborn brush that the machine couldn't reach. The day dragged by even slower than the previous one, and his thoughts were constantly on Babe.

In the early afternoon Matthew drove over to the refilling station to fuel up. He was just pulling the hose out when he heard sharp yells.

He turned and was surprised to find three Japanese guards surrounding him. They screamed at the top of their lungs. He dropped the hose and quickly raised his hands over his head. One of the guards reversed his rifle and brought the butt down sharply on Matthew's lower back. He felt fiery pain tear through him, and he fell to the ground. The guards rained blows down on him, one after another. Matthew curled up with his hands over his head, trying to ward them off. He had been hit a time or two during his captivity but never like this. A fountain of blood splashed from his mouth. His left forearm throbbed with each beat of his heart. His ribs twisted and snapped under loose skin beneath the soldiers' boots. Matthew tried to speak, but they didn't understand him, and the blows continued. A crashing midnight embraced him, and he welcomed the shadowy nothing.

A splash of water woke him. He didn't know how long he had been unconscious. He blinked, trying to understand where he was or what was going on. He was in a stone room. A single bare lightbulb glared down from a ceiling wire. Japanese soldiers surrounded him. An officer sat on a stool directly over him. He held a wooden switch. He whipped it and then lashed Matthew across the face. The blinding pain nearly knocked him out again. The officer spoke to him in broken English.

"How you help your friend break store?"

What is he talking about? "I . . . I don't understand you."

The officer struck him again, this time across his back. "You lie. You help this one, this one Babe break into our stores. He your friend. You two always together. Work together. You tell the truth now or you die here."

"I don't know what you're talking about." Babe had obviously done something. What did the officer mean by "stores"?

Matthew felt the switch again on his back. The pain invaded his muscles and seared his spine. He gasped and shouted, begging for them to stop.

"We find your friend in stores today. He singing and drank up all the *sake*. You take him to hospital last night, close to stores. You knew. You plan with him."

"I don't know anything. I swear. It's true that we took him to the hospital last night. He was . . . he was sick. But I don't know what you're talking about."

The officer struck him again. "You lie. You going to die with Babe. He steal from Japanese. You steal from Japanese."

"I didn't. I swear I didn't know anything."

They didn't believe him. They kept beating him and questioning him for what seemed like hours. Matthew tried to resist the pain, but it consumed him. They tied his arms behind him and then looped the rope through a hook in the ceiling. Between each question they would jerk the rope, lifting him nearly off his feet. The officer would laugh, the rattle of his hysteria in harmony with Matthew's screams.

Matthew thought his arms would be pulled out of their sockets. Finally, he told them everything he could. He told them about Babe's drinking problem, about the hidden alcohol all over the island and how he had run out of it. He told them of the plan to nurse Babe back to health in the infirmary. They kept beating him despite his confession. One of the guards bashed him in the face with his rifle butt. Matthew spit out blood and a tooth. Another crack to his head with the rifle and he was knocked out once again.

When Matthew regained consciousness, he was lying on the floor in the same room. He was alone. He felt a dull ache everywhere on his body. He could only see out of one eye. His mouth was bloody and his gums swollen. He ran his tongue over his teeth, feeling the missing spot. Another tooth was loose and wiggled back and forth like a door on a rusty hinge. He was terribly thirsty but too weak to even call out.

Matthew remembered what he had said, what he had told them. He had betrayed his friend. Sobs racked his body, and he retched, the bitter taste of bile in his mouth. Why hadn't they just killed him? He didn't want to live anymore. He was weak. Why couldn't he have been more like his father? His pa would never have betrayed a friend. He would have stayed true, no matter what. Matthew had never measured up to his father, something his mother had reminded him of more than once. He had tried so hard to live up to her expectations, but it had never been enough. He tried to roll over, but he didn't have the strength. He closed his eyes again, thinking of his father, whom he loved and respected so much, thinking of his mother.

Matthew awoke again to strong hands picking him up and dragging him from the cell. He half opened an eye and saw that several Japanese were holding him. They must be taking him out for execution. He thanked God, anticipating a release from all this misery and his failure. His mind wandered for a while, but when he came to again, he realized with surprise they were carrying him toward his barracks. One of the guards barked a command as they neared the door. Another guard opened the latch, and Matthew was tossed through the opening to crumple on the ground. He lost consciousness again.

When he stirred again, he saw hazy figures hovering above him. There was whispered discussion. His good eye focused, and he realized John and Martin were kneeling over him.

"Thank God you're awake," said John. "We didn't think you were going to make it."

"Where am I?" whispered Matthew.

"You're in the infirmary."

"How long have I been here?"

"Two days."

"Where's Babe?"

"How are your ribs?" said John, lightly placing a hand on Matthew's chest.

Matthew tried to rise, and he fixed his eye on John. "Where's Babe?" he repeated.

He saw John's expression turn to sadness. "He's gone, Matthew. They killed him. The fool broke into their canteen and drank up a bunch of their hooch. They found him drunk as a skunk, singing away happily. After that they staged a kangaroo court and sentenced him to death."

"How did they kill him?"

"Don't worry about that. You need to—"

Matthew reached up and grabbed John's arm. "Tell me what they did."

John refused to meet his eyes. "They beheaded him, Matthew. The bastards dragged him out to the airfield and cut off his head with one of their God-cursed swords. They . . . they made some of us watch."

Matthew closed his eyes, his jaw working furiously. "Did he suffer?"

"It was over too quickly."

"I mean before."

"He . . . he was as brave as anyone could be."

Matthew looked closely at him again. "Don't lie to me. Please. Please tell me the truth."

"Don't torture yourself, Matthew."

"I want to know, damn it!"

John hesitated. "He died badly, Matthew. He was begging them not to do it. Who wouldn't? Who wants to be dragged out to their death? The movies are fine and dandy for portraying noble deaths and acts of courage. I've watched plenty of men die now. It's all screaming and fear and pissing their pants. If they showed that to the world, nobody would ever go to war." John turned his head and spat.

Matthew laid his head back down on the pillow and closed his eyes. "It's my fault. I killed him."

"What are you talking about?" asked John.

"They tortured me. I told them everything about Babe. About the drinking and the hidden caches."

"You told them nothing. They already knew everything. I guess they'd been watching him for some time. They wanted to see if there were more people involved. Maybe people smuggling. They pulled a few people in and tortured them. Everyone talked. Everyone does when they keep beating you."

Matthew turned his head into the pillow and sobbed. He was relieved he hadn't directly caused Babe's death, but his friend was dead all the same. Without Babe, his only close friend, he was here all alone. He couldn't shed the thought that his father would never have betrayed his friend, regardless of the pain and the cost.

John tried to pull him back around, but Matthew threw his hand off and kept his face turned away, buried in his pillow. He just wanted oblivion. Why didn't they kill him? A moment of pain, and this would all be over. He wanted to die. He didn't want to face another day of this hell. If he had the strength, he would rise and charge the guards. Surely one of them would shoot him. Perhaps tomorrow—if he could find the courage. His mind wandered through a maze of despair, but he could find no escape. Exhaustion overwhelmed him again, and soon he faded into the darkness.

CHAPTER EIGHT

Beecher's Hardware Store
Snohomish, Washington
Monday, August 24, 1942

Jonathan sat across his desk from Sarah and finished the last bite of his sandwich. He skimmed the paper as she poured him a cup of coffee. Margaret was out in the store proper, galloping down the aisles, riding a yardstick. Sarah collected the wrappers from their lunch and then brought out a bundle covered in cloth from her basket. She carefully unfolded the fabric to reveal two slices of apple pie. The tops of the pastries were decorated with leaves hand cut into the dough and then baked into buttery designs. Jonathan loved everything Sarah made him, but most particularly her pies. He was glad she had brought lunch again today; he needed relief from the store.

As if she knew what he was thinking, Sarah spoke to him, addressing his fears. "How do the books look?"

"They're okay. They could be better."

"You don't have to fib to me, Jonathan Beecher. I know how much you worry."

He sighed. She was right—why pretend? "Truth be told, they get worse each month. I don't know how to fix the problem. It doesn't matter how hard I work, or what I do to keep the expenses down. I can't control the cost of the things I have to buy, and I can't force people to purchase them. What I'm particularly frustrated about is I've been conservative. I've saved every penny I could, in the store and at home. I was making this business work. Then comes this war and everything has changed."

He could see the grave concern in her eyes. "Can't you sell the store, or close it down?"

He bristled. This store was everything to him. Besides his family and God, what else was there? A retort burned on his tongue, but he swallowed it whole. She didn't mean anything, he realized. He waited a moment and then answered her.

"I don't know. I've never thought of selling it. Who would want to buy it? Not only that, but what would I do if I didn't have the store? I'm too old to find a new job."

"There are so many jobs out there now. Jobs paying good money. The shipyards at Everett and Seattle are full of workers, but they need more all the time. Boeing, too. There's that wing assembly plant on Grand Avenue."

"Seattle's too far to drive. I could work in Everett, but that doesn't solve any problems for me, Sarah. I would owe hundreds of dollars to Max Weber. I also owe a lot on my inventory. I'm trapped, and I don't see a way out of it." He turned his face away, pretending to examine something on the wall. He fought back tears.

"We just need this ridiculous war to end."

"Amen to that." The war was far from over. It seemed that the fears of invasion were at least fading since the victory at Midway in June, when the US fleet had smashed the Japanese carrier force. However, that battle did little more than start the needle moving a little in their direction. Everywhere else, the war was burning and the outcome uncertain. The Germans battled the English in Egypt and threatened to capture the

Suez Canal. The Nazis had blazed through southern Russia all summer as well and were within a stone's throw of seizing the oil fields and then driving south into the Middle East. In the Pacific the Japanese continued to control just about everything, although earlier this month the marines had invaded some island called Guadalcanal—a first step, according to the radio stations and the *Everett Herald*, toward seizing the initiative.

Jonathan had mixed emotions about the war's progress. On the one hand he was hopeful that he would finally have news of Matthew and, even more importantly, that Matthew would be released. On the other hand he knew that Luke would likely be thrown into combat, and he was afraid for his younger son and what might happen to him in the fighting with the Germans or the Japanese.

Margaret scrambled into the back office, her face flushed from prancing all over the store. She came around the desk and hovered near Jonathan, reaching down to pick up his fork and steal a bite of pie off his plate. Jonathan stretched his hand out and mussed her hair a little bit. He loved this girl—she helped in a small way to fill the gaping hole he felt with all of his children gone.

All of his children. They weren't all really gone. Mary was back in Snohomish, or so Jonathan had heard. He had not spoken to his daughter since the night she ran off—fleeing school, Jonathan, and the future he had planned for her so she could marry Robert. He had heard she was living in a rental house a little north, up toward Blackmans Lake.

In the past few months, there were many times he had wanted to go see her. He knew she was likely ashamed, that she was probably waiting for him to come to her. Something stopped him. She was the one who had defied him. She should come to him and apologize. Robert should come, too, hat in hand. Sarah disagreed with Jonathan. She thought he should be the bigger person, that he was being petty. He just didn't know what the right thing was to do, and so he was doing nothing. *Patience.* In time he hoped they would sort out the situation. He prayed daily for guidance, but none seemed to come.

Margaret took another bite of pie, then laughed and ran back out of the room. Sarah smiled up at him. He felt a moment of confusion again. *What am I doing?* He asked himself this question over and over. Here he was condemning his daughter for her actions when he was spending so much time with a woman. Nothing had happened, he reminded himself. He had kept the proper distance that friendship required, but he wondered if he was truly being honest. He had grown closer to Sarah these past months. He found himself looking forward to his time with her, to her company. He was sharing things with her, thoughts and feelings he might not even have shared with Helen—his hopes and his dreams. He could feel the emotions rising, even as he fought to keep them down. *Patience. You will fight the feelings down, or you will have to send her away.* He couldn't bear to think of that.

Were they still merely friends? Was he truly being faithful to his promise to Helen? Was that a fair promise for her to make him keep? The last question ran through his mind as it had a thousand times. *It doesn't matter. Fair or not, you agreed to the commitment. You cannot break your word before God. Not ever.* Could he continue to keep that promise and spend time with Sarah? He had to.

Sarah was dressed in a pink dress today. Always a dress, always with a little design of flowers traced over it. Her neck was exposed, her bones standing sentry perfectly and drawing his eyes downward. She was a waif, a feather. He loved her delicate figure. His eyes moved up to hers. Her gaze was a scorching fire, burning him. He knew what she was wondering, what she was hoping. He felt the loss of control again, the panic. *Patience.* They sat in piercing silence for a long time in the warm afternoon of the office, the sound of her daughter playing in the background as they watched each other.

Jonathan rose, stretching, launching throbbing waves through his lower back. *I don't have the same body I had as a young man.* He smiled to himself. That was okay; his body wasn't any use to anyone in any event. He stretched a bit more, then walked out of the office and into the store. He could see Margaret sitting in one of the aisles, surrounded by cans and boxes. She had fashioned a kind of fort all around herself and looked to be preparing for a siege. The store was otherwise vacant. He felt a jolt of reality. *Another day without customers.*

He sighed and walked up and down some of the racks, adjusting a hammer here and a saw there. He checked a few prices to make sure they were updated. He heard Sarah's voice behind him. "Jonathan, do you need some help?"

He started to answer, but his attention was diverted. The front doorbell clanged. *A customer.* He turned to help them and froze, unable to move or speak. Mary and Robert were standing tentatively near the entrance, hands held in a protective clasp.

~~

"Hello, Father."

"Hello." Moments passed while he took them in with his eyes. Robert's legs stood firmly rooted to the floor, his eyes sweeping as if for threats. Mary clung to him like a wilted flower, her cheeks scarlet, watching the dusty ground intently. She looked different. Older—but also something else.

"Is this an okay time for us to talk to you?" she asked. Her voice played the same note in an even, steady tempo.

Sarah had come up behind him, holding Margaret's hand. He motioned to her.

"It's all right, Jonathan. We need to get going."

"Please stay."

She looked up at Mary and then Robert, seeming to weigh the moment. "I don't think that's the right thing to do. I think you need to be alone right now." Her eyes bored into his. He knew what she wanted him to do. He wasn't sure he was ready.

He didn't want to talk to Sarah in front of Mary. She would see . . . too much. Instead he simply nodded, and Sarah left, taking her daughter with her. He could see surprise and a questioning look in Mary's eyes. He realized Mary might not know about their friendship, or might not approve. He felt a flash of irritation. What right did she have to question his life, after what she had done? He forced himself to remain calm. *Patience.* "What can I do for you?"

"We . . . we've been wanting to come talk to you for some time."

We. What a strange thing for her to say. His daughter had become a part of someone else's *we.* He wanted to steal her away, to embrace her and take her home. He forced a neutral tone. "Say your piece."

She took a step forward, reaching out to him. Jonathan remained still. "Oh, Father, I've missed you so much. I wanted to come see you right away, but how could I? I knew you must be furious with me. You're probably still angry now. But you don't understand. We were in love. We *are* in love."

"I didn't say you couldn't spend time with him."

"I know, but you wanted us to only be friends."

"I wanted you to follow the plan we both had for you. Graduation. University. A future."

She threw her arms up. "*Your* future, Father. I never wanted any of that. I know you think I'm wasting my life, but that was never a life I wanted for myself. I just wanted to find the man of my dreams and get married. I wanted to stay at home, to start a family someday. That's the future *I* wanted."

"You could've told me. We could've talked about these things."

"You never listened to her," interjected Robert, his voice a frozen stone.

Jonathan turned to Robert, his anger rising. "Who asked you? This is between my daughter and me. I think you should leave."

Mary rushed between them. "No. He can stay. This might not be easy for you to hear, Father, but I have to say it. Everything doesn't have to turn out the way you wanted it to. I know you loved all of us and wanted what was best for us, but you wanted it the way *you planned it.*"

"Your mother and I just wanted you all to be happy, to be safe."

Mary snorted. "My mother? She never wanted me to be happy."

Jonathan felt his blood rising. "I'm not going to listen to you insult your mother."

"You never want to hear anything about her."

"This isn't about her; it's about you."

"Fair enough. If you don't want to hear it, then I won't say it." She took another step toward him. "Please, Father. Whatever the reasons, whatever you believe, I love you. I want to be a part of your life. I know you're upset with me, that you're upset with Robert. But we're married now. We're going to start a family. We want you to be a part of all of this."

What should he do? He was as baffled as ever. He loved his daughter. She had defied him and broken her promise to him, but now she was here before him, asking to still be a part of his life. Had she acted any differently from Matthew or Luke, who both had gone against his wishes? He realized he didn't want to lose his little girl. He had done nothing wrong, nothing against his faith or his promises. Or had he? That worry passed again quickly through his mind. In any event he knew what he had to do. First she needed to admit her sin. He wanted to have this conversation in private. Robert loomed too closely, but there was nothing to be done about it. Jonathan spoke sternly.

"You lied to me. You deceived me. You broke your promise to me."

"I know, Father. I did all those things. I've asked God's forgiveness for all that. I'm asking for your forgiveness, too."

Jonathan felt relief. Mary's defiance and deception were what had bothered him the most. She was eighteen, after all, and had the right to choose her own life. Now she had apologized and sought forgiveness for her mistakes. He didn't want his girl to leave his life forever.

Jonathan stepped forward with arms open. Mary smiled and rushed into his embrace, holding him fiercely. He felt better immediately as the cares and worries for her he had felt over the past few months melted away. She had chosen her own life, and he would respect those decisions and support her. At least she had done the right thing and married Robert.

Now he had another issue to deal with. Jonathan focused on Mary's new husband, his voice ringing in iron strokes. "You, sir, are going to have a conversation with me another day. You took my daughter away without my permission, without my blessing. You should have taken more time. You should have courted her and then come to me before any decision was made."

He saw an unexpected expression on Robert's face. Was it pride? Anger? Resistance? The hard look dissolved, replaced by a cat's smile, his pupils onyx pinpricks. "I apologize. I understand you're upset, and I would be happy to talk to you. Please realize your daughter is as big a treasure to me as she is to you."

Was he sincere? The words mismatched his expression. Jonathan half began to challenge him, then stopped himself. Time enough to study this man. For now, his daughter needed peace, and so did he. Jonathan stepped forward and extended his hand. Robert took it, and for a moment their eyes locked. Again the steely glare. They held a viselike grip for a few moments, and then Jonathan released his hand.

"We will have that conversation *soon*," stressed Jonathan. "But for now, you are both welcome in my house."

Mary hurried forward again and wrapped her arms around Jonathan, holding him tight. He returned the embrace, feeling his daughter's love. "I'll come over in the next few days, Father, for dinner, or you can come see us. I have so many things to tell you. You've made me so happy."

Mary let go of him and walked back over to Robert. They both smiled and turned to leave. Jonathan noticed that Robert's gaze lingered on Mary for a few seconds—a lion about to pounce. He felt his skin prickle. Something was wrong. Something he couldn't put his finger on. He would know more when he had an opportunity to quiz this young man. He prayed his instincts were mistaken—but he knew they were not.

CHAPTER NINE

Wake Island
Japan-Occupied Territory
Sunday, September 27, 1942
(Across the International Date Line)

Matthew worked robotically with the spade, shoving away the sand as he attempted to pound a wooden beam in place. After Babe's death the Japanese had reassigned him to work on a crew building concrete pillboxes all along the perimeter of the three islands that made up the Wake atoll. The labor was backbreaking—endless hours of digging and then pouring forms for the concrete.

Worse than the work was the lack of food. Matthew had grown used to the watery rice gruel and the absence of meat; however, the Japanese had cut their meager rations in half, then cut them again. The men were scarecrows agonizing in a field of sand. Even the guards were on reduced rations. Matthew felt dizzy with hunger and weakness. Each day was a passion of heat, thirst, and fatigue.

"A little deeper and we can set another form," said Tom Kadyk, one of the contractors on Matthew's crew. Under Tom's torn clothing undulated muscle that had not yet eroded away. He came from Boise and had been a foreman on Wake before the Japanese invaded. Matthew hadn't known Tom at all before the invasion, but they had become friends in the months since Babe was executed.

"Give me a few minutes to catch my breath," said Matthew. He leaned against his shovel and sank to his knees. He was so exhausted already, and the sun wasn't even to its zenith yet.

Tom put a hand on Matthew's shoulder. "Sure thing, kid. Take a little breather. I'll keep an eye out for the Japs. You want any of this ham sandwich I'm saving for lunch?"

Matthew chuckled. A ham sandwich. What he wouldn't give for real food. He was thankful Tom could still joke. After Babe died, Matthew had felt lost; he'd wanted to die. When the Japanese changed his duties, he was full of despair, but Tom and the others had welcomed him right away. Tom had taken Matthew under his wing, showing him how to work with concrete and over time giving him more and more responsibility.

"Guard coming," whispered Tom, not moving his head but watching out of the corner of his eye.

Matthew pulled his spade off the ground and drove it in, pulling away sand and clumps of rock. He was exhausted again in a few strokes. He didn't know how he could keep going day after day when he felt so weak. Somehow his body kept functioning, but he didn't know how much longer he could make it.

The day dragged on, minute after agonizing minute. Matthew's muscles trembled, and sharp pain galloped through his shoulders and down his spine. He was barely able to hold on to the shovel. He felt feverish. He knew he didn't have much longer before he would fall ill. So many had died already from sickness and starvation. He could feel Tom's eyes on him, silent but observant. They both knew this could not last.

At the end of the day, Matthew was too weak to rise. He propped himself against a pillbox. Tom pulled him up and shepherded him closely back to the barracks, avoiding the guards and keeping to the middle of the returning prisoners.

Matthew's mind spun, and his vision blurred. The ground in front of him kept shifting out of focus. He was sure he would fall, but he kept walking under Tom's iron grip. They made it past the guards and into the barracks. Matthew collapsed onto his filthy blankets. He closed his eyes and slipped into semiconsciousness. His forehead boiled. His limbs jerked and shivered.

He awoke sometime later to Tom's gentle prodding. "Matthew, you have to wake up. You have to eat."

Matthew wanted to keep sleeping, but he willed himself awake. Tom drew him up to a sitting position. He was surprised to see a full bowl of white rice and another full bowl of gruel. The steam embraced his nose with its nutty scent, and he attacked the bowl of sticky grain, shoveling handfuls through his teeth with greedy fingers.

"Slow down," warned Tom. "You'll throw it back up."

Matthew forced himself to chew. The rice seeped through every part of his tongue and seemed to melt into his body.

"Where did you get this?" he mumbled, battling to take his time.

"Don't worry about it. The boys took up a collection."

Matthew pushed the bowl away. "I can't take from others . . ."

"I said don't worry about it," said Tom, a hint of steel in his voice. "We've got a few connections in the kitchen. We manage to get a little extra food out now and again. We save it for people who need it. People who are starving. Right now that happens to be you. Now slow down, and take your time. I can't afford to get you more if you puke this up."

Matthew reached down and took another pinch of rice with his shaking fingers. He had never tasted anything so wonderful. His hands were trembling so badly; he didn't know if he could keep feeding himself. Tom reached out and guided his fingers into his mouth. Matthew ate the rest of the rice over a half hour and then sipped at the gruel. Tom kept holding him back, forcing him to eat and drink more slowly. When at last all the food was gone, Matthew fell back onto his blankets, feeling satisfied for the first time since the Japanese had come to Wake. He was soon asleep again.

He woke up the next morning feeling a little stronger. Tom had another bowl of rice for him and another full bowl of gruel. That night he had the same, and the pattern repeated itself again on Tuesday. He could feel the new strength and energy. Tom had saved his life.

On Wednesday morning Matthew awakened feeling renewed. He felt strength coursing through his muscles. The dizziness and fatigue had faded. He ate the full rations again that morning, enjoying the flavor of the white rice but without the same desperation.

"That's all I can give you," said Tom. "There's another guy who collapsed yesterday. The committee has decided we need to move on to him."

"That's fine, Tom. This was more than I could ever hope for. I didn't know how much longer I could make it. Now I feel like a new man. I owe you everything."

Tom shook his hand. "Don't you worry about it, kid. We have to stick together, or these bastards will tear us apart. We can't resist them by escaping. We can't fight them. We can steal from them, and we can keep our boys going until Uncle Sam comes back for us."

"That's never going to happen."

Tom squeezed his hand. "Now don't you say that. One day we'll look up and it'll be our ships on the horizon. Those bastards can't win this war. They know it, and we know it. It's just a matter of when we'll be rescued. Our bombers have already been over a few times. One day it will be carrier planes. When that happens, you'll know our fleet is on its way."

They returned to work that morning. Matthew couldn't believe how much energy he felt. He realized this was probably an artificial sensation. It would take far more than a few meals to return him to his regular strength. However, Tom had brought him back from the brink. He would be able to work, to stand on his own. That was something.

As they set to labor on a pillbox, Matthew actually enjoyed himself. The sun was out, and it was warm early as usual. The heat felt fine, and the sky was blue with cotton clouds.

Matthew was so grateful for Tom. During this entire ordeal, two older men, father-type figures, had stepped in to save him. He did feel a nagging feeling of inadequacy, and he thought again of his own father. Jonathan wouldn't need someone else to care for him, to aid him. His father would be the one helping everyone else. His father was more like Tom. Had he always been that way? Was he more uncertain of himself when he was Matthew's age? More likely to depend on others? Matthew couldn't imagine that. His father seemed to be forged from iron out of some earlier age of men. Why hadn't the nut fallen closer to the tree? It didn't seem that any of the Beecher children had taken after their father. Luke was even more different from Jonathan. At least Matthew was quiet and hardworking. Luke seemed to represent everything that Jonathan was not—lazy, loud, arrogant, a goof-off.

Matthew smiled, thinking about Luke. He wondered where his little brother was right now. Had he joined the military? He must have. Then again, his father would have tried hard to keep him home, particularly with Matthew missing. Oh, how his father must be worrying about him. Matthew had expected to be able to write to his family, but the Japanese weren't allowing any mail out or in. *He thinks I'm long dead by now. They all do.* Mary must have taken it hard. His younger sister was a perfect but fragile little flower. A tear traced his cheek.

"Chin up, kid," said Tom. "If they catch you dreaming, there'll be hell to pay. I just got you back into working order."

Matthew laughed. He started to respond, then felt the blood drain out of him. On the horizon, he saw the distant outline of a ship. He knew no single American vessel would come this close without a fleet and without air cover. The ship was Japanese. "Tom, look out there."

Tom turned his head the direction Matthew was gesturing. "A ship coming in. Don't you worry, Matthew. It doesn't necessarily mean bad news. Who knows? Maybe they've brought a bunch of steaks and potatoes."

Matthew laughed again. "Trust you to try to make the best of a bad thing. They could be coming for us this time."

"What if they are? We don't know if it's worse in China or Japan. At least we would be at a real camp. There might even be better food or at least some mail. I don't feel like they're even following the rules out here."

"I doubt it's better anywhere else. Hell, we didn't think they'd even keep us around. Not that we're better than dead."

"Now you knock off that talk," said Tom, looking at him sternly. "Alive is alive. You stick to life no matter what, kid. While you're alive, there's a chance. A chance you'll get home someday."

A guard came by and shouted at them to resume work. They weren't able to talk again for some time, but Matthew kept glancing up quickly and watching the progress of the ship as it swallowed the horizon. By early afternoon the massive transport vessel had arrived and docked near the old Pan Am facility.

The Japanese guards appeared again and shouted angrily for them to follow. Tom and Matthew exchanged looks but couldn't talk. Their crew followed the guards and were soon joined by others. Everyone was marching toward the transport ship. *So this is it,* thought Matthew. *The Japs are finally shipping us off this sandbar.* He could imagine the terrible conditions on board, and, despite Tom's hopeful view, he feared the camps in Japan and China would be even worse.

They arrived at the vessel within a few minutes and were quickly herded up the ramp. When they reached the top, Matthew breathed a sigh of relief. The deck was full of supply boxes and crates, all strapped down or in containers. The Japanese shouted at the prisoners to begin unpacking and unloading the boxes. *"Isoge!"* they shouted over and over. *Hurry up!*

Matthew didn't care. Let them shout. At least it wasn't a prisoner ship after all—it was just bringing supplies. Matthew smiled, remembering Tom's optimism; perhaps they had brought steaks and potatoes. He prayed there was more food and that they could return to full rations. He grabbed a heavy sack of what felt like rice, and Tom snatched another. They threw the bags over their shoulders and lugged them off the deck and down the ramp.

They made numerous trips, and soon Matthew could feel the weakness returning. Under the constant threats of the guards, there was no time to rest, and the effort of climbing up and down the gangway with heavy boxes and bags taxed his fragile reserves. He noticed other prisoners stumbling, and one even fell on the ramp. A guard ran over and butted the man hard in the side with the stock of his rifle. A couple of other prisoners helped him up and continued on.

After a few hours they had completed the unloading. The supplies were stacked neatly in a semicircle fifty yards beyond the dock. The guards herded prisoners back off the ship and then lined them up in two rows. Matthew noticed they had set up several machine guns on tripods, facing the prisoners. He felt the fear reaching up to smother him. Had they come this far and endured so much just to be killed now? Why would the Japanese execute them at this point, with so much work still incomplete on the island? The prisoners stood that way for a few minutes in the heat of the late afternoon. Matthew could hear moaning and the whispers of a prayer. Then a number of guards fanned out and began shouting again, pulling men out of the group and herding them toward the ship.

Matthew realized they were taking some but not all the prisoners. A guard approached him and stared in his face for a moment, then turned away and moved to Tom. The guard started shouting and grabbed his friend, pulling him toward the ship. Matthew turned and started to follow, but the guard pointed a bayoneted rifle at him and glared menacingly.

"You can't leave me here!" begged Matthew. "Please, say something . . . do something."

Tom shrugged, a look of compassion on his face. "I can't fix this one, kid. Don't you worry about it. You'll be fine. Just keep your chin up, and you'll get through it. Remember, each day's a victory."

"I can't do this without you!"

"Yes, you can. You're stronger than you think, Matthew. You need to step up and take the lead now here. Someone's got to resist these bastards. It's your turn."

Matthew wanted to follow, but he knew they would kill him. His jaw twitched in fear. First Babe was taken from him and now Tom. He was going to be left on this island to face the Japanese with no friends, no support. He glanced around. There were fewer than a hundred of them left in line. Tom wanted him to become a leader. He wanted him to resist the Japanese in any way he could. How could he? He wasn't Tom. He wasn't his pa. He stood there with the rest of them, facing the ship as it began pulling away from the dock. Tears ran openly down his face. He was alone.

CHAPTER TEN

Snohomish, Washington
Monday, September 28, 1942

Mary Miner cracked the eggs carefully, placing six of them in a bowl. She beat the whites and yolks together briskly with a fork until they were uniformly yellow. She covered them with a towel and set the mixture aside.

Next she pulled out the bacon she had purchased from the local butcher on First Street yesterday afternoon. She frantically unwrapped the thick-cut, maple-cured strips and laid them in a pan. She placed this skillet on a burner and tended it judiciously as the individual slices snaked and sizzled around. She whispered a prayer. She needed the strips well browned but not black.

Mary drew in the rich smell, closing her eyes for a moment to enjoy the sensation. She carefully poured the egg mixture into a second skillet, then immediately whisked the contents with a spatula before the eggs began to stick to the bottom. She continued stirring until the scramble was light and fluffy with no visible moisture. Finally, she flicked salt and pepper over the pan. She looked at the clock and took a deep breath. Almost time. She had to hurry.

When the bacon was done, she used metal tongs to slowly remove each of the pieces and placed them separately on a waiting porcelain platter. Thankfully the meat was well crisped, just the way Robert liked it. Once all the pieces were removed, she turned around to the back counter and retrieved a bowl of premade batter. She reached in with a measuring cup and filled it with the pancake mix she had made earlier that morning from scratch. She brought the cup over to the pan and gently poured the batter into the still-hot bacon grease, grimacing as a few drops of oil spattered out of the pan onto her wrist and forearm. Mary quickly scooped out two more servings of the pancake batter and poured them into the grease. Soon the pancakes were frying up golden brown in the hot oil. She removed the bronzed circles from the pan and then cooked two more sets of three. Her hands trembled.

With everything ready she spooned up the bacon, eggs, and pancakes and placed them on two plates. She moved everything around until it was just the way he liked it, then carried the plates over to their little kitchen table and set them down for breakfast.

Robert materialized a few minutes later, tucking his uniform shirt into his trousers. He was dressed all in blue with a brown leather belt and a holstered .38-caliber service revolver. He walked casually up to the table and picked up a piece of bacon, fumbling for the *Everett Herald* she had placed next to his plate. He stuffed the bacon into his mouth, yawning as he scanned the morning's headlines. He reached over to pick up his coffee cup and absently took a sip.

"Why don't you sit down, sweetie, and let's visit for a few minutes?" asked Mary.

Robert grunted in response as he continued to read the paper. "Did I tell you about the night I had last night?" he said between bites of bacon. "Boy, oh boy, were the crazies out. Two bar fights and a couple of drag racers. I think the goddamn full moon was out or something. It's gonna be another late one tonight, I'm sure."

"Please, Robert, are you even listening to me? Can't you sit down for a few minutes? You didn't get home until past bedtime last night. I never see you."

He looked up. His eyes flickered, and his forehead creased. "No time for that. I have to get in right away and fill in the reports for yesterday." He picked up a pancake and started toward the door. She stood up, blocking his way.

"Please, Robert."

His face flushed an angry scarlet. He lunged toward her, halting a hair's breadth away. "What do you want?" he hissed venomously.

"I just want to spend a little time with you. You've been coming home late almost every night." She hurried on. "When you're home, you're sleeping or reading the paper or listening to the radio."

He snarled and pursed his lips as if to spit. His words poured out in viscous lumps. "You knew I was a policeman and wouldn't be home each night like some lazy shopkeeper."

She ignored the barb. "I knew that . . . I just want you to talk to me when you're home." She forced the last words out. "I'm all alone here."

He shrugged dismissively and stood. "You're the one with the problems, not me." He looked her up and down. "I thought when I married you that you were going to be content and happy. Now all I get is complaining every day when I get home. You've changed, or something was wrong with you in the first place. Your duty is to serve me as my wife. That's what your Bible tells you, doesn't it?"

Mary felt a stab in her heart. She was confused, defensive. "I . . . I have been happy. I am happy. I've taken care of the house every day, made you dinner, taken care of you."

"Then why are you complaining now?" He looked around. "Maybe you need to spend more time worrying about this pigpen. Frankly I've seen houses much better taken care of than this. There's dust everywhere.

Your food leaves something to be desired, too. Undercooked or burned. My mother did a much better job with all of this. She was a good wife to my dad. Not like you."

"Robert! How can you say such a thing? I'm new at this. You have to give me some time."

He reached down and grabbed another slice of bacon. "I guess I can't expect too much with your mother dead. You've only had your father to teach you. Still, maybe you should talk to some of the other wives around town. You have a lot to learn . . . about everything."

Mary blushed. She knew he was referring to the bedroom. She remembered their first painful night together and then every time since. He had complained about *that*, too. She was inexperienced, he said. Wasn't she supposed to be? How did he even know what it was supposed to be like? She was afraid to ask him that question. She felt so inadequate. He was older and so worldly. She thought she knew about taking care of a family. She'd spent so much time taking care of her father and Luke after her mother died. But he was right; she hadn't had much guidance. She felt terrible. How could she be so bad at all of this? Who could she talk to? Her friends were still unmarried. She could ask her neighbors about the cooking and cleaning but never about the *other* thing.

"I'm . . . I'm sorry, Robert. I'm trying very hard to learn all of this."

He took a step forward and put his hand under her chin, looking in her eyes. "It's okay, sweetie pie. You're just a little dumb and a little slow. Boy, are you pretty, though. You give it some time, and you'll figure it all out. Now I've got to get going here." He grabbed another slice of bacon and wrapped it in a pancake, then turned and walked past her to the door, slapping her on the rear as he left. He didn't say good-bye.

Mary stood there for a few moments, and then the tears started. She crossed her arms and rocked back and forth, collecting herself. *I will be okay.* She slowly collected the plates and scraped away the food into the garbage, returning to the table to remove an unnoticed flower she had set out in an attempt to brighten the table. She crumpled its petals and cast it into the garbage before she began washing the dishes. She couldn't finish them, and she turned off the water and sat down, her back against the lower cupboards of the sink. She tucked her face in her knees and sobbed uncontrollably. She didn't know how she could face another day like this. She was a terrible failure as a wife. She sat there long into the morning, unable to move, unable to go on.

∿

In the early afternoon Mary decided she had to do something. She thought she knew who to go and see. She cleaned herself up, did her hair, and finished the chores around the house. She then set out from her house, walking along the quiet streets. Being outside improved her mood. Snohomish was so beautiful this time of year. The sun was out and warm. She loved September in Washington. The birds chirped, and the leaves of the many trees lining the avenue were just starting to glow in multiple colors. She felt better walking and drawing in the rich aroma of autumn.

Mary's destination was about a mile from her house. She walked past Avenue D, the main north-south street, and turned east on Tenth. The road meandered up and down before eventually darting down a steeply declined hill. At the bottom of the slope, Mary turned right, heading south again on Maple. Finally, she came to a small two-story house built in the thirties. She walked up the pathway and knocked on the door. A few moments passed, and then the door swung open. Sarah was there, her eyes registering slight surprise, which she quickly recovered from. "Mary, hello. What a nice surprise. What can I do for you?"

"Hello. I'm very sorry to disturb you. If you're too busy, I can come back another time."

Sarah stepped back and motioned into the house. "No, please—I was just finishing up a couple things. Please come in." Mary followed her inside. The front room was simply decorated, with a sofa and a couple of end tables. A few lamps and pictures adorned the room as well. To the right, a hallway led down toward the kitchen, with a stairway leading upstairs about halfway along the corridor. The house was tiny, clean, simple, and pleasant. Sarah motioned Mary to follow her to the kitchen to a table and chairs. A sewing machine sat on the table, and fabrics were spread out all around it.

"My working area," Sarah explained. "Would you like some coffee? I was just going to put some on."

"That would be nice."

Sarah cleared off part of the table and then set to work making coffee. Mary sat self-consciously, still not sure she should be here in the first place. She kept looking around, trying to think of what she would say exactly. Sarah busied herself with a few dishes until the coffee was done. Then she brought over a tray holding two blue-and-white porcelain cups, a bowl of sugar, a small pitcher of cream, the pot of coffee, and some butter cookies.

"How nice of you, Sarah. Thank you."

"Think nothing of it. Now how can I help you?" Mary noticed that Sarah leaned forward, giving her full attention. She wasn't sure how she felt about this woman who was so obviously a part of her father's life, but now she felt a warmth coming from her that she deeply appreciated.

"I . . . I don't really know where to begin. It's . . . it's my husband. I feel guilty even coming to you, coming to anyone. It's just that I love him so much, but I don't seem to know what I'm doing."

Sarah's eyes narrowed. "What do you mean?"

"I can't seem to do anything right. I'm trying so hard, Sarah. I cook and clean and make sure everything is perfect for him. But he doesn't even seem to notice. He comes home from work at night, and he's so tired. I understand that. He works such long hours. But he doesn't take any time to talk to me. He just wants to listen to the radio or read the paper. Other times he goes out with his friends and is gone until all hours of the night."

Sarah's face contracted. "Is everything else okay? You know, your family life?"

Mary felt a hot blush. "That . . . that seems to be fine. I mean, I think it is. Although when you ask that, it doesn't seem like we're together. It seems more like he's just doing what he wants but not experiencing it with me. I need help, Sarah, and I didn't know who to turn to. I don't understand any of this. I need some advice. Were things like that with your husband?"

Sarah hesitated before she answered. "Every man is different, dear. I don't think it would be fair to compare my husband to yours. Men are hard to understand sometimes." She looked out the window, lost and far away for a moment. "I'm sure time will heal all of this. You've just been married a few months. He's a young man, and he must be so busy with his job. I'm sure if you keep showing him all your love and are just *there* for him, he will realize how important you are and start paying more attention to you in return. A woman has to take control sometimes, without it seeming like we are. Men need to feel they are in charge, but they also need to know that they have a woman in their life who loves them, who needs them."

"So you think if I just am patient and keep doing what I'm doing, things will get better?"

Sarah reached out with her good hand and grasped Mary's. "I'm sure they will. Pray about all of this, too. God helps us with all these problems. Not always in our time, but in His. I'm sure if you keep being loyal, loving, and caring, Robert will come around and realize just how important you are to him and to his life."

Mary felt so much better. This was just what she needed to hear. She had hoped she was doing the right thing, but all of this was so new, so confusing, and so different than she had imagined. She looked up at Sarah.

"Is that what you're hoping for from my dad?"

Sarah's face clouded for a moment, and she looked away. "What do you mean?"

"I've heard you two spend a lot of time together. Both of you lost your spouses. I'm sorry. That's probably a very forward question of me."

"No, that's all right, dear. Your father and I are just friends. We both enjoy each other's company. We are both grieving the loss of our spouses. But we are only friends. That's what God has seen fit to give us."

Mary didn't press her further, although she didn't understand and wanted to know more. She tried a different tack.

"Are you enjoying your time with my father?"

Sarah's smile sparkled like a shining pool. "He is a wonderful man. Perhaps the best man I've ever met. He's plain, simple, honest, faithful, hardworking. He loves you dearly, as he loves all of his children. He doesn't talk much about your brothers, but I know he's dreadfully afraid for them, particularly for Matthew."

Mary felt guilt knocking. Her two brothers were gone and in danger's way. Their lives were at risk, and here she was with her petty worries that her marriage wasn't working out exactly the way she wanted. "He's worried, and so am I," she said. "Knowing him, I'm sure he doesn't talk about it very much, but he's deeply concerned. We all are. It makes my problem seem silly."

Sarah smiled at Mary. "No, dear. It's true they're risking everything, and we need to honor that. But the challenges in our lives are important, too."

Mary felt better, and her warmth for Sarah grew a little more. She was so kind and seemed so wise. Mary felt a trickle of bravery and pressed a little. "Why do you say you and my father will only be friends?"

The sun set on Sarah's smile. "I don't think it's my place to say."

"Let me guess. It has something to do with my mother."

"Why do you say that?"

"You didn't know my mother. She had a way of doing things. It's hard to explain. I'm sure my father has told you."

"No, he hasn't. He doesn't talk about her very much. I'm sure he loved her deeply, though, to be so devoted."

"My father is a simple man, and loyal to a fault."

"What do you mean?" Sarah looked carefully at Mary.

Mary could tell she wanted to ask more. She realized that with Matthew and Luke gone, there was nobody else in their family that Sarah could have asked about Jonathan. This was probably the first time she had ever had the chance.

"It's probably not right for me to ask, but could you tell me a little about your mother?"

"I don't know if I should." Mary felt the memories whipping around in a maelstrom. "Maybe I didn't really know her. I was younger and so busy with my own life. I spent more time with my dad than my mom. I remember her laboring in the kitchen each day and always cleaning—shooing us out when we were too loud or in the way. Then she got sick. That's what I remember the most. My mother lying in bed. In pain. My father at her side. The house filled with worry." Mary felt the tears welling up again. "I'm not a very good visitor today."

Sarah came around and hugged her, placing a hand on her shoulder. "You've been wonderful, and I'm so glad you came by. I don't want you to be a stranger. I'll be happy to talk to you anytime you want, about Robert or about anything else."

"Thank you so much. I appreciate it. I'll be honest—I've had a little bit of a hard time with Father spending time with another woman. I don't even know why. He deserves happiness and companionship as much as anyone does." Mary turned to look up at Sarah. "Please don't tell him about Robert. I don't want him to worry. He already has so much to worry about."

"I promise I won't. Maybe we can talk again soon. I'd love to hear more about the past."

Mary rose. "Thank you so much, Sarah. I would like that."

They embraced again, and Sarah led her to the door. Mary felt better about everything. She knew what she would do. She would be patient, and she would try even harder. Her husband deserved it.

~~~

Mary left Sarah's house and strolled down Maple farther south to First Street. She turned right and continued along the busy main part of town until she arrived at the Piggly Wiggly. She spent the next hour shopping for groceries, mentally checking off a list of her husband's favorite items so she could make him the perfect dinner. Sarah was right—Mary just needed to do everything she could for Robert and take charge a little.

She turned in her ration cards at the counter and paid for her food. She would have to make the sugar count—they could only get a little. Then she carried her groceries the mile or so home. The walk was partially uphill, and she was winded by the time she reached their house.

Mary checked the clock on the kitchen wall. She didn't have much time to do everything she wanted, but she glowed with purpose and serenity. She peeled and cut up some potatoes and then sliced carrots. She placed a roast in a deep oval pan and then dropped the vegetables in with some sliced onions. The oven was already on and warmed by the time she placed the main dish on the middle rack.

Next Mary retrieved her largest bowl out of a lower cupboard and then sifted fresh flour into it, the white flakes cascading like snow. She added some sugar and cut in fresh butter and a little precious cream. She hand stirred the mixture and then divided the dough in half for a bottom and upper crust. She carefully rolled out each clump. She took the extra time to cut out tiny oval shapes in the leftover dough and then placed little creases up and down them, creating decorative leaves.

In a separate bowl she cut up apples and then poured over a mixture of sugar and cinnamon with a dash of vanilla. Her fingers danced. She pressed the dough for the crust into a pie pan and then spread the fresh filling into it until a mountain loomed over the crust's edges. She lifted the dough set aside for the upper crust and carefully molded it over the filling, pinching the ends all around the pan up into perfect folds. She melted some butter and dipped in the leaves, then carefully adhered them in a pattern on the crust.

Hours passed as Mary worked in the kitchen. She carefully scrubbed their table and then ironed a white tablecloth until the creases stood at attention. She placed the cloth carefully and set the table with their best dishes. She brought out their candles and put them in holders.

As evening fell, the smells throughout the house mixed together in a delicate symphony. Mary had timed the meal so everything would come out warm at the same time, right at six o'clock, when Robert should be home from work. In addition to the roast and pie, there was fresh, warm bread and a salad. She had also purchased some Rainier Beer for Robert, his favorite kind. She quickly removed all the food from the oven, burning her wrist in her haste to make sure everything was perfect. She moved all the pans and trays onto matching kitchen towels on the table and arranged the setting until it was just so. She had also changed into her prettiest dress and carefully made herself up. She sat down to wait, humming softly.

Minutes ticked by. He didn't arrive. Six o'clock became six thirty and then seven o'clock. Mary moved the pie and roast back into the oven to stay warm. She began to worry. She called the police department, but Robert wasn't there. The officer in charge said he had left at the normal time. Her father was never a minute late. Her mother wouldn't have stood for it. *She took what she wanted.*

Eight o'clock passed and then nine. Mary sat in the darkness as the candles burned down slowly, the wax dripping unnoticed down the candlesticks and collecting in hardening pools on the tablecloth. Mary felt a swarm of emotions: frustration, worry, anger. Ten o'clock passed, and still, he had not come home. She served herself dinner and picked at it, the food ashes in her mouth, her appetite gone. Finally, at almost eleven, she heard a jingling at the door, and Robert stumbled in. He'd been drinking. She could tell by his unsteady gait. He looked around in the darkness and focused on the candles. His eyes finally rested on Mary, and he jolted a little in surprise, attempting to straighten up.

"Hello, darling. What are you doing there in the dark?" His words slurred, and she breathed in his fetid breath across the chasm between them.

"Where have you been?" She felt the anger rising. She had done everything for him today, and he had been out drinking. He hadn't even bothered to call her to let her know he wasn't coming home.

"I've been at work. *Ish* was a long night out."

"That's not true. I called the station. You left at five thirty."

He lurched toward her and pointed a wild finger. "Checking up on me, are you? Who the hell do you think you are?"

"I'm your wife." Her rage brought her courage.

He took a few more steps, nearly falling over. "That's right. You're my wife, and you'll obey me."

"I didn't call to check up on you. I called to see when you would get home for dinner. I made the best dinner for you, Robert. All your favorite things. And you didn't even bother coming home or letting me know where you were."

"I just went out with the boys for a drink. I can't even have a moment of fun anymore since you burdened me."

"*Burdened* you!" She was yelling now, the fear and worry exploding out of her. "I've burdened you? All I've done is taken care of you since the moment we married. I took care of you and this house, and you've treated me like dirt in return! I'm sick of it! You've changed, Robert!"

She could see the anger in his eyes. "What in the hell are you talking about? I work all day and bring home the money so you can sit here and stuff your face. You've gotten fat and ugly, and you won't even take care of me like a man deserves." He looked at her with accusing eyes. "Maybe that's it. Maybe there's someone else coming over and taking care of you during the day!" He took another step toward her, standing above her just a couple of feet away. "Have you been cheating on me, you little slut?"

Mary burst into tears. "No, Robert, no! I would never cheat on you! How could you even say such a thing? I've only ever loved you. I just want you to be happy."

"I was happy before I married you. I had friends and money to spend on what I wanted. Then you trapped me with your smile and your innocence. Oh, how that changed after we married. Now you're a lazy, ungrateful shrew and frigid to boot."

Mary continued to sob. She had given him everything. How could her life have come to this? She had thought she would marry Robert and live happily ever after, but all her dreams were falling apart. "Please, Robert, don't say that. Please, let's just work things out." She reached for him.

He slapped her hard across the face with the back of his hand. She flew out of her chair, banging her head on the table, then hitting the ground hard. Pain scorched through her. She tasted blood, warm and metallic, filling her mouth. The room spun. She felt his hand on the back of her head, tearing at her carefully groomed hair. He snapped her head back and struck her again, a granite fist crushing her down. She tried to rise, but she couldn't. She felt everything whirling. In the distance, as if her ears were full of cotton, Mary heard dishes crashing against the wall. She was splattered with gravy and vegetables from the roast. Robert was screaming with anger. She heard another crash, then only the silent ringing of her ears.

"Well, you little slut, you've gone and done it now! You've ruined my dinner. Look at you. You're filthy. This house is filthy. You better have this place spick-and-span when I wake up. If you don't, you'll have more of the same!" She heard the stomping of boots down the hallway and then up the stairs.

Mary lay in a broken heap in the darkness for what seemed an eternity. She shivered on the icy floor, her face absorbing wave after wave of crashing agony. Her mind reeled. Robert had hit her. She had never imagined her husband striking her. Jonathan certainly had never raised his hand or even his voice against her mother. What was she supposed to do? Was this really all her fault? She had thought she was such a good woman. She had been beautiful and hopeful. She knew how to cook and clean long before she married Robert. None of it was good enough for him. She was a failure as a wife, worse as a woman. He told her she was no longer pretty, that she was getting fat. That wasn't even true. She still fit all of her clothes exactly the same. Maybe it was true? She didn't know anymore and didn't know what to do.

Slowly, she pulled herself up from the floor to her knees. She felt nausea grip her with steely fingers, but she fought it back. She moved one leg up and then the other, dragging herself to a standing position, using the table to help herself up. She moved to the wall and turned on a light. The kitchen and eating area were in chaos. Brown gravy dripped down the walls. The pan containing the roast had shattered near the refrigerator. The glass pie pan was in pieces with bits of crust and filling splattered near the pantry. She started to sob again. Her hands trembled violently. What was she supposed to do? *I'll think on this tomorrow,* she told herself, reaching down inside to try to find something to desperately cling to. She closed her eyes and said a prayer, asking for forgiveness, for patience, for understanding. Then she began to pick up and clean, tears streaming. She didn't finish until nearly dawn. Exhausted, she fell asleep on the sofa in the living room, a kitchen rag filled with ice standing guard over her wounds. Her soul felt as numb as the flesh on her face.

CHAPTER ELEVEN

Beecher's Hardware Store
Snohomish, Washington
Friday, October 2, 1942

Jonathan and Sarah worked together at the store in the early morning, sorting out a large delivery of new hardware. He watched her labor, admiring her quiet, industrious manner. She helped him out more and more now. He tried to pay her, but she refused, always stating she just enjoyed working with him. He liked it, too. Today she was wearing a white lace top with a white undershirt and a flowery ankle-length skirt. He could see her thin frame, and he watched as she bent over to pick up a box, her smooth elbows and upper arms a milky canvas. Her hair tumbled out over her back. She turned her head around and looked at him as he watched her, smiling in return.

He shook his head and turned away. What was he doing? He could see the pictures scrolling through his mind. Impure thoughts. He wanted this woman, he admitted to himself. *No!* He could not, would not want her. He had promised himself and promised God he would remain friends with her. Only friends. Wanting her was a sin, almost as bad as physically taking her. He had made a promise . . .

The oath angered him now. Sarah wanted to give him every part of her. All of this was new to him—almost incomprehensible. Helen batted love around, catching it by the tail, releasing it, and pouncing again. He'd enjoyed the game at first—until her sharp claws pierced him. *That doesn't matter. She died of cancer! You made a promise.*

Jonathan turned his mind to other things. He had plenty to think about, things he *should* be doing. He picked up the shipment manifest and continued to check off the items that had come in. He tried to ignore the number at the very bottom. A huge number, double what it would have been a year ago. He grunted in disgust. He didn't know how much more he could afford. Well, one problem at a time. He needed to unload everything first; then he could worry about how much it all cost. Regardless of the price, he had to have the inventory.

They continued to put away the items in silence. They often worked together quietly, always near each other. Most evenings he came over and she made him and Margaret dinner. Then he would sit in a chair and listen to the war news on the radio while she sewed late into the night. He would do the dishes or make repairs around the house. They stayed close to each other as they did today.

After the inventory was all sorted out, they went to the back office. Margaret was at school, and they were alone in the store. Jonathan poured them both some coffee from a pot he kept on his back bar. He walked around the desk and placed a cup next to her, his hand accidentally brushing hers. He felt the electric jolt again and pulled away. He shuffled around to the other side and sat down across from her. He tried to avoid looking at her face just now. He felt ashamed about the thoughts that had flashed through his mind. This was a widowed woman. He was a widower. He uttered a quick and silent prayer, asking the Lord to protect him, to protect *them*.

"You seem distracted this morning," she said finally.

He glanced up, looking into her mischievous eyes. "No more than usual. There's a lot on my mind."

"Like what?" she asked playfully.

He chuckled. "Like these books for one. I'm no magician, and I can't seem to make them balance anymore, no matter what I do."

She laughed in return. "Well, you won't take my advice and burn this place down, so I'm at a loss about what to tell you to do."

If only it was so easy. He loved this store, but since the war started, it was an albatross around his neck, slowly dragging him under the waters.

He pulled the inventory receipt out of his pocket and then retrieved his ponderous ledger from a desk drawer. He added in the inventory debit and then set to balancing the books from September. He had experienced an increase in business in the late summer and hoped he would turn a profit for once. He hadn't proceeded very far when Sarah spoke.

"Jonathan, I have to tell you something."

He looked up. "What is it?"

"Mary came to see me."

"What? What about?" He placed his pen down and looked up, surprised.

She flushed and turned her face away from him. "I feel badly even telling you. I told her I wouldn't say anything, but she is just a child, and you are her father. You need to know. Someone has to stop a woman from going through this."

"What did she say?"

"She came to talk about her marriage. It doesn't sound like things are going very well with Robert. She said he's unhappy all the time and complains about her. I tried to give her encouragement, but I didn't really know what to say. I'm very worried about her." She placed her hand on his for a moment. "He sounds awful."

Jonathan grunted. "She should have listened to me and followed my advice, and she wouldn't have to worry about a bad husband." Internally he felt a mixture of satisfaction that his daughter's rebellion had led to some difficult circumstances, but he had a stronger feeling of concern.

"You don't really mean that. She's young and was in love. I don't think you understand, Jonathan. Women are so often unprepared for the real world. We are told over and over that we need to keep ourselves beautiful, learn how to take care of a home, and find the man of our dreams as soon as we can. So often, the reality once we are married is far different from what we expected." Her face darkened.

"That's why she should have waited. In a few years she would be able to judge better for herself."

"That's not necessarily true, Jonathan. Love is a bright sky at twilight. You cannot see easily what lies in the shadows beneath it."

"Does that count for you as well?"

She looked up at him. "What do you mean? Do you mean, how do I feel about you?"

Jonathan felt lightning strike. That wasn't what he had meant. "No, I mean with your husband."

Sarah shifted and averted her eyes. He could tell that was not what she had wanted to talk about. Her face flushed. "I don't like to talk about him with you. Not about when we were together."

"Why not?"

"It just doesn't seem proper somehow."

He pressed her. He wanted to know. "Tell me. Was your marriage to him different than you expected?"

"Jonathan . . ."

"I want to know. It's not important, after all—we're just friends."

She flinched at those words but then finally spoke. "He was a hardworking man. He loved our daughter. He did his best."

"I'm glad you had that time with him. I'm happy he was a good man," said Jonathan. He affected a neutral tone, but he felt jealousy well up inside him. He controlled his emotions with difficulty. He was angry at himself about his emotions. He had no right to be jealous. *You weren't supposed to be in this position again, ever. You've fallen.*

"That doesn't matter anyway," she said, quickly changing the subject. "What matters is what's going on with Mary right now."

"I don't know what I can really do about her marriage. If she had followed my advice, she'd be at the university right now and not caught up in something she rushed into. She's on her own now."

Sarah glared at him. "You don't really mean that."

"I do mean it. I'm frustrated. I taught all my children to keep life simple: God, family, work. All of them disobeyed me. All of them are struggling or in harm's way now." He didn't tell her that in the darkest hours he blamed himself. *I'm failing my own faith—here and now. My children can hardly do better with my example. There must be more I cannot see. I'm riddled with sin and weakness.*

"I know you've been hurt, Jonathan. You wanted to protect your children, and they have all chosen their own paths. Isn't that what they are supposed to do at some point, though? Aren't they supposed to have their own lives?"

She might be right. She was wise. He couldn't force his children to live life the way he wanted them to. *Control is another sin I drowned in.*

"I'll talk to her. I'm not sure what I can really do about things, but I will at least listen to what she has to say."

Sarah brightened. "You are always so sweet and kind, Jonathan. I know it will make her feel better just to see you, even if there isn't anything you are able to change."

She rose and came around the table, placing her hand on his neck. "You must be in knots with these books," she said, and began gently kneading his neck and shoulders. He resisted in the beginning, but then gave in to the luxurious feeling. He felt the stress drain away. Her warm fingers soothed his worries. He closed his eyes and sat in silence. Time ticked by; he didn't know how long. He didn't think or worry. He soaked up the minutes, not resisting. Finally, she stepped away and returned to her seat. She watched him with wary eyes, a cornered doe. He smiled, thanking her with unspoken words.

Jonathan returned to his balance sheet, letting the moment go. As he completed his books for the previous month, his apprehension returned. He found several discrepancies as he compared the bank ledger to his handwritten books. All the changes were negative. He realized with growing anxiety that regardless of the step-up in business, the cost of inventory had outstripped sales. There must be some kind of mistake. A missing deposit or a double entry of expenses. Somehow, despite his expectations, September was the worst month he had ever had. He had lost almost a thousand dollars. Jonathan checked and rechecked the tally, but the numbers were correct. He felt panic. He had already spent much of his savings, little by little, to keep the store operating. He didn't have enough money left to cover the deficit and pay his suppliers. He had run out of money. He couldn't believe it. All these years of hard work and frugality hadn't saved him. First all his children had abandoned him, and now he was losing his business. Why was God forsaking him?

"What's wrong?" Sarah asked.

"I'm done," he mumbled brokenly. He didn't want her to see him like this, but he couldn't bear to send her away. "The store is done."

"What do you mean?"

"I mean that I don't have enough savings left to cover September. I thought it was a good month, but my suppliers keep raising the prices on everything. I've lost money again. I only have six hundred left in savings. I can't afford to pay the rent for next month." Jonathan's voice shook. He never thought it would come to this. He was so proud of his frugality. He thought his nest egg would last through any troubles. The war had reached out with its greedy hands and harvested yet another thing from him.

"There must be some kind of mistake. How could you lose that much in one month?"

"I've checked and rechecked. The numbers are correct." He tossed the books across the desk at her. She scanned the bank ledger for a few minutes.

"You're right. The last few shipments of inventory have eaten up all your business reserves and left a deficit."

"There's nothing I can do. I'm going to have to close down the business, sell the inventory, and somehow try to pay the rent back."

"How long is your lease with Max?"

"Another four years."

"I could loan you some. I have a little savings."

"That's kind of you, but it would be like throwing pebbles in the river. What if I just lost more money next month? I could never borrow money from you that I couldn't pay back."

"What about talking to Max?"

"What do you mean?"

"Remember? You told me earlier this year that he said if you ever had a problem to come talk to him. What if you went and told him your situation?"

Jonathan bristled. He had refused credit his entire life. He had saved up the money for his house and paid cash for it. Then he had saved the money for his initial outlay of inventory. He had never carried an obligation out longer than a month. He wasn't about to start now. "There would be no point in asking for a loan or a forbearance on the rent," he responded, his voice a little tense. "I'm going to just have to sell the business and find work somewhere else." His heart broke as he said this.

Sarah leaned across and touched his hand again. "Jonathan, I'm so sorry. I know how much you've worried about your business. I know you've done everything you can to keep it going. Maybe you should at least talk to Mr. Weber and see what he could offer you?"

"You've told me over and over I should just get rid of this shop. Now you want me to try to fight to keep it? I don't understand." He was having a hard time concentrating with her hand still on his. She was tracing invisible patterns on the back of his hand, her fingers moving gently back and forth. His blood rushed through him.

"I know what I've said, Jonathan, but I also know how important this store is to you. I don't want you to lose it if you don't have to."

"I won't become a debtor."

"People have to borrow money all the time, Jonathan. You've done wonderfully to never have had to do so in the past. But the war has hurt your business badly. I don't think you have a choice now, unless you are truly willing to just let it all go."

He didn't know what to do. He was dead set against borrowing money from Mr. Weber or anyone. By the same token, he had put his whole life into this store. He had worked for others for years, and then finally, by saving and sacrificing, he bought this place. This was his security, his family's future. Perhaps she was right.

"I'll go see Mr. Weber. I don't know what good it will do, but I'll at least talk to him."

Sarah squeezed his hand with both of hers. She had never touched him with her bad hand before. She always kept it in her lap. She seemed to realize that, and her cheeks filled with color, but she didn't remove her hand. Jonathan thought his heart would beat out of his chest. He could smell the honey and rose water of her perfume. Her hands were burning hot. He squeezed her good hand and then slowly drew his away.

"Thank you, Sarah. Thank you for being here for me."

"I will always be here for you."

He rose and tucked in his shirt, straightening his tie in a small mirror tacked up on an otherwise bare wall. He looked presentable enough. "I guess I'll go see Max now. Best to get it over with."

"I'll pray for you, Jonathan. I hope there is something he can do for you."

"Would you mind watching things while I'm gone?"

"Of course not."

He smiled by way of thank you and then left the office and walked briskly out the front door onto First Street. Max's office was only two blocks east, on the river side of the street in a two-story redbrick building that was one of his many properties.

Jonathan entered the building. A bell clanged as he opened and shut the glass-and-wood door. Max was behind the counter. He smiled and clapped his hand down on the wooden surface. "It's Jonathan. What can I do for you, young man? Your rent isn't due until the tenth. Have you come to pay early?" He laughed at his own joke.

"I have a problem, and I need to talk to you."

Max's jovial manner abruptly changed, and his jowls filled like billowy sails as he leaned over the counter, arms extended. "What's wrong, my friend? Come over and sit down. I will get you some coffee, and we can talk about things. It's not your boys, I hope." Max poured them both a cup from a pot behind the counter and then took his seat at a tall stool.

"No. Nothing new about them."

"Well, what can it be then?"

"It's not an easy thing to talk about."

Max placed a strong hand on Jonathan's, pulling him closer. "Come now, Jonathan. We've known each other a long time. I think I suspect what this is about. You're having money issues? Is that it? It's this *Weltkrieg.*"

Jonathan breathed in deeply. He hated having to be here. "You're right, Mr. Weber. It's the cost of inventory. Everything is double or more what it used to be."

"You don't have to tell me. It's the same all around. And no money for anyone to buy anything, either? Correct?"

Jonathan nodded. "I have more expenses and less sales. It's never been this bad, even in the thirties when times were plenty tough."

"They were tough, but not so much for us, yes? The farmers always could make a little money, and they had to buy things. We provided them."

"I don't know what to do. I've used up all my savings."

Max shook his head and waved a pudgy finger. "Tsk, tsk. You shouldn't have. I told you six months ago to come to me with any problems you were having. I can help you, Jonathan. I know times are tough, but they won't stay that way. We are starting to slowly win this war. What's more, our industry is ramping up. There are more people employed than ever. You just need a little relief until things turn around; am I right?"

"I hesitated to even come here. I've never carried a debt longer than a month."

"I know that, and that's what makes you a safe bet for me. I want to help you out. How about if you don't pay me any rent until April? After that, you can pay me the regular amount plus a little extra for a year until the debt is paid." He frowned. "I do have to charge you a little interest, or Mrs. Weber would never forgive me. I'm sorry about that. How about if you pay me an extra two months of rent for the six months of relief I give you? I hate to say it. I would do this for free. But the missus!"

Jonathan was of two minds. He hated to borrow money, and paying back more than the principal would hurt him. By the same token, having six months of free rent could save his business. "I agree to the terms, Mr. Weber. That's very generous. Should we sign something?"

"Come on now, Jonathan. Your oath is all I need. You're good for it. Let's shake on it, and we will call it a deal."

They shook hands and finished their coffee, chatting about the war and mutual friends in the community.

"You don't know what it's like to be an American from Germany, *mein Freund. Ach.* That little monster ruined my country and made us pariahs to the world. *Gott* knows what's happening in my dear old country."

"You brought this on yourselves."

Max waved a hand. "I don't expect your sympathy. We started this. But you see only Germany. I think of my cousin Gretta and nephew Karl. I remember my little village and the Alps reaching to the sky. I can't imagine marching boots, cruelty, and hate. For me, just like for you—there is only family and friends in danger."

Jonathan excused himself as quickly as he felt was polite, thanking Max again for his generosity and then fleeing the office. Once he was back on the street, he breathed a sigh of relief. He didn't have to close the store. He would work as hard as possible for the next six months and save more money. He would talk to friends, advertise a little. The business would come in somehow. With any luck, at the end of the time he would have enough savings to pay back the debt in one payment, with more to spare. He stopped and closed his eyes, offering up a silent prayer to God. No matter how desperate things seemed, the Lord always provided for him in the end.

He thought of his other burdens: Luke and Matthew. Luke was safe for the time being. He had written and was getting by. His tone had changed in his letters; he seemed to finally be finding a humble spirit. Jonathan still had no word from Matthew. He hoped he would hear from him soon. Some letters were trickling home from the Japanese POW camps. He could get one from Matthew any day. Then his thoughts turned to Mary. He needed to see her.

Jonathan hurried back to his store. He told Sarah the good news about the rent and then asked her if she would mind watching the shop for a little longer while he went and talked to Mary. He hugged her and departed, turning right outside his door and then walking down to Avenue D. Before the war he would have driven, but with gas rationing he walked wherever he could. Besides, the exercise never hurt. He took another right and then walked up the avenue, his breath increasing a little on the long, gradual slope. He walked past the redbrick Snohomish High School on his left and the huge auction barn on the right, then continued uphill for another mile or so until he neared Blackmans Lake. He took another right on a dirt side street and marched into the residential neighborhood where Mary and Robert had their home. He had never been here but had driven by a number of times. The house was a small one-story tract home built in the twenties. The dwelling was painted yellow, with white trim, and stood before a postage stamp–sized yard that was perfectly manicured.

Jonathan hesitated. Now that he was here, he wasn't sure what he should say to Mary. He felt the strain of the past few months, and a twinge of anger rose again over her hasty decisions. But this was his daughter. He would love her no matter what. She was in need, and he would find out what was going on. He walked up the short pathway and climbed the steps to the porch. He paused a moment more and finally knocked.

A few moments passed, and nobody came to the door. He knocked again. Still no sound. Perhaps she wasn't home. He banged loudly on the door and heard some footsteps within. The door opened, and Mary was there.

Something was wrong. Jonathan sensed it right away. His daughter faced away from him, lost in the door frame.

"Hello," she said, her voice a crumbling whisper.

"Hello, Mary. What's wrong?" he demanded.

"Nothing," she said, but the lie streamed down her face. He reached his hand down and turned her toward him. He gasped. Her right eye was a dark shadow. She had a cut on the upper corner of her lip, and bruises caressed her cheeks. Jonathan felt hot fire welling up inside.

"Where is he? Where is that son of a bitch?"

Mary flung herself at her father, holding him tight. "Please, Father, no. He didn't mean it! He has been so sorry!"

Jonathan tried to pull away from her, but she clung to him. "I don't care if he's sorry. I want to see him, and I want it now!" He struggled to break free.

"Father, no! Please come in, and I'll explain things. It's not like it seems. It's okay."

He wanted to ignore her, to break free and find Robert. He would kill him. The anger raged through Jonathan like nothing he had ever experienced. But his daughter needed him. She was begging him to listen. He needed to take care of her first. Jonathan willed himself to calm down, closing his eyes and taking a few deep breaths. "Okay, I'll come in for a minute. I'll listen to you."

He felt Mary wilt in his arms. She stepped back and led him into the house, motioning for him to sit at a white flower-print sofa positioned against the front window in the tiny living room. He sat down, still angry, trying to fight down his rage. He took another deep breath.

Mary sat down across from him. She kept tilting her face away to mask her injuries. She told him the story of their first few months of marriage and the terrible evening when Robert exploded. Jonathan started to rise again, the details fueling his fury.

"Please, Father. Please wait! You haven't heard everything. The next day he was sorry. Sorry for everything. He was back to his old self, the man I fell in love with. He apologized, not just . . . for touching me, but for how he had treated me this whole time. Since this happened he has been an angel. He comes home every night on time. He brings me flowers. He tells me he loves me. He's been everything I ever wanted, everything I dreamed of. I'm so sorry I didn't come and tell you right away. I would have if he hadn't changed. But it's been perfect now." Her smile was overbright, her eyes filmed with glaze.

"It doesn't matter. He laid his hands on my little girl. I never touched your mother. Not one time. I don't know any man worth his salt who would strike his own wife." Jonathan's mind was reeling, and he didn't know what to do. He had heard of this sort of thing now and again. Marriage was a solemn relationship before God, though, and he'd been taught that others shouldn't interfere. Even if he did, he wasn't sure what would come of it. Divorce? That was preposterous. Mary would be a pariah in their small town. Divorce was a sin.

"I know it's terrible, but please don't do anything or say anything. He promised he would never do it again. Everything is wonderful now. It was awful before, but it'd be worse if he hadn't hit me and carried on like he did this whole summer. I've prayed and prayed about this, both before and after. God has finally granted me my wish, and I now have the husband I always wanted—the one I thought I had married."

"That's not enough. I need to speak to the boy."

She stood, terror in her eyes. "Please, Father, don't! I'm begging you. Everything is finally the way I want it. If you go and talk to him, he's going to get angry again. He might change. I can't live like that. I can't survive with him treating me the way he was. It's okay now. I'm asking you to leave things alone. He learned his lesson. He's a gentle soul, a loving and kind man. He just has such a hard job. All day long he deals with criminals. If you heard the things he tells me about, you would understand."

"Nothing gives him the right to hurt you! He has no excuse." Jonathan's voice was stern. His mind searched frantically for a platform to rest on.

"No, he doesn't! You're right. But he will never do it again. He was so tortured by what he did, so regretful. I know he will never hit me in the future."

Jonathan grunted and then was silent, trying to think through this problem. In many ways he had no right to interfere. Once his daughter married, she left his household and entered Robert's. It wasn't proper to interfere with another family, regardless of what went on. *A promise must be kept—no matter the pain another brings you.*

Still, this was his daughter. The hate for Robert rose in Jonathan's heart. He had been right. His instincts were dead-on. Yet he hadn't been able to protect Mary. He had counseled her; he had tried to compromise with her. He had forgiven her after she ran away. He had prayed and prayed, yet it had all come to this. He felt the pain of all three of his children. All three had defied him. All three were in harm's way. What was he doing wrong? What was his sin? Pride? Control? His daughter wanted him to trust her, to let her live her life. He needed time to think.

"I'll trust you for now. But this better not happen again!"

He saw the relief in her eyes. "It won't. Thank you so much! You make me so happy. I know you probably won't want to see Robert for a while, but I hope you will forgive him. He's changed. He's so different now." She rose and ran to Jonathan, hugging him, the tears rolling again down her cheeks. He held her for a while and then departed, promising to visit soon. He left the house and walked down the street quickly, keeping his head down so nobody could see his tears. He headed south and entered a small park, seeking out a bench situated near some trees, far away from anyone. He sat down and bowed his head in prayer.

He stayed for what seemed hours, talking quietly to God, trying to understand. Just a few short years ago, everything was so simple: He had a wonderful family. His hard work had enabled him to buy the store and a small house. He was respected; his family was loved. Then his first son unexpectedly left. Soon after, Helen came down with cancer. He stood by her side, watched her pain and suffering. Then she left him, and he experienced more pain than he had ever known. He kept his faith, he battled, and he did his best with Luke and Mary. Then came the war. Luke left him; Mary eloped. The business failed. Everything was falling apart. He had believed if he worked hard, saved his money, went to church, and kept his faith, all would be well. Instead his life had fallen apart. The only things that remained to him were God and Sarah.

Sarah, his best friend. Was he sinning with her? He asked himself the question for the thousandth time. Was his sin with Sarah what was causing his world to fall apart? What could he do? He couldn't live without her. *I'm bound.* They were friends only. He wanted more, so much more. So did she. *My thoughts already betray her.*

Everything had started to fall apart before he met her. He knew that. Was Sarah a test? If he sent her away, would his condition improve again? Was that what God was waiting for?

He felt the hot guilt again, and the uncertainty. He prayed for guidance, for forgiveness. The light began to fall. Still, he sat, his eyes closed, seeking answers that did not come.

CHAPTER TWELVE

Fort Benning, Georgia
Saturday, October 3, 1942

Sergeant Dempsey stood before the Sherman tank and addressed the platoon. Much to Luke's dismay, they had not sent everyone out to different units after boot camp. Nor had Sergeant Dempsey remained behind to lead another group of draftees or recruits. The entire platoon had stayed at Fort Benning, where they were going to be trained in tank warfare. The only new addition to the platoon was Lieutenant Terry Alanyk.

Alanyk was a short man of slight build with curly brown hair. Glasses guarded his knowing eyes. He was an intellectual from Astoria, Oregon, straight out of Officer Candidate School and the University of Oregon. Alanyk was technically in charge of the platoon, although he deferred to Sergeant Dempsey in all things.

The past months had been extremely difficult for Luke. Dempsey continued to keep a close eye on him. Luke had made it through the rest of boot camp with no passes and constant latrine duty. Dempsey had shadowed him the entire time, finding fault in everything Luke did, for every momentary lapse in attention. Dempsey delighted in punishing the entire platoon for Luke's mistakes.

Most difficult of all for Luke was the way the other men treated him. He was a stone fallen far from the mountain. There were no more reprisals, no more beatings. Instead conversations ceased when he came around. People would look the other way and refuse to speak to him when he tried. Ironically Private Wenzel had become his closest friend. Wenzel seemed to think Luke had redeemed himself when he confessed to the prank. The young introvert from Indianapolis rarely took his weekend passes, either, and the two of them gradually became companions, sharing information about their homes, friends and families, and future hopes and dreams.

Perhaps more surprisingly, Sergeant Bonelli went out of his way to be kind to Luke. Although Luke couldn't classify him as a friend, Bonelli, who was now admired and respected by all, would not allow anyone to pick on Luke. He had stopped any additional reprisals, and his protection of Luke had kept the platoon at least negligently neutral about him.

Luke tried to understand Bonelli, but he just couldn't. He still attempted to reason through what had led him to take responsibility, to take punishment in his place. Luke had never known anyone like him. He had grown to respect and admire Bonelli and had joined the rest of the platoon in congratulating him when he was promoted to buck sergeant at the end of boot camp. Several more men had received promotions to sergeant or corporal. Luke had not, and hadn't expected any.

After their initial training the platoon moved to barracks on the other side of Fort Benning and learned they were being assigned to a newly formed division, the Tenth Armored Division. Luke was delighted they were going to be in tanks.

Dempsey turned to the tank behind him. "This is a Sherman M4 tank. This beauty has a 470-horsepower engine and a 75-millimeter cannon. Enough speed and power to get you into a mess in a hurry, and let you fight your way out of it."

The sergeant explained further. "Each Sherman will carry a crew of five. In addition to the main gun, there is also a .50-caliber machine gun and two .30 calibers: plenty of firepower to get you out of trouble quicker than you get into it. Do you see this sloping armor in the front of the tank? Shells will bounce off if you get hit. That means if you're lucky, you won't blow up and boil to death like a bunch of stewed peaches. Now come on over, and let's take turns getting into this thing and figuring out the different instruments and duties."

Luke joined the rest of the platoon breaking into small groups to sit inside the tank. He was shocked at the cramped interior. With the five-man crew all in position and the turret closed, there was barely room to move. Fuel fumes filled the space, even when the tank wasn't idling. He felt claustrophobic for the first time in his life, and he struggled to keep from panicking.

The platoon looked over the tank for a couple of hours. Then Sergeant Dempsey called them all back together and asked the NCOs to come forward and select their crews. Sergeant Bonelli was assigned a tank, and Luke was surprised when he picked him to be part of his crew. Private Wenzel was also named to his crew. Luke was delighted. He was already close to two of them. At last he felt a part of something. The segregation into smaller groups made his isolation seem less severe.

Luke approached Bonelli after the crews were sorted out. He felt sheepish and unsure of what to say, but he needed to show his gratitude. "Thank you so much, Sergeant. I didn't know if anyone would want me. Thank you for trusting me after what happened before."

"You're welcome, Beecher. Don't make me look a fool. I'm going to take some heat for picking you, but I don't care what they think. I know there's more to you than other people want to see. You took your medicine these past months, and you haven't complained much. Still, you might have more mistakes left in you. People are watching closely, Dempsey most of all. I need your best. Can you give me that?"

"Yes, Sergeant, I will." Luke was so pleased. Finally, a chance to redeem himself, to get back into the good graces of the platoon. He had thought joking around would work, but he had failed miserably. Now he hoped if he just kept his head down and his mouth shut, he would finally be accepted by the people around him. He might be able to eventually win them over and be popular again. He had struggled all these months being disliked. He wasn't used to it and didn't like it. He yearned for the days when he was adored by everyone, when he was everyone's favorite guy.

There had to be some way to restore things. Look at Bonelli. He was beloved by everyone. For what? For allowing himself to get in trouble. Luke realized it was more about the bravery. Maybe he needed to do something brave. Was that the trick?

The thought stuck with him over the next few days of training. Luke was selected to serve as the gunner. He was delighted at this role, and happier yet that Wenzel was selected to be the ammunition loader. Private Sam Collins was appointed the driver, and Private Kelly Hudson was the assistant driver and bow gunner. Sergeant Bonelli was, of course, the tank commander.

Collins sat at the front left-hand side of the Sherman and fumbled with the foot pedals, trying to move the tank. To his right sat Hudson, his hands on the trigger of a .30-caliber machine gun. Luke sat above to the middle, his eyes peering into a scope and his hands at the controls, ready to move the main turret to any target ordered by Bonelli. Once he found a target, a foot pedal would fire the 75-millimeter cannon. Wenzel sat behind Luke and would load the shells.

For the first few days of training, they didn't drive or move their tank. They spent that time simply sitting inside and going over the various instruments that made up the complex Sherman. They then moved on to practice simulations of driving and loading and firing the weapons. Only after hours and hours of familiarizing themselves with the tank were they allowed to drive it. Even when they were permitted to move, they had to train for another week before they fired their first round.

As the days passed, Luke felt better and better. The crew had become a team. His past transgression seemed to be forgotten as they worked intensely together, becoming used to each other's actions, thoughts, and idiosyncrasies.

Luke hadn't known Collins or Hudson well before. Collins was from San Bernardino and matched his dark skin with snow-blond hair. No matter how exciting things were, he was always yawning, and he could fall asleep at his controls in a moment anytime there was a lull in training.

Hudson was his opposite. Tall and stocky, he had bushy black eyebrows and jet-black hair, with pale skin. He came from Wichita Falls, Texas. Hudson's family had a cattle ranch, and he was a real cowboy. He walked bowlegged from years in the saddle, and he always had a plug of chewing tobacco in his mouth. Hudson rarely talked, but when he did, he usually had some homespun comment to make. He was terribly prejudiced against the North, and called Sergeant Bonelli "Yank."

After a few weeks of training, Luke learned they would be grouping up with larger tank formations to practice for the first time at the regimental and divisional levels. He was excited to work with larger groups and advance in his training. They had drilled with platoons and companies, but never anything larger.

"I'm proud of all of you," Sergeant Bonelli told them. "I think we'll be the best tank crew in the division. We've got a big day tomorrow. I want you to hit your bunks early so we're fresh. We'll be sleeping by our machines in the fields for a few days to come."

Luke lay in bed wide awake that night, basking in his enjoyment of the past month. He was happy he was part of this crew now, although he still felt some of the distance from before, particularly from Collins and

Hudson. An idea formed of how he might be able to redeem himself and win the approval of his whole crew, and of the old platoon. He fell asleep with immense satisfaction.

∾

The next morning Luke decided he would implement his idea. He went to the latrine early, before anyone else was up. Looking around carefully to make sure nobody was watching, he took one of the bars of soap and scraped off a number of shavings with his fingernail and placed them in his pocket. Again observing his surroundings to make sure he hadn't been seen, he returned to his cot and waited.

A bugle woke the men with the familiar sound of reveille. Luke sprang out of bed with everyone else. The men were excited and talking loudly. Today would be an interesting and exhilarating experience, their first chance to work together in battalion-sized formations. The men dressed quickly and then formed up for roll call. Afterward they swarmed to the mess hall, impatient to eat their breakfast and get on with the day. Luke lined up with the rest of the men and took his tray of eggs, bacon, and pancakes. The eggs were powdered and not to his liking. They were all hungry, though, and were soon sitting at tables with their crews, discussing what today would bring.

After a few minutes, Luke excused himself. He walked over to the coffee and poured two cups. He unobtrusively dropped some of the soap into one of the cups of coffee, along with a lot of cream and sugar. He returned to the table and offered the doctored coffee to Sergeant Bonelli. Bonelli thanked Luke. He liked his joe with plenty of cream and sugar, and Luke hoped he wouldn't notice any difference.

Luke watched carefully as he took the first sip. He was concerned that Bonelli might detect the soap, but he didn't. Luke relaxed. He didn't want to hurt his friend. He felt some shame in doing what he had planned. But this would just make the sergeant a little sick. As the gunner, Luke was second in command. He had been cross-trained as the tank commander. If he took over for a little while, even for just a day, he hoped to prove his worth as a leader and regain the respect of the crew, and hopefully of the platoon.

They finished breakfast and were soon out of the mess hall on their way to their tank. They climbed in and started their system checks. In a few minutes they started the Sherman and rumbled slowly into line behind other tanks, all crawling away from the base and toward open fields where the maneuvers would occur.

The Shermans took half the morning to move into position. The crews were unused to working in such large groups. Several of the tanks broke down, blocking the road and causing lengthy delays. The interior of Luke's tank grew stuffy. He kept an eye on Bonelli, but the sergeant seemed to be totally unaffected by the soap.

The radio sounded. It was Lieutenant Alanyk, who was commanding a platoon of five tanks. Sergeant Dempsey led another one, along with two more NCOs.

"I just heard from company HQ. We're going to join up with our whole battalion. HQ wants us to simulate a group attack over an open field. Our company will be first, followed by Dog and Easy. Form up on my tank and move out. Understood?"

"Yes, sir," said Bonelli. "Okay, people. You heard the lieutenant. We're following him to the edge of some fields about a mile up. When we get there, we'll spread out a bit; then we'll roll out at full speed into the field, simulating a surprise attack. Fox Company is first, followed by Dog and Easy. Any questions?"

"Sarge, I don't wanna be a turd, but just how's we supposed to get our whole battalion in line in the next few minutes when it's taken the whole darned morning just to get over to the starting line?" asked Hudson.

"Good question, Hudson. But we have orders. Let's do our best. We're going to get better at this stuff as we go. We just need to . . ." Bonelli stopped midsentence. He groaned and doubled over.

"What's wrong?" asked Hudson.

"I don't know . . . I'm fine. I just feel a little sick." Sergeant Bonelli hunched over again. His groans increased. He rose, quickly opening the turret to vomit violently outside the tank.

"He's not doing well," said Luke. "We better radio this in." He grabbed the receiver and called the lieutenant to inform him of what was going on.

"That's real bad luck," said Alanyk. "We don't have time for this right now. You better get him out of there and to the hospital. After that, you'll need to take over for now, Beecher. Can you handle the gun and the command?"

"I'll make do for now, Lieutenant."

"Roger that. Hurry up now. We're going to be very late."

Luke helped Wenzel and Hudson pull the sergeant out of the tank. They flagged down some medics that were nearby. The medics laid Bonelli on the ground and checked him out. A few minutes later they brought a stretcher.

The sergeant was in terrible pain, but he didn't want to leave. "Take care of my tank, Beecher. I'm trusting you to do a good job. Take care of the men, too."

"I will, Sergeant. I'm sure you're going to be okay. We'll see you later today."

Bonelli reached out his hand and squeezed Luke's arm. "You'll do just fine, Luke."

They carried the sergeant away. Luke felt the hot guilt wash over him again. He brushed it off. He needed to do this. Bonelli was brave and had won the platoon over. He could do the same. This was the only way he could restore his reputation. Bonelli would be fine. He was a good man, beloved by the men. He didn't need this as badly as Luke did.

Luke climbed back in. He could tell the crew was less than enthusiastic about him taking command. The tank rolled forward. Luke began issuing orders in a clear and decisive manner. Their tank caught up with the rest of the platoon within a few minutes and followed along until they came to the edge of the field. Hudson had guessed correctly—instead of taking a few minutes for the entire battalion to form, the maneuver took more than an hour. Their own tank was always in the correct position.

Luke was surprised to find he was a natural at commanding a tank. He noticed as the day went on that the crew responded more enthusiastically to his orders. When the actual mock attack occurred, Luke moved the tank out with crisp and confident commands, keeping them behind and to the right of the platoon's lead tank in a tight formation. The other vehicles labored to keep up. As the day went on, the battalion practiced the attack over and over. Luke displayed an uncanny ability to keep his tank in formation. Finally, as the light was failing, they lumbered back to base.

The crew congratulated Luke on a superb job commanding. Lieutenant Alanyk was even more impressed.

"That was an excellent job, Beecher. You seem to be a natural. Great work today."

Luke beamed. The lieutenant had said this in front of the entire platoon. He could feel the admiration from the others, something he would have said was scarcely possible the day before. He still felt badly about what he had done to Bonelli, but now it was all worth it. He had accomplished what he had hoped and dreamed of all these months. He had restored himself to the platoon. Even more, he was now looked up to—even admired. He finally felt the way he had always felt in life before he joined the military: a golden child, liked by all around him.

The crew visited Sergeant Bonelli in the hospital, and Luke's sun swiftly set. Bonelli was connected to an IV, and he was unconscious. The nurse said he had been severely poisoned and was terribly ill. They didn't know how long he might be out of duty. He might not ever recover. If he did, there could be permanent damage to his internal organs. The crew visited with the sergeant for about an hour and then returned to their barracks. The discussion all the way back centered on their poor leader.

Luke was stone silent. What had he done? All he had wanted was to set up a situation where he might redeem himself and possibly even shine. But he never would have done this if he'd thought there was any chance Bonelli might be permanently harmed. He thought the sergeant might be sick for a day, two at the most, and then his friend would be back in charge. In the meantime Luke could display some leadership and try to clear up the cloud that had dwelt over him for all these months. Instead he had caused serious damage to Bonelli. What the hell was wrong with him? Was his own petty desire for popularity so great that he would risk his friend's life to achieve it? He thought about going to Dempsey or Alanyk, but the responsibility was too great. He wanted to wait and hope things improved.

The next day Bonelli was no better. At least he wasn't worse. Luke led their tank again, and just like the day before, he performed brilliantly. There was no joy today, however. When the exercises were over, they visited their sergeant again. There was still no improvement.

The maneuvers lasted for an additional three days. Each evening they checked on Bonelli, and each time his condition was the same. He was gravely ill. Luke was riddled with guilt. He spent much of his free time at the hospital at Bonelli's side. He prayed over and over, begging for forgiveness, hoping for a miracle. Still, there was no improvement in his friend.

Finally, the maneuvers were over. Lieutenant Alanyk reviewed their progress.

"We did good work. Not as good as we'd hoped going into this, but better than our worst fears. Each day we moved faster at every organizational level. The formations were quicker, tighter, more complex. There were more breakdowns than we expected, but we learned about that, too, and learned how to fix them up on the go. The next time we do this, we'll be using ammunition as well, and eventually live-fire training. For now, I'm proud of you boys." He turned to Sergeant Dempsey. "Sergeant. I think there was something you wanted to do."

"Private Beecher, come forward."

Luke was shocked to hear his name. His heart sank. They had found out what he did. He would be court-martialed, likely jailed. Who had betrayed him? He stumbled forward reluctantly.

Sergeant Dempsey stood before him and ordered Luke to attention. "Private Beecher, I have something to say to you in front of the platoon. You displayed great leadership in taking over for Bonelli. Leadership that, frankly, I didn't think you possessed. You are a natural talent as a tank commander. You will be happy to know that Sergeant Bonelli will be back soon. He is greatly recovered this morning. I have more good news for you—Lieutenant Alanyk has recommended you for promotion to corporal. Battalion HQ agrees. Congratulations, Corporal." Sergeant Dempsey offered his hand.

Luke was in shock. He wasn't in trouble. Instead he had been promoted, and Sergeant Bonelli was recovering. Everything had worked out the way he hoped it would. He smiled to himself. The shame already seemed to fade away with the cheers.

CHAPTER THIRTEEN

Mukilteo, Washington
Tuesday, October 5, 1943

Jonathan and Sarah nestled on a blanket in a park overlooking the Puget Sound. The sun was out, and the day was unusually warm, although fall was progressing toward winter, and soon it would be too cold to picnic outside. Knowing this, Jonathan had closed his store for half a day and invited Sarah to drive across the wooden trestle from Snohomish to Everett and then over to Mukilteo so they could enjoy the spectacular views. The sparkling blue water of Port Gardner Bay spread out before them. Tiny Hat Island poked out in the center of their view; Whidbey Island was to the left and Camano Island to the right. The fingers of the isles all reached toward them. The bay contained a few sailboats racing along, also taking advantage of the unusual weather, which was climbing above sixty-five degrees.

Sarah sat with her legs extended out on the blanket. Her elbows were against the ground, and her head was thrown back, her smile soaking up the warm afternoon sun. Jonathan watched her, grinning to himself. She was beautiful to him in every way, her thin frame, her pale skin. Her disfigured hand only added to her fragile appeal.

He turned away and busied himself with a picnic basket he had prepared for their day. He unfolded the red-and-white gingham cloth and pulled out a fresh loaf of bread still warm from the oven. He retrieved some cheese and fruit, placing everything carefully on some plates, and then poured them some white wine. Sarah smiled at him, pulling herself up and taking a glass. They touched their drinks together and shared a quiet toast amid the breeze and the protesting chatter of seagulls.

Jonathan thought back to the past year. Not long ago he had thought his business on the brink of bankruptcy. Then he had found Mary, bruised and broken. Now things were so much better. His store had slowly recovered and was at least breaking even, although he still owed Mr. Weber some of the back rent. The letters from Luke were encouraging. His unit was beginning training in tanks. He was preparing for war but still safe. Mary and Robert had continued along under a distant but wary eye from Jonathan, seemingly without any new incidents.

"I never thought the Germans could be beat," said Jonathan. "Now they've had their tails whipped in Africa and in Russia. I don't know if they're whipped or not, but at least they're starting to fall back a little bit. The Japs, too."

Jonathan had hoped with the defeats in the Pacific that the Japanese would send him word of Matthew being safe. He prayed every day as he retrieved the mail that he would get a letter. Something, anything. There was nothing. Even as some things at home looked better, there was a gash in his soul for his son.

He looked up to Sarah, and he felt his sadness fade away. In a year of growing light, she was the brightest ray. She had taken away his loneliness and filled it with joy. She was a beautiful, kind, faithful woman. He had never known anyone like her. Somehow they had maintained their boundaries as friends. He respected and loved her for that, perhaps more than for anything else—despite the aching desire that coursed through him every time they touched.

They ate in silence, watching each other, enjoying the dancing wave tops of the sound and the rich emerald of the forests reaching up to the Olympic Mountains in the distance. Could there be a more beautiful place in the world? He poured them some more wine, and then she came over to sit next to him. Both of them faced the water, a hairline apart.

"What are you thinking about?" she asked at last.

"This past year."

She looked at him and smiled. "It's been a wonderful year. Who would've believed it possible with this war going on?"

"Wonderful because of you," he said.

Her face illuminated. "I would say the same. You've brought life back to me." She hesitated. "Even as friends."

"Your friendship has meant everything to me."

"And yours to me." She turned away, looking out over the water.

"What's wrong?"

"My back. Leaning over the sewing table so many hours. I feel a pinch sometimes." She giggled. "I'm not as young as I used to be."

"You don't look a day over twenty," he said. "Turn around and sit in front of me."

She gave him a tentative glance.

"Just do it, please."

She shuffled forward a bit until she was sitting directly in front of him. He moved forward and placed his hands on her back. She felt like a trembling doe.

"Where does it hurt?"

She motioned with her hand to the middle of her back on the left side. He pushed down hard with his palms, gently kneading the area.

She pushed back against his hands, arching her back slightly. "That feels so good."

He kept his hands pressing, moving against her. He felt his heart crashing against his chest. Her back was warmed silk. He had never touched her like this. He knew he had to keep control; he was only helping relieve her pain. Gradually his hands worked up to her shoulders, and then he moved slowly down the smooth pathway of her arms. She was leaning back now, into him, her eyes closed. His hands reached the cloth covering her hand. He began to slowly remove it. He didn't know why he wanted to do this, but an irresistible urge drew him on. He felt her stiffen, and she pulled her arm away. "It's okay," he whispered.

She hesitated, and he could see the pinpricks form on her arms. Then she drew a deep breath and moved her hand back to his. He carefully removed the mitten. He had never seen her damaged hand before. All this time she had kept it from him. The hand was withered and bent, the bones fractured and crushed from the accident, the skin alabaster and transparent except for scars branching out in complex deltas. He gently moved his fingers over hers, caressing her lovingly, softly. She opened her eyes and watched him, her eyes clouds of uncertainty. He smiled at her reassuringly. She laid her head back again and shut her eyes.

He drew her hand up to his face and ran her fingers across the landscape of his cheek. His blood quickened. His mind spun. He closed his eyes, enjoying the warmth, her fingers walking back and forth.

She leaned farther against him, and he gathered her in, surrounding her with protective arms. He knew he should pull away, but he simply couldn't. They sat that way for hours as the sun arced over the sky. They didn't speak but instead watched the waltzing water and the sailboats singing by. Jonathan hushed his mind. He was tired of thought and prayer. There was simply just him and Sarah.

He had crossed a boundary. No doubt about it. She had allowed him willingly. They had never touched—not like this. He felt the vibrations in his core. He knew he was starting down a path he had promised never to travel. Still, he didn't want to think about it, not today. The landscape before them was too beautiful. He wanted one day for himself, for her. They sipped wine in the warmth and watched the sun disappear below the Olympics to the west. Only when the light faded did they pack up their blanket and basket and walk slowly away. Jonathan thanked God for a perfect day with this angel on earth. He would think about the future tomorrow.

∾

The next day came swiftly. Jonathan worked through the company bills and balanced the books. He couldn't help but be distracted from his task. His smiles marked the minutes. He felt peace and a happiness he had never felt before. He knew he should feel guilty. He had most assuredly broken his promise by touching Sarah in such a way. Somehow he couldn't manage that emotion. Instead there was contentment and joy, a delight he knew he had never felt with Helen.

That thought brought a drop of guilt. He didn't even know for sure anymore what he had felt as a young man. He had certainly wanted Helen, and he had courted her and married her. But then what? They had settled into a domestic life of hard work and hard times. They had matured during the Depression and raised their kids when putting food on the table was all that mattered. He hadn't worried about happiness and love. He was proud that he could take care of his family when millions could not. Her illness appeared to drain the last of their happiness, which faded away to a dull misery they had both borne as best they could.

Jonathan shook his head. He needed to concentrate. He was acting like a boy, with his thoughts scattered around his head. He quietly chastised himself and went back to work. His labors brought new darkness to his door. He hadn't realized it, but the bills this month were far greater than he expected, again. It seemed that every quarterly and half-yearly obligation had all come due at the same time. He tallied and retallied, but the numbers didn't improve. Another unexpected month. He had gone backward a considerable sum.

Jonathan felt the growing panic like an icy claw. Just when he thought he was finally climbing out of debt, it looked like he was facing another crisis. He wished Sarah were there, but she was spending the day working. He thought of going to see her, but he wasn't ready to talk about yesterday yet. He knew what he was going to have to do; he would have to talk to Mr. Weber again. Jonathan felt incredibly frustrated. He thought he had pulled out of the worst of his business problems. Now it seemed one bad month would erase a year of hard work and careful saving.

He reluctantly rose and shuffled woodenly to the front door. He placed the clock return sign on the glass and headed out to Mr. Weber's office, the peace of the morning destroyed. He found Max at his perch near the front desk.

"*Guten Morgen*, Jonathan. Ha! I mean good morning, of course. How are you, my old friend?"

"I've been better."

Max's face grew full of concern. "Now, now. Come in here and have some coffee with me. Tell me what Uncle Max can do for you."

Jonathan took a seat on a stool at the front counter. Max left the room, returning shortly with a tray of coffee and some dessert. He poured both of them a cup, and Jonathan helped himself to a couple of chocolate cookies.

"Now tell me, Jonathan, what is the matter?"

"It's the store again."

"*Ach!* What? How can that be? You've been doing so well. Sure, you're a little behind in getting our payments caught up, but you've made such great progress. Surely things are still going well?"

"I thought they were. I've made a lot of progress this past year. But darn it if October didn't reach up and bite me again. I've got more bills than money. I hate to ask it of you, Max, but is there any way you could spot me a couple more months on the rent?"

Max's face grew thoughtful. He paused to think, a sausage finger pressing a deep well into his fleshy cheek. "Now, Jonathan, you know I think the world of you, right?"

"Yes."

"I want to help you, but now this is the second time. I am a businessman, after all." He raised his arms wide and then returned his hands to his cheeks as if he wanted nothing more than to capture his last words and take them away. "I've an idea. I can defer rent again through the first of the year, and you can pay me back with one additional month so long as you're caught up by the following December."

"That's very generous, Mr. Weber . . ."

"I wasn't quite finished. I will need you to give me some collateral this time." He paused, and his hands fanned out in front of him. "Now don't you worry. It's just a little security between friends. I would like you to sign over your inventory, just to guarantee the debt. Don't fret; I wouldn't try to collect on it. It's just to help me sleep at night, you understand—so the missus doesn't get angry with me."

Jonathan felt a rush of uncertainty. Mr. Weber wanted him to pledge the inventory of the business. Didn't he trust him anymore? He hadn't kept up like he was supposed to. He felt anger and embarrassment. This was the reason he never wanted to borrow money. He didn't want to feel beholden to any other man. Still, what could he do? He needed the financial relief. Things hadn't gone well for so many months. But the war news was improving. Soon the government would begin easing some of the restrictions on items and the prices would go down. He just had to push through for a while longer. Even though it pained him, this deal would buy him time.

Max stood, taking a step toward him. "I've hurt your feelings, haven't I? I'm sorry to have suggested it, but I know you understand—it's only business."

"No, Max, I just had to think about things. You've been so good to me, and it's only fair that you have some protection. I agree to your terms."

Max's smile spread across the pink ocean of his face. "Excellent. Don't you worry about this a bit. It's just a formality." He rose and shambled rapidly over to a file cabinet. He shuffled through some paperwork and retrieved a form. He returned to the counter and then worked away, filling in the details of their agreement. "Now then, look this over and make sure it's all correct, then sign when you're done."

Jonathan reviewed the document. The terms were as proposed, including pledging the entirety of his business inventory. He read through the paperwork one more time to make sure, and then he fixed his signature to the page.

Max snatched up the agreement and returned the document to the file cabinet, turning a key to lock it away. When he was done, he patted the top of the cabinet contentedly. "Now then, my boy, let's finish our coffee and visit for a while."

Jonathan sat with Mr. Weber for another half hour, doing his best to listen and to talk, but he had a difficult time concentrating. He excused himself as soon as he thought it polite and then retreated down First Street to the Snohomish River shore.

He felt like he had just sold his soul. He knew he had no other choice. There were cheaper rents off the main street, but most businesses struggled to make a go of it in other parts of town. Jonathan closed his eyes and prayed, asking God to protect him, to protect his business and his family. He paced back and forth for quite some time, watching the crawling current of the river, trying to shake off a feeling of foreboding.

A thought kept entering his mind: What if God was punishing him for what had happened yesterday with Sarah? He kept telling himself that was ridiculous, that nothing had *really* happened between them, but he knew he wasn't being honest with himself. He had crossed a line, a forbidden line that he had guarded for more than a year. He had broken a sacred promise to Helen and to God.

Perhaps that wasn't fair. Possibly passing this boundary was just another crack around the edges of his faith, of his values. He had chipped away, piece by piece, at what he stood for, and perhaps all the small cuts had finally opened a hole he never intended. All he knew was he had crossed this line one day, and the next day his business crumbled. He shook his head and turned back to his store. He had work to do, money to be made. He would think on all this later. He prayed for answers.

~~

Jonathan spent the rest of the day in the store battling his books. He combed his inventory, looking for missing merchandise and trying to predict what expenses could be coming up in the next few months. He cleaned and straightened the shelves. He wondered if he could come up with some more attractive signage. He'd never had much of a knack for designing. Sarah could help him with that. By the time he closed up in the evening, he felt more confident about the future, particularly with the new relief offered by Max.

He felt less sure about Sarah. She was coming over for dinner tonight as she often did. This evening was different. Her daughter was spending the night at a friend's house. They would be alone together in his home at night, galloping swiftly after yesterday's unexpected intimacy.

He tried to pray for guidance on what he should do, but he didn't receive any direction or comfort from doing so. It was as if God were leaving this entirely to him. He felt the scalding excitement of her touch again, and his breath quickened. He toyed with plans for tonight. After dinner they could sit on the sofa, her feet on his lap. He would massage her calves, gently stroking her soft skin. Then he would pull her head gently up to his and kiss her on the cheek, then the lips . . .

He shook his head. Where was he getting these ideas? Even if he wanted to, what did he know about romance and seduction? Certainly Helen had viewed such things for procreation only. He had to regain his control. He forced himself to reconsider what he must do. They would eat dinner. He would talk to her afterward and apologize for his actions in the park. He would shake her hand firmly and nothing more. She would be disappointed, but she would understand. They could go on as friends—the only future they had together.

He felt better after he sorted out his feelings. His flesh was weak. He had spent his entire life fighting against sin, and he wouldn't surrender now. Sarah would agree with him. She loved him for his strength. Hadn't she told him this over and over? Another part of him admitted she would not be pleased, that she would not understand. Well, what could he do? The world was full of difficulty and suffering.

Bolstered by his conviction, Jonathan felt renewed and strengthened. He walked down the road to the Piggly Wiggly and spent a few minutes shopping for dinner, nodding at friends he saw there. He even whistled a little, feeling better. A half hour later he was home and preparing for their meal.

He first opened a package of fresh lettuce and carefully peeled away the outer layers, removing any brown or discolored pieces. He sliced the rest into roughly equal parts. He cut up an onion and carrots, then celery and radishes. When he was finished, he placed it all in a bowl and carefully washed and tossed the salad. He drained the excess water, and when he was sure it was perfect, he covered the bowl with a cloth and set to work on the dressing. He poured oil into a smaller container and then added mustard, vinegar, a dash of salt and pepper, and two spoons of honey. He whisked the liquid until the color was consistent. He tasted the dressing. It was perfect: tangy with a hint of sweet.

He unwrapped a fillet of fresh Puget Sound salmon. He poured a little oil into his baking pan and then positioned the salmon in the middle. He squeezed lemon and lime juice over it and then sprinkled over salt and pepper. He placed the tray into the oven.

He set the table for the two of them, bringing out his cloth napkins and white china. *Our china,* he thought guiltily. He placed two warm loaves of bread from the store in the middle, along with a bottle of white wine he had chilled ahead of time.

With dinner on the way, Jonathan moved upstairs to the bathroom. He ran water through his hair and then towel dried and combed vigorously until he was satisfied. He put on a crisply ironed shirt and tie and looked himself over in the mirror. *What do you think you're doing?*

He heard a gentle knock at the door. He could feel his heart race. His resolve disintegrated. He closed his eyes for a moment, breathing deeply to calm himself down. Then he walked to the entryway.

Sarah stood at the threshold in the dusk, the bright light of the sky illuminating the halo of her hair. She was dressed in a simple cotton dress. Her eyes held the future, the past, forever. He invited her in, taking a shawl she had draped around her left arm. His hand touched the back of her arm as he removed it. She shivered for a moment.

"How are you?" he asked.

"You look so handsome."

"Come in, please."

They were formal and awkward in a way they hadn't acted in months, perhaps longer. They couldn't hold each other's eyes. He led her into the dining room and motioned for her to sit, pulling a chair back for her. She smiled again shyly and then took her place. He stepped up to the table, very near her, reaching out to pour her a glass of wine.

"How was your work today?" she asked.

"It went well." A little untrue, but he didn't want to talk about work, about the further debt, or about his worries. He just wanted a night with her, near her. He tried to hold the fortress of his resolve together. Yet he felt a terror of the future as well. He felt his earlier resolution crumbling. He didn't want to talk to her; he wanted to enjoy her.

"I'm glad. I worked all day on a sewing project for Mrs. Hamlin. I thought it was going to be quick, but the pattern was much more complex than I expected."

"Will she pay you more?" He was relieved to talk about trivial matters as he stood at the precipice.

"I don't think so. I should have asked more questions before I quoted her a price."

Jonathan poured himself some wine, and they sat in the candlelight together. Once in a while he would catch her eye and quickly look away. The conversation gradually receded, the pauses growing longer. Soon they were sitting quietly together, sipping their wine and enjoying the flickering darkness.

A ding interrupted the quiet. Jonathan rose. "Let me check on dinner." He walked quickly into the kitchen and pulled out the salmon. He tested the fish with a toothpick. The meat was flaky, perfect. He removed the cloth from the salad and slowly poured the dressing over it in a circular pattern. He carried the dinner into the dining room.

"That smells delicious."

"Thank you," he said. He hadn't cooked for her much, and he was nervous. He certainly knew how to cook. He had enjoyed making dinner sometimes, even before Helen had passed away. However, tonight was different. He wanted perfection. Again the inconsistencies pressed in on him. He tried to erect a wall against them, but he was out of time. He knew the dance was over. They must become all one thing or another.

He placed the bowl and the tray carefully on the table and then lifted her plate. He cut some salmon and placed it on her dish, along with the salad and some bread. He then did the same for himself. They bowed their heads in a prayer and then began to eat.

Sarah took a bite of the salmon. She closed her eyes and gave a groan of pleasure. "Oh my, Jonathan. That is so wonderful. Why have I been cooking for us all this time? You should be doing all the work and all the chores!"

He smiled. He was so happy to give her pleasure. He could tell she truly meant what she said. "Try the salad. I have a special homemade recipe for the dressing."

She took a bite and nodded approvingly. They ate together in silence. Afterward she tried to help him with the dishes, but he insisted she sit down and enjoy her wine. She had taken care of him so many times, and he wanted to do the same for her.

After he was finished, they carried their wineglasses to the sofa in the living room. He lit a fire in the fireplace and then came over to sit near her. He was conscious of her closeness, of her beauty. She had grown more attractive and desirable to him with each passing month, he realized. The wine made him feel relaxed and at peace.

"I wanted to thank you again so much for the picnic. I had the very best time," she said. She reached down and put her wineglass on the coffee table.

"I did, too."

"You'd never touched my hand before. I was afraid, Jonathan. Afraid you would find me terribly ugly because of it."

"I could never feel that way," he said. He reached out and removed the white cotton cloth slowly from her hand again, running his fingers through and over hers. "You are beautiful, Sarah. Your hand is a part of you. I love touching you, feeling you." He knew he shouldn't be saying those things. He wanted to stop himself, but his heart and mind warred within.

She leaned closer to him. He could smell her perfume, her skin. He kept his eyes downward, afraid to look at her, watching his fingers caress her hand. He pulled her fingers closer to him and brushed his lips against her hand.

"Oh, Jonathan," she whispered.

His will eroded and slid away. He kissed her hand again and then her forearm. He could feel her heartbeat in her wrist. He looked up to her eyes. She smiled. A tear streamed down her cheek despite or because of her joy; he could not tell. She leaned forward, and he drew her toward him, kissing her lips, pressing her face against his. His soul shouted warnings and praise in two voices.

He felt his head exploding with light and dizziness. He had never felt this way. Not when he touched her hand. Not the first time he had kissed Helen. He was in ecstasy. She was trembling beneath him, but she kissed him with deep passion, pressing harder against him, her hands going to his neck. He loved this woman so much. He had never loved anyone like this.

The screams increased in his mind. He had broken his promise, his oath to his wife, his commitment to God. There was no way he could rationalize this last action. Their friendship, the occasional touch, the way he felt about her—all of it could be explained away as sacrifice in the face of his obligation. This was irrevocably different. He knew he had leaped across the final line.

He gasped, pushing her away. She laughed nervously at first, and then he could see her body grow rigid. "What's wrong, Jonathan?"

"You know what's wrong."

"You aren't still talking about that ridiculous promise you made?"

"It's not ridiculous." He squared himself.

"Yes, it is. Worse, it's selfish beyond anything I've ever heard of. Your wife had no right to demand that of you." Her voice shook.

"What do you mean?"

"She was leaving this world. You still had a whole life to live. She had no right to bind you."

"It was my choice. She didn't force me to it." His anger grew. *She was my wife.*

"What choice was that? A man of honor and faith like you facing a promise on her deathbed? You would never have said no. Who could deny her under those circumstances?"

"Maybe I had no option. Perhaps she was pleased to deny my future. A parting wound. What difference does it make? The promise was made before God."

"What are you saying?"

He looked at her, afraid to say it, desperately wanting to hold back. Somehow he forced out the words. "I'm saying I cannot break my promise."

"You already have."

He pulled away. "That doesn't help, Sarah."

"What do you expect me to do? What do you want from me?

"I want you, *us*, to follow the commitment we made when we started this friendship."

She leaned closer to him. "How can we do that? How can we go back? My feelings for you have grown until I can't take it anymore. I know you feel the same. I love you, Jonathan Beecher. I love you!" Her voice was soft, pleading.

He was silent. He could feel his heart breaking.

She continued, grabbing his hand. "Are you going to deny you love me? Look at me, and tell me you don't."

He looked up and saw her eyes, now red and full of tears. "I . . . I can't talk about this tonight, Sarah. I need time to think."

She stood quickly. He tried to stop her, but she wrenched her arm away from him. "You're despicable to do this to me," she whispered through clenched teeth.

"I haven't done anything . . . Nothing has changed."

"Everything has changed. If you don't understand that, you're a fool. Now you want to turn this off? You want to pretend we're just friends again, that you don't love me, and that I don't love you. I can't do that!" She turned and rushed for the door.

"Don't go! Please don't go," he pleaded. She stopped and turned, watching him for a moment.

"What do you want, Jonathan?"

There was nothing he could say. He turned away.

"That's what I thought," she said. "I love you. I want you. I want to be with you forever. I won't go on pretending that's not the truth. I want you to be with me, Jonathan, and I know you feel the same. But this is so much for you to address. I understand. Think hard about our future. I'll give you a little time, but if you're asking me to go back, that is something I cannot do. Good night." She walked out the door.

Jonathan sat in the semidarkness in deepest misery. He cursed himself. He had finally allowed things to go too far, and now he had crossed the line forever. He fell to his knees in prayer. He was a weak, terrible sinner. He had hurt this woman that he loved. His weakness destroyed them.

CHAPTER FOURTEEN

Wake Island
Japan-Occupied Territory
Tuesday, October 5, 1943
(Across the International Date Line)

Matthew sat with other contractor prisoners in the shade of a palm tree, taking a midday break. His bare back was pressed against the base as he tried to catch his breath. He looked out at the skeletons of these men he had known in captivity for almost two years now. They were all starving, emaciated, with hollow cheeks and sunken chests. They hardly had clothing left. He looked at his own tattered shorts, all that remained of his Morrison-Knudsen uniform.

The rations had improved with that last supply ship but had dwindled gradually down again to almost nothing. The conditions were so bad on the island that even their Japanese guards were starving. At least this made their enemy listless and less likely to bother the Americans.

Providentially, most of the work on the atoll was complete. They had built the pillboxes and installed the air and shore defenses. They had rebuilt all the buildings and improved the airfield. They still worked on the maintenance of the various structures, but they lacked the strength to labor full days, and the guards had neither the energy nor the will to force them. Unfortunately, with nothing to do, time seemed to stand still, making each day an agonizing one of boredom and hunger, punctuated by the occasional work detail.

Matthew thought of Tom, gone now a year. He wondered what had happened to his friend and to the others that were taken off the island. Did they find better conditions in a formal prisoner camp? Perhaps Tom had been able to send news home about those left behind on Wake.

He remembered Tom's charge to become one of the resistance leaders among the remaining prisoners. He had failed him badly. Despite a few attempts to talk to some of the other leaders, they didn't seem interested in what he had to say. He couldn't blame them; he didn't know what he was supposed to do in the first place. After a few meetings he had found it all too easy to fade back into the crowd.

Days had passed and then weeks. Leadership drowned in the boredom and fatigue. The bombings increased. They were afraid of the bombers, but they gloried in the attacks. Their friends were coming. It was simply a matter of time before they were rescued. They must be winning the war. The little, precious scraps of information they had gleaned confirmed this. Matthew had hoped that the Japanese might become more lenient if they were losing the war, but the opposite seemed to be the case. Facing dwindling rations themselves, and with the war possibly lost, the guards became angrier, more violent.

Matthew heard some chatter. Prisoners and guards alike were looking north out over the water. He turned his head and saw there were several ships on the horizon. There must be another Jap supply fleet. He was no longer afraid because things could hardly be worse anywhere else. He did dread the prospect of trying to unload the ships. He didn't think he had the strength to do the lifting anymore.

He was surprised to see some flashes from the ships. A few moments later he heard an explosion behind him, then the delayed report of ship guns. These weren't Japanese ships—they were American! More flashes and more thunder detonated all around him. This was a fleet—an invasion fleet! They were coming finally to take the atoll back and save them all. Matthew realized he might be killed by the shelling, but he didn't care. Either he would be rescued, or there would be an end to this agony. If he was killed, the Japanese would be, too. He smiled and closed his eyes as the blasts crashed, a melodic percussion.

He felt a sharp stabbing and looked up to see a guard prodding him with his rifle and shouting. He stared back for a moment, feeling defiant. The guard hesitated. He could see the fear in the man's eyes. *Finally, it's time for you to be afraid, for you to suffer.* Matthew was sure the guards would be tried and executed for their conduct with the prisoners. He didn't know the rules of war but was positive the Japanese had violated many of them. For now, he couldn't press too much. He rose slowly to his feet and followed the man and other prisoners as they retreated away from the defenses. He could see other Japanese rushing to the machine guns and antiaircraft installations. The guards herded them south into the heavy brush near the airport. They were forced to sit down in the tall vegetation, which provided camouflage but no protection against the shells.

The attack droned on for hours. Soon the sound of airplanes joined the artillery, and they were treated to a full-scale attack on the airfield by dive-bombers. Explosions racked the field, blowing up parked planes and hangars. The Japanese blazed away from all over the island, but the American fighters and bombers ignored them and continued the onslaught. Matthew strained his ears, hoping to hear landing craft assaulting the beaches, but they were too far away to pick up anything but the constant sound of machine gun fire and artillery.

The attack stalled as darkness fell, although the ships kept up the shelling. Matthew noticed the guards fading away until there were only a few left. Had the Americans already hit the beach? Were the Japanese pulling away every last man for a final defense? He remembered their own battle to repel the invading Japs back in December of '41. The entire fight had been a mass of confusion, ending with the hope that they had won the day and turning into despair when they had surrendered. The same could be happening here. But half the atoll could already be in American hands, and they wouldn't know it. Matthew bent his head and uttered a silent prayer for their salvation.

They remained in the weeds into the night. In the darkness they moved closer together. The remaining guards made no move to stop them, and soon they could communicate in excited whispers.

"Does anyone know anything about the attack? Are there Americans onshore?" asked Matthew to someone sitting near him in the dark.

"I don't know. I heard a rumor that there are, but who knows if it's true."

"Who's talking?"

"It's John."

"John Gregory?"

"Yeah, is that Matthew?"

"Yes, it is."

John had remained behind after the last selection. He was now one of the leaders of the remaining contractors.

"What should we do?" asked Matthew.

"What can we do? We sit and we wait. I hope they're already on the beaches and fighting their way inland. They might be here before midnight."

"Wouldn't we have heard them? Heard the rifle fire?"

"I don't know. There's plenty of artillery, and that could be drowning out the rifle fire."

"Has anyone been killed?"

"I don't think so. We've done a check. There's some wounded, mostly shrapnel, but nothing too bad so far. We've been lucky."

"If they haven't hit too many of us, then they haven't hit many Japs, either."

"That might be true, Matthew, but there's nothing we can do about that. I just hope they brought plenty of marines."

They sat that way in the darkness for hours, straining to hear something, hoping to see the silhouettes of American soldiers. They did not come. Sometime in the night, the sound of shelling grew sporadic and then gradually faded away. More guards appeared, and the prisoners were herded out of the brush and returned to their barracks.

Matthew noticed damage everywhere. Some of the buildings had sustained artillery or bomb hits, which he could make out by the light of the moon. But there were no marines here, no sound of ground combat. After the contractors were all inside their barracks, a couple of guards brought in a bowl of rice and a jug of water. John and a few others helped ration out the meager meal, which would have barely fed a small family. The men were dejected and exhausted. Matthew ate his handful of rice in one gulp and then lay down. The invasion had not come, at least not today. He prayed for tomorrow.

∾

In the morning the shelling began again. The contractors were moved back out of the barracks and returned to the same location in the deep vegetation near the airport. Matthew realized that in addition to hiding them, it also kept the prisoners away from the beaches and the defenders. Midday they were given a little water.

Matthew's throat burned, and a tiny swallow did nothing to slake his thirst. As the sun rose in the sky, he could hear the moans of others begging for a little more to drink. The guards ignored them and then shouted at them to be quiet. They dragged a machine gun over to their position and trained it on the prisoners. After that, everyone kept their complaints as quiet as possible.

Matthew purposefully sat near John again.

"Did you hear anything else last night? Did they try to come ashore?"

"Not that I know of," said John. "But a few of the Japs were killed. Better yet, every one of their planes was destroyed in the air or on the ground. I don't know if you knew this, but those American planes are off a carrier. If they have a flattop here, they mean business. They must be coming ashore."

"But why wait a day? The time to attack was when it was a surprise."

"I don't know. Let's face it, Matthew. We're not soldiers. There could be all kinds of reasons. Maybe they want to soften up those pillboxes. We built pretty good defenses. A bunch of little boats trying to come up in the face of all those machine guns would get shot up pretty good."

"I guess you could be right, but I want them to come today."

"I do, too. But today or tomorrow or next year, we have to hold on."

"What do you mean next year? I can't take any more of this." Matthew's jaw contracted with the stress.

John looked at him sternly. "Now listen here. We don't know they're invading. Don't get your hopes up. If you do and they don't, you'll die of despair. They come when they come."

"It has to be today."

"I want that as badly as you. But we can't put all our eggs in one basket."

Matthew chuckled weakly. "Don't mention eggs."

The sun climbed the sky. The bombers returned, raining steel destruction on the airfield and the surrounding buildings. The crescendo of artillery and bombs swelled with each passing hour. Fortunately, the Americans didn't attack the area where the prisoners were hiding. They were huddled close together, and a direct hit could have killed them all.

As the daylight again began to fade, Matthew felt increasingly desperate. He had been so sure the marines would land today. They had to. Why else would they be here, attacking this worthless rock? Surely they had destroyed enough of the defenses to safely bring in the landing ships. As his hopes receded, he felt himself falling apart. He was so thirsty. His tongue remained a dry lump in his mouth. What if they didn't come? What if they weren't invading? He prayed a bomb would just kill him. He couldn't go on.

Darkness fell, and the sound of airplanes faded away. Just like the day before, the shelling from the ships slowed down and eventually stopped. The guards gathered them up again and marched them back to their barracks. This time there was no food or water. The men grumbled in anger. John forced himself up to check whether any food was coming. He returned a half hour later.

Matthew observed immediately that something was wrong. John's face was pale and troubled. A few men gathered around him, and Matthew joined them.

"What's going on?" he asked. "Is it the invasion? Did they fail?"

"They didn't fail. They haven't tried."

"Are they leaving?"

"I don't know. That's not the problem."

"What else could it be?" asked Matthew.

"I heard a rumor from the cook. He speaks some Jap, and he overheard a conversation between a couple of the guards. It sounds like the Japs are as worried about the invasion as we are. The commander doesn't want us around, telling stories about what's happened here. They have orders to shoot us tomorrow."

"How can that be?" demanded Matthew. Their salvation lay a mile away. He couldn't believe the Japanese would just murder them. "They can't kill us. Not with the Americans at our doorstep. They'd all be executed."

"You've seen these maniacs for two years now. Do you think they care about getting killed? They're all over themselves, trying to die honorably for their stupid emperor. I don't know if it's true, but if it is, they won't hesitate because they're worried about consequences."

"What can we do?"

"I don't know, Matthew. How many of them are there? Far more than we have. They're all armed. We're so weak we can barely move. But if it comes to it, I don't want to die sitting down. I'm going to fight."

There was murmuring among the men. Matthew was in shock. Why would God allow them to come to this point so close to rescue and then take everything away? The rumor couldn't be true. The cook was a gossip, and not everything he said was accurate. Even the Japs weren't this stupid.

He tried to fall asleep, but he couldn't. Nobody could. John's rumor flashed through the men like wildfire. They all lay awake, suffering with thirst, alone with their thoughts and fears. John had said that he would fight at the end. How? With what? Matthew heard Tom Kadyk's words again echo in his mind. *Step up and take the lead now here.* He thought of his father. He could never live up to them. He wasn't made for it. He felt ashamed.

The next morning, they were rushed out of the barracks. Again there was no food or water. Matthew was so weak he could barely walk. The prisoners helped each other stumble along to the cover where they had spent the last two days. The artillery fire began again, as did the rumbling of airplanes above. Nobody looked up. After two days of hope, they were crushed. At noon the guards finally brought food and water. Matthew was surprised by the quantity, a full pot of white rice and plenty to drink.

A Japanese officer appeared. Matthew recognized him as Lieutenant Commander Tachibana. He addressed the prisoners in broken English.

"I have a good news for all you. We have made promise with Americans. They will leave us here and stop fight. They will take you away in agreement for stopping bombs. You are very lucky to be here still. You are first prisoners given back during the war. We bring this food and water to celebrate with you. This rice is from Americans as token of goodwill. Eat your fill, and we talk after."

There was a ragged cheer. Matthew couldn't believe it. The Americans knew about them and were going to take them off the island. They weren't going to die after all! The euphoria swam through him. He was going to see his family. He thought of Snohomish and his father. He imagined walking down Avenue C and knocking on his front door. He could see the smile on his pa's face. Mary would be there and maybe even Luke. He would go to work with his father and never leave his small town again. He realized that the shelling had stopped. This was real. They were saved.

The men joked as they ate. Even the guards were sitting down and talking a bit with them. Matthew was shocked to see how quickly they transitioned from enemies to friends. The war wasn't over, but for this small moment in time, they were just a group of men all together.

Soon Tachibana reappeared and ordered them to form up. They set out all together, marching toward the north part of the island. The men chatted and joked with one another. Matthew hadn't heard anyone laughing in so long. They had given up hope long ago. Soon they were passing through the trees and were standing out on the beach at the north end of Wake. This must be where the landing craft would come in to pick them up.

A contractor directly in front of Matthew jerked sharply back. Matthew watched in disbelief as a hot scarlet fountain washed over him. Time stopped. The prisoners in front of him danced and flailed. He tasted acrid air. His ears roared. The sky crushed him, and sand swallowed his limbs. White fire burned his shoulder. *I'm hit. They're killing us,* he realized. *They lied to us.*

Matthew closed his eyes. He felt a strange peace. All this agony was going to finally end. He thought of his father. He would be so sad when he learned Matthew was gone. What would Mary do? How about Luke? He would never see home again or be able to tell them what had happened to him. He thought of Tom. He had broken his promise to him—he had never quite found the courage to lead. He thought of Babe. His poor friend beheaded for nothing, for stealing a little drink. He could hear Babe cussing him out. *You've got yourself dead now, boy, just like me.*

Matthew waited for the darkness to overwhelm him, but it didn't. He could hear the machine gun fire and the screaming. He felt something inside: unexpected anger. The Japs had promised freedom, and they had lied. They had forced them to slave away here for two years. They had beaten and starved and killed them. He remembered John's words from the other night. His friend would not give up without a fight.

Matthew rolled slowly over and opened an eye. His shoulder raged a sharp fire. He forced his mind to function. He was facing the jungle. The flashes were coming directly in front of them. Most of the prisoners were already down, but a few were huddled together, trying to hide from the bullets.

Matthew made a decision. *I will die on my feet.* He rose to one knee, then to a crouch. He expected the killing bullet any moment, but somehow it didn't come. He took a deep breath and leaped up, racing with every ounce of will and energy he had left toward the jungle to his right. He could hear the screaming of the guards, and he felt the bullets flying past him. He would never make it, but at least he was up; he was fighting.

The jungle loomed closer, and then miraculously he was inside. He expected to find the Japs waiting for him, but there was no one. He rotated sharply toward the thickest part of the jungle and kept running, waiting for the shot that would end his life. Somehow the bullet did not come.

Matthew slowed down to catch his breath. The pain from his shoulder was blinding. He hid himself in the deepest cover he could find and checked his wound. He was surprised to see that the bullet had only skimmed the skin, tearing out an inch-deep trench across the top of his left shoulder. The gash was deep and bleeding, but the bullet had passed through. He reached down with shaking hands and tore off a piece of his shorts, then shoved the cloth down into the crimson crevice, pressing against the pain and holding the makeshift bandage in place. The injury throbbed, and he feared he would pass out, but he kept up the pressure. He could hear shouts of men calling out to each other in Japanese. They were searching for him. They would assuredly find him soon, but he didn't care. He had defied them. He had run away rather than standing there to die. Now they were having to work to find him. That was enough. He felt his teeth gnash, but he forced them to freeze. Nothing to fear now. *I finally stood up to them. I finally led. I am my father's son after all.*

Hours passed. They did not see him, though one soldier must have passed within a few feet. The shelling began again, and soon the search had ceased. They had other things on their mind. Matthew chuckled to himself. *How hard did they need to look now? I wasn't going anywhere.* They would continue the search after the fighting stopped, and they would find him.

He removed the bandage and checked his wound. The bleeding had stopped. Matthew didn't know much about medicine, but in the hot jungle, this wound would soon be infected. Without proper bandages and antiseptic, he would die. He laughed to himself at the possibility that maybe the Japanese would treat him if he turned himself in. He couldn't worry too much about the infection; there was no point.

The late afternoon turned to evening, and soon the jungle was covered in darkness. Matthew crawled as quietly as he could through the vegetation until he was out on the sand. Then he made his way as silently as possible back to the scene of the massacre. When he arrived, he saw that the bodies were all gone. In the dim light, he couldn't tell whether there was even a sign of the killings. The Japanese must have cleaned the entire area. He wondered where they might have buried the bodies until he came across a portion of the beach above the high-water mark that he knew had contained an antitank ditch. The ditch was completely filled in, and he had no doubt that the Japanese had buried his friends and companions here. He felt tears flowing down his cheeks, and he fell to his knees. Everyone left to him was dead here, John and Martin and all the rest. He was the only American left on the island, unless someone else had miraculously escaped. He closed his eyes and said a prayer for them.

Matthew felt a sharp prodding on his back and heard a barking word of command. He raised his hands up over his head and turned slowly. A guard had snuck up on him while he prayed and now was pointing his rifle at him. Matthew felt the return of the hot rage that had burned in him earlier, and he remembered John's words: *I'm going to fight.* He rose slowly to his feet and stumbled forward as if off balance. At the same time, he reached out quickly and grabbed the end of the rifle, pulling it out of the hands of the surprised guard, who rushed forward and grabbed him. Matthew fell backward but held on to the guard, dragging him down into the sand. They rolled back and forth, struggling to get a hold, to gain a position of advantage. Matthew saw a flash of light and realized the guard had drawn his bayonet. He grabbed the guard's wrist and held the knife back, struggling to keep his enemy from stabbing him.

They battled for long minutes. Matthew could feel the strength leaving him. With a final desperate effort, he smashed his forehead against the cheek of the guard, who snapped his head back in surprise. Matthew pulled the bayonet loose and slashed it across his enemy's neck, rolling over on top of him in the same motion. He shoved his left hand over the guard's mouth and held him down. The Japanese soldier struggled for a few terrible minutes and then lay still.

Matthew collapsed on top of his foe, unable to move in his exhaustion. He gathered enough strength and rose to his feet to grab the ankles of the guard and drag him toward the jungle. He could only pull the body a few feet at a time before he needed to rest. His muscles were in agony. His wound pulsated in hot pain. Little by little he made progress, and eventually he was able to reach the vegetation. He searched the guard and found a canteen and some food. He was far too exhausted to bury him, so he covered him as best as he could with leaves and branches. He then returned for the rifle.

That was when he saw the boulder. On the beach, not too far from the mass grave, protruded a large rock only a yard from the tide. Matthew smiled to himself. The rock stood sentry over his friends as well as any man-made marker might ever serve. Still, it wasn't enough. Something had to be done. The world had to know they had died here. It had to know of their sacrifice. Matthew walked over to the boulder as carefully as he could. Then, keeping an eye out for other Japanese sentries, he drew the bayonet out and began to carve into the stone. The surface was extremely hard and the work laborious. He had to be careful not to make too much noise, and he kept one eye on the jungle, but he made gradual progress. He wasn't sure how long he worked that night, positive he would be shot at any moment. The gunfire never came. Finally, with the first hint of dawn, he was done. He stepped away from the rock and examined his work. The inscription simply said:

98 US PW 5-10-43

He looked at his engraving closely. He didn't feel he had time to add anything else, and the beach was getting lighter by the moment. He looked around to make sure nobody was watching him, then darted back into the jungle.

JAMES D. SHIPMAN

Matthew kept hidden for the next several weeks. He had held out hope that the Americans might still come, but the attacks had ceased, and the ships had disappeared from the horizon. He was alone on this tiny island without any chance to escape. He had to dodge search parties for the first few days, but over time the enemy stopped looking for him. Perhaps they assumed he had died. He carefully guarded his water and was able to steal two additional canteens from unsuspecting guards. He was starving, but he didn't care. He had defied them. He had escaped their massacre, and he had paid tribute to his fallen friends. He had killed one of his enemies with his bare hands. His father would be proud of him. His friends would be, too. His mother? It didn't matter anymore. He would have time to talk with her soon enough.

Eventually he grew desperate for water and food. He decided he would honor Babe and sneak into the Japanese canteen. He waited until the early hours of the morning and carefully made his way into the camp. He crept past several guards and opened the unlocked door to the canteen. They had no reason to lock it any longer. He found a jug of water and took several long drinks. He then dug around and found some cooked rice in a container. He sat down against a cupboard and dug his fingers into the white soft grains, savoring each bite. He stuffed himself until his stomach gurgled and groaned with pain, finally full. He hadn't felt full in years. He closed his eyes and soaked up the pleasure. He was jolted awake with sharp barking. He no longer cared.

Matthew was taken prisoner, but there were no blows this time. The guards hung back as if he were a ghost. He had killed one of them and evaded their searches for three weeks on a tiny bit of sand. He walked with them slowly, his head up proudly. He was led into the office of Admiral Sakaibara himself, the commander of the entire Japanese command on Wake.

"You are the prisoner who escape?"

Matthew looked directly into the admiral's eyes. "I am."

"Did you kill Japanese soldier?"

"I did."

"The penalty for killing a guard is death."

"I'm already dead." Matthew said the words calmly, his voice never faltering, his gaze never moving. His face was still.

"You are very brave," said Sakaibara.

"No, I'm not. But I've known many brave men."

The admiral rose from his desk and spoke to the guards in Japanese. They grabbed him and led him out of the office into the square. The admiral followed. The sun had risen, and Matthew saw there were many Japanese lined up at attention. Hundreds. He had never seen so many in one place at one time. He was led by the guards to an area in front of the center of the group. The admiral addressed the men in Japanese, then turned to Matthew. He bowed, and Matthew was surprised to see the lines of Japanese all bow in unison. He didn't have time to consider this. They shoved him down to his knees. Sakaibara drew his sword—a steel rainbow in the morning light.

Matthew closed his eyes. He smelled the morning warmth. A breeze blew through his hair. He dreamed of Snohomish, of his family, of his life. He saw his friends smiling down on him. He was going home.

CHAPTER FIFTEEN

Snohomish, Washington
Wednesday, October 27, 1943

Jonathan sat bolt upright in his bed. He heard himself take in a sharp breath and gasp. Sweat rolled down his forehead. What had he been dreaming about? He tried to concentrate, but whatever he had experienced was already fading away, the edges just out of reach. He looked out the window. The eastern sky hovered with the dim gloom of the approaching dawn.

He closed his eyes for a few moments, trying to relax. He whispered a brief prayer. Then he was hit again. Sarah. What to do about Sarah? He had called her the day after their dinner and told her he could only be friends. Since then, she had avoided him. He had tried to call, tried to see her at her house or at church. She refused to talk to him or discuss what had happened. Was that what he was dreaming about? It didn't seem like it, but something filled him with a terrible foreboding.

Jonathan rose out of his covers and quietly made the bed, shuddering a little in the crisp morning air. Summer had faded away. There would be frost on the ground soon—at least on some mornings. Washington never stayed cold for long, although the months of constant drizzle and gray could be worse than frozen air and snow. He shuffled downstairs and piled kindling and wood into the stove, stamping his feet to stay warm. Soon he had a fire going. He stayed near it for a while, warming himself, lost in thought.

Next he washed up in the bathroom and dressed for the day, then sat at the kitchen table, sipping some coffee and eating a piece of dry toast. He didn't notice that he had failed to butter the bread. He kept turning the Sarah problem in his mind over and over. He didn't know what else he could do with her. He was sure if they sat down together, he could make her come around. He knew she was upset, but by the same token, she was not being fair. He had never lied to her. He had told her from the beginning about his promise, that he could only be friends. Granted, they had both come to care about each other—to love each other, but that didn't matter. A promise was a promise. The fact that they had allowed their weaknesses to get the better of them didn't change anything. Surely she understood that? Even if it was difficult for both of them to bear.

There had to be some way to get through to her. What was the answer? He thought about sending her flowers or a gift, but that seemed to send exactly the wrong message. How about having Pastor Miles talk to her? That was an idea. No, he couldn't tell his pastor what he'd done or admit he was in love. That wasn't a solution.

Jonathan finished getting ready and left his house, driving the few blocks to his store. He felt sandy eyed and exhausted from his lack of sleep, and plagued by uncertainty. Despite the bad start to the day, he conducted a brisk business in the morning. A local farmer from the Krause family made a large order for tools and supplies, one of the most significant sales Jonathan had made that year. He felt wide awake, and he pushed his doubts and fears aside. The sun shone through the windows of his store. He felt immeasurably better. The terrible dream, whatever it was, faded into the recesses of his mind. Even the problem with Sarah seemed more manageable. Still, he needed some advice. There had to be someone he could talk to.

The upswing in sales continued throughout the day. A local family he had never seen in his store bought lumber and nails to replace a deck. They paid extra for the clear cedar, his most expensive exterior wood. They thanked him for his help, and he was sure they would come back and hopefully become consistent customers. They had hardly left when more people streamed in. Jonathan couldn't remember the last time he had been this busy. By the time he closed up for the day and tallied his sales, he realized he had sold more on this single day than at any time since the war began. Maybe with all the good war news, people were regaining confidence. Perhaps the government would ease some of the restrictions soon and the prices would fall? Jonathan felt his spirits soar, and a peace came over him he had not felt in a very long time. He closed his eyes and whispered a short prayer.

Mary. The thought came to him suddenly, seemingly out of nowhere. Of course! He could talk to Mary about all of this—well, some of it. She was a woman. She understood such things. Sarah and Mary liked each other, seemed to comprehend each other. Perhaps she could give him some insight into what to do, what words would calm Sarah down and convince her to return to their friendship. Why hadn't he thought of this before? Jonathan finished closing up the store and decided to walk. The evening was so nice, and surprisingly warm.

Halfway to Mary's, he passed the auction barn on his right. The property was quiet tonight, except for some workers making repairs to the grandstands. On Friday nights the seats would be full with farmers and their families, coming for dinner and to bid on livestock. The fence surrounding the arena area would be filled with lingering teenagers, leaning against the rails and watching the auction sales—one of the many free events that passed for entertainment in this small town.

Jonathan marched on toward the heavily wooded area near Blackmans Lake, the houses thinning out as he walked farther away from town. In a few more minutes, he was at Mary's door. He knocked. The door opened. Robert was there, standing over him. He looked irritated for a moment and then poured on a sugary smile. "Jonathan. What a surprise!" His voice was pleasant, but he didn't smile with his eyes.

Mary materialized behind him, her face full of joy. "Father! You never come and see us! What are you doing here? It's dinnertime—would you like to join us?"

Jonathan had forgotten about the time. He apologized. "I'm sorry, Mary. I didn't think about it being time for supper. I can come back later."

"Nonsense," she said. "We would love to have you, wouldn't we, Robert?"

Robert stared half a second before he answered. Again that strange look in his eyes. "Of course, we would. Come on in."

Jonathan could tell his son-in-law wasn't enthusiastic that he was here. He felt the same emotions he always experienced around Robert. Something just wasn't quite right with this boy. He tried to drive the thoughts away. He hadn't wanted his daughter to run off and marry. He was still angry about the incident last year. But Mary was right; nothing had happened since then. He knew he needed to give Robert a chance, but he could not shake these feelings about him.

Jonathan followed them into the kitchen. Mary busied herself with setting another plate at the table. Robert perched near the stove, making no attempt at conversation.

"How's work?" said Jonathan finally.

"Same as always."

"Do you like police work?"

"It's fine."

"Anything interesting going on around town?"

"Not really."

Jonathan eventually gave up and simply stood and looked around. Mary seemed oblivious to the uncomfortable situation, and she hummed lightly, obviously thrilled that her father had come to visit. Soon everything was ready, and she motioned them over to the table. Robert and Jonathan sat down, and she served them chicken and potatoes with a rich brown gravy ladled over the top.

"How are things at the store?" she asked.

Jonathan brightened. "Funny you should ask that. Today was the best day I've had in a very long time—since before the war. I wonder if things are starting to turn around. What do you think, Robert?"

His son-in-law grunted, not looking up from his plate. Jonathan saw a flush on Mary's face. She was clearly embarrassed. He changed the subject to try to smooth over the situation. "I'm wondering if I can talk to you after dinner."

"What about?" asked Mary.

"Just a couple questions about Sarah."

Robert climbed out of his chair. "You can talk to her now. I've got things I need to do tonight."

"Robert, please don't," said Mary. "Stay awhile."

His son-in-law looked at Mary for a moment and then snorted. "I'll give you all the time in the world for *your father*. Like I said, I've got things to do." He turned and stomped out of the kitchen. They could hear him clunking around in another room for a few minutes, and then the front door slammed shut.

"I apologize," said Jonathan. "I didn't mean to impose on your dinner. I should have phoned ahead of time, or come a different day."

Mary blushed. "You didn't do anything wrong. I don't know what gets into him sometimes."

"What do you mean?"

Mary hesitated, then turned to her father and smiled. "It doesn't matter. He's not usually like this. He really looks up to you. Did you know that? He talks about you all the time. How you own your own business. That you managed to save money up and buy the store during the Depression. I know he acts strangely around you, but I think that's just because he's intimidated by you."

Jonathan laughed wryly. "Yes, I'm *sure* that's it." He wanted to say more, to ask more. Mary was clearly covering something up by defending her husband. He had thought things were better for her, but now he wasn't certain. Still, this was between a man and his wife, and it was not for him to interfere.

Mary looked at him closely. "Why did you come here tonight?"

"Can't a father come see his daughter?"

"Of course you can, but you never just drop by. You always call ahead. What's this about Sarah? Have you finally broken down and asked her to marry you?"

"Mary!"

"Why shouldn't you, Father? You know that's what she wants, and it seems like what you want as well."

"I can't, Mary. You don't know everything. I can't because of your mother."

"My mother. What does she have to do with anything?"

Jonathan felt himself growing angry. "Now you watch yourself about your mother."

"Why should I? She was hardly a mother to me."

"What do you mean? She loved you. She took care of you."

"You never saw it, Father. You never see anything bad in anyone." Mary leaned over the table as if to emphasize her point. "You were always there for us, always a wonderful father. But she wasn't a mother of any kind."

Jonathan felt like he had been hit with a stone. "How can you say that? She cooked and cleaned for you every day, took care of you when you were sick and when you were tired. She did everything for us."

"She did all those things, Father, but that was *all* she did. The rest of the time she complained. Complained about you, about us, about her life and everything in it. She gossiped about the neighbors. She made every moment darker. You know that. You had to know that?"

Jonathan rose in his seat. "You stop right there, Mary. It's bad enough that you ran off without a care in the world. Don't come back and try to blame this on me or your mother. I won't hear another word about her."

"You always had your head in the sand. Why do you think Matthew left? What about Luke? They were running away from her."

"She was gone long before Luke left. Long before you pulled your trick."

"You're wrong. She's still here. She's still haunting all of us. Most of all you."

"What are you talking about?"

"That ridiculous promise she made you make."

"How do you know about that?"

"Sarah told me."

Now Jonathan was angry. "She had no right to share something like that with you. Your mother and I made a solemn promise before God."

"A promise I'm sure she forced on you! She didn't care how it would affect you. She wanted to have her claws in you from beyond the grave!"

"I won't hear another word about it! I was coming to you for advice, but I see there's no point in talking to you about it."

"Father, please listen to me."

"So I can break my word like you did to me?" Jonathan knew immediately he shouldn't have said that, but he was so upset by what she was saying.

Mary gasped. "Father, how could you say that? I was in love. In love like you are, too. Only I wasn't afraid to do something about it."

"A lot of good that's done you."

"Get out!" she screamed. "Get out of here! You have no right to say that to me!"

Jonathan tried to step toward her, but she pushed him away, a stone unyielding in her seat.

"Leave me alone! Go away!"

He tried to talk to her again, but she wouldn't look at him. She pointed to the door silently. Defeated, he turned and left, walking out into the darkness. He had come to his daughter for help, and somehow he had made everything worse. He had hurt Mary.

Jonathan felt his own doubts more powerfully. Mary had been so young; yet she had seen her mother with clear eyes. The knife of conflict cut him again, and he warred to reconcile his strife. He shook his head—it didn't matter. He had married Helen before God. Just like Mary had married Robert. As he walked home, he realized more than ever that he had to stick to his convictions, to his commitments. He arrived at the door twenty minutes later with a renewed vow to follow his faith, regardless of the sacrifice and pain. He washed the morning dishes and made his lunch for the next day, turning things over and over in his mind and then steeling his convictions. His thoughts were interrupted by a loud knock. He opened the door and nearly fell over in shock.

Mary was at the door, beaten and bloody, with barely the strength to stand. She fell into his arms, sobbing.

∿

Jonathan held on to his daughter tightly, trying to understand what on earth had happened. He asked her over and over, but for a long time she wouldn't answer. She clung to him, her head buried in his chest, unwilling to look up, unable to talk. She answered with a shaky whisper.

"After you left—he came back. He was so angry. Screaming about you coming over without his permission and ruining our dinner. I tried to calm him down, but he threw a dish against the wall. I told him I was sorry, that I would make it up to him, but he didn't care. He grabbed me and slapped me across the face. Again and again. I tried to pull away, but he held my throat. Then he slammed me against the table. He ripped his belt off and beat me on my back and on the top of my head. I begged him to stop, but he wouldn't. Finally, he said he'd had enough, and he stumbled out of the house."

Jonathan exploded. "I'll kill him!"

"Please don't! Please leave him alone! Stay here with me. I don't want to be left by myself. I don't want anything to happen to you."

Jonathan helped Mary over to the sofa and then picked up the phone. Fortunately, nobody was on the party line and he was able to call out right away. He talked for a few moments and then went quickly to the kitchen. He ran cold water over a towel until it was soaked and brought it to Mary. He carefully dabbed the cloth against her face.

He battled to control his emotions. He had never felt angrier than at this moment. He had put up with this young man swooping into his daughter's life and carrying her away from all her hopes and dreams. He had trusted Mary against his own judgment the first time her husband had hit her. He would tolerate no more. He had to take care of his daughter. He controlled his temper and sat with Mary as she cried quietly, gently administering to her bruises while he tried to calm himself.

There was a knock at the door. Mary sat bolt upright.

"Don't worry; it's just Sarah."

"Why is she here?"

"I need to go out and attend to some things."

"Father, please! What are you going to do?"

He placed a hand on her cheek. "Don't worry, my dear. Nothing stupid. But I want to know something from you before I go."

"What?"

"Do you want to stay with him?"

She looked at him for a moment. Jonathan knew his question had enormous ramifications for her and for him. You married for life. What happened between a husband and wife was their business, nobody else's. He knew he was leaping over those boundaries. If Mary left Robert, tongues would wag all over town. They would lose friends. He might be breaking God's law. Jonathan thought about all this and made his choice: He didn't care. This was his daughter. She deserved better. He could see the light fading out of Mary—not much longer, and she would fade for good.

"Do you know what you're saying, Father?"

"I do. He's a monster, Mary. He's destroying you. I want you to stay here with me. I want you to divorce him. We will face the town together. There are worse things in life than a little gossip."

She started to cry more deeply again and threw her arms around him. "I don't know. I don't know if I can do that."

"I want you to think about it. I'm going to go now. I have some words for *your* Robert."

"Don't go! Please don't. I don't want anything bad to happen."

"Don't worry, dear. I won't do anything stupid. I'm calm now." That was a lie, but she didn't need to hear him say it.

Jonathan rose and answered the door. Sarah was there. She wouldn't face him.

"Thank you for coming."

"You're welcome," she said, her voice frigid.

"Sarah, can't we talk about things?"

"No. You asked me to come over for Mary. Do you still want me here for her, or should I leave?"

He wanted to talk to her, but he didn't have time to do so at length, and Mary needed her. "Please stay and help her."

"Where are you going?"

"To go see Robert."

"Why?" Now he could hear a splinter of concern in her voice.

"I've got things to say to that boy. Things that should have been said long ago."

"Jonathan. He's a police officer. What are you planning?"

"Just talk. Nothing worse. I appreciate you coming." He turned away. He felt her hand on his arm.

"I don't think you should go."

"I have to. Don't worry; I'll be careful. But there are words that must be said."

Sarah didn't let go. He looked in her eyes for a few moments and smiled, trying to reassure her. He gently reached down and pulled her hand away.

"Thank you again. I'll be back soon. I've asked Mary to stay, to end the marriage with him."

Sarah's eyes widened. "Jonathan. Are you sure that's the right thing to do?"

"I am. He's hit my daughter twice now. I'm not going to allow it to happen again. I'm going to fix things up."

She threw her arms around him. "Please be careful," she pleaded.

"I will be."

Jonathan left the house swiftly. He knew what he intended to do. Before he drove off, he went into the garage, scrambling in the darkness with a flashlight until he made it back to his workbench. He opened a drawer and rummaged through the tools until he found what he was looking for, a soiled cloth bundle. He carefully unwrapped the rag, revealing a .38-caliber revolver. He clicked open the wheel and checked the ammunition. The gun was fully loaded. Jonathan placed it in his right jacket pocket and then walked to his truck, making sure that he wasn't watched from the house. He tore out of the driveway and headed down the street.

He wasn't sure where he would find Robert. His son-in-law wasn't on duty tonight. He knew from Mary that Robert liked to frequent the bars on First Street, so he started there. He looked around a smoke-filled tavern near Avenue D, but didn't see him. The bartender looked surprised to see Jonathan and nodded without saying anything. As a rule, Jonathan didn't visit drinking establishments.

He searched two more bars near Union Street, but with no luck. There were still a few more places he could try. Then, back on First Street, he spied Robert stumbling toward him in the middle of three other men, laughing and talking.

Jonathan reached into his pocket and gripped the revolver. He could feel the frozen steel. He closed his eyes for a second, thinking through his plan. He was ready. The group grew closer. Robert was in the midst of a joke. He looked up and saw Jonathan at the last moment; his eyes squinted, trying to focus.

Jonathan lunged forward, grasping Robert by his shirt with both hands. He shoved hard. Robert was taller and larger than Jonathan, but he was intoxicated and caught by surprise. He fell back from the impact and landed hard on the sidewalk pavement.

"What the hell was that?" Robert demanded in slurred words. He tried to rise.

Jonathan could hear the grumbling of Robert's friends around him. He didn't have much time. He reached down, grabbed Robert by the shirt again, and jerked him up. He quickly backed Robert against a store window.

"Jonathan. What are you doing?" he asked, finally recognizing his father-in-law.

"You laid your hands on my daughter. You dishonored her and me. What kind of a man strikes his wife?" The rage overwhelmed him.

"It wasn't like that," stuttered Robert, stumbling over his words. "You . . . you don't see her at home. She's always yelling at me. She doesn't take care of the house. She's lazy and disrespectful . . ."

Jonathan struck Robert across the face with his right fist. Robert's head snapped back, cracking the window. Blood sprayed out of his nose. Jonathan held him hard against the window. "You shut your mouth now, boy, and you listen here. She's not coming back to you. You're done with her. I've sat back long enough. You have no honor. No faith. I'm done with you, and so is she." Jonathan felt hands on his back. He tried to jerk away, but several of the men pulled him away and held him. Robert put a hand to his nose and looked at the blood. Then he turned to Jonathan, his face red hot with anger. He was smiling now, blood filling in the gaps of his teeth.

"Now *you* listen here, Beecher. I've wanted to say this to you for a long time. Your little whore of a daughter belongs to me now, old man. There's nothing you can do about it. If she leaves me, I'll ruin her and ruin you. You've no business interfering in my life."

He stepped forward and struck Jonathan hard. Jonathan heard a crunching sound, and his jaw exploded in pain. He was dizzy and might have fallen if the men didn't continue to hold him up. Jonathan struggled to keep awake, to maintain his balance. He sprang forward again so quickly that he broke away from Robert's friends. He crushed his son-in-law in the chest, knocking him down again and driving him to the pavement. This time he fell on top of Robert, holding him down and lying on top of him. He struck with his fists over and over, driving his hands down as hard as he could.

"Get him off me!" screamed Robert. "Kill him."

Fingers groped at Jonathan, but he rolled away and tore the revolver from his jacket. He aimed it at the men.

"Boys. This isn't your matter. This is between Robert and me. I'm done with him now. I don't want any trouble with the rest of you." The men stepped warily back, arms in the air. Jonathan rose, cautiously. He looked down at his son-in-law, who was writhing slowly back and forth, a wounded snake. He kicked him again.

"She won't be coming back. You will allow this divorce, and you will keep your mouth shut. You're a newcomer in this town. If you start something, I've many friends and family that'll finish it. Do you understand me?"

Robert nodded, his face turned away. Jonathan backed up, keeping his eye on the men. Finally, he turned and retreated rapidly toward his truck. Jonathan's heart beat out of his chest. He hadn't struck anyone in anger since he was a boy. He didn't know if what he had just done was in the right. Had he sinned? He didn't think so. He had stood up for his daughter and protected her honor. He wondered if he would be arrested. Doubtful. Men in Snohomish settled these matters of honor with blows. Robert was a police officer, but the chief was a friend of Jonathan's. They had gone to high school together. Certainly he wouldn't approve of Robert striking his wife. Jonathan was sure this would stay between him and Robert. That would be the problem. The bastard would want revenge. He would have to watch himself, and Mary.

A few minutes later he arrived home. He sneaked back into the garage and placed the revolver back in its hiding spot, then returned to the house. Mary was still on the sofa, Sarah sitting next to her. Both of them looked relieved when he walked in.

"Jonathan, thank God you're back," said Sarah. Then she looked down. "What's happened to your hands?"

Jonathan realized his fingers were covered in blood. Several of his knuckles were cut. His jaw ached as well. Now that he was home and safe, the surge of energy departed. He felt exhausted, even nauseated. "I'm all right," he answered, then walked to the kitchen sink and turned on the faucet, running cold water over his fingers. It stung as the frigid liquid poured over his cuts. He didn't know if he had done the right thing, but he felt the justice for his daughter burning through him, along with the crisp, cold pain.

~∽

"What did you do, Father?" asked Mary. Jonathan could see the fear in her eyes.

"Don't worry, dear. I put an end to his bad behavior."

"How? Tell me."

"I confronted him. I gave him back a little of what he gave you."

Jonathan could tell she was upset, but he hoped a part of her felt vindicated, too, and protected. "That was it?" she asked finally.

"That's it. I meant what I said, though. I want you to stay here."

"How can I do that? We would be ruined. Could you imagine the scandal? I won't do that to you. I'll go away. I can move to another town. Marysville, perhaps."

"You'll do no such thing. We have plenty of friends and family here. When the story gets out, folks will understand. I can't stop everyone from having an opinion, but there'll be plenty of people who'll stand by us, sure enough. It will be okay. It's up to you, though, Mary. I know men. You may be tempted to believe he will change, but I know he won't. We are weak, and we give in to temptations. His is violence. If you go back, he will hit you again. It's just a matter of time. Think of your future children."

"I won't have any children if I divorce." The tears were starting again now. "Who will ever want me? Think of it. A divorced woman!"

"You don't know that. Only God sees all things. I've known more than one divorced person to find love again. Now isn't the time to worry about that." He stopped and looked at her carefully for a moment. "Will you stay, Mary? Will you stay here with me and face this together?"

She returned his look. Confused. Hesitating. Then she nodded slightly. The tears came now in rivers, and she ran into his arms again. Sarah came forward, too, putting her hands on Mary's back, holding her gently while still refusing to look at Jonathan. They held Mary that way for a long time. Then they helped her back to the sofa, laying her down this time with a pillow and a blanket. Soon she fell asleep, her breath coming in even rhythms.

"Did you tell her the truth about Robert?" Sarah asked finally, drawing Jonathan into the kitchen where they could speak more freely.

"As much as she can handle."

"What does that mean?"

"Don't worry. I didn't do anything too rash." Jonathan chuckled. "Do you think I'm a killer?"

"No, I don't. But that man hurt your girl, your *little girl*, as you still think of her. I was worried you might lose control."

"I could have," he admitted. "But I didn't. I did warn him to leave her alone."

"Do you think he will?"

"I don't know. I've never met anyone more arrogant. A police officer at that. I'm going to have to keep eyes in the back of my head for a long time to come."

"Who will watch her during the day?"

"I'll bring her to the store."

"Where she first met him? That's no good, Jonathan. That place is full of memories for her, and there's nothing to keep her busy. I have quite a bit of work backed up now. Why doesn't she come over to my house during the day? You can drop her off, and she can work with me. That will get her mind off things, and she can make a little money as well. Besides, it would be nice to catch up on my orders."

Jonathan smiled at her. "That's very kind of you."

Sarah blushed, turning her head away again.

"I've been wanting to talk to you," Jonathan continued.

"No, please, not tonight."

"There are things that need to be said. Things we need to discuss."

"I know that. Haven't we been through enough this evening already?"

"Will there be a better time?" he asked.

She looked up at him again, pleading in her eyes. "Perhaps you're right. There won't ever be a very good time to do this."

"Have you had some time to think about what I said?" he asked.

"Yes, I have."

"Well?"

She hesitated for a moment and then looked deeply into his eyes. "You're right, Jonathan."

He felt a warmth flow into him. She had come around. Oh, how he had prayed for this to happen. They could go back to being friends. He knew it would be difficult, but they would make it work. They were both so disciplined. "I'm so glad you said that, my dear. I know this isn't easy, but . . ."

"You didn't let me finish."

"I'm sorry. Go ahead."

"You're right that I haven't been fair to you with this. I did tell you we would always remain friends. You were so wonderful to be honest with me from the beginning. I respect you so much for the promise you made to your wife, for your faith, your strength, your everything."

"I respect you as well, Sarah. You are the strongest woman I've ever known."

"Not strong enough to do what you're asking of me. I'm so sorry, Jonathan. You were truthful and upfront with me, and I promised you in return I would remain your friend. I can't, though. Along the way I fell in love with you. Maybe I loved you from the moment I first saw you. I don't know. What I do know is that my feelings have grown until I feel I will burst. I don't want just your friendship anymore. I want you, Jonathan. *All of you.* I want to be your wife. I want to live with you and spend my nights and days with you. I want to have your child growing inside me—if there's still time. I want my whole future with you—forever. I can't go back to friendship. That shore has faded into the distance, and I can never return."

Jonathan was stunned. Sarah was right, of course. He knew in his heart that she spoke the real truth. He loved her as deeply in return. She was beautiful and faithful. She seemed fragile, but she was a rock—stronger than him, he realized, and wiser. He thought her perfect, his angel on earth. She had stood by him during such difficult times. She had followed his wishes, and they had journeyed together through time in this beautiful town he loved, while the war tore everything apart around him. In the intervening time, he had fallen for her. He needed her with every part of his heart and his soul. He wanted nothing more than to fall to his knees and beg her to marry him. He would spend the rest of his life with her.

Sarah wanted a child with him. He hadn't thought of that possibility until she mentioned it: a new life in the world that was part of both of them, another little one to love, a new adventure. He had learned so much about what it was to be a father. Sarah offered the world to him, and he had but to reach out and take it.

She drew closer, placing her arms around his waist and gently resting her head against his shoulder. "I love you, Jonathan Beecher. I love you," she whispered.

Jonathan held her closely in the silence of his home. He could hear a trickle of sounds: Sarah's heart, Mary's breathing in the next room. He enjoyed Sarah's feel, her smell, their gentle touch in the darkness of the kitchen. He didn't know how long they stayed together, hanging on to each other—to life. Finally, he stepped back, letting go. Sarah looked into his eyes, waiting, hoping. His whole future was there in front of him.

"I'm sorry." He heard the words come out of his mouth as if another's voice. As he spoke, he could see the light dying in her eyes, a lantern without fuel. His heart was a sunken rock in his chest, dragging him down. He wanted to take his words back, but he couldn't speak. He dreaded the pain and loss that would come.

"I know that's what you would say." Tears were streaming down her face. More tears. The night was full of them. She stepped forward again and put her hands around his neck. She pulled his head down and kissed him lightly on the lips. A farewell kiss. He felt her dreams, their future, pass between them, drawn out of her forever. "I love you so much, my dearest."

She retreated out of the kitchen and over to Mary. She bent down, moving the blankets up around his daughter. She kissed Mary on the forehead lightly. She picked up her coat from the edge of the sofa and turned again. She looked up at Jonathan. He was still in the kitchen, unable to move. Everything inside him screamed out to him to run to her, to ask forgiveness, to beg her to forget his foolishness. Still, he did not move.

As if she knew his struggle, Sarah stayed a moment—giving him this last chance. Then she smiled at him as if to express how much she admired his strength, even in this moment of deepest despair. She turned and strolled, head high, to the door. In a moment she was gone.

Jonathan wanted to go after her, to stop her from leaving. What was the point? He knew he was doing the right thing despite the loss, despite the pain. What would he say to her if he did try to stop her? That he was sorry? That he hoped she would forgive him? There was only one thing she wanted to hear from him, and he couldn't say it.

He sat down at a chair in the kitchen in the darkness. He was stunned—raw. What had he just done? *I'm a fool. But don't I have to follow my God?* The pain would come tomorrow, and it would be enormous. He would bear it as he bore all things. For now, he pushed all of that from his mind. He wanted to revel in their last moment together. He turned each word she had spoken over and over in his mind. Savoring their music, her earnest declaration of love. Sarah was so much a part of his soul. He closed his eyes. He painted their past on a canvas of joyful sadness. He remained in the kitchen through the night, stirring with the first streaks of dawn.

CHAPTER SIXTEEN

Mars-la-Tour, France
Saturday, November 4, 1944

Corporal Luke Beecher's Sherman tank platoon rolled up a narrow road near Mars-la-Tour, France. Luke sat in his familiar seat at the gunner position with Wenzel next to him, ready to load. Sergeant Bonelli was on the radio, talking over logistics with First Lieutenant Alanyk. Collins and Hudson were below Luke, to his respective left and right. The crew had trained for this moment for more than two years, including more than a month in France. Now they were on their way to their first taste of combat.

The Tenth Armored Division, nicknamed the "Tiger Division," was part of the famous General George S. Patton's Third Army. The entire division was moving up to this area in northeastern France, in an effort to capture Metz, capital of the Lorraine region. Bonelli told the crew that they had passed Verdun on the way, the site of a colossal months-long battle during the Great War. Now the guns sounded again. Luke could hear the thud of artillery ahead. They had experienced these sounds before in training, but this wasn't an exercise. These guns were firing live ammunition, shells that would rain down on them—kill them.

Much had changed for Luke in the last two years. He had grown close to his crew. They felt more real than his family ever had. He could hardly remember home. This was his family now. They had trained together, slept and ate together, endured drill after drill for years—all so they could arrive here at this moment.

Luke felt the fear chasing him. Combat had always been something out in the distance, a vague future event that would happen tomorrow, or next month, or next year. Now combat was here. Despite all his training, he felt unprepared. Soon the Germans would be in front of him, shooting at him.

"Collins, head right," ordered Bonelli. "HQ says there's a German position up ahead. Estimated a couple of companies of infantry, maybe with some tank or antitank support. Our platoon is going to lead an infantry attack on the position. They want us to hit them with the whole shebang."

Luke felt the tank veer to the right and angle down the side of the raised road. Heading cross-country, the tank bumped along as it moved forward over the uneven ground. The Sherman traveled that way for more than an hour. The tension seemed to build with each passing minute. Luke wondered if the others felt the crippling fear he was experiencing. He wanted to jump out of the tank and run the other direction. How could Bonelli remain so calm? All of them were acting like this was no big deal. *I'm a coward.* He tried to concentrate on his job, but doubts kept flying through his head. He felt the panic. He couldn't breathe. He wanted to open the turret and get to fresh air. He closed his eyes, trying to calm himself.

Now they could hear the sound of small-arms fire. Machine guns echoed in staccato bursts, mixing with the notes of artillery and mortar shells. Sharp echoes clanged off the tank as bullets hit the Sherman, bouncing off of its armor.

"Okay, we're in position," said Bonelli. He listened on the radio for a few minutes. "We're going to move forward in ten minutes." Bonelli stood with his head out of the turret, allowing him to man the top machine gun and also to spot enemy targets. Bullets kept ricocheting off the tank, but the sergeant seemed unafraid and kept his position. Luke looked through his scope and surveyed the terrain. They were at the edge of some woods, looking out over a grassy field. The field extended about three hundred yards to another line of trees. Luke could see flashes of fire from the distant woods. That must be where the Germans were. He strained his eyes, looking carefully. He couldn't make out any tanks or other vehicles, but that didn't mean they weren't there.

"Get ready, boys. The attack is about to start," said Bonelli. Luke looked out again, preparing his instruments. He moved the turret to the left and then the right to test that everything was in working order.

"Okay, Collins, the infantry is ready. Let's move out!"

The Sherman jerked into motion, the engine roaring as the heavy tank lurched forward. Luke couldn't see the other tanks of their platoon, but he knew they were out there. His Sherman cleared the trees and rumbled into the meadow. The trees across the way exploded in light. At the same moment, Hudson and Bonelli opened up with their machine guns, tracers walking among the trunks. Bullets clanged off their tank in increasing number. An explosion erupted directly in front of them, the shell of an enemy tank or artillery.

"Beecher, hit the woods!" yelled Bonelli.

Luke peered through his scope, searching for targets. He still couldn't see any tanks. Bonelli hadn't named a specific objective, so he must simply want a shell fired into the trees. Luke looked for a location with as many flashes as possible and moved the turret slightly to line up the sight. He depressed the foot pedal, and the Sherman jerked, its main cannon firing a round toward the woods. The shell exploded a few yards in front of the trees.

"Short!" shouted Bonelli.

Luke raised the cannon angle as Wenzel loaded another shell. He fired a second shot, and this time the shell exploded just inside the woods.

"Good shot, Beecher. Give 'em another!"

Luke moved the turret to the right slightly and waited for another round to load. He depressed the pedal again. Another explosion. Luke could see other flashes. The platoon was pouring cannon fire into the woods. The Sherman kept rolling forward. They had covered half the distance to the woods.

Their tank shook and jarred hard to the right. What was that?

"We're hit!" yelled Bonelli. "Tank to our left. One hundred fifty yards! Load an armor-piercing round! Now, Wenzel!"

Luke looked where Bonelli was directing. He spotted the enemy. Their turret was pointed directly at them. He knew the German crew was reloading to finish the job. Luke desperately turned his turret. The cannon moved so slowly. They were going to be killed.

A flash. The German tank fired first. Luke waited for the shell to hit, but it didn't. They must have missed. Finally, the cannon lined up on the enemy tank. Luke depressed the pedal, and the Sherman bucked again. The German tank lifted off the ground, then landed hard. Smoke billowed out of a huge hole.

Luke was amazed. He had hit it! Just like in practice! He watched in wonder as the turret opened and a figure crawled out. The German was on fire and jumped to the ground, running around wildly in circles before finally falling. There was too much noise to hear the screaming, but Luke was shocked. He had just killed another human. He had never imagined it would look like that. If the German had hit them first, they would all be dead, or at least terribly wounded. He didn't have time to think, because there were more targets, and more shells coming in.

The attack continued. They were almost to the tree line. The flashes were more infrequent. The Germans must be on the run! They were within twenty yards of the trees.

"Collins, stop the tank!" yelled Bonelli.

The Sherman halted. Bullets still clanged off the armor, but the shooting lessened. Luke could see American infantry now, passing in front of their tank, moving in among the trees, spreading out under cover of fire. The firing continued for another half hour or so and then faded away.

"We did it!" shouted Collins. "We knocked those Krauts back."

"I figured when we got hit we were goners," said Hudson. "Didn't figure them Germans as skedaddlers."

"Great job, everyone," said Bonelli. "Good shooting, Luke."

Luke sat in his chair, not responding. He was surprised how cool he had felt under fire. Now that they weren't in danger anymore, the fear rolled back over him. He saw again the burning German, crawling out of his tank, running around, dying. That first hit on the Sherman could have destroyed them. The shell must have struck a lucky spot on the tank and bounced off. The second shell had miraculously missed. Luke and his crew had been seconds from death. He couldn't do this. Couldn't face that again.

"We have orders to head back to HQ," said Bonelli. "We're done for the day."

Collins pushed the tank into reverse and moved back a few yards before circling around. As they turned, they saw a burning tank, one of their own.

"Oh God, that's Alanyk's tank," said Bonelli. The Sherman command tank was a burning husk. Black smoke billowed out of twisted metal. The 75-millimeter cannon was bent midway down toward the ground. There were no bodies. No one had escaped. Luke stared at the tank in disbelief. They had all grown to love their lieutenant. He was small and an intellectual, but he was brave and kind. He had never acted like he was better than them. He had trained and learned with them. He had slept out in the field with them, shared their miseries and their joys. Now he was gone, killed on his first day in combat. Luke felt the fear overwhelm him. That could have been him; that could have been their tank. As the platoon returned to battalion headquarters, one thought filled Luke's mind: *I have to find a way out.*

～∽

The men arrived back at headquarters without further incident. They climbed wearily out of their tank and jumped down to the ground. The initial elation of their victory and survival was gone. Five of their friends were dead, including their lieutenant. Gone in an instant to a fiery death. Luke knew just how close they had come to the same ending. How would they ever survive the war? They were so lucky to have lived through this first engagement.

The panic wouldn't leave Luke. As they rested against the treads of their tank, munching on K-rations, terror consumed him. He was glad he had performed in combat. But he wondered if he would have been able to do the same if he weren't in close quarters with his friends. If he were one of the infantrymen, out in the open with bullets flying everywhere, he was sure he would have fled. He felt the hot shame. He didn't measure up. He had faced combat, but he hadn't passed the test. Now he just wanted out of here, away from the fear and the horror.

"We're moving out again soon, boys," said Bonelli, returning from a meeting at the operations tent. "A battalion is bogged down about two miles up the road. They ran into some infantry and maybe a battalion of German armor. A bunch of Panthers and maybe a Tiger or two. They want our battalion to move up and take them out. It's going to be tough business. I've heard stories of our shells bouncing right off the Tigers. The only reliable kill shot is from the rear."

"How we supposed to get behind 'em?" asked Hudson. "Why the hell didn't they build us a better tank?"

"Ours is not to wonder why; ours is just to do or die," joked Bonelli. He became serious. "I don't know why the Germans have better tanks,

Hudson. But we have plenty more Shermans, and we have a job to do. We have about an hour, boys, and then we need to move out."

Luke felt the panic growing. They were going back out in an hour, against tanks that their shells couldn't even penetrate. He couldn't do it. He had to figure out a way out. In his desperation he came up with a plan. He threw himself on the ground, clutching his stomach, groaning in pain.

"What's wrong?" asked Collins. "Sarge, something's wrong with Beecher."

Bonelli was there in an instant. "What's wrong, Luke? Are you okay?"

"Pain! Terrible pain in my stomach! I don't know what it is!"

"Medic!" yelled Bonelli.

In a moment, a soldier with a Red Cross on his sleeve was there. "What's wrong?"

"He's doubled over in pain. Says it's his stomach."

The medic examined Luke, gently prodding. Luke winced from the touch, groaning even louder. He felt ashamed, but he didn't know what else to do.

"Let's get him to the hospital," said the medic.

A few moments later Luke felt himself loaded on a stretcher. He continued to moan, holding his stomach, his eyes closed. The medics sat him on the front hood of a jeep, then drove him as gently as they were able over to the hospital. The trip took less than five minutes. Luke could hear Bonelli talking to the medic as they went.

After arriving at the hospital, Luke was lifted off the jeep and carried inside. He opened his eyes a little to look around. He sat among a group of soldiers on cots. He heard screaming. There were real wounded here. One soldier cried over and over for his mother, his cries high pitched and pitiful.

A nurse wandered over to Luke and asked what was wrong. The medic explained his condition. She asked Luke if he could show her where the pain was. She prodded again with her fingers, and he grimaced more, jerking around on the cot.

"What is it?" asked Bonelli.

"I'm not sure," said the nurse. "It could be food poisoning, or even his appendix. He's going to have to stay here for a while. We can take it from here."

Bonelli leaned down. "You're going to be okay, buddy. You stay here and get some rest. We'll go give those Germans a bloody nose, and I'll be back with the boys to check on you tonight." Bonelli gave his arm a squeeze; then he turned and walked quickly out of the tent.

Luke lay back on his cot, tears welling up in his eyes. What was he doing? He loved his crew with everything in him. He was faking an injury and leaving them behind. They would end up with a replacement gunner, someone they didn't know, hadn't worked with. The difference could make a delay of a second or two in the reaction time of the whole team. An instant could mean life or death. He understood that he was deserting his team to save himself. Even though he wanted desperately to get up and join them, the crippling fear overwhelmed him. He couldn't go back and face combat again. He'd almost died. He had killed people. A bunch of Germans, yes, but really, they were just other men, men a lot like he was. They had brothers and sisters and parents. They had hopes and dreams for the future. He had taken the future away for all of them. He couldn't do that again.

"Beecher. Are you okay?"

He was surprised to hear the voice. He looked up. It was Sergeant Dempsey, moving among the wounded.

"I . . . I don't know, Sergeant. I felt this terrible pain in my stomach. It was worse than anything I ever felt. It keeps coming over and over again. I don't know what could be causing it."

"Maybe someone put soap in your coffee."

Luke felt a stabbing surprise. "What do you mean?"

"You heard me, boy. I saw you put soap in Bonelli's coffee all that time ago. Do you think I'm a fool? I knew what you were doing, but I didn't understand why. I decided to sit back and wait. I thought you were trying to shirk your duty, to get out of the maneuvers, but instead you rose to the occasion. You took command, and you ran that tank with a leadership I didn't think you had in you. I was disgusted by what you did, but I tried to understand the reasons you did it. You didn't intend for Bonelli to get that sick, did you?"

"No, Sergeant. I just thought he would be gone for a day. I would have never done it if I thought he would be that sick."

"Why did you do it?"

"For the same reason I left mud in your bunk. I wanted the guys to like me. I thought if I led the tank for a while, if I did okay, maybe people would forgive me for the past. I just want people to respect me."

"You don't get respect by practical jokes, kid. You get respect by standing up with courage. By leading. By honor and truth and decency. You have those qualities, Beecher—somewhere inside you. I saw them that week you led your tank in maneuvers. Problem is, they get bunched up with all the other crap you carry around. At first I was just waiting to tell the lieutenant, to drum your ass out of the army. But then I watched you lead those men. I decided to give you one more chance, and I've kept my mouth shut all this time."

He hovered over Luke and placed an iron fist on his chest. "You're a leader, Beecher, but you haven't learned this war isn't about you. This is about your friends, the platoon, the division. I know why you're really here right now," he spat. "You're not sick. You're playing the same selfish game, because you're always looking after yourself first. You tasted combat, and it scared the hell out of you.

"Guess what? We're all scared. But the difference between you and all the rest of us is that you just want to save your own skin. You're still looking after Luke. I think this is your last chance. I'll carry what I saw to the grave. This isn't about soap or mud. This is about your character.

If you let those boys go back to the front without you and they get killed, you will never live it down. If you don't go, you will never forgive yourself. So what's it going to be, Beecher? You might get killed with them. You might not. You have one more chance to be a man."

Luke hesitated. Dempsey had seen through him and apparently always had. He knew the sergeant was right. He felt the tears again. He was so ashamed. He'd been such a terrible man. *This is my last chance.*

"It's okay to cry, Beecher. Get it all out. It doesn't matter about the past. What matters is what you do right now." Dempsey extended his hand.

Luke looked up. This was the moment of truth. He hesitated. He could stay and save himself or walk forward into the unknown—with his honor. He extended his hand. Dempsey pulled him up out of the cot.

"That's my boy. I knew you had it in you. Let's go give the Germans some hell. Just remember, there's no going back and no more chances."

They walked back to the tanks together, Dempsey's arm around his shoulders. Luke didn't feel sure of himself. He still felt the white-hot guilt and the fear. But he was here. He was walking toward his crew, toward his friends. He felt something new: a new life with the possibility of living for others besides himself, without the lies and the games. He could live like Bonelli. Like Dempsey. Simple. Honorable.

Wenzel spotted him first. The crew was still by the tank, finishing their cigarettes before they left for battle.

"Hey, fellas! It's Beecher. He's back!"

They all stood and ran over to him.

Bonelli said, "We're so glad to have you back. Are you sure you're up for this?"

"I'm fine," said Luke. "Finally, I'm fine."

The crew rushed around him, patting him on the back and cheering. Luke felt a surge of happiness surrounding his fear, holding it back. He was here with his friends, his crew. They would face the uncertainty together with honor.

∿

The crew climbed back into their Sherman, taking an extra K-ration each in case they weren't able to get back for any chow later. Collins fired up the tank, and soon they were rumbling off with the rest of the remaining tanks in their platoon. Sergeant Dempsey was the platoon commander until a replacement tank and lieutenant could be found. The tank sputtered and vibrated as it rolled noisily along the road toward the front.

Explosions. Bare minutes after leaving headquarters, the dull thudding of artillery resumed. Luke could feel the jittery fear welling up in him again. He had hoped with his new resolution that the terror would simply go away, but he realized it didn't work that way. He glanced down at Hudson and Collins, watching them as the Sherman rolled along. Hudson was fidgeting with a cigarette pack, turning it over and over in his hands. Collins was tapping both of his thumbs hard against the instrument panel. Luke realized they were all coping with their fear. He wasn't unique. Fear didn't go away. You found a way to handle it, or you didn't.

Luke swallowed hard and looked out his scope. The filtered reality in front of him felt distant, as if it weren't really there. He found that as he looked through the scope, he would calm down somewhat. He had spent hours in training doing this, tracking and looking for targets, preparing the cannon for firing. He had done this very thing thousands of times, and the repetition seemed to have a calming effect on him now. He tried to pretend this was still training, that they were merely on maneuvers.

Artillery shells landed around them. They passed a burned-out jeep to their right. The charred remains of the driver and the passenger still sat upright in the front seats, their mouths open wide in silent screams. A shell hit their tank and bounced off the turret.

Sergeant Bonelli was on the radio again, talking to headquarters and to Dempsey.

"We're getting closer. Just another mile up the road and we reach the attack area. Sounds like the panzers have our boys pinned down pretty good. They're taking a lot of casualties. Two platoons already rushed up to help them, but they took a beating. They're throwing the whole battalion at them now. Looks like this might be the center of the whole German counterattack. If we can stop them here, we may be able to push on through right into Metz."

Another half hour passed as the tanks crept into position. Luke kept straining to see what was going on, but the trees blocked his view. Finally, he was able to see the American position amid the smoke. A mass of infantry was bogged down among a scatter of houses clustered in a village. Directly behind the town a lake yawned its mouth as if to devour them. Flashes of fire erupted from the forest past the water. *That must be where the Germans are.* As Luke watched, explosion after explosion rocked the little village. Chunks of plaster fell down off the walls of crumbling houses. A shell landed directly in the middle of a squad of infantry. Bodies flew, and bloody limbs rained down.

"That's the position we have to take," said Bonelli. "There's artillery, tanks, and infantry. It's a storm."

"I don't see any tanks," said Luke. He was scanning the woods, but just like the last time, the units were invisible and likely set back in the woods.

"They're there. No doubt about it. Let me find out what we're doing next."

As they sat awaiting orders, the artillery fell in among their tanks again. This time it was closer. Luke heard a huge explosion and screams. A tank nearby had taken a direct hit. He felt the fear surging up again. They were going to be hit before they could even start the attack.

Another explosion shook the village in front of them. More bodies flew. Luke saw a soldier turn and run, the artillery too much for him. He was cut down by machine gun fire before he could make it back to the tanks.

"Okay, we're moving out!" yelled Bonelli. "Our battalion is splitting up. We're going to go to the right with two platoons. Everything else is going left. We're going first as a diversion; then the rest of the battalion and all the infantry will hit the other flank and hopefully peel them back. It's going to get real hot, real fast. Collins, get ready for it."

Luke closed his eyes and prayed. He prayed God would protect them, that He would forgive him for his selfish past. Luke thanked God for the strength to come back and for Dempsey, who had restored his honor. How strange to be here. He'd joined the army on a whim, expecting a few months of adventure and then to come back home. Instead he hadn't seen home in years, and here he was in the midst of death and destruction.

"Collins, hit it!" shouted Bonelli. Their tank roared into life, jerking forward and to the right. Luke watched the landscape jumble up and down as the tank rolled over the bumpy terrain. The burning village jolted in and out of view. Another Sherman rumbled in front of them to the right. It jumped and exploded, hit by a shell. A second nearby Sherman kept moving, swerving to the right in front of them and then continuing to roll forward. Another explosion rocked the vehicle, and it was still.

"Tank!" screamed Bonelli.

"Where?" asked Luke.

"To your right. One o'clock, two hundred yards!"

Luke strained and spotted the enemy tank. He turned the turret slowly toward the panzer. They had studied all the German tanks in training. The Panzer V was perhaps the best tank in the world, with better armor and a high-velocity 75-millimeter cannon far superior to the Sherman.

The panzer fired. Luke winced, expecting an incoming shell. It didn't land. They must have been aiming at another tank. Luke centered his sights and depressed the firing pedal. The Sherman jerked, and a moment later Luke's shell landed true. The German tank jolted but didn't stop. The shell had bounced right off the armor. Luke adjusted his sights, aiming at the tread. He could see the enemy turret changing direction, seeking them out.

"Stop moving for a second!" Luke shouted. He wanted a clean shot. The Sherman ground to a halt. He was taking a chance because he was an easy target now. He centered his sights and fired. His tank jolted again. The round landed on target. This time the panzer exploded in fire. The tread curled off the tank like a twisted snake. Smoke billowed. The top of the turret opened, and men climbed out, scrambling for cover. Luke heard the rattle of machine gun fire. Sergeant Bonelli raked them with gunfire. Luke watched the trapped men jerk as they took rounds from Bonelli. One by one they toppled over and dropped lifeless into the mud.

A flash of red caught Luke's eye. He was shocked to see a French family running directly in front of him. A young man and woman were sprinting away from the village. The man carried a little girl in a red coat in his arms. They looked surreal amid the rubble and the carnage. What were they doing here? Why were they trying to escape during the day, during a battle? Shells landed all around them. They kept ducking and moving. The woman was screaming.

"Get the hell out of there!" Bonelli shouted at the civilians, waving his arms out the top of the turret.

The family disintegrated before Luke's eyes. Chunks of flesh flew in every direction. A scarlet wave washed up on his scope, blocking his view. Bonelli groaned above him. The sergeant sank down hard inside the turret, his face covered in brain and bits of bone.

"Did you see that?" he asked, looking at Luke.

Luke nodded in reply. He handed Bonelli a towel with a shaky hand. "You've got to get up, Sarge. We won't last here. We can't stop for them. They're goners."

Bonelli wasn't moving. He seemed stunned. Luke pulled on his shirt. "Come on! We've got to go. We're going to get hit."

"Tanks incoming!" screamed Hudson.

Bonelli finally blinked his eyes, reaching up to wipe the blood off his face. He looked at Luke for a moment and then stood back up. In a second Luke could hear the machine gun fire again from above.

Luke returned to his scope. He could see at least five panzers heading their direction. Muzzles flashed. Shells were landing all around them. They had moments to live. Luke fired another shot, bouncing another shell off a panzer. He screamed in frustration. He knew his Sherman wouldn't absorb a similar shot from the panzers.

The radio blared. It was Dempsey. "They've taken the bait! Pull back! Pull back!" Collins jerked the Sherman into reverse. They roared backward. Luke fired another round and missed. The panzers fired away. He was sure they would be hit any moment, but by some miracle they made it through. Artillery shells started to land among the panzers. A German tank exploded in flame, and Luke saw an Allied airplane arc across the landscape and then rise back up into the sky after a strafing run. Shells fell heavily, American shells. The German tanks jolted into reverse.

"We've got them on the run," reported Dempsey. "The attack worked. We held them on the right, and the left collapsed! They're in full retreat!"

The Shermans rolled in reverse until they reached their starting place behind the village. The buildings were smoking rubble. A handful of infantry remained, the rest having moved forward in the attack. Gradually the explosions faded and the fighting died down. The tanks stopped, and Collins shut down the engine. They climbed out slowly, exhausted. Luke slid down the turret and took a seat on the back of the tank. Collins offered him a cigarette. Luke didn't smoke. He took one anyway and breathed deeply in. The smoke was bitter, and he coughed. He didn't care. He puffed away on the cigarette, trying to erase the memory of what he'd just seen. He saw Bonelli, wiping the blood away from his face with a rag.

Bonelli came over to them. He drew his arms around Wenzel and Hudson and clutched them protectively. Luke leaped down, and the four of them embraced in a tight circle. They held each other for a long time, sharing their pain, their relief. They were alive. At least for now, they had survived.

Luke felt another hand on his shoulder. He turned. It was Dempsey. His face was smudged with powder. He was exhausted, but he grinned. "You did good today, kid. I'm proud of you, Corporal."

Their company commander appeared, congratulating them on a job well done. Sergeant Dempsey received word he had received a battlefield promotion. He was a second lieutenant now. They weren't going to receive a replacement commander after all.

They all congratulated Dempsey. He looked over again at Luke.

Luke smiled. "There's nobody else I'd rather serve under," he said.

Dempsey grinned in return and gave him a wink. "Let's get a little food in us, boys, and some sleep if you can manage it. We're not done yet."

The crew returned to their tank, fished out their K-rations and cigarettes, and sat down for a well-deserved rest.

CHAPTER SEVENTEEN

Snohomish, Washington
Monday, December 18, 1944

Jonathan stood near the counter in his hardware store, watching as Mary rang up a customer. He watched her carefully, always alert for the sadness that would creep into her day. More than a year had now passed since she and Robert had separated, and six months since the divorce had been finalized.

At least the war news is good, thought Jonathan. Everywhere the Allies were ascendant.

Luke was in the middle of things now, which was another worry for Jonathan. His division had entered France in October, four months after the D-Day invasion, and was actively engaged in the northeastern part of the country. Jonathan had only received a couple of short letters from him since then. He was terribly concerned for Luke, but so far God had protected him. Jonathan was astounded by the tone of the letters. His son had grown up so much in the past few years. Jonathan was very proud and just hoped with every part of his soul that Luke would be returned to him safely.

Thoughts of Luke brought Jonathan to Matthew. He prayed for his oldest son every day as well. He hoped for a miracle and wished with all his heart for a letter from him. Each agonizing day Jonathan looked in the mail, and each time there was nothing. He felt in his being that his son was still alive out there, still waiting for a chance to write to his family and tell them he was okay. Jonathan hoped that the entire war would be over soon and that both his boys would be coming home.

He thought of Sarah. After more than a year he still couldn't drive her from his mind, despite all his efforts. They had scarcely spoken this past year, just a nod here and there at church. He had seen her more frequently at first when he had dropped Mary off at her house each day, but it hadn't taken too long to catch up on Sarah's backlog of work, and within a few months he had lost that chance to get at least a daily glimpse of her. Even on Sundays she was frequently absent from their worship service. He was sure she was intentionally avoiding contact. He understood, although it didn't lessen the pain.

Jonathan didn't regret his decision. He felt he had done what he must do. He had made a promise. He had thought he was keeping that promise in their friendship, but he'd deceived himself. They'd fallen in love, and he'd had to end it. A year later the pain still felt as fresh as ever. He might feel he had made the right choice, but the cost had been high.

Mary finished with the customer and looked up at her father, giving him a little smile. "You don't have to watch over me. I'm just fine."

"Are you fine? I worry about you, dear."

"Still?"

"Yes, *still*, and always. You're so sad at times."

Mary's face darkened for a moment. "It's still hard. I'm so embarrassed. I was foolish. I ran away without listening to you and into the arms of a man who was careless with my heart, with my youth. Now nobody wants me. I'm young, but I'm already like an old widow. I don't want to be alone for the rest of my life."

"I understand, dear. Truly I do. I'm sorry for what has come to pass. But I don't regret your decision. He would have destroyed you. He was in the process of doing it already."

"Why couldn't he have been different?" Mary asked. "He was so charming at first. So kind. He told me how beautiful I was every day; he promised me we would be happy forever. The moment we married, a demon filled him. He was never the same."

"He was never the same because the real Robert didn't come out until you were married."

She nodded. "Why didn't I see that before?"

"Mary, you're too hard on yourself. You were a child. A child whose mother died before you were old enough to learn anything from her about men."

"She wasn't my model for men, Father. You were. I should have found a steady, hardworking, kind man. Instead I fell for a con man. All shine and sales, but nothing at the core."

Jonathan understood. *A con or a cat.* Helen had been sharp-witted, bold, sarcastic. She'd chosen him. Simple and honest of disposition, he hadn't comprehended her true colors.

He heard the other voice in his mind, the spirit that always rose to defend. Could he blame Helen? Times had been tough. They'd raised their children in the Depression. They'd been lucky enough to have work and a roof over their heads and food in their bellies. He'd worked ever harder to provide for her, for the children. Then the cancer came. Jonathan had put away his hard feelings and simply served her. She complained about her illness, even about him. Who wouldn't? How could he judge a person in pain, facing the end of her life? He did his best to shield all of this from the world and from his children. *Your voice is fading, Helen. I know you now.*

At last he responded. "We yearn for mystery, my dear. The shiny is often sharp and cuts the deepest. I didn't prepare you for deceit—I didn't know its face. Forgive me."

He heard the doorbell. Two young men and a woman were in the doorway. He recognized them as Bill Sheldrip, Terrance Hunt, and Shelley Hunt, friends of Mary's from high school. Terrance and Shelley had married this past year. Jonathan had heard Terrance was a 4-F and couldn't serve because of his color blindness.

Mary brightened immediately. Shelley had stood by Mary throughout her divorce, and the two had grown close again.

"I haven't seen you in a long while, Bill," said Jonathan. "Where you been?"

"At the University of Washington, sir. I'm studying history."

"You haven't been drafted?"

"Color-blind, just like Terrance here. I tried to volunteer in '42 after I graduated, but they wouldn't have anything to do with me. So off to school I went."

"I haven't seen you around in the summers, either."

"I got a job at Dunn Lumber over on the north side of Lake Union. It started out on the weekends during school, but it turned into full-time work over the summers. So I've mostly stayed down there." Jonathan noticed he kept glancing over at Mary. Bill had always liked her in school. A thought came to his mind.

"Where are all of you headed?"

"We were going to go to the soda shop to pick up some malts. We were hoping that Mary might want to come with us."

Jonathan turned and saw his daughter blushing a little. "That's very kind of you," said Mary. "But we still have a little work to do."

"Nonsense," said Jonathan. "You run along now and have some fun."

She hesitated. "Are you sure?"

"Of course I'm sure. Now get on out of here."

Mary smiled with a shimmer of youth, a look he hadn't seen in years. She gathered her things and left with her friends. Jonathan felt a wondrous joy. He had lived this past year without much happiness, keeping his eye on his store and taking care of his daughter. Except for the war news, the year had been a tough one, with hard work and little to show for it. Now, out of nowhere, a flicker of a miracle, a tiny spark of light. He uttered a little prayer and then went back to work, humming to himself as he sorted out receipts and inventory.

The bell clanged again. He looked up and was surprised to see Max Weber at the door. Jonathan didn't see his friend too often these days, except when he dropped off a payment. Perhaps there was more good news coming his way? Max was always up on the war news and things going on around town.

"How are you doing today, my friend?"

Max shuffled on his doughy limbs into the store. "*Ganz gut,* Jonathan. How about you?"

"I'm doing pretty darned well today. How's business?"

"Business is *nicht gut.* It's about business that I've come to see you."

That sparked Jonathan's attention. "How can I help you?"

Max stepped closer, his eyes darting about. "As you know, my friend, you've fallen further and further behind."

That was true. Jonathan hadn't been able to keep up with all the payments. He owed six months in back rent and had needed to extend his agreement with Max several times. Still, with the war almost over, he was sure he would be able to get back to normal circumstances and pay Max back within the year.

"Yes, that's true."

"I don't know what to say now. I've some bad news, Jonathan. My bank called in my notes. The economy is strained everywhere with the war still going on. I've had to pay out a goodly sum, and I am going to have to ask you to pay the whole six months now."

Jonathan was stunned. "Surely you're joking with me, Max. You've told me over and over that I could have an extension."

"I've had no problem extending credit, Jonathan, but what am I to do? If the bank wants the money, then I've got to pay, and unfortunately, *mein Freund*, that means I need the loan back now."

"I don't have that kind of money, Max—you know that. Besides, there's nothing in our agreement that gives you the right to do this."

Max coughed uncomfortably. "Actually, there is." He reached into his coat and pulled out some paperwork. Jonathan realized it was their agreement. Max thumbed through it and then placed the contract on the counter, his rumpled thumb covering a paragraph in the middle of the page. Jonathan picked up the agreement and read it. He was surprised to see that a clause allowed Max to call in the note in full at any time at his sole discretion.

"You can't do this to me, Max. There's no way I can come up with that money."

"I'm sorry, but I don't have a choice. Maybe there is a way to make up that money."

"Do you mean taking my inventory?"

Max put his hands up in the air. "Now, now. Not all of it, Jonathan. Just enough to satisfy the note."

"There won't be enough left for me to keep up with the current rent. You can't do this to me. We've been friends for years."

Jonathan could see the discomfort in Max's face. However, he continued. "Business is business, Jonathan. I'm sorry it's come to this, but I'm in a hard place, and I have to do what is necessary for my family."

"What about *my* family?"

Max didn't answer. He sputtered, and his face grew scarlet blotches. "Let's not make this worse than it is, Jonathan. I can give you a couple weeks. But if you don't have the money by then, I am going to have to come and take your inventory—just enough of it to square us up. I'm sorry." Max extended his hand, but Jonathan refused it. "I wish you the best of luck, *mein Freund*. Maybe something will come up. Two weeks is a long time." Max raised his hands again, almost in despair, then turned and wobbled from the store.

Jonathan couldn't believe it. He had struggled through this war for three long years now, and everything had fallen apart. He knew he couldn't feel sorry for himself. He had friends who had lost their sons in combat overseas. Luke was still safe and Matthew hopefully so. Despite this, he couldn't help feeling despair wash over him again. Darkness fell on Snohomish, a blackness that matched Jonathan's spirit. He stood at the counter long after closing time, trying to figure out what he could do to hold back the night.

~~

Jonathan spent the next day trying to think of some solution to the problem. He could buy some more merchandise on credit and then hold a huge sale. With the proceeds he might make enough to pay off Max, but then he would be simply substituting one creditor for another, and at far worse credit terms. Could he take out a mortgage on his house? He had prided himself on saving up the money for his home and paying cash. He had never carried a debt on his residence. He might be able to take out a loan on his home, but would the bank lend him money, knowing he was behind to Mr. Weber, knowing he had no savings? Jonathan also considered approaching some of his friends. He couldn't bring himself to do it. He couldn't suffer the humiliation. He had worked hard his whole life and lived frugally to avoid just such a situation.

The morning limped along, and no answers presented themselves. Jonathan prayed for guidance.

Mary came in for the second half of the day. She glowed and pranced around the store. He felt his troubles lift. His daughter's happiness was more important to him than his own. He let some time pass and then finally asked her.

"Did you have a nice evening last night?"

Mary blushed. "Father!"

"I'm just wondering."

"Yes, I did. It's been so long since I could just be a girl out on the town with some friends. I've forgotten what it feels like."

"And?"

"And what?"

"Tell me about the boy."

"Which boy?"

"Mary, don't be ridiculous."

Her cheeks were flushed now. "Father . . ."

"Just tell me."

"*He* was a gentleman all evening. We all sat together and talked for hours. Later Terrance and Shelley left us alone. We stayed until closing. Bill told me all about the university. He's had such a wonderful time there."

"And no girl all these years?"

"There was a girl. They spent two years together. Then she ended it and broke his heart."

"That's *too bad.*"

"You're impossible!"

"Well, that leaves a single young man and a single young woman. Both unattached. I was never good at math, but something about that seems to add up."

"I'm not *single.* I'm divorced."

"Did that seem to trouble him?"

"I don't know."

"Did he ask you out again?"

"Father!"

"Tell me."

"Fine! He said he would like to go to dinner again this week. I doubt it means a thing. I'm sure he just wants to catch up."

"Catching up takes a half hour and doesn't require a second date. He's interested, my dear."

She brightened again. "Oh, Father, do you think so? He's so tall and handsome and brilliant."

"Tall and handsome got you in trouble once already. I'm very happy for you, but let's keep our feet on the ground a little this time. Take your time. Figure out what he's all about. Then you can think about the future."

Mary nodded, but she was brimming with excitement.

Jonathan felt his own joy, but he kept his face as stern as he could manage. "When are you supposed to go to dinner again?"

"He asked me if I could go tonight."

"Did you accept?"

"I was going to ask you if that was all right. If you minded if I left a little early?"

"Leave now. Go home and get ready. Make sure you look perfect. Although with you that's easy to do."

She ran into his arms, holding him tightly. "I'm so happy. I thought nobody would ever look at me again. Thank you so much. I love you!"

"Remember—feet on the ground."

Mary hugged Jonathan again and raced out of the store. He released his smile. He couldn't believe the change in her, and in him.

The euphoria brought the solution to his money problem into sharp focus. Jonathan had tried to determine every way to save the store when God had placed the truth right before him. He would simply sell his inventory and turn Beecher's Hardware over to Max. He had battled all these years, trying to keep this dream alive. Clearly he wasn't meant to own his own business.

Jonathan knew he was a hard worker and there were jobs to be had, particularly with the labor shortage. He would find a job as close to home as possible and with the best wages. He would struggle on, rebuild his savings, and avoid going into further debt. The moment he made this decision, a strange and wonderful peace washed over him. He prayed a thank-you and then set to work mapping out the sale. He grabbed a notebook and began counting his inventory, drawing out what would sell the quickest and for the highest price. Maybe he could even find a buyer for the store itself, and they could take on the debt. There must be someone. He would ask his friends at the auction house. They knew everyone and most of what went on in town.

~~~

Jonathan finished up his work for the day and drove home. He hoped to see Mary before she left, but the house was empty when he arrived. He rummaged around the refrigerator, looking for something to make for dinner, but for some reason he wasn't in the mood to cook. He decided he would go back downtown and enjoy a meal out.

The evening was stunning. A full moon had risen early and bathed the streets of Snohomish in a bright winter light. The air was crisp, and the stars were out. The Milky Way spanned the sky from one end to the other. Jonathan walked down Avenue B, past all the historic Victorian homes. The maple and oak trees spanning both sides of the street were bare of leaves, but their spidery branches stretched out over him in sophisticated designs illuminated by the moon. He whistled softly, his breath freezing in the air. He felt utterly content. He could not remember when he had last experienced such simple peace.

As he walked down the gently sloping hill toward Second Street, Jonathan could see the bright lights of the downtown district. The traffic increased, and the quietness of the night evaporated. He crossed Second and kept moving down to First Street, the heart of the town. He turned left and walked past his store, heading farther down toward the Silver King, where he had decided to have dinner. He was sure that during the week he'd be able to get a table. He entered the restaurant and was seated immediately. He ordered coffee to warm himself and blew on his cold hands until it arrived.

Jonathan looked over the menu and eventually settled on a turkey dinner with mashed potatoes and gravy. He placed his order and then read through the *Snohomish Tribune*, the town newspaper. Stan Bates had led the high school football team to a perfect 9-0 record this year, coming off a 5-1-2 record the year before. The paper carried many of the year-end statistics for the team. Keith Gilbertson, the fullback, had scored nine touchdowns, and Bill "Pete" Peterson had scored five. Dick Rodland was both the quarterback and played safety. Jonathan knew Dick well. He was a Fobes Hill kid, straightlaced and honest. A young man of faith, admired by all. He would help Jonathan out every once in a while with some work around the hardware store. Jonathan had a hard time getting Dick to accept any pay. That was just what kind of person he was.

Jonathan smiled. There were so many good kids in Snohomish. He loved his town and the simple life he was able to live there. The thought made him feel even better. So long as he was able to continue living here, among all his friends and within the community, it didn't matter whether he owned his store or not. There were more important things in the world.

The waitress brought his meal, and he thanked her, accepting another cup of coffee. The plate was heaped with white breast meat and a mound of mashed potatoes. A warm roll and a stack of butter rested on the edge. Jonathan settled in for a delicious meal.

He heard the café door clang open and the bell ring. The sound made him smile again—so much like his own store. He looked up and froze, his heart dropping. It was Sarah. She was with Stan Bensen, a widower in his early fifties and a manager at the cannery on Maple. Sarah's arm was locked around his, and they were laughing together. When her gaze settled on Jonathan, the color drained from her face.

She stared at him for a moment and then leaned over and whispered something to Stan before walking toward Jonathan alone.

"Hello, Jonathan," she said.

"Hello."

"Can I sit down for a second, please?"

"You're welcome to," said Jonathan through clenched teeth. All of his peace was erased. He felt his heart racing out of his chest. He wanted to flee, but she was already here. *His* Sarah.

Sarah sat down. He could see the pain in her face, matching his own. "I've been meaning to talk to you for a while now, but there hasn't been a good time."

"Talk to me about what?"

"About Stan. It's not easy to say to you, but we've been seeing each other for a couple weeks now. I didn't want you to learn about it like this."

Jonathan grunted. "It's not my business. You're welcome to make your own decisions."

"You know it's not as easy as that—for either of us. I've wanted to tell you—but it's very hard for me. Now you've seen it for yourself, and everything is worse."

"It's not worse. You have a right to go on with your life. I'm . . . I'm happy for you. I wasn't able to give you everything that you wanted. It's understandable that you would move on. Stan is a fine man. I'm sure you will be very happy together."

"I didn't want to be happy with anyone but you."

"I know that, Sarah. Life is what it is, though. You didn't make the commitment . . . I did. You deserve a good future, with a man that loves you and will take care of you. I'll be okay."

Her face brightened. "Do you really mean that?"

He forced a smile. "Of course I do."

"Thank you so much, Jonathan. You couldn't give me a better gift. I've been so worried. I know it won't be easy, but knowing you have given me your blessing means everything in the world to me." She looked around. "Well, I should go. Stan's waiting for me."

"Take care, Sarah."

She reached over and squeezed his arm. "You, too, Jonathan."

Jonathan took another bite or two of his meal, but his appetite was gone. He waited for the bill, keeping his eyes away from her. When he paid, he nodded their way once out of politeness and then hurried out the door. He kept his composure through the entire walk home, forcing himself to concentrate on each step as he went. The trip took an eternity. When he reached his house, he hurried his step, closing the door behind him and taking a deep breath, as if he had been unable to do so until then. He took off his overcoat and walked to the kitchen, where he opened a cupboard and strained to look around on the top shelf. Finally, he found what he was looking for. He retrieved a bottle full of brown liquid, a gift from a friend at his wife's funeral that he had never opened. He cracked the lid and poured himself a full glass, then retreated to his sofa. For hours he sat that way in the darkness, taking sips of the whiskey, grimacing at the bitter flavor, his tears silent companions to his grief.

CHAPTER EIGHTEEN

Near Bastogne, Belgium
Tuesday, December 19, 1944

Their Sherman rumbled on in a long line of tanks, moving slowly through the Belgian countryside toward Bastogne. The ditches on both sides of the highway were covered with discarded equipment, the remains of the retreating American divisions who had fled in a panic when the Germans mounted their attack.

Bonelli talked as they rolled along. "Listen up, folks. We got caught with our pants down. There's a batch of Germans out there. They came out of nowhere with tanks and troops. This forest was supposed to be too dense for tanks. Krauts are proving us wrong again."

"Didn't they come right through here in '41?" asked Wenzel.

"Search me. All I know is they have us on our heels. They've captured a whole bunch of us, and the rest scrammed. If we don't stop 'em, who knows how far they'll get. We could lose the whole thing and get our asses kicked back to England."

"What we got to fight them with?" asked Luke.

"Don't know for sure. Our division is sending tanks, but I don't know how many or how much infantry."

"We know any more about what we're facing, Sarge?" asked Hudson. The side of his face stuck out with the huge plug of tobacco in his mouth. He was using his helmet as a spittoon. "Just how many of these damned Germans are we looking at, Yank?"

"Intelligence is spotty at best. Looks like it could be the better part of twenty or more divisions up ahead. Lots of armor, too."

"Hell, I didn't think the Krauts had that many men left in their whole damned army," said Hudson. "The Russians on a holiday? What about all this talk of the war ending by Christmas?"

"Looks like Hitler still has some more surprises ahead for us. How we set for ammunition, Wenzel?"

"We're ten rounds short right now. Any chance we'll get more?"

"I wouldn't count on it. They're rushing us up here mighty fast. Someone's in a hell of a hurry. We'll have to make do with what we have."

"Hell of a thing. You don't bear hunt with half a bag of bullets," said Hudson. "What do we do if we run out, just yell at 'em?"

"We've plenty for now. We just have to hope for the best."

Luke felt unsettled about that. They all did. They had never gone into a fight without a full load of shells. Now they were down not only rounds for the main cannon, but also for all of their machine guns. They also were down to a day of K-rations and no cigarettes. Luke laughed to himself. He'd started smoking just in time to run out. He could feel a deep yearning for a cigarette right now. They would have to try to scrounge something up if they had a chance. Tobacco, food, and ammo.

"How much farther before we start running into Krauts?" asked Collins.

"I don't know yet," said Bonelli. "I wouldn't think it would be much longer."

As if to emphasize his words, the dull thud of artillery shells began to be heard. Luke looked at the sky through his scope. The damned snow just kept falling. That meant no air support and no airdrops. They were out here on their own for now.

Their unit rolled into a burned-out village with a regimental headquarters set up near the town. The tanks stopped, and the men were delighted to get a warm meal. They were served coffee and steaming bowls of oatmeal. Luke and his crewmates shivered as they ate. They hadn't been issued winter gear yet, and the temperature outside was brutal. Thank God the heating system inside the Sherman was functioning properly. The bad news was there were no extra cigarettes and no shells. They were able to replenish their machine gun ammo, so they would at least have a full load for their secondary guns. Luke managed to bum a handful of Lucky Strikes from a regimental guard. He immediately lit one up and breathed in deeply, enjoying the nicotine.

Bonelli came up. "Orders came in. We've gotta get going again now." The men groaned and reluctantly returned to the tank. Luke carefully tucked his five extra cigarettes away in his jacket and climbed back into the turret and down into his seat. A few minutes later they were rolling back down the road again.

The snow continued, coating the roads in a slippery mess. Fortunately, the tank treads gripped the ground and allowed the Shermans to move forward where trucks would have bogged down. The artillery fire increased as they got closer to the front. An hour later they pulled into a snow-filled field. Battalion headquarters was already there and had set up a command post. Sherman tanks were spread out around the post. Their crews were busy camouflaging them with branches and other materials and surrounding them with sandbags to create a protective ring around the command center. Bonelli ordered Luke and his crew to stop their tank but keep the engine running. He jumped out and was gone for a few minutes, then returned.

"Okay, boys. It looks like we're about it. They've rushed us up to help in the defense of this Belgian town, Bastogne. I guess there's a batch of roads that lead into this thing, and we need to help shore up the defenses. If the

Germans get it, it's gonna make a hell of a mess. Battalion told me there's panzers everywhere. They keep coming in from every direction. The town's off that way." Bonelli gestured to the north. "Our orders are to dig in and support the infantry—and stop the damn tanks from taking the town."

"What kind of infantry we got out there?" asked Hudson.

"Airborne, I guess. Shoved up here last minute just like we did. The 101st, I heard."

"Well, at least we got some decent boys to fight with," said Collins. "I'd hate to defend this place with a bunch of greenies."

Luke agreed. The airborne troops had a reputation as good fighters. He remembered they had parachuted into Normandy before the landings began on D-Day and held their own for days until the beachheads were established. They had also parachuted into Holland and caught hell from the Germans when the Allied attack known as Operation Market Garden had gone belly up.

"Where are we headed then, Sarge?" asked Luke.

"Our platoon is going up the road a bit. We'll dig in behind some trees and sit tight."

The Sherman fired up again, and soon they were rolling back down the road, toward Bastogne. The tanks traveled for half an hour, then turned off the road to the right, behind a line of trees. They were waved in by infantrymen, and the tanks then broke into separate areas, rumbling up to the tree line into positions designated by the infantry. Luke and his crew shut down their machine and climbed out. Luke was shocked to see it was just their platoon of five tanks. Lieutenant Dempsey was already on the ground, shaking hands with a captain of airborne troops.

"Boy, are we glad to see you," said the captain.

"Likewise," said Dempsey. "What do we have in front of us?"

"A world of shit. Tanks and antitank guns. A ton of infantry. They're wearing white camouflage, hard as hell to see in this stuff. We don't know what units for sure, but there are a batch of them."

"Do you think we can hold the line?"

"We'll try, but hell if I know. I've got good boys in my company. Hell, the whole 101st is tough as nails. But they rushed us up here with half our supplies. We don't have any warm clothes or warm food. Medical supplies are almost nonexistent. So is artillery. You're about the only good news we've had so far. Any more coming behind you?"

"Not that I've heard of. I wouldn't count on it; that's for sure. I think we came to this party by ourselves, and we carried all the supplies we're gonna get."

"I hope you're wrong," said the captain. "But I'm afraid you're right."

"Anything more we can do to help?"

"Just having you here is a godsend. I'd have you help dig, but we need you boys in your machines. If the shells start falling, the worst that could happen would be having you caught out in the open; then we'd lose our only fire support. I wish I could offer you a hot meal, but all I have is K-rations, and not many of those."

"We were able to resupply a bit down the road," said Dempsey. "We've enough for now. We're going to prepare for what's coming. Holler if you need anything, or radio it in. We'll be awake and ready to fight, come what may." They shook hands.

The platoon returned to their vehicles. They turned on the Shermans periodically to fight the biting cold. Other than the sound of the tanks running, there was nothing to break up the deadly quiet, made more poignant by the falling snow, which sucked all sound out of the air. Even the artillery fire ceased. Whatever was coming their way, it hadn't come yet. When it did, Luke knew it might well be more than they could handle. Five Shermans against God knew what. They waited tensely in the snow, in the eerie calm.

～

Luke awoke abruptly to an explosion. He opened his eyes, jolted from a restless nap. He looked through his scope. It was dark. Flashes ignited all around him. Through the thin line of trees, he could see white forms advancing. German infantry. Their rifles sparked as they ran. Among them moved several German tanks, the biggest Luke had ever seen. Tigers, the monsters of German armor. Luke recalled from training that the Tiger sported a massive 88-millimeter gun that could shred a Sherman in a single shot. Their armor was so thick that they were known to take a dozen shots from a group of Shermans and keep on rolling.

"Get our machine started, Collins!" yelled Bonelli. He opened the top turret so he could man his gun. Bitter cold streamed in immediately. The Sherman sputtered and stalled. The engine wouldn't start.

"Collins, what's wrong?" screamed Bonelli. "Get that thing started now!"

Hudson was already blazing away with his machine gun. Shells landed around them. Luke looked through his scope again. He could see explosions hammering the foxholes. The company returned fire as best it could, but the shelling was intense. Luke focused on the enemy tanks. A shell exploded on the turret of one of the Tigers, but it kept moving forward as if bitten by a fly. The Tiger paused and fired. A massive detonation rocked the woods. One of their tanks had just died. Luke wondered which one. He couldn't see to his right or left. He prayed the men had escaped.

Finally, their Sherman sputtered into life. Luke moved the turret, looking for a target. He centered his sights on one of the Tigers, aiming for the treads. He depressed the firing pedal. The shot landed short! He saw the Tiger's turret wheeling in their direction.

"Wenzel, get that reload in!" he shouted.

The Tiger turret was pointed directly at them.

"Round in!" shouted Wenzel.

Luke fired. He saw the flash of the Tiger at the same moment. His round landed on the mark. The tread exploded, and the Tiger stopped. The German round landed short, showering the Sherman with harmless shrapnel that bounced off the armor. That was close. Luke breathed a sigh of relief. There was no time to celebrate. He looked back in his scope. He was shocked to see a dozen or more panzers rolling forward out of the mist.

"Sergeant!" he yelled. "Do you see what I'm seeing?"

"I do."

"We can't hold against that!"

"We've got to try, Luke. We can't retreat!"

"We have to! We won't make it five minutes!"

Bonelli popped his head in. Their eyes met. Luke saw the pain in his sergeant's eyes. He saw the fear. The sergeant reached out his hand and placed it on Luke's shoulder. He forced a smile. "It'll be okay, my friend. We have to try."

Luke was amazed and ashamed. Bonelli was so brave, so strong. He remembered when Bonelli had turned himself in all those years back for a transgression that he had committed. Luke was filled with love and respect. This was what Dempsey had meant. The moment when you had to be a man, a soldier. Luke tried to reach down inside himself. He wasn't sure he could ever be Bonelli, but he could try. He smiled back. "Yes, Sergeant." Bonelli stood back up. Luke could hear the machine gun above him resume. He turned quickly back to his scope, searching for targets.

"Collins, move us forward!" shouted Bonelli.

Luke felt the Sherman jerk into motion. He squinted in the scope as they moved toward the tree line. In front of him he could see the infantry battling away in their foxholes. What bravery to stay in those positions against this murderous fire. He raised his eyes, concentrating on the advancing enemy. The attack had bogged down midway through the clearing. The infantry was reforming around the Tigers. Luke took aim at another tread and fired. His shell exploded among the huddled Germans, killing a batch of them but appearing to do no damage to the tank. A shell exploded near them, shaking the Sherman and making it impossible for a moment to aim.

Bullets and shrapnel bounced off the exterior.

Luke blinked in a foggy daze. What had just happened? He heard intense ringing in his ears. He looked down and saw Collins, headless, his hands still clutching his instruments. A gaping hole had torn through the left side of the tank, killing their driver. Luke turned slowly, trying to move, trying to call out. The ringing in his ears nearly drove him mad. He saw Bonelli slumped against the back wall of the Sherman. Blood covered his chest and arms. His eyes were open but blank, staring. His mouth was wide in a silent scream. Hudson was still firing his weapon, apparently oblivious to what had happened around him. Wenzel looked stunned but didn't seem to be hurt.

"Hudson, take over the steering!" screamed Luke.

"What the hell for?" asked the Texan.

"Look!" Luke pointed at Collins.

Hudson glanced over and grimaced. "Oh, hell, Collins. Why'd you go and do that?"

Another shell rocked the Sherman but didn't break through. Luke screamed at Wenzel to load another round. He looked through his scope and saw the Tigers, rolling forward, ever closer. He fired another round and hit a tread, stopping another of the massive tanks. Two Tigers fired in return.

The Sherman exploded. Luke couldn't see. The roaring nearly drove him out of his skull. He couldn't feel anything but heat. There was fire everywhere. He opened his eyes, but his left one didn't seem to be working. He could see Wenzel, wounded, looking up at him, trying to say something to him. Luke felt the panic rising. He needed to get out. He looked down and saw Hudson, wounded, his left hand missing. There was fire all around them. He could feel his skin starting to scorch and peel. He turned for the turret and started to climb out. Something stopped him. He turned back and saw his friends in their tank, suffering.

Luke knew this was another moment of truth. His last moment. He hesitated for a second and then reached out, grabbing Hudson's good hand. He pulled with all his strength and drew his friend past him. In a few agonizing moments Hudson scrambled out the turret. Luke screamed. The fire burned his legs. He looked down, horrified. His trousers were on fire. His boots were melting. He turned to Wenzel. He could see the fear on his friend's face. Luke reached down through the pain and pulled Wenzel up and out of the tank. The fire was unbearable as the flames licked Luke's waist. Wenzel looked down and with both arms reached out to Luke. Luke grabbed his hands and felt himself pulled out of the tank. His mouth formed screams, but he couldn't hear anything.

Luke found himself in hell. There was fire everywhere. The trees that had stood in front of him were mostly down and burning. The dead lay everywhere. His entire platoon of tanks was knocked out and smoking. The Tigers were still coming, although there were only half a dozen left. The remaining Allied infantry were still in their foxholes, maintaining their position, firing away with their rifles. They would be overrun any moment. Luke hit the ground, lying in the snow. He felt Wenzel's hands on him, covering his legs in snow, trying to extinguish the fire that still burned his legs. He could see the private's mouth moving, but no words were coming out.

Luke was dragged backward, with Wenzel following behind. He slid in the snow, but he felt nothing. His legs were a charred mess, the pants burned away and the skin a charcoal black. He still felt no pain. He was laid down. He looked up at the sky. Snow was still falling. Medics poured a white powder all over the wounds. He was given a shot that made him sleepy. He floated between consciousness and oblivion. He looked to his right to see more Shermans rolling forward past the aid station. Reinforcements were coming up. There was a chance they might hold the position after all. A miracle. He thought of Bonelli and Collins, both dead. But Hudson and Wenzel were alive; at least they had been a few minutes ago. They had taken out a few Tigers. *He* had. With a Sherman! They might stop the advance! He couldn't believe it. Even more miraculously, he had been part of it. He had stayed and fought with his friends. He had sacrificed to save his crew. Luke closed his eyes, strangely contented. He could sleep now. His job was done.

∿

"Luke." Luke heard the whisper of his name. He fought the groggy sleep, trying to open his eyes. He felt himself sinking again.

"Luke." There it was again. Luke fought harder and opened his lids. He was staring at the top of a tent. His mind was in a fog. He looked around slowly to his right and then to his left. Lieutenant Dempsey was in the cot next to him, his face cut and covered in dirt.

"You made it," said the lieutenant.

"For now," Luke managed.

"We stopped them. I heard we stopped them after all."

Luke breathed deeply. They had accomplished their mission. "We lost Bonelli and Collins."

"I know," said Dempsey.

"Hudson and Wenzel made it out, though."

Dempsey's face darkened. "Not Hudson. He caught one outside the tank."

"How about Wenzel?"

"He made it. He's wounded, but the doctor said he's going to pull through just fine."

"How about you?" asked Luke.

"Leg's gone. Right one. I'm going to make it, but the war's over for me."

Luke smiled. "You'll be going home."

"So will you," said Dempsey. Luke could see in his eyes that the lieutenant was lying. He didn't need that confirmation. He remembered his wounds. Over half his body was burned. He didn't have long.

"I'm going home all right, but not on this earth."

Dempsey watched him for a moment. "I guess not. You did good, kid. Best I've seen. Bonelli would be proud of you. I'm proud of you. You shot the hell out of those Tigers. With a Sherman! And you saved Wenzel. He's going home alive because of you. You've become a man of honor and respect. I will never forget you."

Luke smiled at his commander. "You made me the man I am. I owe you everything."

"No, you did this. I just gave you a little push along the way. The rest was up to you."

Luke lay back again, too exhausted to continue. He closed his eyes. He saw Snohomish clearer than he had in years. He imagined his dad and Mary, waiting at the kitchen table at breakfast, a worried look on their faces when he returned from a night on the town. He remembered his friends, the trouble they got into, the old high school . . .

Luke felt himself moving, lifted onto a stretcher and carried into another tent. A doctor hovered over him. "Don't worry. We're going to operate on you," he said. "We'll be putting you under soon. Don't sweat it, kid. You'll come out of this fine."

Why did they all want to lie to him? Luke knew the truth. He thought he would be afraid, but he wasn't. Finally, in the end, he had done his duty. He had sacrificed himself for others. They had held the line. He had saved Wenzel. A nurse placed a mask over his face. She smiled down with understanding eyes—a little sadness in them. He winked back with his good eye before the darkness washed over him.

He dreamed in peace. Wandered in his past, in his beautiful town, among his friends and crew. He dreamed of Matthew, who stood with a smiling face, surrounded by light, his arms held out to greet him.

CHAPTER NINETEEN

Snohomish, Washington
Saturday, December 23, 1944

Jonathan walked through his hardware store, filling out price tags and tying them with string onto pieces of equipment. He had decided to try selling the items at auction himself and pay out Max with the money. That way he would get the maximum amount in the sale. Jonathan had inquired about a potential purchase of the whole business, but nobody in town knew of anyone who was able to take on the store, particularly with its back debts. So he had settled on liquidating the inventory to pay out the balance. To work more efficiently, he had closed down for the week. The only interruptions were from friends knocking on the door, asking why he was closed. He tried his best to answer their questions cheerfully, but he wasn't sure he was doing particularly well.

As Jonathan worked away, he stopped periodically and took a small sip from a bottle he had tucked away in one of the aisles. This was his third bottle of whiskey in a week. He didn't want to think about things anymore—didn't want to consider the future or the struggles of the past few years. He just wanted to get through this inventory liquidation and find a new job. He promised himself that he would take stock of the future after he was settled in with new employment. Over the past week he didn't even have Mary for company very much. She was out almost every evening with Bill now. Jonathan was happy for her and hopeful for her future, although he admitted selfishly that Mary's change in circumstances couldn't have come at a worse time. Not only was she gone when he needed her, but her newfound love poured gasoline on the fire of his own emotions.

He had missed church this past Sunday, for the first time in so many years he couldn't even remember when. He recalled vaguely that he had skipped worship a time or two when things were at their worst for Helen, but this was the first time without a real excuse. Jonathan just couldn't face his friends right now, and he was terrified that Sarah might bring Stan to a service. He wasn't ready to see her again.

The worst part of all of this was there was nobody he could talk to. Jonathan had always been so strong, so faithful; he was far too embarrassed to admit what he was going through emotionally. He knew the pain would fade eventually. It always did. He just needed to keep his head down and get through this inventory sale. At least that gave him something to do each day.

For some reason Jonathan feared for Matthew so much more deeply right now. He worried that he had deluded himself this whole time, that his son was dead and he would never hear anything about him. If so, this war had taken nearly everything from him. His store was gone. His son was gone. Sarah had come into his life and then left again, causing only pain and anguish. Mary was divorced. Luke was in danger.

Jonathan took another nip from the bottle. He no longer grimaced at the sharp flavor. He had never drunk hard liquor before in his whole life, except a sip or two out of politeness. He knew plenty of people who did so regularly. Before, he'd disapproved, although he'd kept his thoughts to himself. Now he understood. He needed the dulling of his senses and the light euphoria to pull him through this time. *Only until the store sells,* he promised himself.

There was a knock at the door. Jonathan looked up. Mary and Bill were there, waving at him. He felt a little warmth when he looked in his daughter's eyes. She was so happy. He was glad for her. He let them in, and she gave him a big hug. He shook Bill's hand.

"How are you today, Father?" asked Mary. "Are you making progress?"

"Things are going fine enough. It's quite a bit of work going through all these things."

"Do you have a buyer yet?"

Jonathan grunted. "Doesn't look like I'm going to have one. Much of this stuff will fetch a decent price at auction, though. I'll be able to get out from under this lease at least."

"You should've done this years ago. You've worked so hard, and this store has never given you back what you put into it."

"True enough." She was right, after all, but this was *his store.* He was his own boss, beholden to no one. He was about to lose that forever when he rejoined the ranks of the workers. He knew he would be just fine, but there was something he was giving up and would probably never regain again.

"Bill and I are going to ride the bus into Everett to Paine Field. They do fighter training out there. There are planes taking off and landing all the time, and practicing up in the air. They say it's quite a show if you get there at the right time."

Jonathan nodded. "I've heard that, too. Everett has many nice places to visit." He was thinking of another place in Mukilteo, and a warm afternoon long ago spent watching the water.

"Maybe you should come with us. This stuff can all wait a few hours."

Jonathan was tempted, but he shook his head. It was a struggle to come in here and face the end of his dreams, and he needed to get through it as quickly as possible. Getting away for a day would only delay the inevitable. "No, you two go on ahead and enjoy yourselves." He turned to Bill. "You take good care of Mary, you understand."

"I always will," Bill said. Jonathan saw his daughter blush at those words. They shook hands again, and Mary embraced him. Then she made a strange face.

"You go on ahead, Bill. I want to talk to my dad for one more minute."

After Bill left, Mary turned to him. "Father, have you been drinking?"

Jonathan felt hot shame. She must have smelled the alcohol on his breath. He didn't want to tell her, but he couldn't lie. "I've just had a sip to keep me going here and there. It's cold in here."

"You've been working here for years, and you've worked in far colder places than this. I've never known you to take a drink. What're you doing?"

"I'm doing fine, Mary. I just need to get through this inventory and get out of this store. Now that I know I can't keep it, I don't even want to be here anymore. Please don't be cross with me. It's only for a while longer."

Mary looked like she wanted to say more but must have changed her mind. "Please be careful, Father. There's so many people who ruin their lives with alcohol. I never imagined I would have to say something like this to you. Be careful."

Jonathan felt even more embarrassed, but he only nodded. Mary gave him another hug and then turned and left. He had disappointed her, probably for the first time in her life. He felt the guilt burn through him. He wished she hadn't come here today. Still, it wasn't the end of the world. He would be done with this in a few days, and then he'd never touch the stuff again. She'd see.

Jonathan went back to work, taking another sip out of the bottle before he began. He was working on the back wall that contained all the handsaws, hammers, and screwdrivers. He remembered fondly when he had designed this display, carefully measuring the spaces and then drilling in screws so that the various tools would hang in a pleasing way. This was one of the most difficult parts of his store to set up. He had been so happy then, with the whole future in front of him. He had imagined droves of daily customers, all his friends and family visiting him and buying their hardware from him. Things had started out that way. He had prospered, but then this war came. This damn war. He didn't swear any more than he had drank in the past, but the words were beginning to come into his mind more often now. Well, a little swearing never hurt anyone too much, either.

Jonathan heard another knock at the window on the front door. Mary must be back. How could he get anything done with all these interruptions? He hurried forward with a handful of tools, not paying attention. He placed the tools at the front counter and then looked up to see who it was. It wasn't Mary. He froze. Two uniformed men were at the door. One of them knocked again. He knew what they signified: Matthew. Matthew was dead. He had dreaded this moment for so long—prayed against it, refused to believe it might be possible. Now they were here to tell him his boy was gone forever.

He hesitated. He didn't want to go to the door, didn't want to face this. He felt a moment of wild hope; maybe they were at the wrong store. Maybe they were looking for directions, for another family.

He walked slowly to the front, reaching up a shaking hand to unlock the dead bolt. "Can I help you?" he heard himself say, his voice a dry, cracking whisper.

Both men looked uncomfortable and sad. They weren't here for someone else. They were here for him. He knew it. The older soldier, a first lieutenant, stepped forward. "I'm sorry to bother you, sir. Are you Jonathan Beecher?"

There was no doubt now. His boy was gone forever. "Yes, I am."

"Sir, I regret to inform you that your son Corporal Luke Beecher was killed in combat in Belgium on December 19, 1944, bravely serving his country."

Luke. He couldn't believe it. For some reason the thought that Luke could be dead hadn't entered his mind. Of course it wouldn't have been Matthew. His older son was a civilian contractor. They wouldn't have sent soldiers to tell him of Matthew's death, would they? For some reason this detail of protocol seemed terribly important right now. He couldn't understand how it could be Luke. He had always felt that Luke would be safe, that he would come out of the war all right. Luke always made it out of all his trouble.

"Sir, are you okay?"

Jonathan was a long way from okay, but that didn't matter. "Yes, I heard you. Do you know what happened?"

"I'm sorry, I don't." The soldier reached out and handed Jonathan a telegram. When he took it, both men stood at attention and saluted him. Jonathan nodded again and then stumbled in disbelief back into the store. Mary. The store. Sarah. Helen's death. Now he had lost a son. Luke was gone forever. His little boy. Jonathan found his whiskey and took a deep drink. Then he hurled the bottle against the tool wall, splattering liquor and glass all over. He fell to his knees, his eyes closed.

∾

Jonathan stayed that way for a good while. He felt the whiskey soaking his pants. He didn't care. He felt misery he had never known washing over him in cruel, sharp waves. A bottomless chasm opened in his heart. His problems from just a few hours before seemed trivial. Now he would happily take them all on and much more if he could just have his boy back.

He felt anger and a righteous fury at God. What had he ever done to deserve all of this? He had gone to church every Sunday. He had prayed multiple times a day. He had lived his life devoutly, following his promises. He had given up the love of his life for that faith. His reward for all of this? He had lost everything. God had abandoned him and didn't care. Jonathan rose to his feet and stumbled into his office, retrieving another bottle from a drawer. He cracked it open and took a deep drink, choking on the fiery liquid as he gulped it down.

He had wasted his life, he realized. Faith and church and God had been worthless. Was there even a supreme father? Who would let all this suffering happen? *The world's burning, and you don't give a damn. If you're even out there.* Jonathan took another deep drink, trying to wash away the pain, trying to understand. He couldn't drive away the lancing sting, no matter how much he tried.

He knew he should be doing something different. He should go see his friends, go see his pastor. He didn't want to. He was tired of trying to see the positive side of everything and believing that things would surely get better. They weren't going to, after all. Things would be this bad for good, maybe even worse. He still had another son out there, and he hadn't heard from him all this time. Luke's death made Matthew's future so much more uncertain. Jonathan had only one son left now, and he knew he couldn't survive another loss.

All afternoon and into the evening, Jonathan sat in his office, drinking out of his bottle and brooding over the future, and over the past. Finally, he was feeling a little of the numbness set in. He looked at the bottle. It was more than half gone. He felt tired, but the anger kept him awake. He kept going over everything in his mind, looking for some glimmer of hope. He felt only the ash of his life, burned away.

Jonathan rose and stumbled out of the office, taking the bottle with him. He walked unsteadily to the door and then out the front, neglecting to lock it. Who cared what happened to the inventory anymore? Let them come and take it. He turned left and walked as quickly as he was able, trying to avoid anyone that he knew. He took another quick turn and walked past Second Street and up Avenue B, fleeing the populated downtown. He couldn't stand talking to anyone right now. He took drinks of the bottle as he went. As he walked without purpose, the darkness was his friend, hiding him from others.

Jonathan couldn't think straight. One thought kept wandering through his mind: Should he take his own life? He mulled it over. No. As desperate as he felt, he knew that was never a path he would take. He would endure this devastating world to the end.

He felt cramps in his stomach. He was going to be sick. He ran into the bushes of one of the big Victorian houses on Avenue B. He fell down and retched, his stomach heaving. He heard a yell from the dwelling. Someone must have seen him. He stood up as quickly as he could and lurched away into the night.

He kept roaming for a long time. He wasn't sure why. Despite the fire in his gut, he kept at his bottle until he realized he had drunk it all. There was a roaring in his ears. He was having a difficult time focusing, remembering where he was. At last he decided where he wanted to go, and shambled off in that direction.

Jonathan found the house he was looking for eventually. He wasn't sure how long it had taken him. All he knew was he needed to be here. He stumbled up the pathway, falling one time hard on the pavement. He looked at his hands: they were cut and scratched from catching himself. He didn't feel any pain anymore. He crawled to the front door and knocked over and over, using the knob to drag himself back up. The door opened. It was Sarah.

She was surprised to see him. "Jonathan . . . what are you doing here?" She looked more closely. "What's wrong with you? Are you drunk?"

"I've had a little to drink," he said, stumbling on some of the words. "Can I come in?"

"I don't think that would be right. What's going on with you?"

"It's Luke. He's . . . he's dead."

"Oh, no! Oh, I'm so sorry. Please come in. I didn't mean to be rude. It's just . . ."

"I know what it is. You don't want Stan to think anything bad. Or the neighbors."

"Let's not worry about that right now. Please come in."

Jonathan stumbled past her and sat down hard on her sofa. The room was spinning, and his stomach was starting to hurt. He'd never been truly drunk like this before. Sarah sat across from him on a chair.

"Tell me what happened," she said.

"I was working on my inventory." He fought to keep his voice steady. "I have to sell my store. You probably don't even know that, or care for that matter."

Sarah looked more concerned. "Of course I care, Jonathan. I'm so sorry."

"Well, anyway, there was a knock at the door, and two soldiers were there. For some reason, all I could think of was Matthew. But then they told me Luke was dead. I never even thought of him." Jonathan buried his face in his hands, sobbing in his grief.

"Jonathan, I'm so sorry," Sarah repeated. She moved over and sat next to him on the sofa, placing a hand on his shoulder. They sat that way for a long time, talking about Luke and the past. She changed the subject.

"What happened with the store?"

He explained about the deal with Max and the lease. Sarah already knew he had fallen behind, but she didn't know he had never caught up.

"I had no idea, Jonathan. I'm surprised Max would pull that. What's wrong with him? The two of you have always been friends."

"I can't blame him. I should never have gone into debt. I promised myself I wouldn't do it, and then I gave in to weakness. I'm just getting what I deserve."

"Don't say that. You don't *deserve* bad things to happen to you. You're one of the best men I've ever known, maybe *the* best man."

He looked up at her. What a kind thing to say. Sarah had always made him feel so much better about things. She was smiling at him with understanding. With encouragement. She was so beautiful. She was what he had always wanted. All the pain of this past year without her welled up again inside him. He felt the biting agony.

"I've lost everything. Everything. I've spent my whole life living in faith, and I've still lost everything." He raised his hand to his forehead. "God abandoned me, and so did you."

"I didn't *abandon* you, Jonathan, and neither did God. You know that isn't fair. I wanted you more than anything, more than anyone. You chose not to accept me."

"You could have remained my friend. You left me when I needed you. You knew about my promise, and then when I needed you most, you left me for good. Now you've replaced me with someone else. You're going to marry Stan someday. How could you do that to me? I still want you so badly."

She was quiet for a moment and didn't respond.

"Why couldn't you remain my friend?" he continued. "I loved you so much, and you turned me away. Why do you need another man in your life now? You've betrayed me for someone else. I've lived with my sacrifice; why couldn't you sacrifice for me in return? We were meant to be together, even if we could only be friends."

"Jonathan, you're not being fair. Please stop. I deserved more than that. You know that. We both realized our relationship had reached a point where we couldn't go back. You can't blame me for something we both knew was true."

He leaned in and kissed her on the lips, kissed her deeply. She tried to pull away, but he held her head. She shoved him back.

"Jonathan, stop it. You're drunk. You can't do that to me anymore. I'm with someone else now."

Those words stung him deeply. He knew what she was saying was true, but having her voice it out loud cut him so much more profoundly. "You could have been with me. You should have stayed with me."

"There was no *us*, Jonathan. You made that choice. I never wanted our relationship to end. But that's all in the past now."

"I love you, Sarah. You shouldn't have left me." He tried to kiss her again. She slapped him hard across the face. Jonathan reeled back in surprise and pain. She stood up and moved away. What was he doing? He felt shame again, then a wave of nausea. He dashed for her bathroom and vomited in the toilet. He could barely keep his balance. He threw up over and over, his eyes stinging, his stomach on fire. He felt the dizziness overwhelming him.

He laid his head down on the bathroom floor and looked up at the ceiling. The light above him was spinning violently in a circle. He could feel blood on his lip. Sarah appeared above him; she was spinning, too. He could see the hurt and concern in her eyes. There were tears coming down her cheeks. "Why did you come here tonight, Jonathan? Why did you do this to me? I'm sorry I hit you, but you don't have the right to do that to me. Not anymore." She reached down and placed a blanket on him. He could see the misery in her face.

She shut off the light and left him. The spinning tore at his mind. He was sick again. He had never felt more miserable. He thought of Luke again. His wonderful boy, gone forever. What had become of his life? Jonathan sat his head back down and wept, letting the darkness mercifully overcome him.

❧

The room still spun. Jonathan could feel the circles spinning in his head. He opened an eyelid a crack, and stabbing light assaulted him. His head was a maelstrom of pain. He sensed a pillow under his head, and his back lay against something soft. He waited for a few more minutes, then opened his eyes again. The spinning continued but seemed to be slowing down a little. He was surprised to see he was on his sofa, in his own house. Why did that surprise him? He tried to focus, to remember what had happened the night before.

Luke. His son was dead. Jonathan remembered the visit from the soldiers with sudden, terrible clarity. His heart sank again. His boy was gone. He remembered his despair yesterday and felt it again. What had he done after that? He remembered drinking, more than he had ever drank in his entire life. He had left his store and walked around Snohomish. How many people had seen him? How embarrassing. He had drunk the entire bottle. Then he had gone . . . Oh, no! Jonathan remembered. He had gone to Sarah's. He had poured his heart out to her. He had kissed her. She had slapped him in return. He felt the hot shame burning through him. How could he have allowed himself to act so stupidly? He couldn't believe it. What a fool. He would have to apologize to her immediately.

He tried to rise but sank back into the cushions. He felt the nausea again, the swimming and spinning. He was sick. He felt worse than he had ever felt in his life. He would have to wait. Maybe Sarah would come over and check on him and he could apologize. Then the thought struck him. He remembered falling asleep on her bathroom floor. Yet here he was at home. How had he ended up here? He had no memory of walking home. He wasn't sure how he would have even moved.

He heard footsteps. Mary must be here. Had she been involved in moving him last night? That would be even worse. She had warned him yesterday about drinking. He looked up. Mary wasn't there after all—it was Pastor Miles. His friend carried in a tray of toast and a cup of coffee. He looked down on Jonathan with a mixture of sorrow, pity, and understanding.

"Tough night, wasn't it?"

Jonathan groaned, closing his eyes again and letting his head sink back on the pillow. "Maybe the worst night of my life. How did you get here?"

"Instead of *how*, you might ask *how long*. I've been here all night."

"What are you talking about?"

"Sarah called me late and told me you were at her house, passed out. I assured her that could not be possibly the case, so imagine my surprise when I drove over and she proved me a liar. Then she told me about Luke. I'm so sorry for your loss, Jonathan."

"Where's Mary?"

"I sent her over to my house. Mrs. Miles is taking care of her. She knows about Luke. I didn't know if I should tell her, but you're burdened enough right now. I thought I would take one over for you. She's distraught but even more worried about you. I told her you would be all right, that I would take care of you."

Jonathan was relieved that Mary hadn't seen him like this. He was so sick the grief felt distant and dull. "Thank you, Pastor. When I heard the news, I didn't believe it at first. I'm still not sure I believe it now."

His friend set the tray down on the coffee table in front of Jonathan and handed him a piece of dry wheat toast. Jonathan's stomach still felt unsettled, but he took a little bite. The bread tasted wonderful, and he took another bite. He finished it quickly and then had another piece. They were quiet while he ate. When he finished two full slices, his stomach felt better. He was able to sit up, although his head still throbbed.

"You missed church last week, my friend. Something I didn't think would happen unless you were dead or nearly so. Would you like to talk about things?"

"I don't think I'm ready."

"I know it can feel that way. If you don't want to now, I understand, but I think the sooner we get this all out, the better."

Jonathan didn't want to talk, but Pastor Miles was one of his closest friends. He started with a few small things, and then the whole story stormed out in a flood: the impending loss of his store, his fears for Matthew, his concern for Mary, his loss of Luke, his loss of Sarah. He found it difficult, but he even talked about his loss of faith. "I feel abandoned by God. I've worked hard and lived my life the right way for so long, and everything has been taken away from me. I've lost my way."

"You haven't lost your faith, Jonathan. You've just misplaced it. No wonder, with all you've been through. God didn't promise us an easy journey—even for the faithful. He promised to love us and care for us along the way. He gave us friends like me to share the road with. We come to this world, we suffer, we die. Our path is easy or hard. Our only choice is how we respond.

"You're one of the most faithful men I've ever met. You have inspired everyone around you with your joy, your devotion, your kindness, your hard work. You find yourself in your darkest hour now. God is still here with you, and so is this town, our people, your friends. You are beloved, Jonathan. We will all get through this with you, together."

"I have guilt, Pastor. Terrible guilt about something. I am grieving for my son, but in the midst of all of this, I find myself even more in pain about Sarah. I don't understand how she could have come into my life and brought such light, such joy, only to be taken away from me." Jonathan told his friend the whole story about Sarah—their time together, his promise to Helen, and the end of their relationship. "I've tried this past year to forget, to live with the comfort of my commitment and my oath. I thought I was over her, that I had moved on. Then I saw her with Stan. I felt terrible jealousy, terrible anger. I know it's not fair, but I don't want her to be with anyone else, despite my promise, despite my limitations."

"I have never understood that promise."

"What do you mean?" Jonathan was surprised. This was his pastor. Surely if anyone would support his decision, it was this man.

"Jonathan, this won't be easy for you to hear, but I didn't think much of Helen. Frankly I don't know anyone who did. She was your wife, and I took the both of you part and parcel. We marry, and we live our lives, but she was a cold and selfish woman. More than one person came to me and complained about her. People didn't understand how you could put up with her. If anything, they admired you more for your patience."

"Who came and talked to you about Helen?"

"Matthew for one, and plenty of others. Does that surprise you? All of your children struggled with her—even Luke. Perhaps Mary least so; she was still young when her mother died. Matthew couldn't stay in this town with her. She was jealous of him. She belittled him when you weren't around. She preferred Luke to him; everyone knew that. You would think Luke would have responded to that attention, but he seemed to understand her game. He spoke to me about her, too. They all had complex feelings for their mother, and they were concerned for you. They never wanted you to know how they really felt. I've kept that secret all these years, but I think it's time that you know the truth."

Jonathan was stunned. He knew Helen had been hard to live with, but she had been his wife. She was the mother of his children. "Why didn't you tell me before?"

"There never seemed to be a reason, although when you and Sarah stopped spending time together, I was sorely tempted to let the cat out of the bag. If I'd known more about things, I would have told you right then and there. Sarah filled me in on the whole story last night."

"There's nothing that can be done about it. I love Sarah. I always have, and I always will. But I made my promise before God."

"I don't know what to make of that oath. I never have. Helen had a right to expect you would be her husband. You made your pledge before God on your wedding day. I don't condone divorce, sorry to say, even in Mary's case, at least until every other possibility is explored. Spending your life with Helen was your commitment, but it was a selfish and unfair act for her to bind you for the rest of your life after she fell ill."

"Are you saying the promise wasn't proper?"

"A promise is a promise. I don't know if I can say it was a sin for her to force it, but I can't say it wasn't, either. Life sometimes is complicated like that, Jonathan, and even a pastor doesn't know what to do. Just this once I'm going to step in where maybe I shouldn't. I think your oath is invalid. I think you're free to act how you wish. If I'm wrong, I pray that the burden of sin will fall on me, not on you."

"Can you take on that responsibility? Is that allowed?"

"I don't know, Jonathan. But I just did. I will tell you what I think you should do. I think you should lie here for the rest of the day and recover. When you're done, you should take a bath and put on your best clothes. Then you ought to drive over to Sarah's house and sweep her off her feet, and never let her out of your sight again. It's your life, of course, but if I were you, I wouldn't let another day pass by without her."

Jonathan's mind reeled. Did his pastor really have the power to absolve him? He didn't know, but he felt the excitement rising in him. He could be free of the promise. He could be with Sarah. Was it too late? He had been such a fool. He had let the best thing in his life get away from him. In the midst of that, he had abandoned God. No, Pastor Miles was right—he'd just misplaced Him. He smiled.

"There's the grin I was looking for. You are a great man, Jonathan. You've had a tough road these past years. We have a lot of grief before us about Luke. I'll walk down that road with you, but there's another person who wants to walk with you as well, and you need to go get her before you miss your chance."

"Thank you, Pastor. Thank you, my friend."

Pastor Miles grasped his hand. He reached down and embraced Jonathan, holding him close for a few moments. "I will be with you every step of the way. Now get some rest, and go find some happiness."

His friend departed. Jonathan lay back on the sofa, still sick, still exhausted. He was shocked by what Pastor Miles had said about Helen. Over the years many people had hinted at their feelings, and a few had come right out and said them. Even his own children had complained about her, although he'd rarely allowed them to go very far. Helen had been difficult. But she had been his wife. He had honorably lived with her, loved her as best he could, and done his best to live with her shortcomings.

What about Luke? He knew his grief was just beginning. He wished he could see him now, talk to him, tell him how proud he was and how much he loved him. There would be plenty of time to grieve for his boy.

Sarah. His Sarah. He closed his eyes and thought of his beautiful friend. He wished he could rush out and see her now, but he was too ill. He needed to sleep, to recover from the poison he had drunk. Tonight he would do just what the pastor had suggested. He would go, and he would finally have his girl. For the rest of his life. The thoughts of her whirled around his mind as he drifted off to a happy rest.

CHAPTER TWENTY

Snohomish, Washington
Sunday, December 24, 1944

Jonathan slept the entire day. He awoke to darkness, surprised at how long he'd been out. He arose cautiously. The spinning and nausea were gone, although a headache remained. He walked into the kitchen and turned on a light, checking the time. Six o'clock. Not too bad. There was still plenty of time to get ready and go over to Sarah's. A sudden thought crossed his mind: What if Stan was there? It was Christmas Eve, he realized. He decided it didn't matter. He had waited for Sarah long enough; he wasn't going to wait any longer. If Stan was there, he would forge forward regardless, and trust God.

He rushed upstairs. Mary wasn't home; she must have stayed at the Mileses' house while he slept today. He was glad. He needed to apologize to her about his actions. Luke. He had forgotten about Luke. Mary would be crushed. How could he go over to Sarah's when Mary was dealing with the death of her brother? How had he become so selfish? He heard Pastor Miles's voice in his head. His friend had already talked to Mary about Luke. He wanted Jonathan to take care of Sarah first. Jonathan decided to see Sarah, and then he would come home and drive over to pick up Mary.

He stepped into the bath. The water was hot, almost too much so, but he stepped in anyway, relishing the heat. He eased himself in and then turned off the water, leaning his head back against the tub and luxuriating in the warmth. He lay that way for a long time, half asleep again, dreaming of what the evening could bring, thinking over the future. At last he roused himself and picked up the soap. He took a towel in his other hand and scrubbed his entire body thoroughly, then lathered his hands and washed his hair. Fifteen minutes later he was fully dressed and combing his hair. He brushed his teeth several times, gargling to remove the stale taste in his mouth.

Jonathan looked in the mirror. He looked about as good as he was ever going to. He was no longer young. There were wrinkles now. Streaks of gray ran through his hair. A moment of doubt ran through his mind. What if Sarah didn't want him anymore? What if she chose Stan over him? He would have to do his best and leave all of this in God's hands. He whispered a prayer of hope and also asked forgiveness for his brief loss of faith.

Jonathan stepped out into the darkness to walk to Sarah's. He had considered driving, but something seemed proper about making this pilgrimage on foot. He also hoped the crisp December air would clear the remaining cobwebs from his head. He traversed the few blocks to Sarah's house in a matter of minutes. He could feel his heart racing faster as he drew closer. *Don't worry,* he told himself. *It's only your whole life, after all.*

Finally, he arrived. There were lights on in the house. Sarah was home. He strained to see if he could make out anyone else inside, but he could not. He was prepared for Stan to be there, but he hoped he wouldn't be. He would like to face Sarah alone. What about her daughter? He hadn't seen Margaret last night—at least he didn't remember seeing her. What if she had witnessed all of his actions? A new thing to worry about. Well, he would know soon enough. Jonathan walked up to the door and knocked gently. He heard footsteps, and the door opened. It was Sarah.

Her face didn't register any surprise—as if she'd expected him. For an apology, he realized. "Hello."

"Hello," she said.

"May I come in?"

"I don't know. Are you sober tonight?"

"I think you know I am."

"I would expect so. But I've never seen you act like you did last night, so I don't know what to expect anymore."

"Are you alone?"

"For now."

"What does that mean?"

"Fortunately, Margaret has stayed with my mother this past week. Or she would have witnessed your little scene last night."

"Who's coming over then?" He was sure he already knew.

"Stan is picking me up. He made dinner for us tonight. He'll be here at any time."

"Can I at least come in for a minute?"

She hesitated again. "Sure. But only for a bit."

He stepped into the house. He half expected to see a mess from last night, but everything was clean and tidy. Sarah was an excellent housekeeper and would never have allowed things to remain a mess all day. "Your house is all in order."

"No thanks to you. Really, Jonathan, I would never have expected you to act that way. I know you've been through a lot, and this news about Luke is the worst possible. But I would never have expected you to be drunk."

"I'm so sorry about that. You're right, I've never drank until the past week. Losing the store has been tough on me. That and . . . well, that and other things have made life almost unbearable. I don't know what happened, but I needed something to drive away the pain."

"You made a fool out of yourself last night. You placed me in a terrible position. You were unfair to me, and you took advantage of my feelings for you."

"I know that, and I'm here to apologize. I was wrong in everything I said and *did* last night. That's not all I've been wrong about."

She looked at him closely. "What do you mean?"

"Sarah, I love you . . ."

"Yes, we went through this last night. Please. I appreciate your apology, but I can't . . ."

"Please listen to me. I need to say this." Jonathan took a step toward her. She backed away. He felt a pit in his stomach. She was afraid of him now. He almost gave up and left, but he knew he had to tell her what he wanted.

"Go ahead. But you can say it from over there."

"I was wrong. I was wrong a year ago to allow my promise to Helen to get in the way of my happiness. You are the most important thing in the world to me. I want to spend the rest of my life with you, and I don't care anymore who knows or who cares."

Sarah looked confused. "What are you talking about, Jonathan? Are you still drunk? Don't say these things to me." He could see her growing hurt and confusion.

"Please, I'm trying to explain. I've come to realize that the promise I made to Helen was wrong. It was wrong for her to ask it of me. I don't know; maybe it was the right thing at the time, but then you came into my life. For whatever reason, we became friends and then we became more. At that point, I thought I was having courage by drawing a line. I thought that's what I was supposed to do. I realize now I made the biggest mistake of my life then. I realize that I want you, that you are the light of my life on this earth. I believe that God will understand this, that he blesses us." Jonathan fell to his knees. "I want you forever, my dearest. I want you to be my wife. To spend the rest of your life with me."

Sarah was quiet another moment and then took a step farther back. He could see her face redden. "How dare you!" she screamed. "How dare you leave me alone for a year and then wait for me to finally be happy before you come back and do this! You broke my heart. I cried until I couldn't see anymore. For months I hoped you would do what you're doing now, that you would show up at this door and beg me to marry you. I waited and waited, and all I ever saw was that lonely door. Finally, almost a year later, I woke up one day and felt I could go on without thinking of you every minute, without crying myself to sleep." Her voice broke, and her hand clutched a table. She hesitated and drew herself up.

"Then Stan came along. He has taken care of me, treated me well. He had no restrictions, no loyalties to anyone but me. Now you want to swoop back in and have me give him up? Give up everything? For what? So you can change your mind again? I don't believe you, Jonathan. I don't believe you." She burst into tears and slumped onto her sofa. He tried to step forward to comfort her, but she motioned him away.

"Sarah, please."

"Please, what? Please pretend this last year didn't happen? Please forgive the pain you caused me, the hurt you've caused Margaret? Why are you here, Jonathan? How could you do this to me? You could have at least had the decency to stay away, to let me finally live my own life."

"I want that for you. I want a life with us *together*. I'm ready to accept that."

Sarah looked up at him, her eyes bleary and red. "Well, that's just fine, Jonathan Beecher, but you're too late. I waited long enough, and you never came. I can't go back to that place anymore. I'm sorry, but I can't do it."

He tried to take a step closer again, but she put both her hands out, and he stopped. "What do you want me to do?" he asked.

"I want you to let me go. I want you to let me be happy. I want you to be happy, too, Jonathan, but it's too late for us. There is too much pain, too much harm. I hope we can be friends again someday. Not like it was, but at least able to see each other at church, to be happy for one another. For now, I need you to leave me alone. Leave Stan and me alone. I can't have you showing up here anymore. I'm sorry, but I just can't."

Jonathan didn't want to let her say this, but he had pushed as hard as he could. If he hadn't tried to kiss her last night, he felt he could try to stay longer, to fight for her. But he had clearly frightened her, and he would not let her be afraid of him. He had been true to himself. He had told her how he felt. He owed her even more. If this was what she wanted, he would honor it, regardless of the pain.

"I'm sorry, dear," he said. "I'm so sorry it's come to this. I don't want to do what you're asking, but I understand. I made my decisions a year ago. I'm forever sorry how I have hurt you. I would love to make it up to you by spending the rest of my life with you, but if that's not what you want, then I will do the next best thing. I will go away and leave you alone."

Sarah didn't look up again. She was dabbing her tears with a blanket. "Thank you," she whispered, her voice broken and quiet.

There was a knock at the door. Jonathan felt his heart sink. Now it was too late. There was nothing more he could say. He waited a second more, but she didn't speak again. He turned and walked to the door, opening it up to find Stan on the porch, flowers in his hand. His face registered surprise to see Jonathan standing there.

"Take the best of care of her," said Jonathan. "I had my chance, and I let her go. I'm a fool. I hope you are not." He brushed past Stan without waiting for a response, and retreated into the darkness.

He walked all around the dark residential streets of Snohomish that night, not returning to his house for an hour or more. He was terribly sad but also satisfied. He felt no inclination to drink again—he knew he never would. No matter what, he was the Lord's and the Lord was his. He had said his piece to the love of his life. She had rejected him, but he understood why. Now he had a daughter to take care of. He must get through the loss of Luke. He must sell his business and find a decent job. He must live his life, in faith, in his beautiful little town.

∿

Eventually Jonathan headed home. He had allowed himself a little time to experience the loss of Sarah. He would need far more, he knew, but for now this was enough. He had other responsibilities. He needed to pick up Mary. He hoped she was still at Pastor Miles's house. At least they would know where she was if she had left. He hurried his pace and within a few minutes was back at his front door. He unlocked it and walked into the darkness after closing and locking the door behind him.

"Hello, Jonathan." He was shocked by the voice. He turned around. There were no lights on. He strained to see into the living room in the darkness. He couldn't make out the figure, but he knew the voice well.

"Hello, Robert."

"Where's my Mary?"

Jonathan stepped cautiously away from the window and into the darkness. From the sound of the voice, he guessed Robert was sitting on his sofa. "What are you doing here?"

"I'm the one with the questions. Where's your daughter?"

"She's not home."

"I guessed that. Is my wife out with her new boyfriend?"

Jonathan took another step into the living room. "I don't know who you mean, but Mary's not your wife. Not anymore."

"She'll always be my wife. And you know exactly who I mean. That little bastard, Bill. I've followed the two of them all over town. She thinks she's sneaky, but she's not. They've been holding hands, and he's even kissed her a time or two. Pretty poor behavior with another man's wife, wouldn't you say?"

Jonathan took another cautious step into the room.

"That's about enough of that," said Robert.

Jonathan heard fumbling in the darkness. A light flashed on. He took in the scene quickly. Robert was sitting on the sofa, one hand on the lamp next to him. A gun rested in his lap, and his other hand rested on it, caressing it.

"Now, what are you doing with that?" Jonathan asked.

Robert looked down. "What? This? This is my service revolver. A .38 special. A police officer is never without it. You have one yourself, as I seem to recall from the last time we were together."

"What are you doing with it in my house?"

Robert looked up with a sly grin. "Well, there's an answer to that question, too, Jonathan. But first, you haven't told me where my wife is. I want to celebrate Christmas with her."

"I don't know where she is. Now why don't you go on home? I'll have her phone you later."

Robert laughed. "Funny, Jonathan. That's real funny. If I left, you'd call my boss and I'd be out of a job. No, I don't think so. I think I'll stay right here, and we'll sort this out when she gets home. Maybe she'll bring her boy home, too, and we can get everything out in the open at the same time."

"Robert, she's not your wife. You've been divorced for six months. I don't have to call your boss. We can forget any of this ever happened. You just step out of here, and I won't speak another word about this to anyone."

"You must think I'm as big an idiot as you. I know you'd say just about anything to get me out of here right now. But you're not calling the shots here tonight, Beecher. I am, and I already know I'm not leaving until Mary and I've had a little talk."

Jonathan took another slow step forward. He was within eight feet of Robert now. The policeman tensed, grabbing his revolver and raising it to Jonathan. "Now I told you not to get any closer, boy. I know all the tricks. Slow or fast, if you take another step, I'm going to put a bullet right into your heart. That'll be the end of your meddling."

Jonathan raised his hands. His heart was beating out of his chest, but he tried to remain calm or at least appear so. "What do you mean by meddling?"

"Don't you think I know who convinced her to divorce me? She would never have done that on her own. She's my property, damn it! We loved each other. She would've never walked away if it wasn't for you. And for what? A little smack now and again. A little attention getter. She has a mouth on her, that one. You didn't do anything about it while she was growing up. Nor did that dead wife of yours. I had to step into your shoes and teach her right. Not like in the bed. She didn't need a lot of learning there. She took to anything I wanted, just like that. She's a regular little whore; I promise you that."

Jonathan felt the anger rising, but he didn't move. Robert was baiting him. He was enjoying himself and waiting for Jonathan to charge him. He could guess what would happen after that.

"Robert, there's no point in saying things like that. Mary was a good wife to you, but all that's over now. Court says the marriage is over. Why don't you just drop that thing and go on home?"

He saw a flicker of impatience and anger cross Robert's face. "I already told you—I'm the boss here! You won't stand up for your little slut of a daughter, huh? I guess you know the truth the same as me. Now she's fornicating with some new man. Of course, you're no better, with that crippled slut you make time with. She probably taught Mary everything she knows."

If Jonathan had a pistol in his hand right now, he knew what he would have done. He didn't. He knew he was unlikely to survive the night, but he had to try. He swallowed his fear and forced himself to remain calm. At the worst, he wanted to disable Robert and save Mary, even if he couldn't save himself. He had to wait for the right opportunity. He would only get one chance.

He heard the door start to jingle. He closed his eyes. His worst nightmare was coming true. He could hear the sound for a moment longer, and then the door swung open. Mary walked in, a look of excitement on her face that turned immediately to horror. "What's happening?" she asked.

"Mary, how nice of you to join us," said Robert. "Why don't you come in and have a seat?"

She turned to Jonathan. "Father, what's going on?"

"What's going on?" said Robert, mocking her voice. "I'll tell you what's going on. Your father and I were just discussing what a little whore you are. He agrees with me, of course. By the way, where's your new man? I would just love to meet him."

"I don't have a new man."

"You're as bad a liar as your father. You know exactly who I'm talking about. Where's Bill?"

Mary's face flushed. "I don't know where he is. I wasn't planning on seeing him tonight."

"Well, that's refreshing," said Robert, thick with sarcasm. "You've managed to see him every other night. Dinners and walks and hand holding. Did you think I wouldn't notice?"

"I don't understand, Robert. We're divorced."

"You wanted that! I never did. You and your bastard of a father. You forced me to do it, and you lied to the judge to get it. I was lucky to save my job. You did everything you could to ruin my life. I'm here to return the favor."

Mary took a few steps into the room. Robert waved her over toward her father. Mary walked quickly over and clung to Jonathan.

"Oh, what a beautiful scene we have now. Father and daughter together again. This is just how I imagined things, although I wanted the boyfriend here to also share in the festivities."

"That's about enough now," said Jonathan. "You've had your fun. You can't shoot us here, and you know it. The neighbors would hear, and you'd never get away."

Robert snorted. "Who said anything about getting away?" He raised the revolver up higher, aiming it directly at Mary. His thumb reached up and pulled back the hammer, clicking it into place.

"What do you want from me?" asked Mary.

"You'd like there to be an answer to that, wouldn't you? You'd like to come back to me now and play the housewife. Meanwhile you'd be out whoring around with your new friend while I'm gone doing all the work. I knew that about you the second we married. The second we were in bed. I knew you would be out with other men, all over the neighborhood. All your faith and church garbage was just a giant lie. I see women like you all day long in my job. Dishonoring their husbands for a smile to relieve the boredom. You're no better; you're worse."

"No, Robert, I don't want that. You had your chance to love me."

Robert rose and took a step toward her. "Shut your mouth, you lying whore! You had no right to leave me! You deserved everything you got!" He pointed the pistol at Jonathan. "You and your lying father! You're both going to pay tonight."

"Please, Robert, don't," said Mary. She was using a soft voice, her hands in the air. "Please don't do this. You're right. It was all my fault. My fault, but not my dad's. Please leave him alone."

Robert returned the gun to Mary. "There won't be any begging tonight, my dear. Nobody is walking out of here until the bill is paid in full. Now, I want you to pick up the phone and call that boyfriend of yours. Tell him your dad is sick and you need his help. Tell him whatever you need to, but get him over here. If you say anything to alert him, I'll shoot your father now."

"No, I won't do that."

He took another step forward. "You sure as hell will!"

Jonathan leaped over the coffee table, landing hard on top of Robert. They fell back together, hitting the sofa hard and knocking it over so the men rolled on the ground. Jonathan had both hands on the revolver, trying to wrest it out of Robert's hand. He could hear Mary screaming in the background. As strong as Jonathan was, Robert was in an insane rage. He pulled his hands back hard, trying to get the gun free. Jonathan kept a viselike grip on the gun, angling the barrel toward the ceiling, fighting to keep control. With a last gasp of strength, Jonathan wrenched the revolver away and then bashed the barrel against Robert's head, knocking him out. He could feel the adrenaline pouring through his body. He lay on top of Robert for a few moments, gasping for breath; then he slowly rose and turned to Mary.

She was still standing where she had been before, but her face was now a pasty white. "Are you okay, Mary?" he asked.

Her eyes were filled with horror, and she pointed at Jonathan. What was she staring at? He looked down, and then he saw it. His stomach was a mass of blood that kept slowly expanding. Robert had shot him when he charged. He hadn't heard the pistol fire, hadn't felt the bullet hit him. Now he could feel the pain. He sat down hard and then laid his head on the floor. Mary rushed over to him.

"Father, are you okay?"

"I'll be fine, dear." Jonathan wondered if that were true. "You need to call an ambulance." His voice was weakening. He felt dizzy. Darkness kept washing over him. He was going to pass out. He closed his eyes. From the other room he could hear the sound of Mary on the phone. A few moments later he felt pressure on his stomach and looked up to see Mary applying a kitchen towel to his wound. Tears flowed down her face. Jonathan smiled up at her. He was content. He had saved his daughter. No matter what happened next, she would be okay. He reached a bloody hand up and touched her wrist. "I love you," he whispered.

"I love you, too," she said.

The darkness covered him.

~~

Jonathan slept peacefully. He occasionally heard the sound of voices or flashes of light, but nothing could reach him. He couldn't remember the last time he had reveled in such peaceful rest, as if the cares of the world were leaving him. He dreamed of Snohomish, but he moved freely about as if he were flying. He passed up and down the tree-filled streets and the beautiful old houses, and down by the river to swirl among the businesses of the commercial district. He felt a little sadness as he passed by friends he recognized, or a building he especially loved, a sadness he didn't understand.

Other images flashed through his mind: scenes with Luke and Matthew, much younger, playing in the yard while Mary sat in his arms—just a baby. He saw Helen again, working away in the kitchen. She was smiling at him, something she so rarely did. There was an understanding in her eyes. Most of all, his mind seemed to scroll through all of his memories of Sarah—the day he met her, their time together at church, their dinners and walks and conversations. Always she was smiling at him with a clear love in her heart.

Jonathan looked up, and before him was a stunning sunset, a rich red sky dotted with exquisite clouds and bursts of light. He was drawn to the horizon, pulled toward the beauty. He looked down at his town, his home. Snohomish lay below him; twilight was falling. For a moment he balanced between the light and his beloved town. Slowly he drifted down. He wasn't ready. Not yet.

Jonathan felt the light again, but this time it was harsh and hurt his eyes. He closed his lids and then blinked several times. When he opened them again, he was able to focus, but he was confused. Where was he? He looked around at the unfamiliar room. The walls and lamps and everything seemed to be a brilliant white. He turned his head and was surprised to see Pastor Miles, asleep in a chair next to him. As he watched, the pastor yawned and opened his eyes. He was surprised to see Jonathan awake.

"Jonathan! Thank the Lord! I'm so happy you're awake!"

"Where am I?"

"You're in Snohomish General."

"Why am I in the hospital?" Even as Jonathan asked the question, he started to remember.

"You were shot, Jonathan. In the stomach. The doctors have been terribly worried about infection. We didn't know if you were going to make it, but yesterday they said you were improving."

"How long have I been here?"

"Five days."

Jonathan was shocked by that. He felt like he'd been asleep only a moment. He'd missed Christmas. "Where's Mary? Is she okay?"

"She's fine. She went to get something to eat. She's barely left your side since you arrived here."

"What happened to Robert?"

"Ah, yes, our good friend Robert. He was arrested that night, and he's in the Snohomish County Jail, awaiting charges for attempted murder. You'll have to be part of that process, I'm afraid, and so will Mary. The good news is he'll be behind bars for a very long time. He's lucky it's not thirty years ago—they might have strung him up without a trial."

Jonathan heard the door open and a gasp of delight. Mary came in and rushed to his side.

"Father, you're awake! I've been so worried! Thank God!"

"Yes, we need to thank God for all of this," said Pastor Miles.

"What happened after I passed out?" Jonathan asked Mary.

"There isn't really that much to tell. I called the ambulance and then did my best to help you until they came. When they saw what happened, they called the police. Fortunately, Robert never woke up—the police had to take him out on a stretcher." She smiled. "You must've hit him pretty good."

"I'm just glad you're safe."

"I am, thanks to you. He was going to kill us; there's no doubt about it. I was frozen with fear. I would've called Bill. I didn't know what else to do. I was so shocked when you charged him. I think he was, too. He didn't expect that."

"He'd done enough to you. I wasn't going to let him do any more." Jonathan eased his head back down on the pillow. Now that he was more awake, he realized he was terribly weak. His stomach felt like his insides had been dug out with a shovel. He glanced down and noticed for the first time several tubes sticking out of his midsection. At least his daughter was okay. A thought suddenly occurred to him.

"My store! I was supposed to sell the inventory! What am I going to do now?"

"I tried to help with the store," said Pastor Miles. "I went and talked to Mr. Weber, but he wouldn't change his position, even though he knows what happened. He's burned some bridges in this town; I'll tell you that."

"Did he seize all the inventory?"

"Well, he would've, but he can't."

"What do you mean?"

"He's all paid up current, and for good measure. The rest of the lease was paid up front as well."

Jonathan raised his head again. "What are you talking about?"

"I'll tell you. When all this happened, we held a special meeting of the congregation. I told them you would be down for a while from this injury, and I also told them about your situation. We took a special offering, and we paid off the lease. There's even some extra left over you can put in savings."

Jonathan started to rise again. "I can't let you do that. You need to get that money back."

"No sense in arguing with me. The money's gone, and I don't see our German friend returning it to you or to us. You'd think that man doesn't realize there's a war going on—a war his people started. In any event your lease is paid, and there's nothing you can do about it. I know how stubborn you can be, but look at it as a gift from God. You can't say no to that. There are a lot of people around here who love you, Jonathan. Maybe more than you know. Just for once let other people take care of you, instead of the other way around."

Jonathan wanted to argue further, but what could he do? Unbelievable. His friends had come together and taken away all his debts. It was a miracle from above. He felt a peace he wouldn't have expected. He decided he wouldn't fight this. "Thank you so much, Pastor. You will never know what this means to me. I'll thank everyone at church when I get the chance. I am so humbled. In the long run I would like to give all of that back, when my business allows it."

Pastor Miles smiled, looking satisfied. "I thought I'd have a harder battle than that with you. Like I said, you're a beloved man, Jonathan. It's time you understood just how much people care about you. Pay us back or not; that's your choice. I'm glad you are willing to accept this."

"What about Luke? We haven't done anything for him."

"We've been working on that, too," said Pastor Miles. "When you're healthy, we'll have a service for him. We haven't forgotten him, but you need to get better first."

Mary stepped forward and hugged Jonathan again. He put his arms around her and held her close. His little girl was protected. She was going to thrive, and so was he. He heard the door open and close again. The doctor must be here. He looked up and was surprised. It was Sarah.

"Hello, Pastor," she said. "Hello, Mary."

They both greeted her in return. "Well, look at the time," said Pastor Miles. "Mary, would you like to accompany me on some errands?"

Mary smiled. "How kind of you to ask. I need some fresh air."

Pastor Miles stood up and walked out of the room, with Mary following him. He stopped to give Sarah a hug on the way out.

"What was that all about?" asked Jonathan.

"I'm not sure," she said. "I suppose they wanted to give us a few minutes alone."

"Why?"

"Because there are things that need to be said."

Jonathan tried to sit up, but still couldn't find the strength.

"Stop that. You'll hurt yourself. Let me come over closer to you so we can talk." Sarah moved around to the top edge of the bed and sat down in the pastor's chair. She was wearing a plain white dress with a blue sweater. There was a ribbon tied in her hair. She wore a blue knit mitten over her hand. She leaned over and looked at Jonathan with searching eyes, not speaking for a few moments.

"Jonathan, there are things I want to say to you. I'm asking you to listen."

"I can do that."

"I don't think you realize how badly you hurt me. I loved you with my whole heart. I . . . . still love you. Letting you go last year was the most painful thing I have ever done. When Stan asked me to dinner, I didn't want to go. I didn't want to move on. But I would never have believed you would change your mind. Then when you came back to me and told me you wanted to be with me, I was so confused— particularly when it was only one night after your *other* behavior. I couldn't trust what you were saying. I was terribly worried you didn't mean it, that you were unsettled."

"I can understand why you would have felt that way. I'm still ashamed of what happened."

"I'm not upset about that. After everything that was happening to you, I can understand. We all reach a point of deepest despair in our life at one point or another. We can't be judged on how we might act at that moment."

"Thank you for that. I'm very sorry about how I conducted myself. I'm even more sorry I didn't see clearly in the past that I needed you in my life—and that God would accept that. It's not easy for me to let you go now, but your happiness is more important to me than my own. Stan is a good man. I know he will make you happy."

"I'm not choosing Stan. I'm choosing you."

"What are you talking about?"

"I ended things with Stan the same night you came over. I made up my mind that I was going to put away my pain and come back to you. You are all I ever wanted, and I couldn't give up my chance for happiness. My chance to be with you."

"Sarah, does that mean that you will marry me?"

"Of course I will. That's all I've ever wanted."

"You've made me the happiest man alive."

She stepped over and embraced him, careful not to disturb the tubes on his stomach. "I love you so much," she whispered, then kissed him tenderly. He kissed her back, holding her as truly his for the first time. He was worried he would feel guilt, some lingering link with his past promise, but he did not. He knew he was doing the right thing, that God was blessing his path. They held each other for a long time, amid the stark white walls, the hustle of the hospital, the pain. An island of joy.

EPILOGUE

Snohomish, Washington
Saturday, May 12, 1945

Two hundred people crowded into the sanctuary of the Snohomish Free Methodist Church. The war was over—at least the war in Europe. Hitler was dead. The healing was just beginning. Millions had perished. Millions more were displaced. In the east, the war continued with the Japanese, who were fighting on alone. The United States was preparing to invade the homeland islands. Many more casualties were expected, but nobody doubted the final result. The war would be won. The boys would eventually come home. Peace would settle once again over Snohomish, over the United States, and over the world.

Jonathan stood nervously at the front of the sanctuary, Pete Brandvold next to him. He was dressed in his best suit—well, his only suit. Pastor Miles was to his right, all smiles and jokes today. The organist struck up the wedding march. Everyone stood as Sarah came slowly down the aisle, beautiful in a light pink dress, her eyes fixed on

Jonathan's. Everyone watched her slowly make her way to him, toward their life together. Jonathan looked over to the altar again. Next to Pastor Miles stood Sarah's daughter, Margaret, sixteen now, taller than her mother, stunningly beautiful. Tears rolled down her cheeks. She smiled at Jonathan, happiness in her eyes.

He next looked out and saw Mary in the front row, a few feet away from him. Bill stood next to her, his arm around her. He glanced down and saw the ring on her finger. He was so proud of his daughter, living in Ballard now, a suburb of Seattle, and working for the phone company while her husband finished his degree. She was signed up to take summer classes at North Seattle Junior College. She wasn't showing yet, but there was a baby coming, too, the continuation of his line. She had everything she had ever wanted, and everything he had ever wanted for her.

Sarah reached the front. She looked at Jonathan again with the deepest love in her eyes. She blushed, almost shyly. She was the most beautiful woman he had ever seen: small, courageous, resilient, his precious angel on earth. This was their moment together, their beginning, a life he never thought they would have. He thanked God for the wisdom He had shown him, for giving a small-town pastor the courage to open his eyes. He thanked Helen, too, for letting him go; he hoped she understood.

Pastor Miles performed the ceremony in the simple and loving way he did everything. They exchanged their vows, watching each other with appreciation and with excitement for the future. They had their second lives together, and the rest of their time on earth would be as one. Finally, he completed the ceremony and turned them toward the guests. "It gives me the deepest pleasure and happiness to present to you Mr. and Mrs. Jonathan Beecher. You may kiss the bride."

Jonathan reached over and placed his hands on Sarah's neck, pulling her in for a kiss. He had intended a swift brushing of their lips, but Sarah had other things in mind. She pressed her lips against his, deeply holding him against her for a few moments, then pulled away gently, smiling up at him with happiness.

The reception followed on the lawn of the church. Mary and some of her friends had made sandwiches and cookies, along with a red punch. They stood behind a long table, serving the guests who then stepped out to mingle with friends and family. Nearly everyone was from Snohomish. Conversations dwelt not only on the happy couple but also on the end of the war. Some of their boys might be heading to Japan now, but others were coming home. Theirs was a mixture of fear and excitement, of hope and dread.

Sarah and Jonathan visited with them all, taking a little time for everyone who had come out. They held hands, and each other, as if to make sure this was for real, that they were truly together. They laughed with friends, shared stories of the past. They cried, too, as they reminisced about Luke and the other boys who would never be coming home again.

The hours passed pleasantly, and soon it was time to depart. Jonathan had closed the store for a few days and booked a room at a resort at Sol Duc Hot Springs on the Olympic Peninsula. They had a long drive ahead of them. They tried to help with the cleanup but were soundly refused.

Jonathan embraced Mary and Bill. "I'm so happy for you," his daughter said.

"I'm happy for you, too, my dear. You finally have the life I wanted for you."

She smiled. "I can say the same for you."

"Poor Luke. He never had that chance."

"Let's not talk about that today, Father. Today is a day for happiness. I know he's up in heaven, smiling down on us, happy as can be for you."

"What about Matthew?"

Her face clouded. "I don't know, Father. What do you think? I pray about him every day. I expected we would hear from him years ago or at least receive news about him. I hope in my heart that he's out there, that he's coming home."

"I feel the same. I hope and pray he'll be on his way back to us. In my heart, too, I feel he's out there, that he will come home someday."

Jonathan embraced Mary again, holding her tightly for a few moments. He shook Bill's hand. Then he and Sarah hugged Margaret, who would stay with Pastor Miles while they were gone on their short honeymoon.

Sarah and Jonathan walked over to his truck, which was covered in decorations and cans. The teenagers of the church had been busy during the reception, creating a mess Jonathan would have to clean up before they could properly depart. He would drive to their house first and take off the worst of the trimmings; then they would be able to leave.

Pastor Miles led everyone in a prayer, blessing Jonathan and Sarah individually, their family, their life together, and their future. Sarah hugged him, and Jonathan shook his hand.

"Thank you, Pastor. Without you, we would never have been together. Thanks for talking sense into this stubborn mule."

"Don't thank me, Jonathan, thank God. I just spoke what I know He wanted to tell you. The rest was up to you."

Jonathan stepped forward and embraced the pastor. Sarah joined them. They held on tightly for a moment. Jonathan thanked the guests for coming. He walked over to the passenger side of the truck and opened the door for his new wife. He helped her step carefully inside, reaching down for another kiss from her. The guests cheered. He turned around sheepishly and waved again, then crossed over to the driver's side. He stepped inside and started the truck, pulling away slowly as friends surrounded them. Cans clanged noisily on the pavement as they turned onto the street, heading south toward Second.

Jonathan reached over and gently removed the pink satin mitten covering Sarah's hand—her damaged hand. He ran his fingers over the scar tissue, gently caressing her as he had the first time he ever truly touched her. Sarah leaned against his shoulder, closing her eyes. Jonathan turned west. The sun was setting, the sky a beautiful red, and they were going home.

SNOHOMISH, WASHINGTON

Snohomish, Washington, is a typical small town in the United States. During World War II, the city experienced its share of loss. The names of the people killed in active service in the war are listed in a mural on the outside of the American Legion building downtown.

Snohomish continued to grow after the war, changing over time from a largely rural farming community to a bedroom suburb for Seattle and the significant Boeing plant next to Paine Field in Everett.

The city limits still hold a population of less than ten thousand, but the school district is large, with two high schools, the original Snohomish High School downtown and Glacier Peak High School across the valley. The town is fiercely loyal to its schools and maintains a small-town, collective sense of spirit. Snohomish High School is consistently voted as "Best Spirit" in Washington.

The Snohomish Free Methodist Church continues in Snohomish but has since changed names and locations. It is now known as CrossView Church and is located just off Avenue D. The church maintains its affiliation with the Free Methodist conference.

Snohomish still contains a number of farms, and tourists will find an array of wonderful markets providing fresh fruit and vegetables and local honey. In the fall, there are corn mazes and pumpkin patches.

The mills and canneries are mostly gone now. The beautiful historical homes remain and are marked with signs. There are periodic home and garden tours.

Much of the draw to Snohomish in the twenty-first century is the antique stores. The downtown on First Street is full of eclectic shops and restaurants. Tourists come from far and wide to visit the shops, particularly in the summer. Snohomish is a must-see for anyone visiting the Seattle area.

WAKE ISLAND

The events depicted concerning Wake Island are written as accurately as possible, with some fictional additions utilized as instruments to tell the story.

Wake Island was a popular stopover during the early part of the twentieth century for Pan Am flights traveling across the Pacific. The US military utilized the island as well and was in the process of beefing up the island's defenses when the surprise attack on Pearl Harbor occurred.

The island, at the time, held a small contingent of marines and a large number of civilian contractors from the construction firm of Morrison-Knudsen out of Boise, Idaho. As war loomed closer, the contractors grew nervous but stayed on the job for the excellent pay with the belief that Wake was a backwater and would not be a primary target of the Japanese.

The defenses were caught by surprise when the Japanese attacked the island very early in the conflict. Despite the surprise and the extremely limited defenses, the defenders held out and even repulsed the initial landing attempt. After this successful defense, Wake became the first victory of the United States against the Japanese, and the defenders were heroes on the mainland.

The US government strove to reinforce the island shortly thereafter, but resources were limited, and the fleet was turned back when news arrived that the island was under invasion again. This time the Japanese took the island.

The defenders were rounded up and left in the central runway area for several days. Survivors reported that they were given no food and little water. They suffered terribly in the open air and were sure that they would be executed at any moment. The Japanese had a well-deserved reputation for executing prisoners, and, in fact, the commander had considered executing the Americans at first but was overruled by the Japanese government.

Eventually most of the Americans were removed from the island in prisoner ships. The journey to prisoner camps in China and Japan aboard these ships was described as a nightmare, with a number of prisoners dying along the way. Those who made it found POW camp conditions of a shocking nature. Many more contractors and marines died in captivity in these camps. At first no mail was allowed, but eventually news arrived on the mainland that some of the Wake Island prisoners were alive and living in camps under Japanese control.

The Morrison-Knudsen contractors remained on Wake Island, assisting in building its defenses. In early October 1943, a force with the US carrier *Yorktown* was off the coast of occupied Wake Island and conducted offensive air operations. The American fleet had no intention of invading the island, but the Japanese commander, Admiral Shigematsu Sakaibara, thought the contrary. Finally, on October 7, he ordered the remaining Americans on Wake Island to be executed. One contractor somehow escaped the execution and survived for three weeks. At some point he carved a message of remembrance on a rock near where the contractors were buried in a mass grave. He was eventually captured and executed by Sakaibara personally.

After the war the truth came out about the executions. Admiral Sakaibara was executed, and Lieutenant Commander Shoichi Tachibana was sentenced to life in prison.

THE TENTH ARMORED DIVISION

The Tenth Armored Division, known as the "Tiger Division," was attached to the Third Army under General George S. Patton. This division was formed at Fort Benning, Georgia.

Combat Command B, a portion of the division, was rushed north during the Battle of the Bulge and took part in the heroic defense of Bastogne, along with the 101st Airborne Division.

With limited ammunition and no cold-weather gear, the Tenth battled wave after wave of German attacks and, together with the parachute infantry, held the Nazis from recapturing the city and moving on to Antwerp.

The 101st Airborne Division has historically received most of the credit for the historic defense of Bastogne, but without the assistance of Combat Command B of the Tenth Armored Division, the Germans may well have successfully pushed through and defeated the American defenders.

ACKNOWLEDGMENTS

I would like to thank a number of people who assisted me in research for this book, including George Gilbertson, Ken and Kiffin Roberts, Russ and Phyllis Roberts, Rip and Carol Krause, and William "Bill" and Susan Pepperell. I also found some great information in the *Snohomish High School Football Record Book, 1906–2010*, by Keith Olson and *River Reflections* by the Snohomish Historical Society. Without their help, I wouldn't have had such outstanding information about Snohomish during the war. Thank you so much to all of you.

ABOUT THE AUTHOR

James D. Shipman was born and raised in the Pacific Northwest. He began publishing short stories and poems while earning a degree in history from the University of Washington and a law degree from Gonzaga University School of Law. He opened his own law firm in 2004 and remains a practicing attorney. *Constantinopolis*, his first published novel, depicts the epic fifteenth-century battle between the Turkish and Roman empires for the fabled city of Constantinople. *Going Home*, his second novel, is based on a true Civil War story. An avid reader, especially of historical nonfiction, Shipman also enjoys traveling and spending time with his family.